THE NIHILISTICS

THE NIHILISTICS

MARK DAMON PUCKETT

Special Thanks

Charles Ardai, Editor at Hard Case Crime, read this novel in its early stages (in one night) and told me to keep going. Wendy Walker (*All Is Not Forgotten, What Remains, American Girl, Mad Love*) encouraged me to get it past 90,000 words. I'd also like to thank Colman Andrews who gave me a list of mystery, crime and noir novels many years ago. I read each one and have never stopped making my own lists of these badass genres. Book designer Daniel Middleton at Scribe Freelance also deserves a salute for his next-level, grand slam cover that has attracted so much attention.

Also by Mark Damon Puckett
The Reclusives
YOU with The Ill-usives
The Killer Detective Novelist

CONTENTS

The Nihilistics   1

Strake   101

The Governor's Niece   201

*For my older brother Farrar,
who died early seeking justice*

THE NIHILISTICS

PART I

"Investigators' initial inquiries made it possible to say that this attack was the work of individuals who, whether by virtue of insanity or of calculation, were resolved to create disorder at any cost."

Jean-Patrick Manchette,
Nada

It was a small town outside Athens. No despair in it.

They were ready. Three of them.

At the stoplight. Idling white Impala convertible SS-396.

Red seats warm on their backs. July 1970.

They gazed at the building. Georgia bank, only cold thing on the block.

The year of the car was 1965. Might not do the job as it sputtered, had to be revved by the foot of the driver.

They were past minding. Called themselves The Nihilistics.

Nixon had just given his special message on Indian affairs on July 8. His warbled voice was on the AM radio, 1460. 10:30 in the morning, the time.

A beep nudged the driver, Tane, a teenager who was fixated on the bank. His crow black hair burned under the sun, aviator glasses mirroring the stoplight in front of him, now green.

Ellman, in the passenger seat, tapped Tane's elbow with the back of his hand to go. He was bald and his head burned. Tane moved through the light, eyes under glasses staring more at the building on his left on Railroad St.

"Park it here," said the very young lady in the back seat with no bra, pointing at a space. Her shoulders and neck stung in the Georgia blaze. Ninety-eight degrees. Southern morning sun. Broken car top. Six eyes with red veins from the wind. Fire above them on the way to Athens. Tane's black hair scorched. Ellman with a singed pink scalp. They pulled into a space by Shep's Diner. Found a tree with almost purple leaves rise out of the sidewalk to shade them. The trio seemed to breathe at the same time.

"What the hell kind of tree is that?" said Tane.

"Norway maple," Ellman mumbled.

"Hm."

There were no masks for the job. Being dead was no issue. Easy to die when you hope it'll happen. The two men opened their long doors. Becca leaned forward to step out behind Ellman. Tane was now at the trunk. He slid the key into the slot. Turned the metal, lifted it upward, the mouth of a beast.

Handed Ellman his weapon. Gave Becca hers. His, he grabbed last.

He left the Impala idling. Whether it would stay running was to be seen. They walked side by side down the empty street, Becca's blond hair swaying in the middle. She carried a long knife made of bone. Ellman had his M1911, a.k.a. the Colt Government. Tane: a hatchet.

No plan beyond a road atlas. In Amarillo each had pointed to a place in Georgia with their index fingers. Found a spot in the center of the three points. They had already forgotten its name. Some neglected place near Athens. It had been a long drive from out west.

A man with white hair saw them and turned away in distress, vanishing around the corner. They knew nothing about the bank before they went inside. Chosen at random. Tane feigned chopping with his hatchet. Ellman loaded his Colt Government. Becca held her long knife with a blank look.

The sun stared, a fierce leerer. Their walk was short. Inside the bank were four tellers. Two men. Two women. The counter was open. No metal bars. No security windows. Small town arrogance. Ellman nodded.

In synchrony the knife rose to a dowdy female. The gun was held on the forehead of a portly male. And Tane aimed his hatchet blade at the other young man and woman hugging each other. Tane liked the hatchet: it could chop and, with a twirl, suddenly be a hammer. Gemini weapon.

There was then a visual feast of blood in the small bank with white walls. Splattering a bowl of free yellow, green and purple lollipops on the counter. Around the tellers, red sprayed. From the knife in the older woman's neck. With liquid splashing out behind the man's head. And the hatchet blade sunk into the side of the young man's jugular, three times to deepen the wound. Handle twisted. Hammer on the other side plunged into the forehead of the young woman, twice.

A neck slash pouring an endless cherry color.

A head hole like an empty eye until it gushed thick, with a spurt.

They seemed to be a couple. Four bodies had dropped. It was easy to grab money from tills. Tane took a purple lollipop. Peeled off the plastic with drops of blood on it. Stuck it in his mouth. He had noticed an Underwood typewriter on a desk and grabbed it under one arm. So he had a sucker in his mouth, a hatchet in his hand and a typewriter under his arm. They left the bank in no hurry. Hands full, Tane told Ellman to drive.

"Um," she said to Tane as they walked, "why did you steal that hunk?"

"I'll be writing this up for *Killers!* as a piece."

"You? You're not a writer."

"Samuel Bunker, that's my pen name."

"No way! You mean 'The Rest Stop Hatchet Killer' stories?"

"Yep."

"That's you?"

He nodded proudly. As luck would have it the seats were red; blood would blend into them. "Still running," Tane noted, setting the typewriter down in the passenger seat then tossing his hatchet into the open trunk by the Colt and the knife.

He slammed it shut.

"Guess it's not our time," Becca said, disappointed.

They found their seats again with Ellman now driving.

Tane took a sheet of paper out of his small travel bag.

Rolled it into the typewriter that sat in his lap.

At the top of the page he wrote, "The Nihilistics."

Streaked with blood on their faces and bodies, they didn't bother to wipe it off.

In a film, credits would flash in red at that instant.

Becca counted the bills as they rode through town at a slow speed.

"More than I thought," she said, impressed.

"No security guard," Ellman had to mention.

"Yeah," said Tane, typing away, "that's right."

"No resistance at all," the girl observed, adding, "wait . . . doesn't that say Sheriff's Office right there?"

They noticed where she pointed.

"Ha," said Tane, "look at that."

Ellman: "This was just a practice run anyway."

Tane: "So the next one?"

"Yeah," replied Ellman, "we'll be dead soon."

"What about that old guy who saw us?" she asked.

"What about him?"

"Who cares?" Tane added.

Hot Georgia wind warmed them. They kept to the small roads. The typewriter clicked and tapped.

"We need to fix this damn top," Becca complained. No one responded.

The old man with white hair reappeared on the sidewalk with Sheriff Strake who had an orange pet hen that walked beside him. They had just missed that car leaving.

"You said a *hatchet*?"

"Yessir, and a knife. And a pistol."

"Three of them?"

"Yeah, three."

"Thank you Jimmy," said Strake, staring at the bank. "Let's see how bad."

Strake was cinematic in looks with McQueen thick straw blond hair cut short. Sideburns halfway down the ears. He had seen *Bullitt* eight times in the fall of 1968; the likeness was not accidental. With a thick chest and shoulders he was a sturdy six feet. His eyes were almost a blue blackness. Short scars on his cheeks and forehead, from the war. Teeth yellowed from cigars. He sauntered over to the massacre after thanking the witness.

His hen right behind. Maude was her name.

It was a dead town, he thought. Deader now.

His son worked at that bank. So did his daughter-in-law.

Ellman and the Colt Government

The gun was a part of him. Had been his father's. Never left the top of the fridge. Except to kill a stray cat. Or black snakes that often fell from the trees in the yard. Snakes could rain on you sometimes.

He lived alone with his dad. After his mother's depression and suicide by pills. Ellman left the house after high school. But he took the gun. You could hitchhike in the late 60s with a pistol bulging in your waist. And the fools would pick you up. He rode on many semis and rarely talked to anyone.

He thought he was numb. It was below that. Deeper than dead. And the Government made noise. It was not the killing that attracted him. It was the sound.

Ellman was twenty now and he was alone. Detached. Except for an abrupt blast that came after each shot. Everything about him was mute until a bullet came. Each person deserved at least one bullet. Including himself. He would get one, one day.

He preferred to walk on blue highways. Forgotten roads through dying American towns. Sounds of his boot steps echoed on the gravel of the roadside shoulder. The noise was a comfort to his mind. A foot rhythm. It meant only he was there. Anyone who disturbed this was an intruder. He had simple walls of silence. The merest sound of others bothered him.

The only public place he could abide was the library. He lost himself in many of them along the way. It was where he first read about nihilism. Much of which he didn't understand. He never liked to stay anywhere for more than thirty minutes. Could only scan books quickly in that time frame. But the word took hold in him. As did its history. He thought about forming a group of similar thinkers. But realized it was counter to nihilism in that the philosophy, if it even *was* that, belied the formation of anything concrete. In other words if it was all baseless, life, wasn't the very notion of nihilism against everything it purported to be? Which was nothing. No thing. So if you went and formed a group of nihilists, didn't you already negate nihilism?

It gave him a headache to ponder it. How could you be a nihilist with other people? You couldn't. Still, he read the crime books and magazines. Knew there were other unhinged minds like his out there. On a whim he bought an ad in the back of one of the edgier mags called *Killers!* that said, "The Nihilistics Meet in Amarillo, Texas."

He had given a month-long range for the date and found a cheap motel address in the Yellow Pages. "Looking to Form a Posse for Random Killings" was the subheading of the ad. He had sent it in as a joke, especially the last part. And they had published it! Every time he bought a copy on the road it was still in there. A gag had turned into something real.

Maybe he would go to Amarillo. See who showed. Yes, maybe he would. He liked the sound of it: The Nihilistics.

A death band. This is what too much library reading could do to you. It gave you ideas that never were anything but. No action. Books were non-action. He'd been reading about nihilism for so long that it had taken shape. Even though he didn't quite understand the concept.

Could killing be considered not nothing? Killing was some thing. So . . . what was no thing? It was a puzzle, this word nihilism. It was a trick. It made you think you could be nothing which was not possible. Killing was the most personal thing you could do. Well, impersonal for sure . . . making a human absent. A formerly present person was now no longer alive. You, the killer, caused nothing, but the act itself was something.

Phew, Ellman thought, I have to stop thinking about this shit. My head hurts. Sometimes he walked in the road. It was so empty, all of it. A lone man with a cigar. Smoke following him like a white cape.

Thoughts of nihilism working themselves into an answer to this mental riddle he could not comprehend.

Cars would stop even without his thumb raised. Offer a ride. If he made it into the car, they got a bullet. Anyone who gave him a ride would soon be dead. It was just how it had to be. A film director could frame Ellman in this moment. A man steps out of the car. Leans into the passenger window to thank the driver for the ride. Lifts his gun from his jacket. Blasts the person in the forehead. Never caring whether he was caught, he sauntered away at his leisure. Vanished into the woods, a place he made sure to see seconds before asking to stop. He always had to see the woods before the shot, a visual ritual.

"This is fine."

The car braked. Ellman opened his door. He stepped out and closed it gently, having made sure the window was down. Gun lifted. Pointed into the open space of the window. A dead driver with the bullet hole in his or her head, slumping. Repetition of this was uncanny. A rewound frame to play again the same, hundreds of times. He wanted to kill thousands. Hundreds were not enough. Each one left him blank as the last. A blank in yourself was an infinity never to be filled. They were dead moments, impressions of the no longer living, image and sound.

His Government stuffed down into his waist. Barrel bushing and front sight still warm from the shot. He liked the 7-round box magazine instead of the 8. The number 8 gave him the creeps, forced symmetry, just two zeroes, one on top of the other. You can't disguise double zeroes, no matter how you stack them. The number 8 was a fraud. Always avoid double zeroes. His jinx. Whenever he saw them, bad luck happened. 7 rounds of ammo, .45 Automatic Colt Pistol. At short range these bullets gaped holes in foreheads.

People died in a democratic manner. No judgment was made. Ellman shot everyone with random disinterest, male or female, old or young. It could be said that when you care very little for dying that it's impossible to kill you. Nihil was Latin for nothing. Nil. You shouldn't say bad things about the dead. No fear of that with Ellman, for he never spoke of them, his many kills. He had looked up the Latin phrase many times in small town libraries and the common translation, he discovered after some research, was wrong.

De mortuis nihil nisi bonum. Don't speak ill of the dead. Versus. Speak *only good* of them. It wasn't about maligning dead folks. It was more about only saying good things about the idiots. Kind of like the difference between an epicurean and a hedonist. One avoids pain, the other pursues pleasure. Body pain, aponia. The Latins sure had some good words, he said to himself.

Often he mumbled aloud when he walked. A monologue no audience would ever hear. For Ellman the dead had never even been alive, so . . . was it really killing them? He shrugged off the thought. Hiked along with sore feet and ate eggs and bacon in little dumb towns and stared at cute waitresses in pink dresses with green eyes without flirting. While walking he waited for that sound of the car to stop on a quiet back road . . . for a final ride. A warm car braking behind him caused a tingle up his backbone.

One afternoon in November 1969 a shot did not come like it was intended. He had tossed a library book in the back seat after the man had stopped. Later, when it was time, Ellman forgot to get out of the car first.

He had been sick. Not thinking right in his debility. Shivering.

He was still in the passenger seat for the shot. Mistake.

His gun did not lift fast enough at the driver, who had put the floor gearshift into neutral to idle. But the man had a pistol too . . . it shot off the bottom of Ellman's earlobe. He blinked once in pain with gritted teeth. Ellman reached over, twisted back the key in the ignition, pulled it out so that the driver could not leave.

Another sudden shot in Ellman's front left shoulder, flaming pain across his skin. He had at least knocked the gun upward to avoid his gut. Sure enough, he now remembered, there were double zeroes on the license plate. His deep fear was to take a bullet in the stomach. That was no way to die. It was too slow. A belly shot never ended. After the shoulder bullet, Ellman gripped the driver's gun, yanked it from his hand. It scalded his palm.

He had both weapons now as blood dripped from his ear, but he was stunned and still sitting in his bucket seat. Those two shots emptied his body. A trickle from his ear. A gush from his shoulder. The former was nothing. The latter was everything.

This everything would, he was certain, lead to his becoming nothing. His reach for the key and lunge for the gun had tired him within seconds. He couldn't move. Why hadn't he stepped out of the car first? Like he had done every time. Never change your procedure. He had been feverish. It was the only explanation.

Before leaving a ride, Ellman *always* rolled down the window, stepped out of the car, shut the door, leaned in to thank the person and shot the driver while looking in the passenger side. Lazy this time. Amateur. These were important rituals. Make sure the woods were there for a quick escape. Roll down the window. Step out. Shut the door. Lean in. Aim. Shoot. Instead, he was tired and had stayed in his seat for the killing. Idiot. After his two shots at Ellman, the short blond driver had opened his door to run. Ellman saw him in a field of short corn, his legs hidden, only his torso visible as he sprinted.

One problem: the car was still in neutral. It began to roll on the slight incline. Ellman's body was warm ice, shivering with trembles. His hand was slow to open the door, forcing himself to fall onto the asphalt on his right shoulder. He hoped the jolt would knock him out of his static state and it did. Not fast enough. The car was on something more than a small hill. Ellman gazed at it rolling off the side of a little mountain. He hadn't been paying attention. Just assumed it was all flat in Arkansas because of the cornfield where the man escaped.

Luckily, he had the two guns which had dropped into his lap before he rolled out of the vehicle. Now he was mad. This never happened. No one ever escaped the Government. He managed to get on hands and knees and touch his ear. The nothing. Blood spilled from his shoulder onto the white strip of the highway, dots of it plopping down. The everything.

Red rain. It might rain red when he died too. Maybe it would snow red. However it happened he knew the color of his death.

And the numbers. Red and double zeroes. He crawled to level ground and here it was the flat terrain he had expected.

The field was long and the man was still there, walking and noticing him, not as far away as he thought. Ellman forced himself up to his knees. He lifted the Colt with his right arm. Aimed as the blond man stopped in a panic. The aim was slow, never forgotten even bathed in blood. The bullet, fired from this terrible rural road, caught the man in the chest with a thump. He fell from sight. Ellman stood with adrenaline from the shot and stumbled toward his victim. What fog in him had caused his first error? It was the fever he had ignored earlier as he hitchhiked. Sometimes sleeping on damp ground at night caused it. Never let yourself be blurry, as he knew he was in this moment. Mind smog. Murder needed confidence.

It was okay to not know things. That was different. He never knew the numbers of roads and wanted to be lost as he roamed. Sometimes he forgot where he was. Nights of long driving would take him four states away from where he had started riding with people, one after the other.

How many dead in their driver seats along the road? It was a clear feeling though, no blur like now. He had loved the road. Until this happened.

The haze in his head was a shroud. Steps to the cornfield were creeping and sluggish. He had to check that the man was not alive. He stopped to breathe. Blood dripped from all over him. Yes, when he died it would certainly rain red. It was a waking dream that filled his mind. Would it be the blood of people raining on him after slaughter? Or would the rain just be drops of dark water that cleansed his blood? And only looked red because of blood dripping down his forehead into his eyes?

Sometimes it was quiet red snow, this final vision of himself.
A sky of red dots that covered the dirt in snow blood.
He saw this field of red many times in his thoughts.
He also saw the red rain.
It could be cold red snow. Could be red and wet rain. He wasn't sure. But he did sense that the dream was true. The last thing he was to see in his life would be red. Red was debt as well. Made sense. To let your attention blur was devastation that led to mistakes. Like now. A dead short blond man in a field. Or *was* he dead? Would the man keep resisting and taking advantage of Ellman's blur? An opossum scurried near him like a corpulent rat ready to hiss, contemplating a road crossing. Don't do it, Ellman thought. Your odds aren't good. Even on abandoned roads, opossums still found a way to get killed.

He left the man's gun on the roadside, would throw it in the trunk later. He walked with slow steps to the cornfield wondering what old highway this was. Why did he blunder *here*? In this void that was bleak. Nowhere was fitting for the beginning of the end. The slide off. He had been waiting for it.

No other car had appeared in the last fifteen minutes. It was fall moving into winter, colder than normal. Soon he was in the field and maybe he wanted death so he moved without care. He aimed his Colt ahead of him.

It was lucky that his left shoulder had been smacked with the bullet and not his right, the shooting arm. There was the man, rising not high but lifting himself for . . . what? He had no gun anymore. Sad sight. The man's chest was a bleeding hole that oozed through his white t-shirt, some kind of sick human canvas stretched for bullet art. Ellman was closer until he was only a few feet in front of him. The corn was ashen and rustled against his thighs. He shot him again, right above the nose. Brick red blood trickled down between his blue eyes.

A car was coming. Ellman ducked into the brittle corn stalks. Lay by the fallen man on the dirt hard from the cold. Where was the opossum? It had vanished, was not dead in the road.

He was dizzy with blood loss and his fever ache made it worse. He began to dig with his fingers. After the top layer of hardness, the ground was soft. He dug until dark. Slid the man in the shallow grave. Covered him. Fell asleep on the funeral mound. He didn't know the days he slept. It was many, he knew, a distortion of time. Wasn't this what his life was? Time shapeless? Only to finish in red debts. Maybe it was the third day that his fever ceased and he felt good enough to stand. Was even hungry. Dirt had been stuffed into his shoulder wound, the ear stopping on its own, only minor.

He checked on the blond man's car. Found it down a small hill, not nearly as steep as he had thought after being shot. Your skull echoed into amplification when a bullet pierced your body. Your eyes saw more yet it was leaden and slow at the same time. It took him a minute to find the key still in his pocket. There was no damage so it started fine. The damage had been in his mind. There was always more damage in him than in true life.

He backed up and turned around. Gunned it up the hill skidding. It was a stick shift so he could use low. Soon he was back on the lifeless southern road. Aiming for where . . . he had no idea. Hours were vapor to Ellman. He had taken the man's money clip before burying him, plenty of cash. A wallet was also discovered later in the glove that had more bills.

In front of him a car or truck or semi roared by the window and he took each vehicular affront personally. He found a gas station after passing the sign. Welcoming him to Oklahoma. Put salted peanuts and a stick of beef jerky and a root beer on the counter to pay. Beside them he sat peroxide, alcohol and gauze with a roll of duct tape. And they sold tourist shirts with the state's shape on them. He bought four. He paid. Asked the clerk to bag his food as he went into the restroom. Where he changed into one of his Oklahoma t-shirts. In the trash can by the leaded gas pump he dumped his bloody shirt.

The clerk hadn't even noticed the red stains as he read a Jim Thompson novel, *After Dark, My Sweet*, and barely looked up to bag his items. Ellman opened the trunk and found the blond man's gun and dropped it in the trash can too. It was dark as he chewed spicy jerky and sipped warm root beer and munched peanuts while driving. Soda sugar made his teeth ache. The fizz bubbled hot on the roof of his mouth. He had gotten it from the fridge, but it must have just been added since the can wasn't chilled.

In a few hours he pulled into a disgusting motel and paid for a room for a night and it was a good sleep, yes, the sleep he needed. He had also taken a warm shower, hot but not quite. The room smelled of pine cleaner and irate souls. He could die in this aberrant womb. Often he wished for death to ease him away from his grim life.

He would move west in the morning, likely alive again. Somehow alive. With a nihil mind. Nihil. Istic. Annihilator. He knew he should feel remorse. It was not in him. He thought of the faces of the people he had killed. Tried to count them. How long could he go and not be caught? Faces multiplied as he drifted into sleep. Red rain came again in his crimson dreams.

The 1968 Ford Torino GT (the dead blond man's) had two doors. Almost new, fastback. So bland in army green color it was a perfect car to drive stolen. What year was it now, Ellman asked himself? 1969 right? He knew it was fall, perhaps November. That blur again. A lost man had no dates in mind. Oklahoma was arid and plain. He stopped in a place called, yep, Norman a bit above the Chickasaw Nation. Just south of Oklahoma City. Pulling "his" car up to an A&W for a cheeseburger and chocolate shake that he ate at a table in the hot sun outside.

His shoulder needed attention. The bullet grinded against a bone and it hurt. Last night, alcohol poured on the wound had nearly caused him to pass out in dizziness on the shabby motel bed covered with blood stains. He splashed peroxide on the wound after the alcohol. Drying it with a brittle and smelly towel, he wrapped gauze around it then duct tape. He would change into the second Oklahoma tourist t-shirt in the morning before he left the depressing motel, glancing at the bloodied bed cover one last time before he shut the door. Guest carnage.

He wondered how people got away with owning tenement motels, but there was one after the other along these forsaken midwestern roads. It was best to move through them at a quick pace. There was no life here. Just the barely living. The cheeseburger in Norman tasted sublime, even though the meat was dry. Somehow, even a bad cheeseburger always tasted good. The chocolate shake was cold and delicious. Norman, just one letter shy of Normal. Back in the Torino he meandered through a few stoplights and stared at some high school girls on the sidewalk. He aimed for Amarillo around four hours away and was there by early evening after stopping many times for gas. And just to stop. There was no prominence ahead of him. No marriage, no woman even.

He had gone bald at eighteen from too much thinking. A job had a routine, a way to find yourself moving into the next morning. It was a future of sorts but any job reduced you to work and little else. He had evaded the war. Started to wander when his draft card came. Maybe he should have gone to

Vietnam. Maybe, if he had, he would not be killing now. But he would have been killing over there. So in the end it mattered none.

Kill here. Kill there. Irrelevant where. He stared at the road as he drove. The once black asphalt was charcoal gray or even white in places, bleached and cracked with sun. A skeletal jackrabbit moved slow in the distance, an old man on a walker. Sometimes he pulled over the car to the roadside. Stared at the fields, usually of corn. Or of nothing. He was a man barely moving forward. The shoulder bled through the gauze. Sopping it like white bread in tomato soup.

At one point he sat on the hood and pulled off his second t-shirt. His naked torso felt good. He doused the shoulder wound with peroxide and alcohol. Pulling out his pocket knife his father had given to him when he was a boy, he dug deep inside the blood. Could feel the bullet against the bone. He cut the wound larger: it gaped like an open mouth at the dentist.

He dug in his thumb and middle finger inside humid flesh. A poem of excruciation, in that moment, was tattooed silently on his tongue. A few cars and trucks zoomed by him. The Torino bounced a little. His index fingertip found the bullet joined with his thumb, digging. The wound stretched as he grasped the piece and freed it from under his skin. Finally the bullet emerged like a tiny baby from a small womb. He stuffed it in his pocket. Doused the womb with white fizzing peroxide. Stuck the bottle mouth into the wound and poured. Semis thundered by him. Blood leaked onto the pavement and splattered his worn boots. Yes, more red rain.

With paper towels he blotted the blood. Spilled on rubbing alcohol. Dabbed some more. From a sewing kit found in a supermarket along the way he had the needle threaded and ready to go. There was no pain as the long needle dug into the damaged slash. The laceration sewn with cheap black thread. He kicked the second t-shirt down the roadside.

Decided to drive with his upper body unclothed for a while. At least that was his last thought until about five minutes later he fainted. Thankfully he knew it was coming. Veered into an abandoned gas station by wrecked cars before it happened. A lavender darkness had come early. The night covered his mind in seconds. He managed to lock his doors. And he was gone. For some time he was gone.

When he was conscious again he left the blond man's car where it was. Hitched. The next person lost her life. He had a new ride, at least for a while until he abandoned it. While he drove he did not kill. Only seemed to shoot them when he was picked up in their cars.

Had money saved from other murders as well. Decided to stay in a motel in Amarillo until March or later. Lie low. Took that long to feel back to himself. For one month straight through December 1969 and January 1970 he vomited many times a day. Followed by days of sleep. Puke acid caused one of his back teeth to drop out one morning. He pocketed it with the bullet from his shoulder. His red dreams filled with dead faces. A bright film of them streamed behind his eyes. The film moved faster. More faces. Sleep was dreaded but he needed it.

His body had many aches and creaks. Too many nights sleeping on cold ground. His goal had been endless death. While he had always known he would be caught, in some manner, the idea remained dormant. Pressed down into him. But it was rising. As his formerly quiet world slid off, this mental payment for his deeds surfaced with retribution. In his bed he wondered about himself as he dissolved. He was no longer the intact man he had been. Fragments of him remained. It had begun during his feverish lapse with the blond man. He had taken two bullets, one nothing, the other everything. This physical torment was a clear emblem of what was happening inside him. His outward body was part of the slide off. His inward mind could no longer suppress thoughts of the end of his life. He thought of a library book on nihilism he had been carrying with him when the blond man gave him a ride. That book had been tossed into the back seat. Was it still there? He wanted to read more of it. But he had switched cars before he came to the motel. Couldn't even remember where he had left the blond man's. Was unable to lift himself from bed. A cruel magnet kept his head stuck on the pillow. He started to see all the bullet wounds in the foreheads he had shot. They widened into a unison of mouths that said nothing. Mute chorus.

So . . . it was all scarred.

More vomit. More sleep. More red dreams.

He suffered. Knew that he deserved this misery. Atone. At one. He had forgotten about his prank plan. Until the end of March. When he noticed the girl at the motel.

Becca and the Bone Knife

She had a knife with her most of the time, even as a little girl on their Kentucky land. Would sit with a pocket knife cross-legged. Throw it into the soft ground, see how deep it sank. Hold it over her eye.

Think bad things about how easy and hard it would be to push it in there. Easy because it would be quick. Once you got past the seconds of pain. Hard because it would not be so easy to surmount that fear. Trying not to be morbid about sinking a knife into her brain, she would stand at a maple tree, fling a knife into the bark. Did a tree feel the blade? Her mother hated it. Her father encouraged her. She watched him skin raccoons hanging upside down from a tree in the front yard. Small bodies of red and blue lines and cords.

After she turned twelve he let her do the skinning. The raccoon became a buck with its throat slit. Her hands were a fast film, more rapid than her dad's. The local newspaper came to do an article on her when she was fifteen. Her mother despised Becca, a smaller version of her father. Her mom sat at the kitchen table, slurring. One night she was so drunk that Becca, now seventeen, skinned her mother's arm up past the forearm.

She didn't stay around long enough to see what happened when she woke up screaming. She would miss her father but never see either one of them again. She became the knife. She was many knives. Was then one knife. She walked near country roads. She knew the woods. No need to go back to school. No idea how to go forward. Family pulled you backward, she knew this. Bad family yanked you backward, held you down by the neck. You could never see ahead. You were always catching up to zero. Maybe family even blinded you a little with its acid.

Her drunk mother almost had woken up as she skinned her, so the other arm was out of the question. A selfish maternal waste. Becca left when she was done. A final gift to the horrify-ing woman.

She was in a forest now. Miles from home. Her back to a tree as she sat and thought. It was time to leave this state of rural nothing. It was nowhere, men in overalls smoking in gas stations off the highway 40 exit. They stared at you like dumb frogs with unmoving eyes.

Another teenage girl would be panicked about rape in tractor trailers, needing to ride in them to get where she was going. The knife kept her from being another teenager. The knife was her confidence. She could do many things with it. She had skinned the smallest of animals, mice, hamsters, gerbils. Increments up to bigger opossum, raccoon, deer. A cow once.

Even a horse. She would never forget that horse. In France they ate them. They ate mule in Italy. There was horse sushi in Japan, raw horse meat. Her father let her skin bigger animals after she perfected smaller ones. This meant many mice and raccoon at first, more difficult than deer. Smaller skins required more skill. She was having a memory of that horse. Strung upside down from a low barn rafter. Shot in the head by her dad. Said it could no longer walk with two broken legs. The cut neck poured blood for a long time.

She had to stand on a stepladder at times to reach high enough. Took nearly four days. Veins and arteries and white tendons filled her vision by the end. She knew she would never skin anything as big. It was when she was done that she wanted to kill and skin a man. Maybe many men.

She had been sneaking copies of *Killers!* from the gas station magazine rack and reading them since she was thirteen. There were stacks of them under her bed. All those animals were just practice for humans. The void of finishing the horse had left her empty. She had sensed this urge before, to kill men. It was at first a firefly in her eyesight, one radiant dot. After the horse it became two or three. More dots filled her eyes with tiny lights. Each seemed to be a man to kill. Followed by skinning. Or she would skin a live man as he died. There were so many dots in the weeks to come that she had to leave. It made no sense: she loved her father. Why men? She was sixteen at the time of this thought. She knew her mind was off. It had not been right before she started reading *Killers!* and its accounts of human crime. That magazine only confirmed it after the fact. There was one story of a musical drifter who walked into a farmhouse whistling and pummeled the entire family with a trumpet. The "true" stories were so absurd that she often laughed at them.

Every once in a while, though, one felt all too real, as if it had happened. These murders got her leaning forward. She liked to read the ads in the back as well. Half the time she couldn't tell what was true and what was false. The magazine profiled actual famous killers on occasion. Outsiders who lived with no rules. Sometimes the kills had a pattern but for the most part they were random. Every killer was insane in some way. It was this insanity pattern that she started to recognize in herself. A person like her would not live a long life.

She wondered if the dead animals affected her thoughts. She found books on skinning. During war the Japanese skinned entire bodies of enemies as torture. She felt for the animals. She had loved them and there was a part of her skinned along with them, each time. A layer of her peeled off. She never tortured them, only skinned them when they were dead.

She got to know death from the inside out with animal bodies. They sold that horse leather she skinned for a good price. They ate horse meat for nearly a year. The dots multiplied but, along with them, the light. Becca had headaches with these small flashes. Her mother was worse, yanking her backward. When she tried to move forward, she came up to zero again.

It was a need to do harm but she felt no anger. Maybe there would be women to kill too, not just men. One thing was certain: the future was vague. However, there would be killing on that path. And human skinning. Here she was leaning her back against a tree. Just turned seventeen. Kentucky was easy. The walk to the Citgo by the highway was about twenty miles. She needed to keep to the woods. Stay out of cars with strange people, men or women, locals who knew her family. She did not like weird men. Odd women who talked too much were worse.

She loved to walk in the woods in the quiet away from the noise of her mother, a gruesome misuse of a person. She took her time walking and came to the Citgo the next day. There, men in overalls smoked inside with their staring frog eyes. They came for the fried chicken and talk of politics. She knew they left keys in their trucks. She had saved money from skinning. Enough to travel and eat for many months.

In an old blue Chevrolet she eased off the parking lot and stole her first truck. On the seat she laid the knife: made of horse leg bone. The truck, she knew, was a hunter's. He left it for a week at a time, sometimes two. Rode with a friend for deer hunting. Becca had been coming to the station and listening for nearly a year.

She heard the local gossip, even participated in it because she too hunted. She stole copies of *Killers!* and hid them under her shirt. Funny, she had cash for the magazines but liked to steal them. Famous for her skinning she was paid by veteran hunters to handle their deer, the reason she had so much money now. There was a risk one of the truck owner's friends would notice it gone from the store. Maybe not. She would at least have time to flee Kentucky, a place she had wanted to leave since she was a girl.

She had money. Had the knife. Had an aim. Some people know they are dead before they die. They feel something and this sense is right. She was a corrupted part of her damaged mother, never to be fixed. However, she had a focused ability for blood. She was a surgeon of dead bodies. She feared nothing. Not even her own death that remained in her as an early vision. She would not live long. Did not need to. She existed as a blank. Vacant as the empty motel rooms she found along the way.

She took her time leaving Kentucky. It was her home after all and she needed to do this slow. What would her father do when he came back from his hunting trip to find her mom butchered? Her arm skinned, perhaps in shock. If Becca was right, he might have extended his hunt to avoid her mother anyway. And maybe she would rot there. Or never wake up. Hard to say. The sheriff would have no problem figuring out who had skinned her. Right now, Becca had a bit of time. Maybe a few days. Maybe a week. Likely months. Things happened less fast in the country.

She could even have longer if Dad treated her himself. And they kept it hushed. As they did so many things. The horror of others knowing about their insane daughter might just keep them quiet. She shrugged. It was moving now. There would never be another move backward. No more yanking. No more catching up to nothing.

There was a small bliss in stopping in gas stations, buying chips and sodas and jerky, sleeping alone in desolate motel room beds. It was enough for a couple of weeks as she made her way west. Yes, it was enough to be alone. No more yelling from that witch. In the quiet truck she rolled through Missouri, Kansas and Colorado, stopping at the Great Sand Dunes near Alamosa. Staring up at the mountains of magic sand. She threw her horse knife into it, practicing. Nobody on the dunes that overcast day.

Half of her was sane. The other half, not. Did the "not" half wish to be dead? She assumed so. She accepted her early loss of life as a given. It might be easier than she imagined. There was no more rational resistance. She smiled at the knife she held. White and smooth. Leaned back her head. Held the knife over her left eye like a sword swallower. If she endured the pain of the sharp tip in her eye, could she stand a few seconds of agony? Be strong enough to drive it into her mind?

This knife was her cyanide. She needed both hands for the force. Maybe not lean back her head. Just look forward with a swift jab. The first time she had these thoughts she was very young. Each year her contemplation of this act grew longer by the minutes. She might start thinking about it. Practicing it. The knives became longer with age too. Sharper as well. An hour would pass doing this with the knife. Only for her to snap out of it realizing it was unconscious. What she later feared was a disease in her head. Sometimes after arguments with her mother she wanted to do it and came close. Like now. Knife cyanide to the eye.

It was drizzling cold mist on her. Whatever was next would be easy and difficult. Easy because there would be no more fight about her future. Difficult because of violence along the way. Much of it. Nothing mattered in a life that recognized its futility. She was set. Little to think about anymore. Just to act. She was certain she would be dead before the end of the year. It would bother a normal person. Which she was not. Sitting in the truck she kept staring at one ad in the back of the magazine. On the road she drove with an empty mind.

Tane and the Hatchet

Tanner had never been called that. Always Tane. The most average and handsome boy you could imagine without a bit of violence in him. That was the impression . . . Meanwhile he read true crime novels in bed with a flashlight, any magazines he could find at the convenience store stands. What he learned about violence was that anyone could do it. You didn't need an education to be violent. To shed blood you just had to murder someone. There were consequences, sure, and maybe your life wouldn't last very long, but no one could stop you from killing. If that was your wish. So many people deserved murder, especially the bland. Dumb killers were bad plotters. Good killers thought it out and looked ahead at what might happen. It wasn't about inflicting pain on people. It was more about human chess slaughter. Why could a soldier kill in war but not come home and do the same? Context. The killer had to have context. He wanted a taste. How? At night his eyes widened as he read about murders in forbidden pages. He had learned how to type in school and tried to write a few stories of his own. They never felt authentic. In the morning the mediocrity of his life choked him. His parents thought he was an ideal boy who loved to go to bed early. They had no idea that he wanted to read all night about killing. His father worked in insurance, his mother stayed at home and cooked every meal for him. His school was average. Expensive. Ordinary nonetheless. The rich were homogeneous.

One winter afternoon in late December when he was eighteen, he chopped wood in the Ohio cold. His father sliced the chainsaw on a dying maple in the yard. It was the first time his dad asked him to try it. Handing him the vibrating saw that chugged as he blew cold air breath. His father smiled, he remembered that, proud of his son. Something twitched in Tane's head. He sliced the blade right into the man's thigh. Without even thinking about it. Dropped the saw by his dad's leg and watched him bleed. Let time pass. Walked inside, told his mother cooking lunch what had happened. She screamed and called the ambulance which never came fast in those days.

He held a fascination for impunity. At the same time he didn't mind being caught. Perhaps being caught inoculated you from capture. Maybe not caring was what gave you power. Deep in him he rebelled against mediocrity. He had to not be average anymore. Although he felt he had never been. O. HI. O. Even the name of his state sounded like a topographical monotony. A state he would leave. In fact he used the mayhem of his father's death to sneak away, something he had planned for months.

Once the ambulance came and said he was dead, Tane vanished through his back yard to the Trailways station.

He was on a bus, right on schedule. No more normal. He had been to a prep school in town, hated vocabulary tests. How could he erase those words forced on him and get back to no language? Everyone wanted to talk. About what? Nothing, that's what. Talk added up to very little. He no longer had to be a part of talking. On the bus ride he thought about the empty hole inside him. He had carried a stack of crime magazines with him to read on the trip.

One ad in the back of *Killers!* had caught his eye as he planned things weeks ago. He was loved more than enough. Why was it never adequate? All of a sudden a nun to his left retched into a white washcloth. She apologized with her eyes. The bus stank of diesel and blue mint from the toilet. Ohio took forever to leave. Indiana and Illinois. Another forever.

Bugs slapped the bus windshield so thick and rapid that he thought at first it was a rain storm. Until he saw the dead bugs skidding down his own side window and realized what they were. Insect genocide. Stops were gas stations, mostly. Missouri and Kansas. A long drive west through nothing states. Places where nothing people lived. At the top of Texas he had to leave the stale bus. He just had to get away from the smell. Wherever he was now, he was sick as he remembered the nun on the bus puking. It was a gas station with nothing much around it. Flat and deserted. He was by himself. No one seemed to be here as he retched on the dry dirt. Then a man appeared. Long white hair and pink skin, brown cowboy hat. Came over to him, out of nowhere, put his hand on Tane's back and said, "You okay, son?"

"I'm all right," he said, wiping bile spittle from his mouth.

"Them buses smell nasty, don't they?"

"Yeah," Tane chuckled, "try being in one for two days."

"Lemme get you a Seven Up."

He sauntered over to the soda machine, found a quarter and the green bottle dropped. Flicked off the top with the embedded opener in the middle. Tane tilted back his head with closed eyes. Poured the clear, sweet, cold soda into his mouth. Sun flashed into his eyes as he opened them.

The man watched.

"Thank you," he said to the fellow.

"Come on inside. Cool in there."

Tane looked around and noticed the garage for car repairs.

On the floor was a hatchet for some reason.

"What's that for?"

"Wut?"

"The hatchet."

"That's mine. Use it for hacking up mulberry bushes that sprout up through the cement cracks."

"Give you ten bucks for it?"

"Hmmm," the man thought, holding his chin with a thumb and finger and propping his elbow with his other palm.

"Not enough?"

"Well . . ."

"Twelve?" Tane tried.

"Cash money?" the man asked.

"Yeah, cash money."

"What about fourteen?"

"Fourteen's fine." Tane stifled a laugh, handing him the bills.

"Thanks."

"Hey, can I ask another favor?"

"Sure."

"Give you another twenty if you drive me south a little."

"How far?"

"Close to Amarillo?" Tane asked him.

"I can drop you there."

"When can you take me?"

"Bus was my last gas-up customer for a day or two probably. Let's go now."

Tane stared at the man. Just because you had a weapon didn't mean the murder urge would come. The weapon could not precede the desire. It was only a prop until the compulsion came. And he liked him. He couldn't kill the guy. The hard part would be learning how to kill nice people. They were in the Texas Panhandle, where, he was not sure. Some random rest stop. He gave the man another thirty instead of twenty. Stepped out of the truck with his hatchet. He said thanks through the window and wished there were more like him. The fellow was not so bad. He was all right. The red truck with the white-haired driver 180ed, giving a casual wave with his right hand. Tane waved back, even feeling affection for his kindness amid the desolation.

On a whim he jumped up into an idling semi in the rest stop parking lot. It was full of diesel. He noticed the annoyed trucker stomping to his rig. Tane stepped back down with the hatchet. One slash to the neck. The blade was dull and slipped off the skin with a bounce. He would sharpen it later. Didn't do the job. Twirling the handle around, he hammered a hole hard into the forehead. The shocked man fell. He aimed for the same hole. Hammered another right into it, practicing his aim. He stepped up again into the idling truck. Had never driven anything this big. Would only need it for a little while.

That felt good, he thought to himself, looking in his rearview mirror back at the body on the asphalt, grinding gears. The semi felt like an airplane taxiing. Fields of abandoned oil wells to his left and right. For a couple of months he would live in the truck. Stay on the big highways. It had a bed in the back and a fridge with food. Then he would leave it somewhere and hitch.

Meanwhile, at rest stops he followed people into bathroom stalls. Killed them as they sat on the toilet, suspecting nothing. A humiliating way to go, he realized. He did feel bad for these practice victims. Easy to kick open the stall doors to slash their necks and hammer their heads. And simply leave them there. He kept a tally on a pad of paper. The semi was like staying in a hotel room almost. He could leave it running and have heat when it was cold. Stealing wallets and purses off his dead gave him plenty of money. He thought of the killing as a daily job. Sometimes he bounced around between five to ten rest stops a day, many of the same ones on a route he liked. This meant up to ten people could die. He worked in the dark also to raise his numbers. Looked at local papers during the day to see if the killings made the news. On a whim he decided to make up a story on his writing pad.

Type it up and send it in to *Killers!* for a submission. Well, not made up. It was what he was doing every day and night with his hatchet. "The Rest Stop Hatchet Killer" sounded risible enough to fit the magazine's sensational slant. They might believe it. They might not. It was in between true and fake that caused readers questions. Is this real, they might wonder? At a pawn shop in a small town he found an old Underwood typewriter that still worked except for the "f" key. He bought a ream of paper at a nearby stationer. Whenever there was an "f" he filled it in later with a pencil. After every fifth murder he wrote up the stories. Mailed them to the editors at the magazine. Waited. Was obsessed with that ad in the back for The Nihilistics. At the beginning of the month he checked the newsstands. Nothing the first month. But there it was, his first story, the second month. His eyes widened in surprise and elation. He couldn't get paid for them because he didn't want to use a P.O. box. Had made up a name too for the author, Samuel Bunker.

He would have to ditch the typewriter at some point, too heavy to carry while traveling around on foot and in cars after he abandoned the semi. Once the stories became popular and in demand, he would still submit them. But handwritten. Samuel Bunker was the ostensible murderer. Tane became Bunker when he killed. It was a new persona that worked. Sam Bunker, for short. Had a killer's ring to it. While he liked the semi for the room it had, it was difficult to drive around. He was stuck parking mostly at rest stops. The very places he committed the murders. He would miss the large bed and fridge he could fill with food, even a television that plugged into the cigarette lighter. It wasn't practical and soon there were many cops all over the rest stops. In a way he did blend in with the other semis. Still, it was too risky. By his count he made it up to thirty killings. That meant six stories since he wrote after the fifth murder. Each story contained five murders. He decided to space out sending his writing, one at a time at the end of every month. This way he would tease the editors and readers.

And if he didn't have time to write on the road, which was likely, he would always have something to send to them. His writing was deeply disturbing, to him at least. As he reread the savagery of his days and nights, it struck him that he was no longer sane. It was not right that he was so happy being a criminal. So it wasn't the slaughter itself that bothered him. But that it kind of made him feel good. A flipped switch had put light on a deranged self. Starting with the death of his innocent dad. After murder thirty and story six he took a break. A couple of months had passed. He was ready for the nihilism the magazine offered. He left the semi back at the same rest stop where it had been stolen. The typewriter was still in it.

And he started to hitch.

Sheriff Strake

Strake knew what was in the bank before he went inside it, a silent fear he had known in Vietnam. Never knew when you might find a gutted body on the side of the road. Flies coming out of the nose. But you expected it, so you were never fully surprised. He told Maude to stay outside and keep guard. The hen clucked. He braced himself. Pulled open the glass door.

The first thing he saw was his son Harris beside his young wife Betty. Harris had been slashed in the neck. Possibly with the hatchet Jimmy had mentioned since the cut was so wide. His boy leaned against her. She had a yawning hole in the middle of her forehead with a creek of brown blood down to her chin. Roger, the manager, had taken a bullet in the head, looked like. And Dolores had maybe been stabbed in the neck, if Strake had a right accounting of the three weapons Jimmy had seen. But . . . a hatchet? Good grief. He knelt down to his son and touched his face. Blood on the white walls flashed across his eyes. Betty had been three months pregnant. It was horrible death. Two generations of his blood erased in a minute.

Outside again, hands on knees, he took in a breath and blew it out. With the dead you could take your time. There was no hurry. As Maude trotted beside him he walked over to the coroner, Meyer, and told him the situation. Dolores was Meyer's sister. Meyer nodded with tears moistening his eyes (but not falling) and said he would take care of it.

"Sorry about Dolores."

"You too, Strake. I mean, your son, his wife, their baby . . ."

"It's the start of a bigger war here. Jimmy said they were young, the killers."

"What'll you do?" he asked Strake.

"Oh," the sheriff said, "I plan to find them."

"How?"

"Chase them down. Maybe give the heel of my boot some practice."

"Good. When?"

"Leaving now. Can you look after Maude?"

"I could use the company."

Meyer shook his hand, looked him in the eye. They each put up a left hand on the other's shoulder for comfort. Maude bobbed her head, her absent but vigilant eyes never closing.

Strake called Jimmy and asked him to watch the sheriff's office while he was gone. He decided not to use the cop car, the old black Chrysler with blue lights on top. No, he wanted something faster. It would have to be his personal ride. That wouldn't matter. He no longer cared about damage to anything since it had all come undone.

The Chevelle SS 454 was a drag racer on the weekends out at the Talson Farm. The V8 could take it up to 160. It was jeep green with two white stripes on the hood. Two doors. Four headlights, two on each side. The sheriff, before his pursuit began, called many other sheriffs in towns around Athens to warn them. They thanked him. For help, Strake called three particular sheriffs he knew well. They spoke of the Crucifix, code word for how they would stop the killers. It was a local trick they had come up with to trap joyriders. He and Sheriff Neaves talked briefly. Strake said he would come see him first to give him more details. Neaves was the next town over.

He would stop to see the other two sheriffs afterward. Life went to a dark place after that. He had only done a year in Nam but had seen at least a few thousand deaths, small children, babies, young girls, farmers. Trained as a tracker, a spotter and a sniper for the Marines, Strake had grown up with guns. His father and his grandfather had both been sheriff before him. His small town only had a few hundred people. The four deaths at the bank would take a long time for everyone to understand.

After he had seen six of his buddies splitting apart over land-mines placed closely together, they shipped him home because of his visions. He could no longer see clearly, in two ways. First, his vision was ruined for a while by the blast. One eye speared with debris. And the second loss was inside his mind. Gradually, his vision improved to near sniper accuracy. He was lucky he could still see out of both. The left eye ached after that landmine fiasco. He had to cover it with his palm to hide from the light.

His spotter, Jim Riley, had exploded into pieces like blood and flesh confetti. Mad visions within his head never left either. He often saw his six friends as sides of beef hanging upside down in a meat fridge, swinging dead men. The loss of Jim, he could never handle.

The Chevelle left his house. He was no longer married after these visions scared his wife off. No one knew where she was. He didn't blame her. She had shadows of her own from a ruth-less childhood. It was an impossibility to live with someone like him. Maybe he had killed "legally" in the war, if there was such a thing, but he was still a killer. An insane one who could blend into the normalcy. Just the person to find these twerps.

His trip might end up being aimless, he knew that. He had become complacent. The quieter it was, the fewer visions he had. Already the blood on the bank walls had brought them back with quick fear. They would only increase, the more blood that was shed. As best as he could figure, he was looking for a white convertible, maybe red seats, with two young men and a lady. One of the men was bald, according to Jimmy. His gut feeling was that they would aim for another small town. It seemed like they had nothing to lose. Jimmy thought maybe they were radicals. Hell, they sounded like something out of a French crime novel.

But why *his* town? There was nothing radical in killing innocents. Or maybe there was. It was random, he was sure of it. Had to be. Random with only more random to come. The world had turned random anyway. It was no surprise. None of it was ever a surprise. Could he fight off the visions, the closer he came to violence again? He couldn't say. Somehow, he was not worried. He did sense, however, that he would never go home. Whatever home was. Blood was bathing his mind again.

On the back roads under an empty sky he drove by trailer parks. Shirtless boys in yards stared at him. Broken men sat in lawn chairs smoking and drinking beer from tin cans. This scene was repeated along the old highway. He passed a fallen Winston billboard that said, "How good it is."

Strake knew these trailers well. His ex-wife had grown up in one, her father heavy into drugs. One night she was in her trailer when, maybe seven years old, they shot bullets at it for thirty minutes. She still had to live in it after the shooting with an aunt who had no teeth and ate lard with a spoon.

His first stop was in the next town over to see Sheriff Neaves, to ask him if he had seen anything suspicious. Neaves consoled him about his relatives, shaking his head in sadness. Neaves was a Scottish Cherokee. His name meant "fists" and these letters were tattooed across the knuckles of his left hand. He was over six feet tall with fair skin and freckles but long black hair and wide brown eyes.

"You said a *hatchet*?" he asked.

"Yep, a hatchet, a knife and a pistol."

"And Jimmy saw them?"

"On the street before they went into the bank, yes. He got a glimpse."

"Hm," Neaves said, pacing around his office with hands in his hair, "but they didn't harm Jimmy?"

"Just went into the bank. Didn't hurt him. Seemed like they *wanted* to die, if you know what I mean. He said they hardly noticed him."

"Well the highway runs right through town here by the Texaco. I think we might've noticed a car like theirs."

"So, nothing?"

"I'll ask around, Strake. So far it's been quiet."

"Thinking they may be on a spree."

"Possible. Lots of radical kids out there at the moment."

"Yeah, radical for no reason. Could be political."

Strake suddenly thought of his son Harris and put his thumb and forefinger in his eyes to stop any pain of tears that might come.

Neaves watched this tableau of a crushed man with patience, let it pass.

"And you said you want some help with the Crucifix?"

"I could use some, yes. I have two other sheriffs also."

"Think it will work?"

"Doesn't have to be perfect."

"I remember we tried it a couple of times, didn't always fly."

"May not even need it."

"Ha," Neaves said, "the Crucifix. Good trick."

"Can be, if we do it right."

"I just worry. Doesn't seem like they care about much."

"That's a factor, yes. We have to be careful, coordinate it."

"Something always goes wrong when there are crazy people involved."

"Well," Strake said, "let's be a little crazier."

"Heh heh. Just follow you then?"

"You mind using your own car? That's what I'm doing."

"I've got a car, ohhh, do I have a car."

In Neaves' garage was his Oldsmobile 442, black with a long white stripe front to back down the lower part. It was a sharp ride. Brand new.

"Four speed?" Strake asked him.

"Yep, fast."

"Sure you want to go?"

"I'm going. That's that."

"Could end up a goose chase."

"In these cars, sheeeee-ut, I don't care. We'll get them."

"I think we need to go now."

"I'm ready," Neaves assured him. "A deputy'll look after things while I'm gone. Delman. More of an office guy, but he'll hold down the fort."

"I'd hate to see your new car damaged."

"Can always fix her. Got a real good body shop I use. We'll put them on standby."

"Let's go then."

They had a bit of luck in the next town with a clue. After Strake had talked to him on the phone, the sheriff there had definitely seen the car with the two men and the girl. They had stopped for gas and eaten at the diner. Rotund and pink-faced from his favorite chicken fried steak and mashed potatoes and peach pie, Sheriff Crowley noticed them from his office and waddled outside, all three chins jiggling. In fact he had been finishing this very meal when they had appeared. Something hadn't looked right with the deranged trio. One of the men limped. The girl was shouting at them both. They had cash in their hands they were counting.

"I thought they was mebbe filming something down here. You know, we get those film crews shooting country shots. Met a few directors who ask us to help out with road traffic sometimes.

She looked like a movie star. They did too, come to think of it. All three wore fancy sunglasses."

"Happen to see where they went?" Strake wanted to know.

"They're keeping on this highway. Back roads are too slow, sometimes gravel. Might've tried them but found out soon enough they couldn't make much progress. You may still catch them if they're on this little highway now."

"Still interested in helping?"

"Hell yes, my friend. Think you can pull it off with the Crucifix?"

"Maybe. What kind of car you have?"

Crowley said his was the sheriff's ride, an indestructible turd brown Chrysler that had no mounted sirens. "Blend in real nice, Strake. Never put sirens on the top, just have one in the seat I put on the dash when I need it."

Neaves smiled. "One more car and we're good to go." He followed Strake, the Oldsmobile and the Chevelle like two bulls running after each other. Sheriff Crowley behind them at a distance in his long tank. It was longer than Strake's car by nearly six feet, a beast of a vehicle.

In the fourth town, no word of the three, but Sheriff Houston, a short black man who had been in Vietnam with Strake and was missing a pinky, also joined the posse with his Ford Mustang Boss 302. It was the only one that stood out with its turquoise brightness, but they couldn't do much about it. "Ride Captain Ride" by Blues Image blasted from Houston's radio.

They smiled at the coincidence of the tune.

"Ready gents?" Strake said, grinning.

They all nodded like little boys.

"Stay spaced out, especially you Houston. Your car could be a target with that bright paint job, not that the line of all four of us is *that* inconspicuous."

"Understand," Sheriff Houston said.

"And you all know the Crucifix, right?"

He went over it again just to be sure, adding, "We may find them suddenly. Stopping will draw attention with the four of us sticking out like sore thumbs, but I have a plan. Now, we've done it before, the Crucifix, and it worked but they have weapons. A hatchet, a knife and a handgun. Plus three death wishes. We're dealing with people here who might even be *hoping* to die, flagrant as they're acting."

"I'll be happy to oblige them," said Neaves.

"One more thing," Strake said, "when we get into a town, you three keep driving through it unless we see their white Impala, then I'll meet you out where the town ends. That way I can stop and ask questions. And you can flank the town line in case they drive past you."

"You doing okay, Strake?" Houston asked him. "I mean, your son . . ."

"I'm fine."

The four men got back into their cars, Strake leading them.

It was a vehicular gang ready for the Crucifix. In his gut Strake knew it wasn't likely to happen. Still, a plan was needed, mostly for unity, with the proviso that it would turn to something else. He was sure there would be no controlled order in the capture of these three idiots. He was soon proven right. In the next few towns they came up blank. Heading west they picked up more little clues. And then they found the body. Beside a . . . typewriter.

In the small towns, if the Impala had been there someone noticed it. With this information they forged ahead, more or less right. They just needed the trio to stop for an extended time. From the looks of it, they were only gassing up or grabbing food on the run. Sheriffs Houston, Crowley and Neaves had also made sure that deputies watching the offices called around to each town to warn them. These calls made every place ready for what could happen, plus CB radio chatter sharing information about sightings. About a hundred miles west of his town Strake found out they tried to rob another bank. Their sheriff had been hiding behind the teller counter, sometimes doing security for the bank anyway. Before they could react, the sheriff fired at the three of them like ducks at a shooting gallery. He had taken one bullet from the handgun in his forearm.

He ran out the back. They grabbed cash, the bank manager found out later. No tellers had been hurt since they had been warned and told to go home. The trio fled in the convertible. This put them on a clear path for being caught. Gas stations were on alert to not serve them. The posse of four was on their trail at this point. The Mustang, Chrysler, Oldsmobile and Chevelle drove to the town line of the recently hit second bank to wait after hearing about it on the CB. The storm before the calm, Strake thought. The next two hours would feel like two days. His visions were darkening again, making him feel heavy and slow. Much would happen. Not all like he had planned. Violence never had a design. It was a rupturer of designs. The showdown would soon occur. What he never anticipated was the persistence of the girl.

Or that body and typewriter on the roadside.

It was all crucifying in the end.

The Nihilistics

At the motel in Amarillo, Ellman was still hurt from his gunshot shoulder. Moving around in pain. There weren't many choices for places to stay. Becca had noticed the same shabby one-story dump with the pool out front by the highway. The one from the ad. He saw her at the pool. She noticed him, thought his bald head attractive. Mirror sunglasses hid their eyes. Looked like he was never coming to her so she went over to him. He sat in a deck chair. She noticed the bullet hole. No bandage during the day, only at night, she found out later. "You on the run?" he asked her, staring at her little body in the orange bikini.

"Maybe. What of it?"

"Sassy one."

"Sassy enough."

"How old are you?"

"Seventeen."

"I see."

"You look like a tragedy," she informed him.

"I want to give you a chance to walk away. No good can come from being around me."

"The hell's that supposed to mean?" she scoffed, hand on a hip.

"You're too young to be a hooker."

"What! I'm not a hooker, you dipshit!"

"My fault," he apologized. "I mean, I just thought . . ."

"What's so bad about you anyway?"

"You don't want to know," he assured her.

"Like, why you got shot up?"

"Something along those lines perhaps."

"Why don't you tell me about it?"

"I'm not baring myself to some dumb teenager."

"I assure you I'm not dumb. I'm here for The Nihilistics."

Ellman leaned closer. "Say again?"

"You heard me."

"You mean . . . you saw my ad?"

She sat on the chair beside him.

In the next few hours of that hot Texas afternoon, humidity moistened their bodies in the sun. Ellman decided to do just that: unburden himself. To this point his every thought had remained in his own head. Never to be shared. It was cluttered in there. She asked him if he had killed anyone. He hesitated. "Yes. Many."

She wanted more details about the murders. Which is when he described the Colt Government to her. Something he would show her later that night in his room. Instead of asking him "why" he had killed them, she wanted to know "how." This was the beginning of The Nihilistics. A dialogue by the pool. Ellman had been dreaming of such a group. He liked to think up names while he walked on the roads. The Nihilists. The Annihilators. A final thing to be a part of as he went down in the red rain. He was not much older than she was. She did *seem* older. Her curious questions began to worry him since she was a minor. So he asked a few of his own. And she had no problem telling him about her disgusting mother, even the skinning of the arm. Stealing the truck at the Citgo, driving across the country. Her own desire to kill. "One day," she announced, "I *will* skin a human."

His eyes widened. "Gross."

"It's beautiful."

"If you say so."

The synchronicity of their meeting here amazed him. As if she had followed him to what would be their future annihilation. It was a fate he now believed was planned. Well, it was sort of a cheat since he'd placed that ad. Soon, they were in his room and she was admiring his Colt. He was consumed by erotic lust for her but could not act. His shoulder ached. He asked her to help him bandage it for the night. The touch of her fingers on his warm sunburned skin made him shiver. She saw the goosebumps.

It aroused her. They did nothing. It was a new and sensual tension between them. Ellman had an odd code. He could murder with impunity but would not sleep with a minor. She seemed to understand. Through the night they sat on the bed. Talked about the peculiar lack of feeling within them.

"Alexithymia," he said.

"Sounds like five-dollar word puke."

"Means we can't find what we feel."

Ellman described each murder to her even though they were in essence the same. He caught a ride. Shot the driver. But the last driver had two bullets for him. He was tired of it. Couldn't do it anymore but something made him. Killing after his mistake would be messy. No longer clean and neat. She wanted to help.

In the morning they had to leave her stolen truck.

"We need to switch vehicles," Ellman said.

They walked around the hot asphalt checking different ones. Found an Impala convertible across the parking lot, keys in it and everything. Headed east where they would begin their work at the banks. Just off the highway they saw a man with black hair hitching. They stopped and let him jump in the back seat. At a diner just over the Texas border in Oklahoma, they talked more with the hitchhiker.

"Tane," he said, shaking Ellman's hand and staring at the young girl.

"Ellman."

"Becca."

"Let's get something to eat," Tane offered. "On me. For the ride."

"Sounds good," Ellman agreed.

As they ate, Tane shared his own story. He pulled out a copy of *Killers!* to show them, not mentioning he was a writer. Ellman's eyes widened.

"You too?" he said, confirming The Nihilistics meeting.

Tane opened to the ad. "I was on the way to your motel to meet you."

Becca was the only one who had not killed a person and said so.

"Well," Ellman told her, "let's change that."

He opened an atlas. With eyes closed they each loosely pointed to towns in Georgia, close to Athens. In the center of their three dots they found one place. "I'm sure there's a bank we can hit to give Becca her first kill and to stock up on money, but if we're serious we won't make it very far."

"They'll think we're some kind of militant group," Becca mentioned.

"Militant groups care too much," Ellman responded to this. "We care about nothing."

Tane nodded. He could not believe his luck being picked up by these two. He would have just missed them if he had gone to the motel in the ad.

"I got here months ago, been on a little practice spree. Wanted to get ready before I came to meet you."

"Kind of name is Tane anyway?" Ellman asked.

"Short for Tanner."

"Sure you want to do this?"

"Would've done it on my own anyway. Might as well go down with some friends."

"Could be fun."

Becca stared at the two: wondered what it would be like to knife them each in the throat. Skin them while they were oozing blood slowly, still conscious. "What are the odds," Tane wondered, smiling his best handsome grin, "of us all meeting like this on the road?"

"It was an inevitability," Ellman said, batting his eyes.

"I mean, I know I was going to the motel, but it looks like I would have just missed you. And yet you still picked me up on the road here."

Were they flirting? Both of them ignored her and excused themselves to the restroom. She had an idea why they went in there and they came out with faces flushed about twenty minutes later.

"Don't even tell me," she said, waving a hand at them, staring down at a piece of bacon that looked like something she had skinned.

After the diner Ellman and Tane poked each other and horsed around more. They got a room together in the next motel. Becca stayed by herself in the one next to it, fuming, wishing she was eighteen. They stayed in one more motel in Alabama. Found out the top to the convertible would not raise, meaning hot wind the entire trip that dehydrated them, hurt their eyes and flamed their tempers. They stopped in the small town in Georgia.

Prior to storming into the first bank, they agreed to lunge in unison with their weapons. There was tension because Becca thought Ellman liked her. Maybe he still did. Tane had ruined that. They could not have been more precise in their coordination against the four bank workers. The knife and the hatchet seemed to work in perfect time, skin plunged right at the moment the Colt shot its bullet. What Becca hadn't anticipated was the thrill at seeing someone die. She had watched animals, sure, and their eyes haunted her, but with people there was no feeling, just awe, like a child seeing parents having sex for the first time and realizing they had flesh.

The woman teller was thirty pounds overweight. Her horse bone knife slid into her neck as blood flew around. Spurted back into her eyes. It was an ecstasy she felt in her body, in the wetness coming from between her legs. Her knife had been made for this moment. As she watched Tane use his hatchet on the younger man and woman, she also noticed Ellman's style and wondered just how many people he had killed. Beyond the ones he had told her about at the motel pool. The three were together. They had killed at the same time.

Almost at the exact instance. After this it would be chaotic and filled with mistakes. There would never be precise killing like this. Maybe it was because they had no fear when they walked down that sidewalk and came into this bank. They had talked about dying. Knew they wanted to die. But had it really been that difficult to maim unsuspecting people? Whatever the case, she felt different when they left the bank. She had a sense that Tane and Ellman had a similar feeling. Elation was only brief. There was fear now.

She noticed the sign that said Sheriff's Office once they were back in the car and leaving. A random witness, a man, had seen them. Tane didn't seem concerned. Why hadn't Ellman just shot that witness? Their death wish seemed inane. While she was thrilled, Becca had a sober reaction. Sure enough in the following towns many eyes were on them. Or at least they felt that they were. But weren't The Nihilistics all about falling apart? Aren't we *supposed* to fall apart? she thought to herself. It was fractured. She decided to accept the splintering.

They were in complete non-control. Each town added more fear. The trio argued more. They were covered in blood. Ellman drove them to their ending. They could not complain. Because they had designed the end from the beginning. Tane had typed up the story of the first bank very fast. Asked to stop at a post office before the next robbery. He ran inside to mail it to the magazine editors.

"Writer," she scoffed, under her breath.

The next bank they hit: no tellers. A sheriff jumped up. Picked them off as soon as they barged through the door. Ellman was already limping because he had slipped on some blood in the first bank and fallen. Becca took a shot in her thigh. Tane's was worse: right in the stomach. Good, she thought, die slow. Ellman, who seemed impervious to death, had the skin of a knuckle shot off. He barely got off one shot from the Government that grazed the sheriff's arm. The man was out the back door before they knew it. Money was in the tills. They grabbed what they could pocket. They wouldn't need much anyway. Days were limited. Perhaps it was down to hours.

Becca and Ellman lifted Tane who had collapsed on the bloody bank floor. Ellman had picked up the hatchet and thrown it in the trunk. He kept driving because of Tane's gut shot. It was very bad, so he sat in the back with her. She stuffed a shirt onto the wound to hold back the blood. The rest would play out just like they had (and hadn't) planned. They thought they were ready. Maybe they were to some extent. Maybe not. More eyes of more towns followed them. It had been a mistake to stay on this same back highway but the country roads were too rough. Places were talking to each other about them. Death seemed bigger, the closer it was. Before, it hadn't appeared to be so bad. Since Tane bled from his stomach, Ellman kept driving. Becca knew what she needed to do.

In one sudden movement she grabbed her horse bone knife. Lifted it over him. Stabbed him deeply in the chest right where his heart was. Or close to it. One last gift for Tane, the fake Sam Bunker. Ellman winced but accepted it without much worry. She watched Tane's eyes blink a few times in thanks mixed with spite. Ellman pulled over the car. She pushed out the body. It fell with a thud onto the gravel shoulder. Then it was just the two of them. She moved to the front seat. Heaved the typewriter onto the ground too. It landed perfectly upright near Tane's head.

"Didn't like that guy," she said, staring at the annoying bullet in her leg.

Ellman shrugged.

"You think he was really Samuel Bunker?"

"From *Killers!* you mean?"

"Yeah, he said he was."

"Guess we won't be around long enough to find out."

"Probably stole the hatchet idea from the stories."

"Or the other way around," Ellman said. "He was the Rest Stop Hatchet Killer and wrote stories about it."

"Doubtful," she sneered. "Highly doubtful."

"I wonder why he only just told us he was a writer."

"He told me back at the first bank," she said. "I never believed him."

They drove on.

Showdown

The four car posse pulled over by the body near the random typewriter. All the sheriffs walked up. Looked down at the dead young man in the ditch. Blood seeped from his gashed chest in a muddy puddle. A bullet hole in his stomach too. They were close to the killers. They'd stopped right here to dump him. But the trio was two now. Strake was going to call an ambulance, thought better of it. Instead they loaded the dead body in his trunk.

"No sense in people seeing this," he told them, tossing in the Underwood too. They agreed. The one who had killed his son and his boy's wife. He knew it was him. *The bald man held the gun,* Jimmy told him. *The man with hair had the hatchet.*

The trunk was still open as they chatted. Before they knew it the young man jolted and flung himself on the ground, landing right on his mouth. The sheriffs winced: had to have hurt. They stared at him as he lifted up his head. Made no effort to help him. Exposed bloody gums, snaggled teeth. A front tooth fell to the asphalt. "She stabbed me!" he slobbered and took off in a sprint. Into a field then the woods. A comic sight that could never be funny. None of the four men had a gun on them. They had taken them off to drive. No one ran after the boy. They stared blankly in the distance like four cows.

"Don't chase him," Strake said. Implicit in his comment was what the three others knew. Strake would walk into those woods. Track the killer of his son and daughter-in-law. Instant justice was good and ugly.

Meanwhile, they kept staring at the boy making a visible trail of blood as he ran. Strake told Neaves and Crowley to drive ahead. Keep on the hunt.

"Houston, you come with me."

To the other two he added: "Be on standby . . . we may still need a last minute Crucifix."

They nodded and drove off.

"Ready?" Strake asked him.

"How is that guy still alive? See that bullet in his belly?"

"Somebody wants me to kill him. That girl."

"The stab wound hole is huge. He should be dead."

"She knew what she was doing," Strake assured him.

"The girl, what do you mean?"

"She just pretended to kill him. Knows exactly where the heart is. She missed it on purpose."

"I wonder why," Houston said.

"I know why."

"Do tell."

"She's the worst of them."

"Hm."

"That's no ordinary knife, not metal. Jimmy said the blade was white."

"Makes sense," said Houston. "They're rare but she must have a bone knife. Not easy to make."

Chasing a wounded animal was cheating. A human was different. Especially a rotting human. You were sort of digging out your own heavy darkness when you went back to what made you bury it in the first place. Strake knew he was doing it. The war was a labyrinth of torment in him. A maze of psychosis where he was always lost. To go back was to be lost again. With a familiar recognition of anguish. Meandering around the old ordeal. Surrounded by high walls.

What would he do when he found the young man, someone who killed as if it were a joke? He also wondered about the girl and her knife. The typewriter: he had no clue. Her purposeful stabbing had missed the heart enough to let the guy survive. She intrigued Strake. Felt she would be more of a problem than the two men. He would deal with her later. Strake had tracked many men in his life. It was an art, sure. For him it was about keeping his eyes alert. Many looked at the woods and saw a blur of sameness, no variation in an intimidating landscape. He saw small things, so minute that the unalert eye would never glance at them. Most could recognize the pellets of deer scat. But reading squirrel and chipmunk and rabbit scat could tell him a lot too.

As they walked Houston told him a story about a Vietnam village where a group of girls, each with a grenade, surrounded a soldier friend. The explosion of humans left a lurid panic in his thoughts for the rest of his life. His Marine friend had been ambushed from the north, east, south and west. Houston had watched his buddy go piss by a tree. Had only looked away for a second when the children appeared. There was nothing to do as the girls exploded one by one and the four blasts annihilated his friend. Houston could not move. He was behind a tamarind tree. He ducked behind the trunk when he saw them expose the grenades. When he peered out again female torsos had been ripped from the tops of their bodies. His friend's head had vanished. "I think they were no older than ten, the four of them."

"Yeah," Strake said, as they walked side by side. Commenting on the past never helped. Yeah was about all that needed to be said.

"You sure you want me along?" Houston asked him. "I mean, I can turn back and let you do your business."

"No, I'll need you. At some point. Not sure when, but I will."

"Okay."

They walked on in silence, Strake stopping to eye the bark or squat to touch the scat. He could smell the young man's blood. So very different from any animal. Any blood smelled raw but humans reeked in a forest, even when they had not been stabbed. The stabbing had made this too easy. Droplets not visible to Houston were easily spotted by Strake. Soon the murderer would have to lean against a tree or sit on a fallen one. One time Strake had tracked a killer for days. He was a new sheriff at the time, just back from Vietnam. Still vigilant from his time there, cutting his hair like Steve McQueen and thinking he was the actor. The fugitive had been on a spree in Augusta and Athens targeting women fleeing up around Brasstown Bald after having been shot in the hand. He had been a mental patient and difficult to track because his movements were so random and sporadic. Had last been seen by hikers. Hadn't even tried to bandage his hand, blood all over the mountain area. Strake had triangulated where he might be. Shadowing him still took two weeks of camping and tracking. The sheriff was dauntless on a hunt. It was always a pitiful sight, the end of a chase, and that man was no different. He had no teeth and was cross-eyed, skinny and frail.

Strake had to keep reminding himself that he had shot four women. He felt sorry for his victim and watched him for a bit, took aim and shot the gun out of his hand, rushed him and cuffed him. But there was a moment when he thought about stomping him to death. With this new chase he had a decision to make. First, it was not a chase if you looked at it. There was no rush and the young man would be found soon. The choice was immediate justice in these woods. Or the sheriff's own prolonged agony as the man faced trial. He knew there was a right thing to do here. Was probably not going to do it. Yes, he was about to do the wrong thing. Because he still had the other man and woman to find once this was done. On the one hand the young man could die on his own. Rot out here. One option. Turn back and focus on the other two at large. What did he want to do to this person when he found him? Thoughts of torture boiled in his forehead. Buried things unearthed themselves leaving a hole.

It took Strake a while for pain to surface in him. He knew his son had been dead on the bank floor. They were probably just getting him and his wife and the two others to the morgue by now. This fleeing man had done it with a barbaric weapon. Yet he still felt sorry for the twerp who had just knocked out a front tooth. Stabbed a short time before that. Shot in the gut at the second bank, according to the quick report Strake heard on one call he made from a pay phone. Limping through the woods with a punctured lung barely able to breathe. How did you calculate the needed justice when there was already commensurate suffering?

Part of him liked this girl who had stabbed the guy, he had to admit. She had style, if he was allowed to think that. It was not easy to just miss the heart. She must be skilled with her knife.

Might be the most difficult of all to bring down. For now he needed to concentrate. Decide what he wanted to do about this fellow who had taken his family away from him in an instant.

Houston said something but he didn't hear him. "Say again?"

"I think he's right up there," Houston repeated.

"Already? Too easy."

"Well, we need more easy in our lives."

"I guess we do."

The young man was nearly dead. He had his hands on his thighs. Wheezing as blood sprayed from his mouth like aerosol. His chest poured red. As if his body were full of wine. The two sheriffs stood before him and said little. There was little to be said. This was a man whose life was dripping out of him. Chest and gut. Knife and bullet. He had killed two (three counting her baby). A knife had been turned on him. The fairness of it was almost sublime. Strake stepped forward a couple of paces.

"Son," he said, "tell me something."

He could not talk.

"Ask him about that typewriter," Houston suggested.

Words would not come. Strake noticed the uncorked blood leak down the front of his shirt. Gushing so fast now. The young man (or was he just an older boy?) stared at Strake. Insides spilling onto the dirt. Houston waited for Strake. A moment of waiting. Green trees and blue sky, bright, indifferent colors. Only the dirt seemed disrupted like hot chocolate powder with cold milk. Blood puddles filled at the boy-man's feet. Dripping down his pants. Painting his chest and stomach. Soon he leaned to the side. Fell gently by the blood in the dirt. Strake moved closer. Lifted his foot. Stomped the head to crush it with his boot heel. He did it a few quick times. The air was damp, ready for rain.

"You know," Houston remembered, "there is a reservoir just around here. Could toss him in."

"Hmm," Strake considered for a second.

"It's not far."

"We'd have to carry him."

"Not more than half a mile from here."

They looked at each other. In their eyes the decision appeared to make itself. "I'll lift the legs first," Strake offered. "You take the arms."

The boy was not heavy. At first. Walking sideways on narrow paths hurt their backs and knees. Strake walked backwards for a bit then they turned around and Houston did the same. The woods, quiet. A chipmunk darted nearby, stopped, twitched its nose and shot off. Bluebottle flies swarmed them as did gnats. At one point they saw a random old white shed falling down. Conferencing hornets swarmed a gray nest under the eave.

"We have to go up a hill in a bit," Houston said to him.

"Let's rest a minute."

"This kid looks like he was still in high school."

Strake stared at the dead boy. Bloodied sternum. Damaged mouth from his fall out of the trunk. Crushed head from the sheriff's boot heel pummeling. Much of the forehead, gone. His brain melted in the dirt like a snake slithering to a hole. They had left a trail of blood, defeating the purpose of hiding the body in the water. "His head is dripping."

"We'll clean it up on the way back. We need to hide him."

"Wonder what got into them?" Strake thought to himself.

Then he spoke the same words aloud.

"Well," Houston began, taking off his brimmed sheriff's hat and dabbing away sweat from the inside band, "I've been noticing a change in the high school kids in our town. Used to be they might joyride and toilet-paper a house, some light bullying here and there, but now everyone's got a knife and they're trying to get a gun. I broke up a fight the other day in a parking lot at a bar. Some Alabama punks were running people off the road for fun and a few of our kids cut them off in their truck out at Sandy's Bar. But the outsiders stabbed one and were about to shoot another. Luckily a tractor trailer driver was idling in the lot and called dispatch on his CB. This kind of thing is happening all the time now when it hardly ever did before."

Strake moved his head from side to side in disgust. He had seen similar things in his own town. "Drugs aren't helping," Houston added.

"I shouldn't've stomped on him like that."

"Let's not forget what he did to your boy and his wife."

"Doesn't matter."

"Sure it does, Strake."

"Didn't feel right. I regret it."

"As far as I'm concerned . . . it was right." They stared at the fractured face. A head smeared with red viscera. Lines of blood trailed back more than a hundred feet on the path.

"We got rain coming. Wash most of this off."

"I don't know, Houston."

"Sometimes, there is no right thing, even if it is right."

"Maybe . . . maybe." Georgia sun in July was dreary with humid heat. Black clouds were ready to cry some bad rain.

"How much further?" Strake asked.

"Not far."

"Your back okay?"

"I'll make it."

They lifted the dripping body again. This time Houston grabbed the ankles, Strake the wrists. As they moved through the woods Strake's vision burst into brightness. They made it up the hill. The reservoir. It was a flash of the sun perhaps that shocked his eyes. He grew dizzy. Fell to the ground. Not fainting but on all fours like a panting animal. Houston leaned down to him. Asked him if he was all right. "Give me a second." Just a few more steps to toss in the body. The hill exhausted his legs. He didn't want to feel compassion for this dead boy. He had wronged him. It was supposed to feel good. His restraint had vanished. This dead and mangled kid was the evidence. "Come on Strake, let's do it."

He stood, shook the dizzy visions from his head. They leaned over and lifted the body, swinging it three times to toss it with a plop. It floated for a moment. Almost like it may not sink. But then bubbled down and disappeared. Now there were those lines of blood to erase. They used their boots to smear it into the dirt. As they walked back through the woods the way they came, Strake thought about how each killing felt random.

In fact all killings were routine. Normal and random at the same time perhaps. Justice didn't feel perfect. Left you raw.

"You all right?" Houston tried.

"Yeah."

At their cars they stood smoking cigars. Fumes hovered around them, keeping away the gnats. Neither one spoke for a while. They wanted to enjoy their smokes before things collapsed. Collapse was near. They had gotten lucky with this one who had been stabbed. Only two to deal with now. Still, something worried Strake about that girl. It gnawed at him and she didn't even have a gun. That white knife. He noticed a precise stabbing of the boy.

Jimmy had definitely said the knife looked white, Houston suggesting maybe bone. A bone knife? He sighed. Breath blew out of him for a few seconds. Houston took a puff on his cigar. Strake wondered what would happen next. There were many ways you could put yourself in the middle of violence to end your own life. He considered it. What his life meant. If it meant anything. Their cigars were ending. They dropped them. Mashed the butts. A little bit of smoke wisped up from each like fumes from warm manure. They talked for a little bit. Needed to call the other two sheriffs. Houston patted him on the arm. Strake thanked him for his help.

"Why do I feel like this is just the beginning?"

"It'll probably get worse, Strake."

They got in their cars to drive. His stomping of the boy was a clicking film reel in front of him. Too late to worry about it. It was done. There would be more. Sweat fell into his eyes. He wiped off the salted wetness with the back of his left hand.

Forward.

To the next pointless death.

Maybe even his own.

Ellman and Becca

Ellman could see his life in minutes. Before, he viewed it in days. Or, the day he was in at the time. The first bank had been a transcendent robbery. Every motion sublime. Except one. Each killing, faultless. Afterward he slipped, yes. That was *after* the killings. He limped a little. Maybe had sprained his ankle, hurt above the knee too. Tane had gotten in his way when he slipped on slick blood and fell. Becca took care of the boy after the second bank. Good riddance.

Now it was just the two of them. The remaining minutes of his life and hers. Perhaps the final nihilism. When you knew it was ending. The gas tank was full. It would be the last time it was. All the gas stations were on the lookout. Becca's thigh was not as bad. She too had a little limp after digging out the bullet with her knife. A bigger nihilism was subsuming them. Shaving them down in numbers. Forcing them to believe something they never quite understood in the first place.

"What the hell is nihilism anyway?" Becca asked him.

"I really don't know," Ellman had responded, slightly amused. "Seems like the more you try to figure it out, the more sense it doesn't make."

They drove on. The road a hypnosis for the almost dead. There was nothing left but termination. While they had known this all along, it was now more than certain. Only so many places they could go. If they meant to die, they should accept it with embracing. Their heads played out the potential escapes. Each one ended with them dead. Their lives had limits on them. Best to drive, not think about it. So Ellman drove. Becca thought what he was thinking. They stopped talking. Stared ahead. Waited for the clear inevitability to assail them. How many mistakes had he made along the way?

Something ate at him. He had forgotten a lot when he had taken the bullet in the shoulder from the blond man. He had passed out on that funeral mound. Fainted later in the car with the loss of blood. He remembered having a fever at the time. A haze veiled his past. A book on nihilism in the blond man's car. He had forgotten to grab it. Then he switched cars. So a book he had checked out from that Arkansas library, under his own name, was sitting in the back seat. Wonderful little clue for the detectives. Amateur!

"Where will we go?" Becca said, interrupting his thoughts.

"Who knows?"

"I need to rest. My leg hurts a little."

"So does mine. We can't stop."

"Would it matter if we did?"

"Probably not."

"So let's stop," she insisted.

"We're NOT stopping!" he shouted.

"Jesus."

"Sorry," he added.

"What the hell is wrong with you?"

"I don't know. I'm trying to remember something about the time I was shot. I forgot all these details. They come back in spots."

They were pulling into another town, or so they thought. Knew everyone must be on alert. They stuck out in a ridiculous way. At a stoplight they slowed at the yellow, but Ellman ran it when it turned red. They kept moving through the streets. Forward, always forward. At the edge of town there was a shabby motel that looked really familiar. "Wait," he said.

"Yeah, same motel. You drove us back to the same town, genius."

"Damn country roads!"

"Nice getaway," she said, pointing. "Just stop here."

"You sure?"

"I'm sure. I have to get out of this boiling car."

"Another lovely roadside inn. Jeez, look at this disaster."

"Get us two rooms."

Five junkyard dogs slobbered up to them at the car, skinny with bodies and ears dotted with hundreds of fat ticks.

"Hello friends," she said, petting each head.

Ellman walked into the lobby. A bell rang. A withered man in overalls stood and nodded and smiled. Human scarecrow? Teeth the yellow color of stained piano keys. His hands were coated with grease. Snuff bulged under his bottom lip.

"How much for two singles for a night?"

"Forty. Twenty each."

Ellman peeled off a fifty. "Keep the ten."

Back at the car he handed Becca her key.

"I want my money," she insisted.

He shrugged. Opened the trunk. Stuffed stacks of bills into a brown grocery bag. Slamming the trunk he stood and gazed at her, squinting from the sun because he had taken off his sunglasses. His head was pink, burnt. She left him without a word and found her room. Inside she thought about what she needed to do. First she tended to her leg with some bandages. It hurt, sure, but not as bad as being cramped in that car seat. On the bed she lay and stared up and thought of her older past and her newer one. Both pasts filled with sadism, dead bodies, animal and human. No emotion arose in her, only thoughts. She was in her mind. Nowhere else. She had never felt anything. Even her desire to kill was a thought, not a feeling. She had imagined it. The bank had happened. Afterward . . . numb blankness.

When Ellman's knock came in the morning, she ignored it. He came back a few times. Said he was leaving. The last words he spoke were muffled through the door: "I went back and paid the clerk for a week for you."

At last the knocks stopped. She heard the car roar to a start and leave. She stayed in the room for five days. Only going out to the front desk for quarters. Then to the snack and drink machines. For chips and peanuts and sodas. And jerky sticks for the wild dogs. Her thinking had been that if they split up they might be less of a target than if they were together. Ellman could ditch the car and find another. That would slow their end somewhat, taking herself out of the chase for a moment. A chase needed two people. It turned out that she was right. Those five days healed her leg, mostly. They also gave her mind a rest. Rest was a type of ammunition. At one point while they were driving and Tane was still with them, Ellman had said: "You know that ad in the crime mag? I did it as a joke."

"A *joke?*" she replied.

"I didn't think anyone would answer it!"

So it had all been a joke in the end. Ellman's joke. His nihilism that he couldn't even define. The Nihilistics, a sham. She did a lot of thinking on that smelly bed in the motel. Fat caramel roaches strutted around the room like guests. But *had* it been a sham? Hadn't they done exactly what she had dreamed of doing? The first bank had been an ideal heist, her virgin killing. Where would Ellman go? Tane was likely somewhere bleeding to death, what she had planned for him, stabbing him just under the heart to make him suffer as much as possible. She really did not like that guy. Sam Bunker, my eye. How long could she stay in this shoddy room? It was the perfect spot for her. One week of respite. Of calm.

She still fantasized about Ellman, he made her wet, she couldn't explain it to herself. His aloof distance. His intelligence. His hot Colt. He disgusted her too. His slick bald head was alluring and hideous. In some ways he was the first man she liked. And hated. The mix was sexual and severe. Hatred and attraction. She slept and dreamed of him. Of blood. Of killing. Of skinning. Her sleep was easy and soft at times. Hard and awful at others. Flashes of dead animal bodies she had skinned. Human death. Where would she go now? She couldn't think about it. Resisted brooding about what was next. She wanted only to sleep. Eat snacks. Drink sodas with ice from the machine. Play with her poor, hungry dog friends. She let them in the room on her bed. Tweezed off all their ticks that she kept living and crawling in a plastic cup.

Becca's leg felt better each day. One morning she could not wake up. Slept for nearly thirty hours. When she did open her eyes she was ready. Her shower lasted a long time. The water was hot. She wanted to stay under the stream. With her grocery bag of money she left. Instead of walking on the road she saw the woods in the distance. Aimed for them. She was in a green field. She took her time. A breeze cooled the sweat on her. She stopped. The five dogs had stayed at the edge, not following her for some reason. She smiled at them. Tilted her head back. Poured peanuts into her mouth. Chewed. Moved on. Came to the edge of the woods. She stared up at the oaks and maples and pines. Then she walked into them. Unsure.

Agent Pierce

Sheriff Strake had called the GBI after his family deaths, Georgia Bureau of Investigation. He knew Agent Pierce from high school. Thought he might want to know about the three killers, if he hadn't already heard. The two of them talked on the phone from time to time anyway. One item that came up was the Bald Drifter. An obsession Pierce seemed to never let go. Each time they chatted there was a new hitchhiker murder. Even Strake heard rumors around the Georgia towns about a similar man. Folks remembered not picking up the killer on the side of the road, only to find out later that one of their neighbors *had* given him a lift and was found dead.

Most of it was talk. Sometimes talk led to something. The description was always the same. Or close enough to let Pierce see a potential blueprint of these serial murders. The same gun and the same bullets had killed these people. Pierce had been called in for most of the hitchhiker murders happening around the country for the last few years.

Many of them in the South. But a surprising number in thirty or so states. After hearing Strake's description of the trio, especially the bald man with the pistol, he felt they were related. He knew it. Had to be the same man. Back in December a car had turned up in Amarillo with a book left in it that had been traced. The man who owned the car, his body had been found buried in a cornfield in Arkansas by the farmer who owned it. The shallow grave avoided by disappointed wild dogs, crows and vultures. In cold winter frozen dirt deterred scavengers from devouring a corpse. It was still identifiable. When Pierce had talked to the librarian in Eureka Springs, Arkansas, she had described a bald man who had asked her many questions on nihilism. The book found in the car in Amarillo was called *Nihilism through the Ages* that this man had gotten from the Arkansas library.

Seemingly using his own name, Ellman. It added up. The dead man found by the farmer. The book. The same book found way out in Amarillo. IN the dead man's car registered in Eureka Springs. Traced back to a library in Arkansas near where the man was found in the cornfield. A library where a bald man was seen asking about nihilism. It had to be him. That book had hand-written notes and circled passages, likely Ellman's marginalia, around the 19th century Russian nihilist movement, specifically the words "nigilizm" and "šestidesjatniki". Beside the latter word that Pierce had finally translated as "sixties", Ellman had written, "The younger generation must kill everything before it." The word "assassination" had been circled four times on one page.

Pierce had been piecing together details about these hitch-hiker murders for years. Strake's call sealed it. He needed to drive to the Athens area and be sure. Still had the book and brought it with him. Pierce had wanted to get out of the cigarette smoke in the Atlanta GBI office. A drive to the country would help clear his lungs. He smoked Gauloises Blue but for some reason hated it when others blew fumes his way. Mainly because many of the agents liked menthols. A mint in a cigarette? Come on!

On the drive he thought of the matrices he had strung together of all the murders of the Bald Drifter. He knew every small town where a killing had occurred. At first it seemed random. But the more that Ballistics returned the same verdict (same gun, same bullets) and the more he interviewed townspeople (bald man, I almost picked up that guy, my neighbor died when he did), the more it made sense that it was one cold man who took his time and didn't seem to care about being caught. Pierce had made himself read the book on nihilism the Texas police found in the blond man's car in Amarillo. Likely abandoned there by the Bald Drifter.

According to Strake's friend Jimmy, he had seen the trio on the street and noticed how cavalier they were with brazen exposure of a knife, a hatchet and a pistol. This too tied in to the nihilism in the missing library book in the stolen car in Texas. They were young. They didn't care. They had killed four people in a bank including three of Strake's close kin, his son, his boy's wife, her unborn child. Based on the number of exact matches for bullets found in the victims shot in their cars, he could closely estimate that there had been fifty-five hitchhiker murders. Fifty-five! Yet this man had never been caught. Likely there were even hundreds of killings. Hard to convince his peers that serial killers even existed. They had found blood in the car in Amarillo and some matched the man buried in the cornfield who also had matching bullets in him. Some blood did not match. Had to be the blood of this drifter.

So something had happened to the man between Arkansas and Amarillo. Pierce assumed he had been injured badly. Lost some of his confidence. Maybe that's when he teamed up with these other two. All speculative but he was close, close to it. A second bank had been hit by the three. They were less successful in this endeavor that had wounded them. As he drove he stopped to call on pay phones to hear more details since he had no CB in his car. Witnesses had seen the white convertible driving through towns. Then with only two, the bald man and girl.

Pierce figured that the third young man deserted them or had been killed. Meaning they were chasing down only two people now. On his last call to the GBI, though, he was told that the bald man was driving around by himself. Of course by the time they found him he would have ditched that Impala convertible. Where was the girl now? Dead? Had anyone even identified her?

Pierce told the agent on the pay phone that the bald man would go into hiding soon like he always did after a killing. Sure enough, after about fifty miles he called in again for more information. The convertible had been abandoned by a gas station. An elderly woman had reported that her white Buick Skylark had been stolen. What astounded Pierce was that no one in the GBI listened to him about the patterns he had discovered with the Bald Drifter until after the twentieth death or so.

His research was correct. The office was lazy. They moved like frozen slugs. Didn't want to do the extra work. Thought serial killers only existed in crime mags. He spent his weekends going to these towns. After a begrudging time his boss signed off on sending him to the places to assuage the locals, even if no larger hunt was issued. Now there was a hunt because they had not been preemptive. Part of the reason for the languishing response to these killings was that they occurred in small towns. The drifter was wise to choose where he did because it took forever to draw any attention to unknown places. In fact, as far as he knew, Pierce was the *only* person who concentrated on them.

Even the local sheriffs shrugged when a murder happened, passing it off to randoms, saying they could do nothing about it. It was the local older folks who helped him. They knew something was wrong. They noticed strangers on the side of the road and in their libraries. While it was hearsay it was still relevant.

Loose facts had a final precision about them. There was scant evidence beyond what these witnesses thought they could remember. Meanwhile, twenty deaths turned into thirty, thirty into forty, now forty into fifty-five. During one presentation to his team of agents he was ridiculed for his dearth of evidence despite the same bullets used.

"It's a good theory, Pierce," said one, "don't get me wrong, but how can we catch a murderer with no real proof?"

"All the bullets match!"

The excoriations continued in subtle banter, implying that Pierce was a monomaniac whose other duties had suffered as his other cases idled. It was true. He was tortured by the Bald Drifter. Perhaps it was because he saw the sadness in the small towns, the loss of an innocent woman or man who had done nothing to deserve his or her death. His interviews created human unions with them, and sometimes he called them to check on how they were doing. They had cared about their murdered neighbors.

Why was the Atlanta Field Office not seeing what these people so easily saw? Soon he would be in Athens. He needed to find Strake whom he trusted. Maybe Strake had already found the drifter. If he understood right, the girl was no longer with him. Which would require two chases, if the drifter hadn't offed her. He was still an hour or two away. A red wasp buzzed at the base of the windshield, half-dead. Crawled around the cracked brown dash inching toward its death. Pierce reached out his hand and swatted it. He couldn't stand to watch anything suffer in the final moments. No matter how small. He needed to synchronize with Strake before something more happened. Yes, he wanted this drifter dead. Pierce was certain Strake and his cronies did too. But they could not kill him. No matter how much they wished it. Why, though, would a man let himself be caught like this after years of easy elusion? Ellman, his name at last learned from the library, could have been killing for multiple years with ease. How come . . . now? Was he bored? Or tired? Maybe he was a nihilist, ready to die.

One of the ironic motifs that struck Pierce and made him laugh was that you certainly couldn't be a nihilist when you were dead. In other words, you had to be alive to embody nihilism. It was fine to contemplate a nihilistic ending. As long as you were alive. There were no dead nihilists. Only living ones. Pierce floored it. He had to catch them before some blunder killed Ellman. Strake had a good heart. But he was, in the end, a killer.

Convergence

Alone on the drive Ellman let his thoughts crush him. To blot out that he was scared of his pursuers. Fear was in his head. After dropping Becca he decided not to speed. They would catch him. It would be ugly. He was not looking forward to it. Another thought kept coming back to him: that damn book in the blond man's back seat. Ahhh, it didn't matter. Just another slip that made him realize he was fading in precision. Enough for him to know that the end was nearer. Once his pristine routine of killing had been ruptured by the man's two gunshots, everything had turned to amateurism.

It would play out in what would feel like a matter of minutes. The old lady would report her stolen car. He wouldn't bother to steal another one. This was the final chase. Any moment he expected police to drive up behind him. How would it end? He knew. At least he had AC in this car. It would be a cool death. Ellman felt he was being chased, so in a rapid reversal he decided to reorder their pursuit. He had the Government behind him and plenty of bullets. For what reason had he let himself become the chased? It began with that ad. When he was alone he never had any issues, except that one time of course. Damn blond man!

There were little changes in him too like not killing the old lady when he took her car. He stopped on the side of the road to think. He would follow them now. Maybe just run right into them. Regardless, he had no desire to be followed anymore. It was a state of mind: the thought that people were after you. Change that thought and pursue *them* instead. Likely, he would run right into the sheriff. Since it didn't matter and he was going to die anyway, why not confront it, end it? He pressed the gas hard. A smile extended across his face as he nodded with satisfaction. The Buick tore down the old highway. Four conspicuous muscle cars in row sped right by him, each man wearing a sheriff hat. His eyes focused on the rearview mirror and they saw many red brake lights.

Maybe this was the red rain. A bunch of goddamn brake lights. All four cars spun around. In a line they came after him. He too u-ied. Drove straight at them. No more being followed. End well, he thought. Not being a coward.

With the Government he shot out a hole in his windshield. He had a clear aim at the first car, a black man in a Mustang. Ellman pushed the Colt through the cracked glass, was able to set the barrel down on the jags for a steady aim. He accelerated and fired. The car slowed with the man's quick death. Rolled to a stop. The two right behind him, fanned out. Just missed a collision. The last car, the Chevelle barely moved out of the line, kept coming at Ellman, head on. Ellman fired again, missed this time. He swerved. The remaining sheriff slammed his brakes, turned and went back to the other three cars. Houston had a bullet hole in his forehead. Neaves' Oldsmobile and Crowley's Chrysler had just avoided rear ending Houston when he was shot. Quick reactions. They were the best drivers around. Strake

CB'ed for an ambulance and to report this setback to Pierce's office at the GBI.

No Crucifix this time. It was sad about Houston. Strake felt relief on one level, knowing the man had witnessed him kill that boy. What now? Jesus! The information had been coming through the CB that this had to be the Bald Drifter. Strake needed to get to a pay phone. Neaves and Crowley said they would meet him whenever Strake needed them. They were ready for anything and knew the back roads, could get to his location with a quick squawk on the CB. Strake got back in his Chevelle. Gunned it. There was nothing else to do but follow the man.

Ellman had picked one of them off. Now he was the chased again, not the chaser. It would come down to the two of them. He had to keep moving but gas was low, almost empty. If he stopped he would be spotted. The gas stations were on alert. Damnit! He had a big hole in the windshield spraying glass slivers at him. Of course it started to rain. Water was drenching the dash, the seats, his legs, mixing with the glass. He missed drifting and walking and getting into one car after the next. Could no longer go back to that. The Buick sputtered. It rolled to a stop and there was nothing around him, just falling drops. At least there was the rain. Not red.

But you couldn't have it all. On the shoulder of the road he opened the door. Found his ammo. He stood from the car, drenched. It was a swift and thick rain. Coming so fast from the humid heat. He could barely see for a moment in the sheets of water. He shut the door with a thump. Loaded the gun as he walked. Him or me. His footsteps sloshed on the asphalt.

He heard the Chevelle barreling at him. This was it. He aimed at the car moving so fast it could have been going more than a hundred. Too hard to aim. It was a straight road. Might get lucky with a shot. Who was he kidding? It was fitting. To die on the road. He'd always imagined a rain of bullets killing him. Not a muscle car cutting him down in daylight. He began to fire his Colt. It was futile. The bullets might as well have been drops of rain, just shooting forward instead of falling down. That was a thought. Bullets were moving in a horizontal way, most of the time. Rain was dropping. Right now the bullets crossed the rain in a final matrix. It had been his road once. No longer. The car rammed his body with force in his pelvis. He fell under as it roared right over him. Stopping in a few yards. He was alive, crushed.

Could not move. On his back, staring up. The drip of blood in his eyes blurred his sight. The rain was not red. Just his eyes. The sheriff stood from his car, approached. He was over him, his black pupils double zeroes. His heel came down on the drifter's forehead. Finished the rest.

Strake stood above the man with blood coming from his eyes. The car had mangled his hips into contortion. But it was the red eyes. Water poured over the dead man's face. Red bubbled up from the eyes like oil from a well. The sheriff could not stop staring at them as the rain drenched him. His car idled. For the second time today, without any conscious intention, he had killed two young men with the heel of the same boot.

More work to do with the girl, if she was alive. He knew she was.

What was he to do now, soaked after a second killing?

He thought, as the rain cooled him, that he needed to find her.

The dead man had come to the end of his road and knew it.

He had been walking right up the middle of the highway.

Made it easy for Strake whose car had two bullet holes in the windshield on the passenger side. A madness of rainfall had saved him from the two shots that hit the glass. He looked at the dead body once more. At the gurgling eyes strangely soothing in their blood flow. Two out of three. One left. A young girl. Who had killed the sister of Meyer, the coroner. Why he liked her, he couldn't say. That bone knife was a weapon of skill. Hell, Strake might be at the end of his own road. He could see her stabbing him, then he would be gone too. Gone from pain. The only way to leave the hurt was to die. He knew this. Without the rain he'd be dead now. What was death by a bone knife? Better than taking a bullet like Houston did while driving. The thing was: he had no idea where to start finding the girl.

Logic had it that she planned to avoid vehicles since people might spot her very easily at this point. Which left a span of woods in Georgia where they might never find her. Strake let out a sigh. He had no desire to get back into his car and drive without purpose. Strangely enough, the blur of his visions had not worsened. Rain seemed to keep falling. The dead man lay dead. The sheriff wasn't confused. He just didn't want to do anything. He understood the drifter, why he did what he did.

It would be easy to just walk, to ride, to kill. Isn't that what Strake did anyway? Just on the "good" side. He leaned over. Grabbed the man's bullets falling from his left hand, the ones in his pockets. In a pants pocket he found a spent bullet and a tooth. He kept them. Back in his car Strake called in the death on the CB, said the man had walked out in front of him shooting with the Colt. He had placed many of the drifter's bullets in his ashtray, in his shirt pockets. Morbid souvenirs. Pierce was close, he was told with a static squawk on the radio. "Where you headed?" asked the dispatcher. Pierce had been calling to let Strake know he was close.

"To find her," he said. His car moved forward. He looked in his rearview one last time at the prone body on the shoulder. Turned on his wipers. They moved from side to side. The one on the right hiccupped when it slid over the two bullet holes that had just missed him. Two splintered glass eyes staring into the empty passenger seat at nobody.

Becca was deep into the woods by now and she was hungry. She had money in a bag and some snacks and could figure out the woods. She had been in enough of them with her dad. Rain had come with surprising speed and smacked her face and she felt miserable in her wet clothing. She had not thought to bring a change of clothes. Now, here she was with a bag of wet money and a false death wish and stupid choices. She had killed someone, a woman. Why? Tane didn't count. She thought it would be easy.

Like Ellman's stories he told her at the motel in Amarillo. About hitchhiking and the Colt. Murder was not a story. She had thought it was. There was a choice to make in this moment. Go back. Or keep heading into the trees. With the plan to not leave the hiding place, at least for a few weeks. This meant a grungy lack of shelter. No clean clothes. Nowhere to go to the bathroom. A horse bone knife. A sopping bag of money. A few snacks. Real prepared. The absurdity of it made her shake her head from side to side.

The rain was the decider. Her hair was wet. This downpour did not have plans to slow, it seemed. Tree cover helped. Ellman had told her something once. They had rehearsed a number of possible situations. In a way Ellman had predicted everything right. He said there would be death. He assured her it would also be random. However, he kept pushing the point that she must never let herself be cornered. An opossum in the bottom of a trash can. When you think that's happening, and it will probably happen to us, he told her, that's when you need to reverse the chase and go after them. Or . . . yourself. Remember, he added, our whole plan has to be relentless, to keep going after them until our own deaths.

"Our ace," he said, "is that we don't mind dying. They do."

Recalling his words Becca retraced her steps and aimed to leave the woods. After three hours she was in the green field again behind the motel where she had stayed with Ellman before they had split. She walked back there. Paid the clerk for a month. Found her same room again. The dogs were happy to see her. Pink tongues sloshing from their famished mouths.

Strake liked the rain. Drove around the places he had already been. Not certain about what to do next. Neaves and Crowley stayed close in their cars, ready for that call to use them. He could CB them directly. Pierce, he heard, was with the dead Bald Drifter, likely trying to confirm that the body was his killer. Strake was on his own. He liked it that way. He smoked a cigar with the nice new ventilation of the bullet holes dripping water from the eerie glass hole eyes. As hot as it had been, this rain was like a sweet shower after a dirty day. Truth was, he couldn't get excited about killing a girl. Even if she deserved it. Probably brainwashed by the other two. The one thing Strake had always been was a little lucky. He ran into what he needed at the right time. By now more GBI were on the way since Houston had been murdered. He needed to avoid the agents. Rolled down his window. Tossed out his cigar.

In the rain Pierce stood over the dead man on the roadside. He had been so close. It was his drifter. He knew it was. Just couldn't prove it quite yet. Once the body was at the morgue he could get confirmation from some of the townsfolk he had interviewed. They had seen his face and would know. It would be the final proof he needed, even if no one else listened to him.

The top of the man's head had been bashed, caved in at the highest part of the forehead, leaving the face identifiable. Knowing Strake very well, Pierce let it go. A news team had pulled up in a white van with a satellite on top. He gave them a short interview and let them film what they wanted. Afterward, Pierce followed the ambulance to the coroner, shaking his head in frustration. So close. He had wanted the man alive.

Becca sat on the queen bed in her room. The knife to her left. Wet money out of the bag by her feet. She drank a cola over ice. Her ticks were still in the plastic cup. The room obviously never cleaned after she left briefly. Dogs whimpered outside her door. In the shower she knew the end was close. Had she confused a wish to kill people with a need to kill herself? The killing was in her. It was tiring. Ellman was probably gone. He had made himself a target in whatever car he was driving at the time. An old Robert Mitchum film was on the black and white RCA. She ate some salted peanuts and greasy potato chips. Opened her door and tossed out some jerky morsels for her drooling pets. In a few minutes her head was on the pillow and she was sleeping.

Nothing would happen for a little bit. The motel owner had not recognized Becca from the robberies and let her be. She slept and ate snacks. Ordered her bills on the bed. Sharpened her knife. Had no escape in mind, just comfort. She let the five nearly tick-free dogs in her room when lonely. Tweezing off ticks gave her something to do. One, the Doberman missing an eye, had about a hundred ticks on him when she first started. It was a strange motley of nearly wild animals. A skinny greyhound with a nose as long as a footlong hot dog. A black Labrador with dandruff. She called him Snow Boy. And two unrecognizable mutts, maybe a pit bull mixed with a mosquito and another spawned from a junkyard with crossed eyes. The five of them, she had seen one afternoon, had chased down a pudgy raccoon near the parking lot and savaged it. Leaving almost nothing.

Strake was back at his office dealing with the four bank funerals. It was robotic. He wrote a check for them all, somehow feeling responsible. Not fair, his son. What was left? His father only. There were no more connections except for a woman he knew in Vietnam. Hanh. But there was no one here. He was alone and would be for a long time. Leaving the funeral home, he went to Shep's for a burger, sitting on a barstool at the counter. His stomach felt raw. He was hollow.

Pierce had ten older witnesses confirm that this was the Bald Drifter. The librarian in Arkansas assured him it was the man who had checked out the book on nihilism. Pierce had sent her a fax. Pierce called Strake one afternoon and asked if he could come by for lunch, as he was still in town. Strake said he had just buried his son, his daughter-in-law and the two others. Was fatigued beyond recognition.

"Sure, meet you at the diner."

They were seated in the pink booth. Maude lying under Strake on the floor. Pierce saw the dark circles under Strake's tired eyes. They had been friends since high school. Knew a secret or two about the other. One was that Strake always wore long sleeves. He had come back with dots on his arms. Pierce knew because he had asked for help. Strake had gotten off the scag. They never discussed it once he was better.

Coffee was brought. Neither one of them drank it. Known to be the worst cup for miles.

"So, the coroner talked to me about this fella Ellman, our confirmed drifter, and how he died."

Strake stared at him. Pierce almost didn't want to ask. Back on the road with the dead body he had promised to let it go. He couldn't.

"Now, you said that after he killed Houston, you went in pursuit. We found out later he ran out of gas so that corroborates what you told us, that he was walking right up the road at you. Raining pretty hard, right?"

"Yes, coming down."

"So he aims his Colt at your car and shoots the two bullet holes we found on the passenger windshield?"

"Yep."

"Anything else you want to tell me?"

"Well," Strake said, "I didn't know his car had run out of gas. Didn't even notice he was walking at me until it was too late. The rain was . . . like a fog."

"Yes, I remember it. I came right after."

"Only saw him at the last minute. I felt the bullet holes seconds before but thought he might be in his car shooting, like when he killed Houston."

"I see," said Pierce, nodding.

"Then this damn walking body appears like a shadow right on the double yellow line and the front of my car must've hit him at close to ninety."

"Okay, I think I got that. Just a few more questions. You don't mind?"

"I don't. It's good to see you. Glad you finally got your guy, by the way."

"Thanks, Strake. Anyway, I arrived at the body later and noticed the head crushed at the top. The coroner pointed out this anomaly too."

"Anomaly?"

"Um, your car hit him in the legs and stomach and chest."

"The back of his head hit the pavement, I guess? I did run over him."

"We know all that. It's just that the coroner thinks maybe something happened after you barreled into him."

"Like what?"

There was a silence between them for the next moment. Pierce knew he should have left it alone. In fact he already knew Strake had finished the job with the heel of his boot. Maybe he just wanted the sheriff to know that he knew. The man looked forlorn. He had just lost his son and much more.

"Ask what you need to ask, Pierce."

Pierce looked down at his coffee that had been untouched. The black color struck him, why, he did not know. This pivoted the subject.

"Don't ever drink the coffee here," Strake warned him with a grin.

"Any word about the girl?" Pierce asked.

"None."

"She has to be close, right?"

"Or hidden in the woods, one of the two."

"What's your plan?"

Strake thought for a moment. "No idea."

"Sorry about your son."

"Thanks."

"And everyone else. Can't be easy for the town."

"It's not."

"So, no plan?"

"I kept trying to come up with one. There wasn't any that didn't seem like a waste of time."

"You'll find her."

"Maybe. Just not sure what to do with her when I do. Jimmy said she looked young, maybe even like a minor."

"Hmmm, maybe she got roped in with the other two?" Pierce offered.

"Uncertain, but she did take out one of our bankers here, related to our coroner, Meyer, by the way. I'm hoping we can find her alive and not have another death on our hands."

He couldn't tell Pierce that she had stabbed the other boy and dropped him on the side of the road. There was a lot he couldn't tell Pierce. They walked out of the diner together.

"I'll be staying in a motel just up the road," Pierce told him, "right off the highway there."

"I know the one. Looks haunted. In fact, I think it *is* haunted."

"Need some wind-down time after this."

"Thanks for coming over, Pierce. I think you know the answers to all your questions."

"Yes, I believe I do."

"Good to hear."

"Oh, wait, what do you think happened to the boy named Tanner?"

Strake looked at him for a long time. But said nothing. They shook hands outside very close to where The Nihilistics had parked that day they had attacked the bank.

Pierce drove to his motel. Paid the clerk in overalls at the front desk. The man gave him a beige plastic ice bucket that had a dead gnat in it. He found his room and fell on the bed in his black suit and yellow tie, eyes struggling to stay open. Even his shoes, at first, did not leave his feet, his exhaustion was so fierce. Before he slept he thought of the tacit yes Strake had given him about the drifter. The vanishing of the first boy, now identified by his parents as Tanner, also a tacit yes, even though the sheriff had admitted nothing.

I knew it, thought Pierce. Strake's boot heel was famous. Everyone was aware of it yet no one talked about it. Pierce had to smile as he drifted into a sleep, managing to somehow surge forward over his growing gut, untie his laces fast and drop his head backward onto the pillow. His black shoes dropped to the stained orange carpet. The suit and tie would have to wait.

Four Rooms Down

Becca watched the occasional t.v. and saw the sheriff interviewed, as well as the GBI agent, Pierce. It seemed that Ellman had gone down firing. Tane's body had not been found but it was obvious what had happened to him. And his stupid typewriter. His mother had contacted the Ohio police who told the GBI, and they had pieced together that he was one of The Nihilistics, after learning of Tane's chainsaw "accident" of his father. Becca had stabbed him and tossed his body right in the line of the chase where the sheriffs would find him. Strake was a Vietnam vet, according to the news, and she put her money on his finishing off Tane. That body was gone forever. It was just her now.

Playing out with exactness but seeming lopsided at the same time. If she left the motel and headed to the woods, misery but possible survival. Already tried it. Not a good option. If she stayed here she had enough money. The overalled hick running the place never asked questions. Too easy, she thought. A good break. Leg mostly healed. Slight limp. Not bad. Lots of sleep and snacks. She was bored. Alone her mind reflected on killing. From the news she also realized that she had knifed the coroner's sister at the bank, a woman named Dolores. Ellman, they were calling the Bald Drifter. Things had died down, but Strake would be on the move again soon. Right now she had to stick close to the motel.

How could she leave anyway? Any local roads were certain to expose her. No, she was in the safe eye of this hurricane and she was staying. It was dark and maybe close to August if not already. She opened her door with the ice bucket. Looked around. Just her crazy dog buddies. Nobody ever seemed to stay at this motel. Basil, the clerk, kept her supplied with rolls of quarters for the snack and soda machines. She had a roll in her pocket. As she passed the fourth door down she saw a light behind the curtain. She froze. Someone was here.

Days were lost in sleep with her. She didn't want to know what day it was. This meant that there *could* have been many guests. She had just slept through them. She thought for a moment. Cars pulled right up to the rooms to park. She saw no vehicles. Maybe Basil had just left a light on after cleaning a room. But if he had cleaned, it meant someone had stayed there. Before getting something to eat and drink she walked around the motel grounds. There it was. A turd brown car clearly driven by someone in government. She waited. Headed to the snack machines.

As she dropped in quarters she heard someone behind her. An overweight man in a robe approached looking groggy. He slid in some coins and a Coke dropped. She bought chips and peanuts.

"Evening," he said.

She nodded to him without speaking. The dogs trotted up to them expecting jerky. "They're harmless," she said, noting his fear. "With me at least." As far as she knew there were no photos of her on the news. Nooo, she said to herself with a stifled giggle of a realization. It had to be him.

"Best restaurant in town," he added, nodding toward her junk food dispenser. Light from her machine glowed under more fluorescence above them. Mosquitoes whirled above, devil fairies. She moved to fill her ice bucket. She also bought three sodas. He shifted to the snacks and got himself a fat Tootsie Roll.

"Desolate place," he tried again.

"I don't mind it," she said.

"It's a catastrophe."

"Say, aren't you that GBI agent on the news?" she said, with a sudden boldness.

"Ah, you saw me, huh?"

"On television just now."

"Crazy murders around here recently."

"You caught the Bald Drifter, right?"

He stared at her and made her uncomfortable.

"Well," he said, annoyed, "technically no. Sheriff Strake took him down. I'd been tracking Ellman for years. Nobody believed me. Until now. It was him. We confirmed it."

"You didn't catch him after all that work?" she goaded him a little. "That's gotta be frustrating."

"Somewhat," he said, chewing his Tootsie Roll turd.

He stared harder at her. She held his gaze.

"What brings you to this area?" he pried, starting to be suspicious.

"Passing through for the summer to visit relatives in Florida."

"Mmmhmm. Runaway?"

"Gosh no. I'll be going to college down in Alabama after that. And . . . is it really any of your business?"

"Um, well, wait, yes, sorry, that was rude."

"Yes it was. Don't be so judgmental. Night."

She headed back to her room, dogs behind her, and slammed her door for effect, leaving the mutts salivating outside.

Agent Pierce. Four doors down. Out of shape. Would he put it together? How could he not? Maybe he wasn't a closer. She knew one thing: she was now staying for a while.

Over the next few days he was friendly and apologetic about his earlier comments. If he only knew. She couldn't hide here anymore. But she could buy herself some time. After about the third day of rebuffing him, she invited him to her room around 3:00 in the afternoon. He was obviously married with that gold band, probably had kids her age. He accepted and said he would be by later. When he arrived at her door he had all kinds of snacks and sodas cradled into his arms. So it was rather easy to plunge her horse knife into his fat gut. It slid in like stabbing a watermelon.

She was careful to avoid the snacks that would be yummy later. They fell to the floor. She would pick them up in a minute. One soda bottle shattered. Gouged in his belly, he started to gasp and fall forward, helpless. She kept him propped long enough to let him fall onto the bed so that she wouldn't have to lift his heavy ass off the floor later (not that there would be much left of him). After he was lying on his back, she gathered the snacks. Cleaned up the brown fizzy soda with a towel from the bathroom.

"Strake's coming," he slobbered, trying to grasp at her.

"Sure he is," she scoffed.

"He is. To meet."

A shudder tickled her fear. "No way." Bluff.

"I know it's you."

"What do you mean?" she asked.

He grimaced in pain.

"They have been surveilling this place ever since I met you."

"You're full of it."

His stomach bubbled blood fast. She almost felt bad for the liar.

"I'm not kidding," he winced. "You're dead."

"Not because of you. I was dead long before you came."

"Everyone knows you're here, trust me."

"Ironic. Since you're the one who looks like the dead man at the moment." She removed his trousers. "So why haven't they charged in yet?"

She could take off skin with the bone knife fast. What if he was right and they were outside? The first leg took time but she finished, including the foot. Skin piled on the bedspread. Figuring his screams would alert them, she worked in a quick manner. No one came. As she had expected, bluffing. Could she do the entire body before they found her? As she came to the second leg he moved into dying. She finished it all. Legs. Torso. Arms. Neck. Face. Scalp. She had to go. But she opened his mouth with her fingers. Poured in the army of ticks from the plastic cup.

She absolutely could not stay here anymore. It was possible that Strake knew she was at the motel. Pierce looked beautiful. At last she had finished an entire human. Too bad it hadn't been her mother. Wait, she muttered. Pierce's car! She riffled through his pants pockets. His room key only. She went four doors down to his spot. Opened the door. On the dresser: his car keys and holstered gun. She took them both and went back to her room. Packed her money and a few clothes. And her white knife stained with red. On Pierce's body she placed a note ripped from a motel pad: "For Strake. Enjoy the meal." Left the door open . . .

In the car she reveled in the fact that she was not somewhere shivering in the woods on the run. It was pleasant to be driving. To have another kill under her belt. She had to get out of Georgia. Her earlier lie about Florida was not a bad idea. She made a plan. To go south. A short-lived one.

She didn't get far.

A Day Earlier

Strake met Pierce at the diner again. He had something to tell the sheriff. Pierce had met a young girl at the motel. At first he didn't make the connection then it hit him that she had to be from the trio.

"You sure?" Strake said, leaning forward.

"Not a hundred percent, but maybe she is hiding in plain sight. I mean, there isn't anywhere for her to go."

Maude sat in Strake's lap. Both men eschewed their coffee, better known as arsenic motor oil (but worse).

"Hmm," the sheriff thought aloud.

"I know it's her. Has to be."

"What'll you do?"

"Not sure," Pierce said to him. "Not sure."

No one had come forward to identify the girl, no parents, nothing. This meant they didn't even know her name. Had only a glance from Jimmy and a few other onlookers who described her as an attractive young blond. There were no photos. They didn't even know where she was from.

"What if it's not her?"

"I thought about that, but nobody stays at the motel, Strake. Doesn't it make sense?"

"Maybe, I think you might be right."

"Can you swing by the place?"

Strake thought for a moment.

"I can try but I'm only one person. I don't have anyone to cover for me, except Jimmy. I'll come out soon."

"That could help."

"Can't you get some GBI assistance at this point?"

"I could, but they're still suspicious about my hunches."

"Even after confirming the drifter?"

"Yeah, they have never taken me seriously. If I was wrong about the girl, they'd laugh in my face."

"Which room?"

"She's staying four doors from me on the left. I'm in the far right room, looking at the building."

The next day Strake decided to talk to Basil at the motel front desk.

"You got a girl staying here?"

"Oh yeah, pretty."

"How long?"

"Couple weeks."

"Weeks!"

"Yep. Stayed about a week. Guy with black hair paid cash that time."

"Shit," muttered Strake. "Then what?"

"Well, then she sprised me and came back. Stayed in the same room. This time by herself."

"And she's still here?"

"Far as I know. Doesn't leave her room much. Good with them stray dogs that sprang up outta hell."

"Okay, Basil, this is important. When she left that first time, any idea where she went?"

"I know where."

"Which was . . . ?"

"She ran down that back field there behind the motel. I saw her."

"Then came back?"

"Ash rye."

Ash rye was translated as *that's right*.

"Okay, thanks Basil. Keep an eye on her for me. Call me if you notice anything strange."

"Will do, Sheriff."

He was about to go to her room then figured Pierce was here to keep an eye on her. His assumption that Pierce could take care of himself ended up being pretty wrong. The man worked in an office and hardly ever stepped foot in the field.

The next day Strake got a call from Basil. Pierce had gone into the girl's room. Had not come out for a long time. Strake bolted. Kicked himself for not checking on her room the day before. Sped off to the motel. As he was getting closer he saw what he was sure was Pierce's brown car pass him going the other way. And she was driving! Not Pierce. Strake slammed the heel of his palm on the steering wheel. He had to think. She had the man's car. This meant Pierce was in trouble. He called dispatch, told them to phone Basil and get an ambulance to the girl's room.

"Tell Basil not to go inside."

"Roger."

"Get that ambulance over there now. Something might've happened to Agent Pierce."

Strake spun his car around and headed after her. She was about a mile ahead. He floored the pedal, closed in. Looked like she hadn't seen him. She seemed to be in no hurry. But when he touched her bumper she hit the gas. He had asked dispatch to call two more people. They would know where to find him. She veered off onto a faster road. Strake right behind. In about eight minutes, he saw one of the two cars appear behind him. The second car emerged in front of her. Sheriff Crowley sped past him in his big Chrysler. Veered left. Off the road into a flat grassy field. Up ahead he could see the other car coming. The girl panicked as Neaves played chicken with her in his Oldsmobile.

She slowed. Strake inched up to her back bumper. Neaves closed in on her front. She was trapped. Moving slower but not stopped. From the field on the left: Crowley barreled at her side door. He did not slow down. The front of his car smashed into her door with such force that she was knocked to the other side. Flew out the passenger window, obviously not wearing her lap belt. Crowley backed up and sped down the road. To the repair shop to hide the car, as planned. Neaves stepped out and checked with Strake. With his two index fingers Neaves made the cross sign. Grinning and nodding, Strake motioned Neaves to go. He screeched off. Now Strake was alone with the girl. She lay face down in the field just past the shoulder. Not a full Crucifix but good enough.

He walked up to her car first to take a look. Saw the bone knife on the front seat. Pierce's gun. And the bag of money. He leaned over to it. He could let her die. Crowley had banged into her hard. He approached her. Knelt down. Just a child. A wasted kid.

"What's your name?"

"Does it matter?"

"We don't know your name."

"Becca. Last name Heath."

"Where you from?"

"Kentucky."

She gave him the town.

"What happened to me?"

"We have a little local trick here."

"Your friends?"

"Something like that."

"I think I'm dying."

"You might be."

"All that money."

"I saw it. You know, your friend with the typewriter killed my son and his wife. She was about to have a baby."

"I'm sorry about that," she whispered.

"One sec."

A small knife surged up into Strake's neck, not the one made of bone. He fell forward on the grass. Never thinking she might have a second knife. Managed to turn to his side. Watched her limp to her damaged car. Screech off. His hand lifted to his neck, he pressed the blood back. Pulled out the bag of money from under his shirt. The only thing he could think was: she still didn't want to kill me. Her stabbing filled him like heroin. Then he slept a little.

Dazed. Her body hurt from the car impact. Blurry double vision. The car side mangled and barely drivable. Only after she had driven about five miles did she realize he had taken the bag of money. All she saw on the seat was the bone knife and Pierce's handgun. Luckily she always carried a smaller back-up blade. It could do some damage. She just couldn't kill the guy. Thinking about his dead son. There seemed to be a standoff between them. A need to chase each other. She could see it in those dark eyes of his.

And she was sure he could see it in her own. An understanding of sorts that it would be a shame to kill the other. He had his chance as he stood over her. Leaning down was his mistake. What did it matter? They would catch her soon enough. Her thoughts were violent too often. How did people live long lives and think these things for a lifetime? She couldn't see herself doing the same. Plus, she no longer had any money. Strake had the bag. She winced thinking about the car t-boning her. Couldn't she just go back? Finish him off. Grab the money. She turned the car around. Drove back to the field. Strake was still there. She parked on the shoulder. After staring at the pistol she grabbed the bone knife instead. Walked toward the man. His eyes opened as she approached. While the thought of an endless chase thrilled her, it also made her tired. One hand stanched his neck blood. It was not a fatal wound.

"I made this knife from a horse I skinned."

He stared up at her.

"I knew it would have a purpose one day."

"You came back to end this?" Strake asked her.

"I really don't know."

"What's holding you back?" he gasped.

"You make me sad," she told him.

"And why's that?"

"I don't know. You look so tired." She eyed her bone knife.

"You can't really run anywhere," he said, getting to his knees.

"Oh, I know. It's inevitable."

"Have you wanted to die all along?"

She thought for a moment. "Yes, for a long time."

"Bad thoughts?"

"So many," she admitted.

The field around them hummed with silent apathy.

"How did you get mixed up with those other two?"

"A stupid magazine ad. In *Killers!* I kept seeing it in the back. We met in Amarillo."

Strake was able to stand. She saw the bulge in his shirt and asked him for the money. He handed her the bag. Since his pants pockets were baggy she didn't notice until he pulled out his own knife and wielded it. Cutting into her arm that held the bag. She dropped the money. Pointed the bone knife at him. Their hearts were not in it, killing each other. He half looked like he was going to let her go. But he was fast and had cut her again on her cheek under her eye before she could even see what had happened.

"Tell me what you did to my friend Pierce back there at the motel."

"He was your friend?"

"Was?"

"I made some dog friends who were hungry."

"What do you mean?"

She told him about the skinning of the man and the wild dogs and leaving the door open so that they could devour Pierce after she had finished. Strake stared her not quite knowing what to say. Their knives were at their sides now. She knew better than to get in an actual knife fight with him. Her abilities in fighting were all about surprise thrusts that lasted seconds. It was clear he had agility with his blade. As he had certainly not expected her to have a smaller knife that cut his neck, she had not anticipated his using a knife either. From his pocket she thought a gun would appear.

"Let me get this straight . . . you skinned him?"

"Yes."

"And then you let dogs in to finish him off. Did I hear that right?"

"You heard what I said."

"I killed your two friends," Strake confessed.

"Doesn't really bother me."

"Why don't you let me take you in?"

"For what? A life in jail?"

"You'll be in an outdoor jail if you flee."

"Probably right. Not many places to go."

"I don't see a lot of options for you."

"It was easy to think about dying when we first talked about it. Now I feel like an idiot for following those two."

"You just sped up a horror show. Not sure why anyone would willingly do such a thing."

She stared at his blond hair. He was a man she could desire.

"I came from trash," she said. "That means I am trash."

"You don't have to be."

"It never leaves you."

"You think so?" he said, not moving his eyes from her gaze.

"I don't think it does."

Strangely, no cars had driven past them. They were alone in the field. In a futile duel. Neither had the heart to do anything. She suddenly felt pain in so many places. There was no way to stop this except through violent action. Kill him and run. Be found in a few days. If she wasn't found she would fear for the rest of her life. What happened when she ran out of money? Why, though, was she worried about it? Wasn't this the very end she expected after the first bank? To come to death and embrace it hard. Not panic when it was time. The man was kind in some way. He affected her as blood dripped from his neck. So this had to be it. She lifted her knife and aimed. It would be real this time. Strake watched as the white blade sunk into her pupil. Her teeth were gritted in final defiance that required a deep, last plunge. Then she fell to the grass. He collapsed by her. Wanted to close his eyes. Just for a minute. He thought of his son. Of Houston and Pierce. The girl had saved him from an impossible decision. He could not have killed her. She could not run far if she had killed him. He left her in situ with the knife jutting out of her eye. Picked up the money. Strolled to his car. He fired up a cigar after he sat at the steering wheel. The second thing he would do was to return both banks' money. The first: head to the motel to see what happened to Pierce.

When he arrived Basil was standing in front of the open door where the girl had stayed. He was in shock.

"Basil?" Strake tried.

The man didn't move or say a word. He heard the dogs before he saw them. Taking in a breath he walked into the room. There were five of them on the bed. Gnashing the guts and bones of Pierce. Jagged white teeth looked like sparks. Hardly noticing the sheriff they feasted on piles of skin from his body that she left beside him. He saw the note on the motel pad paper: "For Strake. Enjoy the meal."

Even the man's face had been skinned. Strake leaned in closer. Saw fat ticks crawling around his lips. Into his nostrils. Around his eyes. The dogs seemed happy more than territorial. Didn't snarl at him. Bellies full they trotted through the motel door. Flew off like vultures when a car approaches. All five of them had a bone or organ in their mouths. Past Basil who remained still as ice. Closing the door, Strake walked up to him and gave his arms a little shake. "Basil, buddy. Come on."

"The ambulance never came," he said.

"I see that."

"Never liked them hellhounds."

"You okay?"

"Yeah, I'm okay."

"I'll tell Meyer about this. Don't worry about the ambulance right now."

"Hey what's all that blood on your neck?"

"Finally caught that girl. Didn't end too well."

"I don't wanna know."

"You sure?"

"Ash rye."

Basil stumbled off with a hand flipped behind him in a wave. The sheriff had seen many dead bodies, mangled and gruesome, but nothing like what the girl had done to Pierce. To her it was perhaps forbidden art. No, the skinning had not bothered him. But the ticks in the mouth had. To Strake this was a grim final touch that maligned whatever work she thought she was creating. He shook his head: he had just convinced himself that skinning was not that bad. Revision: it *all* bothered him.

He understood her better now. The only art she could make was vulgar and inhumane. In other words she could not create without death.

Interestingly enough she had added a living touch to her human knife carving: the ticks in the mouth. They were not dead. For some reason. Poor Meyer. Jesus. The coroner had to look at all these graphic bodies as he did his work later. How did Meyer do it? Time for an easy errand. Returning the money to the banks. He went to the second bank first. Not as much was stolen from there. The manager thanked him. At the first bank where his son and daughter-in-law had died along with two others, there was someone new from the regional office. The man was in black suit with a yellow tie that had dollar signs on it. Strake handed him the crumpled bag of bills. He drove around town taking care of what he had to do. Still hadn't tended to his bleeding neck so he stopped by the hospital. They cleaned the wound but it somehow needed no stitches, just a bandage.

At one point he drove up the reservoir to check on the young man's body. He walked the same path he and Houston used to carry the kid and could still see a few lines of caked blood the rain had not washed off. There was a soughing of the breeze that gave him a chilling memory of war hikes in unknown woods. He looked up and watched limbs sway and creak. Up at the top of the water he could see no floating body. It was still submerged. His secret, dead with Houston.

More details had emerged about the ages of The Nihilistics. The Bald Drifter: twenty. Tanner: eighteen. Becca: seventeen. Young people, erratic and bitter. Their only purpose to join each other and do violence. He feared the worst. He had lost a grandchild in all of this and would not have another chance for one. The reservoir was bright. Sun hit it and hurt his eyes. He squinted in pain. And stood there for a while. Then he walked back down the path. Kicking dirt over any remaining blood stains. Back at his Chevelle he pulled out a cigar for a long, reflective smoke. He thought for a few moments. Sour vapor blew from his mouth. He watched it move away from him and fade. Looking at the road, he imagined the killings of the drifter. The ease with which he rode. And killed. Killed again.

The girl had not killed as much. His thoughts flashed to her own eye as a small target. The white blade of her horse bone knife. He would not rush this smoke. Leaned against his car for a long time. The sun was yellow and absolute. A future of nothing was around the corner. No son. No more family. Only a job that took him down dark paths. He blew out more smoke. It was a good cigar.

He stopped in to check on Meyer, told him where to find the girl's body. Warned him about the sight of Pierce. Asked about Houston's funeral. Maude gave him an affectionate cluck. They walked back to his office together. After that quick conversation with Becca about who she was and where she was from, he tracked down her parents who had been looking for her. On the phone he could tell the father was relieved in a way. He called Neaves and Crowley to thank them. Strake paid for their car repairs. His neck healed. Many funerals that late summer, even the girl's. He was the only person there. Not much of a funeral, just a cremation. Meyer came by the office after it all settled. Gave him the bone knife.

"So you watched her do that to herself? This wasn't another Strake heel special type thing, now was it?"

"No," said Strake, "she did it. I couldn't believe what I was seeing."

"I'll bet. Okay, I had to ask for the report."

"Strange suicide."

"Sure was. It would take an act of pure force and will to drive a knife through an eye and into the brain without stopping yourself."

"Thanks for your help Meyer."

After the coroner left, Strake scratched Maude a little on the back. He looked at the bone knife. Picked it up. Held it to his left eye like she had. Using both hands. The thrust would need to be forceful. What struck the sheriff as nearly impossible was the required aim to do it in one jab. Precise focus. Strake thought about the trio a lot in the coming weeks. The Nihilistics.

At night he kept seeing her knife plunge into the eye, wiping out her life in seconds. He could not stop having nightmares about those ticks in Pierce's mouth, tiny gray humpbacks bloated with canine blood. Dogs feasted on him in horrible dreams. Many things would not leave him. Bodies from different landscapes merged. War images became recent thoughts of murder and suicide. Confused definitions of nihilism rippled his mind. On the one hand it was a negation of values in place. But on the other it was pure unbelief. His deep fear was that he was no different from the trio.

He had to be careful too since his reputation was one of personal justice rather than letting the law do what it should. Conversations at the diner with Pierce and later with Meyer in his office made him see that his boot heel was infamous, discussed around town. Folks tacitly let him do these things. But it could catch up with him. Then again, wasn't justice changing? Weren't deviant people ripping up the laws? Like The Nihilistics. If so, did he not need to be equally deviant to hunt them? Deep down he was not a lawful man.

He spent many nights wondering if this was bad or if this was maybe kind of good. Nothing stopped his shocking dreams. Each tragic thing that happened only fed more images into his nightmares, adding to a visual lexicon that grew as a mind fire. There would always be a body in the reservoir waiting to bubble to the surface. There would always be wild dogs on a bed devouring a skinned body as ticks crawled out of the mouth. He wondered what would happen next. More trios? More nihilism? It could not get better, he imagined. Once people saw in others that they could be lawless too, it allowed ideas to grow. Maybe he was in the right place to do what was needed. Every time he thought of the absurdity of recent events, his mind almost refused to believe the memories.

A man walking down a highway with a Colt firing into a car window as he drove. Thumping into the drifter with such impact that the sheriff's teeth crunched with some chips that he spat into his hand. Stomping the man's face. A girl with a bag of money with no more choices . . . she stabs a knife made of bone deep into her eye and collapses in suicide. A young man carried through the woods and dumped in a reservoir. The body of a skinned GBI agent, also stabbed in the stomach. Eaten by hungry dogs. His friend Houston shot in the head. These were just not normal things. But the butchering had happened. Now they were in memory. Mostly his remembering. What would he do now?

One afternoon he found a copy of *Killers!* at the newsstand. Becca had talked about this ad that she and Tanner had seen in the magazine to meet up with the Bald Drifter named Ellman. He wanted to see if it was still there. It was not. He thumbed through the psychotic rag to see what had drawn in the trio. Killers sharing stories as if it were normal. A chill rose in his back when he saw a story called "The Nihilistics." By Samuel Bunker. No, he thought. Not possible. It was a short account of the first bank robbery where the four had been killed including his son and his wife.

The same weapons. A horse bone knife held by a girl. A Colt Government used by a bald man. A hatchet used by a young eighteen year old. The same four deaths. In a small Georgia town outside Athens. The Impala convertible. How? One piece now fit. A spark of a nearly forgotten impression. The typewriter by the boy's head. On the side of the road when they found his body. Strake had to sit down. He could not stop after the first line: "If you're reading about what the three of us did, we'll be long dead by the time you do."

Either some writer had found out about The Nihilistics in the news and stolen the story. Or one of the trio was sick enough in the head to write it as a perverted glorification after it had just happened. Both possibilities were equally frightening. Odds were the young man Tanner had written it, since the typewriter had been by him when they booted him from the convertible.

Strake hadn't given it a second thought. Tossed the Underwood in the trunk of his Chevelle before dumping that body at the reservoir. Come to think of it, the typewriter was probably still in there. What was, he wondered, next? If his small town was not immune to massacre, he thought about how this carnage was to be multiplied in cities. It was starting to be godless. Without rules. Reacting to the violence would necessarily have to be subversive, at best. One time his father, also sheriff, told him about ritual suicide in Japan, how he actually had seen seppuku happen to a shunned man during WW II.

A self-slicing of the belly to die, what his dad sometimes also called harakiri. As much as he resisted defining himself like the trio, Strake felt that after he had watched Becca's ocular harakiri, he had no choice but to be subsumed in the nihilism to come. It was coming. Had already arrived. He read all the stories in the magazine obsessively. Sent in the card found inside the pages to order a subscription. Maybe he would learn something about deviant homicide. In a few weeks the death died down. For the moment. Even so, he could still not stop thinking about it.

Or how in some strange way, she had done him a bold favor. When it came down to it, he knew she wanted to die. And this made him realize that he didn't.

He supposed he liked living.

Thought, however, that life had no intention of relenting.

Maybe he just liked not being dead.

What could be done?

Nothing but to wait for it.

STRAKE
PART II

"The landscape had changed."

Edward Bunker,
No Beast So Fierce

Strake strangled a man in his dreams that morning. The neck would not give. As much as his hands pressed. Shadows of his palms separated from him, a ghost slipped into a smoke body. His hands, invisible vapors. He was in Cà Mau. End of January 1969. Still ninety-six humid, warm degrees. They had finished him early at Camp Lejeune. Scout Sniper School to train some young ones.

Now riding on a barge down a milk chocolate river in the middle of a filthy city. Watching a group of Vietnamese men cut up a cooked brown turtle to eat. In the past month thirty headshot kills. He tried for one each morning. The city filled with Viet Cong. He had been in the Marines when he was a teenager. Continued to do work for the government after that for over a decade. They never told him what he was. Fine with him. Not a spy, sure, sure. What was not defined had freedom. Their lack of defining let him roam. And kill with indemnity. Never spoken but assumed: figure out your own justice. In February alone in the rain he turned thirty-six. Creaked more in the legs. Knew he was an unspoken label they would never admit. A loose spy with a gun. As long as he killed VC they were elated.

No one had more single, confirmed kills than Strake. Sometimes the kills were very close. Yards from the victims. One time four of them playing cards. Four quick pops in the head. Faces fell on red, white and blue poker chips. Blood poured. Tiny human rivers that came out of the dead when shot. Other times he roamed. Rode barges and boats with garbage and poor toothless folks. Killed at a distance too. Received orders about locations, sometimes. Orders didn't always reach him. They trusted him to do it anyway. He ate skewered prawns, rubbery and charred. Not much appetite for anything else. Except the rice lager, 33 Beer.

Strake justified his killings. Fewer of them meant they wouldn't kill his friends. The military moved him around to different Viet Cong strongholds, all over the turf. Kills accreting. In his mind he was clear in the daylight. In darkness came the dreams. About his body separating away from his skin. Into a new vaporous form strangling necks. But he could not hurt them since his hands passed through like smoke. He was smoke moving through a country. The smolder of a man floating with a sniper rifle. M40. Bolt action. Easy to murder in brightness. Difficult to remember in the dark. The smoke of him was dripping into blood. Clean kills. Dirty dreams. That's how he thought of himself. His young son Harris was on his mind. Strake loved him very much. The thing he was good at . . . ruined everything else.

Soon it was October 1969, nine or so months later. A blur of constant murder. Seven Marines hiked through a forest so green that it hurt his eyes. Strake and six others. The color was brilliant and blinding. Jim Riley, his spotter, was in front of him with the other five. Strake in the rear. Already he had been having eye problems. Humid air gave him stye blisters on his lower eyelids, blurring the white sclera to red. What he saw next was luminous, terminal. Six men turned to blood and skin confetti on triggered landmines. A spray of new candor. The truth had been changing for a while. Now here it was in full gospel. Each body explosion much like the smoke of himself. As it dripped into blood. You did not know what was smoke, what was blood anymore. It was all mixed in the wind of human flares. In front of a green so ugly. A wet country. A dripping place. Dripping with death.

If he wasn't causing the death count, he was witness to it. Landmines were like mousetraps for men. They snapped in the same way. Abrupt and shocking. It could have been one landmine that killed the six. Or six landmines, as if they each had one of their own. One of the many times in Strake's life when something spared him. Being spared, though, a man became an endless witness. Drenched in memory. And maybe it was not the bursting of flesh that stayed with him. It was that *snap* of the human mousetrap bomb. His father called it gralloch after a deer kill when they strung up a buck to be gutted. Watching the entrails spill like vomit.

One of the six soldiers, his body left nothing. Gone, no sign of him. Guts drained on the ground from the other five. Two blue eyes still on rods stared up at him like an alien plant. Scalps of hair ripped. Intestines, piles of them, attacked by flies. Strake stared for a minute. He had to keep moving through the woods. Needed to avoid more mines. The beginning of his visions. Sometimes he saw extended images that were not real. He had not escaped damage himself, although at the time he had thought he would be fine. The landmine blasts had hurt his left eye. His ears could hear only muteness.

He was about to move into the tree cover when he saw Jim. Strake had not even considered that his friend might be alive. The horror was voiceless. Jim's mouth was gone, his bottom jaw too. Teeth scattered like white rice. He pointed at Strake's gun. No, Strake motioned without words, I won't. Faster nodding. A butchered face. A permitting. He looked at these puddles of blood and bowels. Nodded and aimed. Jim's head spasmed. Then he was calm. Strake had been in shock many times. Best to move forward. Even in walking slumber. In that first week of wandering there were no villages for miles, only rice paddies.

His hearing returned in a slow way. Screeched pitches of ringing, a squealing insect. For a month he wandered. He didn't want to find anyone. A helicopter chopped by and ignored him. Maybe it was all right. To be lost in this place as a fragment. He kept to the trees. Had plenty of ammo. Took out Viet Cong when he sensed them hiding. He stumbled on a makeshift refugee camp. Anorexic children with bloated bellies. Men and women with only gums. Fat flies on their necks. He passed random insane grunts. Wandering or escaping or both. A US soldier crawled. Looking for something on the grass. He tilted up his face when Strake approached. Only sockets where his eyes had been gouged. "Are you all right?"

Clearly the boy was not, with head trauma.

"I can't find them! I can't see!"

Strake could not stop for long.

"My dog tags!"

"Son . . ."

"I lost them!" he moaned.

Reluctant to leave but knowing he had to go, Strake left the eyeless kid. Thinking of similar punishments meted out in an Italian poem. At dusk a journalist dropped from the belly of a helicopter. Rushed at Strake with a Speed Graphic. A flash came from the massive camera in a crisp small blaze. The man handed Strake a 33 Beer and a paper bag. He looked inside: greasy cheddar cheese and broken crackers covered in flies. The journalist was already scaling the rope ladder into the chopper. Strake stared upward. In his eyes the flash glare was dazzling with throbs. Rain came but he hid from it. Afraid to be wet even though it never fell below sixty degrees after dark. Nights were not easy. The dreams deepened to austere salience. Smoke and blood. Blood made of smoke. He counted his kills sleeping on the ground. Not sleeping fully for many weeks.

He found some grunts one morning. One young man missing a front tooth gap-smiled at him. Had a skimpy mustache like long eyelashes. Others joined them. Strake told him he was a roving sniper. Talked about the landmines, his friends. About the boy with no eyes crawling. Why was he looking at him so oddly? Had he been listening? The other grunts took notice of him. Seemed to be in awe of something. Finally, he asked: is there something wrong?

"Your forehead," said Missing Tooth.

Strake reached up. Wiped at it. A piece of skin with blood peeled off. Dry and brittle. Not his.

"They're all over your face," he let him know.

Strake felt his cheeks. Had he not touched his face in a month? The men waited as he rubbed off the skin of dead friends. Pasted onto him for weeks from the landmine blasts. This is when the heroin came. They injected the sleepy toxin to calm him, perhaps. More, to make him suffer with the crowd. They lay around a fire in false bliss. He did not resist that first time. Had seen scag all over the country. Nodding, he took the first injection that would begin another type of wandering. The flash of the journalist's Speed Graphic triggered a reliving. Each kill returned in a magnified wickedness. He saw no difference between a soldier and a serial killer.

He needed to leave these men who seemed to be on their own, not fighting, not reporting to anyone. Just sitting around a fire and pressing heroin in their veins. One night he left when they were asleep. He took no needles. Had to quit as quickly as he started. An arresting repetition of scenes. Wading in rice paddies. Dots of squeaking mosquitoes peppered his face and neck and arms. He was sure he had dengue. Copters above. Lost humans falling past him, hiking, wounded, some about to die. Camps of starving Vietnamese. Emaciated, humped Feng cattle. Still doing his job. Those months of late October and November 1969 were not clear to him. How he managed to even keep moving. The left eye stayed blurred for a while. Heavy inertia was in his body from stopping the drug so quick.

A swirl of dengue kept him in a smog of incoherence. His mouth salivated in craving. Cramps and aches. Awful bouts of squatting over a dug hole, liquid diarrhea shooting from him. Heat caused a different kind of sweat than the heroin as it oozed out of his skin. One prolonged fever lasted ten days. He moved through it. Forward. *Don't stand still.* Start walking. He notched more VC murders. Unsuspecting campers never realized he stood feet from them. By mid-November the worst was done. At least with the junk that had polluted him.

Aches from dengue remained. He had a map, hadn't really looked at it. He unfolded it now. Searched for a small American base and made that his aim. His memory was stained in black. Hard to remember names of places. He never stopped walking. Never stopped killing. His future would be to kill. To stop killers. To sometimes kill them. And not always in the *right* way. He would never escape being sheriff. He had been shadowing his dad, Strake Senior, ever since that first time back from the Marines. Even before that as a boy. Had already seen more than enough with his father, who trained him.

In some ways worse than the war itself. Soon he would be home, although he knew what waited for him. A job yes but an insecure wife who grew up poor. Would never be able to deal with him once he stepped into the house. These foggy, painful months were the last of a certain type of autarchy. Ha, autarchy. How in the world had he remembered this word? Self-sufficient. Free to drift into drugs and landmines. Heroin was just an internal landmine.

He decided to be in no rush. To see what he could. Turn it into a hiking trip. With an occasional sniper kill. Jesus, he was demented. He looked up for a god but only saw the empty blue. At one point he came to a massacred village. Bodies of children and women on the ground. Men ripped in half. A torso here, legs over there. Two dog carcasses gnawed by birds. Another scene of many scenes here.

A young woman peeked out from a straw hut. She was perhaps nineteen or twenty, at first glance, but she could've been thirty. She stared at him with jaundiced brown eyes. He looked at her. Without speaking he entered her small home. Didn't leave until the end of December 1969. Her name was Hanh. Strake spoke limited Vietnamese. Understood some French.

"Les cadavres," she rasped, her first words to him.

He understood. Found a shovel outside leaning against the hut. Began to dig into the moist dirt. Rolled bodies into the graves. Including the two vivisected dead mutts. He dug as deep as he could to keep stray dogs off them. A charcoal blob, upon a closer glance, made him wince. He laid the baby in the same grave as a woman. Found the torso and legs of a man. Gathered them into one hole. Bodies scorched black. Others hacked into separate limbs. It was a ruthless chore. By the state of her clothes and face it was clear Hanh had been raped. Strake worked hard. Wanted to collapse into one of the graves himself. Would be so easy. The grave was dug. Why not?

No one to throw the dirt on him, that's why. You couldn't bury yourself, in the end. A final human joke that you could never really do anything on your own. So much for autarchy . . . He slept on the floor for many nights. Drank tea and soup with her. One night she took his hand. Motioned for him to come to her. Their breathing was erotic. They only slept. For a night or two. Soon she wanted him. He slid into her body. Joined with her skin. Their touch was silent. He washed her legs and back in a small metal tub. She washed his feet and naked body. She shaved off his beard with a sharp straight razor. Even twisting the blade up in his nostrils to cut nose hairs. He could hear the scrape of the razor. He felt clean for the first time in a long while. Lying on their thick bamboo mat on the dirt floor.

"Toujours," she whispered, "je t'adore."

They walked on a long hike one day past rice fields. "Marble Mountains," she said in halting English. He could not see them. Her hand gestures meant they were in that direction. She pointed with four fingers of her right hand: "Da Nang." There was that Air Force base there. On the South China Sea. She had trusted Strake despite his rifle. He knew he had to go. One morning they kissed outside in the hot air. Their dry lips were coarse. He walked for a week to find his friend Houston. To see if he was still alive. He was. They shook hands.

"Thought you were a goner, buddy."

"Not gone yet," Strake told him.

Strake finally had his eyes and ears checked.

Stayed in the military hospital tent for a week.

Houston would be sheriff in a few towns over from Strake outside Athens, Georgia. They flew home together. Told stories anyone around them would have a hard time believing. Home always seemed better when you weren't near it.

The first thing Strake did after he flew into Atlanta was to rent a car. Drove Houston back to his town first. On the way home they were quiet. Strake forced himself to remember his wife. He hadn't written to her the entire year. The same thing had happened in the Marines when he was younger. Doing his time. Coming home. Working for Strake Senior at the office. Learning how to become a sheriff. Since he had been a boy he had ridden around the patrol car with his father.

Often stopping at falling houses on bleak farms. Where old couples could barely walk. What Strake recalled was the tenderness in his dad as he dealt with their problems. One woman had tripped and fallen backwards on the stairs after a stroke. Was dead. Sprawled upside down. Pantyhose on varicose legs. Veins so thick they bulged in the brown nylon. Her farmer husband stared at her, unable to do anything. Strake Senior percolated coffee and sat with the man. While the ambulance, which sometimes ran out of gas, took its time arriving. Strake, as a boy, saw death early. Many times. His father never shielded him. In fact they talked about the last death in the patrol car as they rode to the next one.

"One death after the other," Strake Senior sighed. "Get used to it."

For a small town there was more than you would expect. Mostly folks in their late seventies, eighties and nineties, too poor to leave their houses. Many of them smoked and their homes reeked of cigarettes. Gruesome orange wallpaper streaked with tar. Smoke stains like ghosts. His father inhaled three packs a day. Strake's mom was no longer around, dying shortly after she had him. It gave his dad a lonely sadness that he himself never understood until he grew older. And lost everyone. As he drove back home from the Atlanta airport with his friend Houston, he thought a lot about Strake Senior. Who had fallen sick right before he left for Vietnam. Frail, stuck in his bed, fifty pounds lighter. Lungs black with cancer. He was not looking forward to his doomed marriage either.

Their son Harris worked at the bank with his wife. It would be good to see them. They were trying to have a baby. Had married young like Strake. Strake's marriage was an expected disaster. He and Mary Mae met at high school. Even though his father warned him about her trash family, Strake couldn't help himself. A pixie blond with green eyes. Who looked innocent. But was not. Her parents were known to be into drugs and the messes they caused. So Strake had to hide his time with her.

Which made it more deceptive and erotic as he lied to Strake Senior. His friends were Houston, Neaves and Pierce, the first two becoming sheriffs like him in nearby towns and the third,

Agent Pierce, working for the GBI office in Atlanta. Neaves was a tall Scottish Cherokee with FISTS tattooed across his knuckles. Houston was a black man missing a pinky he lost in the war. Pierce was white and kind of a dowdy fellow, so it was surprising when the GBI hired him. The four of them played football, basketball and baseball on championship teams.

Strake Senior was their hero. The three friends warned him about Mary Mae. It never mattered what anybody said: he couldn't think straight around the girl. She twisted his head into mad mazes. EmEm, as he called her, fought against her family inheritance. Hated where she came from. Both parents did drugs or dealt them.

When they were sixteen they parked at a nearby pond. Couldn't keep their hands off each other. It had consequences. She had a baby, their son, at the end of December 1949. One of the first baby boomers. Harris was twenty now, about to turn twenty-one, somehow a decent kid who had ignored his parents and their bickering. His son always had jobs even as a young boy. The town knew him well. He had no interest in taking over sheriff. Started work at the downtown bank at eighteen. What was today?

It was December 31, 1969, New Year's Eve. There would be no celebration at home with his wife. He dropped Houston at his house. Dreaded the final leg. Knowing what waited. Once EmEm knew she was pregnant, Strake had to tell his father.

"And you're ready to raise a kid?! You're still in high school."

"Didn't **you** have me when **you** were in school?"

"Wellll, that's different?"

"Is it?"

Strake Senior thought for a moment. "I guess not."

They lived at his father's house for some time. His dad helped out more than he thought he would. Strake made it through high school. Joined the Marines to get away from her scream-ing. The child occupied her. She didn't want him around any-way. Once he served his time, he promised his officers that if any big wars came up, he would be available. In the decades leading up to Vietnam they had him surveil certain criminals around the South. He also kept tabs on radical groups. At thirty-six when he found himself back in the war after training some kids at Scout Sniper School in Camp Lejeune, it was just to get away from her. Again. EmEm knew. Now, about to turn thirty-seven in Febru-ary 1970, after a year in Vietnam, he felt old. Not ready to start back sheriffing.

It was about to be a new year. Didn't feel like it. January 1 was tomorrow. He sighed, knowing he needed to visit his bed-ridden father. He was at his home after parking the rental in the driveway. Felt like he had to knock. She opened the door. Stared coldness into him. The one thing she had resisted while raising Harris was to fall into what her parents, the Reeds, had. Or so he thought. It was clear that she had been using, as soon as he saw her face. Ragged and tired. She barely gave him an apathetic wave. Plopped on the couch. Stared at the television.

"Didn't think you'd come back," she hissed.

"EmEm."

"Don't you EmEm me. Call me Mary Mae! Why didn't you die there? I thought you would DIE."

"Good grief."

"I thought the war would kill you," she said, as if muted.

"What do you want?"

"Go away."

"I want to be home."

"Sure you do."

The next morning, the rental was gone and so was she. "I won't be coming back," a note said.

With a long breath Strake resumed as sheriff at his desk. Jimmy, deputy assistant, shook his hand with vigor, so very glad to see him. They talked about cases Jimmy kept organized for him while he was gone. He stopped in at the bank to visit Harris and Betty. They were happy he was home. He waved hi to the teller Dolores (Meyer, the coroner, his sister).

January 1, 1970. A new time. He met his son and daughter-in-law later for lunch in the cafe diner and told them about EmEm.

"She *is* acting strange," his son said.

"Drugs?"

"More than that. You think she's coming back?"

"Not this time."

They talked a little more. Betty said Strake could be expecting his grandkid soon. "We're not sure about when, but the doctor is hopeful for me," she assured him.

"When will you know more?"

"In a few months."

"We're hoping by May or June," said a dejected Harris, avoiding his eyes.

"I can't wait. You two will be wonderful parents."

Harris and Betty turned to each other, in love but somehow wounded. Strake was proud.

"Betty, can I talk to Dad alone for a minute?"

"Sure hon. I'll head back to the bank."

"Something wrong?" Strake asked, after she left.

"Yes."

He went back to his office, avoiding a visit to Strake Senior. Trying to also absorb what Harris had told him. Sorted through tilting piles of forms and papers. Old cases. A grandfather at thirty-seven! But with complications. He anticipated a bad time with EmEm. Never expected she would leave the minute he returned. It was a relief in some way. She sliced at him with cruel words. Hated his aloof way, his casual disappearing. He gave her only stoic indifference. Sad, he muttered to himself. I wonder what will happen to her. Jimmy stopped in at the office again. He loved Jimmy, eyes of the town.

Later Strake would see Meyer, to check on the latest coroner news. It never ceased to surprise him that crime happened in what was just a little southern village. First he needed to go to the cemetery. Mom's grave. Being around her memory helped. Strake Senior was a logical man who read Poe, Doyle and Christie stories from the local library.

"Now," his father once said to him, "murder happens everywhere. Just like there are beautiful girls in small places. Sit around and keep your eyes open and wait. The ugly little world comes to you. Just like the beauty does."

After a quick stop at the cemetery, Strake called the rental car company. Was surprised to hear that his car *had* been returned to the airport. So . . . she flew somewhere. I wonder where she's going. Strake couldn't get his mind off Hanh either. She filled him with soft memory. Wondered how she was in her forsaken place, one they had turned into a short time of bliss. Time to work, Strake said aloud to an empty office. He stood for a second over the mound of papers. Sat in his wooden chair with rollers that creaked. Called his father, said he would visit tomorrow. Vietnam behind him. But still in him for a long time.

The next day he drove to his father's house. Strake Senior was in bed, reading. His hair white and face tan. Lung cancer from a life of filterless Lucky Strikes.

"Hey boy," he coughed.

"Dad."

"Welcome home."

Strake Senior first took Bartholomew Reed to the dump after the parents of many young girls in town had talked with the sheriff in private. Bart and Strake Senior were the same age. Picked up hay together on farms for extra money, as boys. Bart liked to steal cars and wreck them. He put distance between him and Bart after he saw the Reed boy punch a kid's mouth at school. With the intention of knocking out each tooth, one at a time. Bart's trouble grew in increments. As the boy became a man he had to top the last problem he made. The two had scraps, fistfights here and there. Mutual amusement, shirtless boxing matches many in town watched with awe. Then something changed when they were teenagers. Bart, no other way to put it, liked sin.

They might visit the same prostitute, but Bart was just a little bit too rough with her. She would slam the door on them the next time they tried. One offense became a misdemeanor leading to arrests and jail. Bart turned eighteen. Fell right into doing time at Arrendale State Prison for robbing a liquor store. Reed, a sadist. Liked to punch out people's teeth. Pointless violence. Bart did it to anyone, old people, children. The town feared his outbursts. If he made you a target, he stalked you with malice. This was why Strake Senior had no trouble taking Bart Reed to the dump. He tried to knock out a tooth at a time to make his point.

Reed didn't care. Walked around with a fanged mouth, bleeding gums. Probably thinking it made him look even more deranged. So Bart liked to hurt people. He liked the pain of being hurt too. Then his kids came, Fletcher, Bubbo and Mary Mae, the three inheriting his sadistic mess. Somehow Strake Junior fell in with her. Of all the people to choose, his son had picked EmEm.

He knew what she was up to when his son was first in the Marines then back to Vietnam. It was bewildering to see Strake

Junior think this girl was loyal to him. She cheated with about every man in town and beyond. His thoughts were disrupted when he saw his son out on the porch. Strake Senior could no longer walk.

"Come in!" he shouted from his bed.

He liked the cool air from the screen door even in winter, so he left the main one open. Kept a pistol with him by mystery books strewn across the blanket. Right now he was reading Ross Macdonald's *The Way Some People Die*. His son pushed open the screen door.

"Hey boy," he coughed.

"Dad."

"Welcome home."

"Some welcome."

Strake had told his father what happened with his wife over the phone.

"EmEm just up and left?"

"Barely saw her. Seemed angry."

"Been telling you all your life."

"Well aware," Strake Junior said.

Over the next hour the two men talked a lot about the Reeds.

"You can turn them on each other easily," Strake Senior said.

"How?"

"They're paranoid. Pour salt on human wounds, watch them writhe."

"I think Mary Mae got mixed up in something."

"You surprised?"

"I suppose not."

"Don't even let me tell you what I know about her."

"Wait . . . what's *that*?"

He pointed to a three-wheeled device on the other side of the bed he had just noticed.

"Motorized tricycle! Runs on gas, not electric. Can drive it to the Texaco station in town a few miles. Made sure the tank was big but it does stink of gasoline in the house a little."

Mud tracks were visible on the wood floors.

"Is it a wheelchair?"

"Sort of. I had heard about the Harding design after I was in double dubya two. One of my vet friends used it. But this one here is made custom. I worked on it with a local mechanic before I lost the use of my legs. I could tell they were giving out on me."

He fired up a Lucky and coughed fumes. Both nostrils sprayed down smoke like dual exhaust pipes on a muscle car. Still holding the cigarette with his left hand he reached over to a coffee mug. Spat a phlegm of blood into it. Mottled red snot hung from his lip. His son reached over. Wiped the mucus off so it dropped into the cup.

"Thanks buddy."

"How do you feel? Still don't want to go to the hospital?"

"Too late."

"Wouldn't you be more comfortable there?"

"I hate hospitals. All that *white*." He shuddered.

Strake Junior smiled at him. "What's wrong with white?"

"Think about it. Why in the world do they wear the ONE color that makes blood stand out the most?"

"You have a point," he chuckled.

"I mean, make the scrubs red!"

"Ha ha, you can tell them next time you go."

"Plus, they wouldn't let me ride around in my tricycle wheelchair."

"And you drive this into town?"

"All the time, my friend. It's fast."

"How quick can you go?"

"We put this extra engine on it. Doesn't have a speedometer, but I cranked it up one time and couldn't stop. Flew right out of it! Had to crawl back in the dirt because no one was around."

"That's not good."

"What I need on it is a siren."

His son smiled then grew serious. "What do the docs say about your lung cancer?"

"Not too long now. Course, *not too long* to a doctor could be six years. Doctors say a lot of things, most of it inaccurate. They're not accountants."

"Anything I can do?"

"It's all in order. You'll get the house, as you know, and by not staying at the hospital I'll still have a little savings for you."

"Hey, I have to run."

"Glad you came."

"Need any food?"

"Nah, not much of an appetite. Just drop in when you can."

"I will."

"Bring me good cigars next time you come."

"Because . . . you need more nicotine?"

"Wisecrack!"

"I'll bring them."

"Hey, son, I do have a favor."

"Shoot."

"If you need help taking down the Reeds . . ."

Strake Junior stared at him. "I'll think of something."

Back at sheriff central the next morning Strake telephoned his old high school buddy, Agent Pierce. In the Atlanta GBI office. Checking in to see what he might be on his radar.

"These hitchhiker murders. Been obsessed with them, as you know."

"Any progress?"

"No one listens to me."

"Why not?"

"They think serial killers are only in crime mags."

"You have proof?"

"Same bullets used every time, shot in the head. I make it as some kind of Colt. Leaves victims in their cars behind the steering wheels."

"Hmm."

"My boss lets me look into them. This drifter picks small towns where no one cares, so no one's putting together the pattern like I am."

Strake told him about EmEm and about possibly being a grandfather in the near future. They said goodbye. Strake cradled the black phone receiver. It hit him that he was alone. His left eye ached but the vision had gotten a little better. Never would be perfect again. He was just happy he hadn't lost his eye during the landmine blasts. Right at that moment, he happened to stand from his desk to stretch his legs. He looked out the window into town.

In the middle of the street Strake Senior zipped down the road on his gas-powered tricycle. Wearing pilot goggles and a cowboy hat. Heading to the station for gasoline and cigarettes. Madman. As he sorted through boring triplicate files he thought of his father's words. About waiting for the ugly to come to you. His father had been right. One perpetual local nemesis of the Strake family had been EmEm's father, Bart. And their retinue of drug scum, including many out of towners. Strake Senior had often taken care of business on his own, roughing up Bartholomew. A derelict waste of a man who abused his daughter every day until she moved in with Strake.

It was known around the neighborhoods that Fletcher Reed, one of his sons, sold drugs to high school kids. Whenever Strake Senior caught him red-handed, he took him out to the junkyard. Boxed his face with hands wrapped in bandages, just like had done with Bart. Fletcher Reed began to so resent these thumpings that he became vengeful. Nothing worse than a toothless drug addict in bib overalls (and no shirt) with revenge on a fuddled mind. Well, maybe there was something worse, his brother Bubbo. Bubbo Reed was lecher who had violated EmEm many times at night, maybe even raped her.

She wouldn't talk about the details. Bartholomew Reed and Strake Senior had grown up together. Their brawls were legends. Fletcher and Bubbo, when they weren't selling drugs to kids, were terrorizing them. Strake at six feet was intimidated by these idiots. While they were short they were thick with muscly fat. And deranged. Many times he rode in the car with his father. As they took a handcuffed Fletcher or Bubbo, or both, out to the junkyard for some face disfiguring. It was the first time that Strake understood that justice didn't always have to come in a jail cell.

"Is it legal?" he asked one time in the patrol car, noticing the shredded skin on Strake Senior's knuckles.

His father chuckled. "*Legal?*" Said nothing else.

It was a tacit fact that Strake himself would take over the beatings once his father died. Fletcher and Bubbo were still at it. Drugs on the rise with hippie use. More mysterious black suits snooping around town. With EmEm out of the picture he couldn't quite allow himself to care. Until his conversation in the diner with Harris. He didn't want to schlep them out to the junkyard and torture his knuckles just because his father had started a perverse tradition with Bart. He needed to find a way to nab them. The town allowed the abuse to happen because Bart owned the local pawn shop. Many owed him money. He was a crook. Everyone knew it.

Suspicious men in black suits came to the back of his store a lot. Bart had done a bit of time for mail fraud and pornography. As a teen, state pen. His sons kept the shop while he was gone for six months. They lived in a series of trailers off the main highway all about a mile apart. Strake wanted to finish off the Reeds. For good. How, he wasn't sure. It was a lull time after the new year. Maybe he could come up with a plan. About that time he heard his father again. Coming back down the main street the other way barreling home. This time, puffing a cigarette looking like a train shooting up cotton smoke. Quite a ride. "I need to get me one of those," Strake thought.

Out at Fletcher's trailer he told him about his sister EmEm splitting.

"Not surprised." He dug out some more Red Man. Stuffed it into his right cheek that already stuck out with a bulge. A stream of tobacco spit shot out of his mouth. Landed in a small puddle near a rusted Schlitz tin can in the yard. Fat red ants gorged on a littered Twinkie. Strake leaned forward.

"I heard a rumor," he lied.

"A rumor?"

"About Bubbo."

"What rumor?"

"Can't be sure, but is he working with your dad to push you out?"

"Push me out!"

"Yeah, drugs, the pawn shop, all of it."

"Whard you hear it?"

"Around town. Some men in black suits came by the office too."

Strake had made up the last part, based only on rumors he had heard. The suits concerned him. At first it was only one or two. Now it seemed like five or ten. Fletcher slapped his thigh. "I knowd it!"

"You did?"

"Heeeeeelllll yes, they been trying to get rid of me."

"I'd watch your back."

"Thanks Strake."

"Wanted to let you know. And to tell you about Mary Mae."

Strake waved and got in his Chevelle SS 454. Next stop was Bubbo.

"Hey Strake, come to take over for your dad's little trips to the junkyard?"

"I have no interest in continuing that," he said.

"Well, my face is happy to hear it."

"I *have* been hearing rumors though."

"Rumors!"

"Yeah, about your dad and Fletcher cutting you out."

"Cutting me out! Of what?"

"Everything, the pawn shop, selling drugs to the hippies."

"You have GOT to be kidding me."

"Just telling you what I heard from the suits."

"I knowd it all along. Never trusted that peter head."

"Keep your eyes peeled."

"We had a falling out. Thought something was fishy."

"Gotta go."

"Thanks Strake. Preciate ye."

Strake did the same at the pawn shop. Told Bart both his sons had something planned. With Jimmy and Meyer dropping the same "rumors" around town the Reeds simmered to a boil. It took about a month, well into February. He had almost forgotten about his scheme when the black rotary phone rang.

He answered it. Nodded, took down some notes. Made a quick phone call for some help. In the fields of Vietnam Strake had thought about the Reed enmity he inherited from his father. Did he hate the Reeds? He didn't hate anyone. Strake Senior's antagonism might have been fueled with righteous gas, true. But what he wanted to know was if he even cared to continue the grievances. Only because of Harris now.

He had mulled it over many times as he wandered with his M40. Mixed in with his past was the fact that he had become a daily walking assassin in a vain battle. It took time to absorb the constant killing. Moreover, he had been given a freedom to roam. Trusted as a sniper ninja, given spy blessing to kill VC. That was the deal he made with his commanding officer. Strake had already done his stint in the Marines when he was younger.

He was just back to fulfill an internal obligation he sensed was, in a way, mandatory. What was important to him, regarding this hereditary loathing from Strake Senior, had to be a separation from it. He could not simply pummel the boys because his dad began it with Bart. After much thinking Strake saw a clear line. It divided his own hate of the Reeds from Strake Senior's. Because of EmEm. She refused to talk about Bubbo and Fletcher's raping, and possibly Bart's. But Strake knew. She feared them.

The sons terrorized her even when she was pregnant with Harris. One time pushing and tripping her on a public sidewalk. Jimmy saw the whole thing and ran to the office to tell Strake. He was still young then, going on seventeen. That was the first trigger he needed. To learn about his own spite toward the Reeds. Strake's plan had an origin. In himself. Not one merely accepted from his father. He had learned how to separate Strake Senior's hostility from his own. Revenge could not be someone else's. It would be false if it was. For every murder Strake had committed he had justified it with something. Playful as his scheme was

to cause friction between the Reeds, it was holding a magnify-
ing glass on an eye. Watching the iris melt as sun shot a bolt of
light through it. To justify matters even more, his diner talk with
Harris sealed his decision.

He arrived at the pawn shop with his rifle. Fletcher, Bubbo
and Bart were spitting words. Near the register. At the glass case
filled with guns. Wearing faded overalls. Each had some form of
tobacco in his mouth.

In Bart's hand was a pistol, smoking. Some customer had
been in the pawn shop when it started. Before Bart fired the
gun, the man had left to call Strake. Fletcher looked at the blood
sliding down his arm. Maybe multiple shots had been fired by
the father. He noticed Bubbo had been hit too, also in the arm.
"Strake, don't mess in our bidness," warned Bart.

"Family bidness," Bubbo added.

"Yeah," said Fletcher.

"Looks like he shot you both."

"A bad habit of his," Bubbo notified him.

"He shoots you often?"

"Sometimes," Fletcher said.

"Warning shots," added Bubbo.

Strake stared at the scene. The Reeds must have been shocked
when Strake Senior's gas tricycle bumped open the door. With
the red siren mounted sideways on the back. Flashing cherry
strobes but making no noise. He drove inside to knock over a
shelf that fell forward. They watched the cheap trinkets crash to
the floor. He had a few fat pistols in his lap. A Winston Churchill
long cigar clenched in the side of his mouth (from a stash Strake
had dropped off, as promised).

"Hey Bart, you withered turdeater."

"Stop calling me turdeater."

"Never had a taste for the turds like you do."

"You know I don't like it."

"I can't help what you eat for breakfast instead of sausage."

"Shut it!"

"Whatever."

"You owe me for the damage."

"Double whatever."

"We'll see about that."

"What's going on here then?" Strake Senior asked.

The boy's arms were bleeding faster from Bart's earlier shots.

"They're trying to get rid of me," Bart told him.

"You're the one trying to get rid of **us**," challenged Fletcher.

"Shoot again," the sheriff informed Bart, "I'm putting one in you."

"Shut up Strake!" Bart shouted. "Why don't you track down Mary Mae? She ain't so innocent."

Strake ignored him. Noticed guns rising. Fletcher and Bubbo lifted pistols out of their overall pockets to kill their dad. Strakes Junior and Senior fired on the brothers. The Reed father did not go down easy. Blitzed wildly at his sons. A chaos of bullets. Bart had multiple shots in him. Dropped his pistol smashing the glass case. Fell, his chin hitting the glass as he died. Using his M40 Sheriff Strake moved in front of Fletcher and killed him with a shot above the nose. Strake Senior finished Bubbo with two pistols shot at his heart about ten times.

"Three turds with one stone," Strake Senior said.

At that strange moment the pawn shop door opened.

In walked Basil who was the clerk over at the motel.

"What the?"

Strake Senior eyeballed the entrance. An open threshold.

In the idling tricycle with siren still flashing, he sped through the door.

Basil ducked out of the way.

"That your dad?"

"Hey Basil. Yeah. Don't mind the mess."

He had a black case. Looked like it held a musical instrument.

"What's in there?" Strake asked him.

"Oh, this?"

"Yeah."

Basil stared nervously at the three dead men as blood creeped around the white tile like ink.

"A trumpet, looks like."

"What's it for?"

"Not sure. Some man in a suit stayed at the motel in January, didn't pay his bill and left this."

"How much you think it's worth?"

Strake moved behind the glass case and opened the register.

"Hm, well, the motel bill was around a hundred."

The till clanged open. Strake lifted eight twenties.

"You said a hundred and sixty, right?"

"Um . . . ash rye."

Strake handed the dumbfounded clerk the bills.

"Don't forget the tip, Basil."

"Tip?"

"Yeah, *your* tip."

"Ohhhhhh, MY tip. Ash rye."

Strake found a fifty and gave it to him.

Basil dropped the trumpet case by Fletcher's forehead. A brain bullet spewed red from the hole.

"Just leave it here?"

"Or take it home and learn how to play jazz."

Basil thought for a moment.

"I do like the modern jazz."

"Tell you what," Strake offered. "Why don't you give me twenty for it and it's yours."

"But I just sold it . . . ohhhhhhhh."

He gave Strake a twenty that the sheriff put back in the cash drawer.

Basil lifted the black trumpet case, now with blood dripping from the bottom, and sprinted out of the place.

Strake would have to call Meyer to clean up the bodies. He needed to put his M40 on the trunk of his Chevelle, not let anyone see it. It was stolen military property after all. Meyer would write up an appropriate report attributing this to internecine quarreling. Blurring justice so the lens was never transparent. Over time Strake knew this lens would be smeared with mud until it was opaque. His father's "justice" had been blurring the glass way before him. Justice, in the end, was never clear. Or clean.

"Sometimes," Strake Senior said to him once in the patrol car, "you make up what you need so the right thing gets done. Main thing is, you don't talk about it once it's over. You start talking about it . . . you can't do it anymore. Someone will find out."

The Chevelle roared to a start. He smiled a little at the thought of Basil annoying his motel guests with unbearable jazz trumpet riffs in the middle of the night. At the coroner's office he discussed the Reed situation with Meyer. Back at his office the phone rang. It was Pierce telling him about uncovering more hitchhiking murders, same bullet, same shot to the forehead, victims left slumping over their steering wheels. Some were dead on country back roads for months before anyone found them.

"The cars look broken down so no one stops. We've found bodies in vehicles four or five months later."

Strake didn't know what to do with this information. He liked Pierce and listened, even though he could see why his colleagues thought he was a nut. Apparently no one at the GBI took him seriously. Their indifference might prove fatal if Pierce was ever proven right. It was nearing the end of February. He had just turned thirty-seven. Many months to kill in boredom and isolation in rural Georgia. He considered tracking down EmEm. Why had she vanished so suddenly? Where was she? What had Bart meant by saying she wasn't so innocent?

She had returned the rental car. He assumed she had flown somewhere. Or wanted to give that impression. She had no friends or even family; they were all here. Well, three fewer of them at least. He had redressed her past. The Reeds were done. Drugs would still rise. They had cousins. During March and April he decided to clean the office. Find any old files that needed addressing. The days flowed like a drip from a water faucet.

Paperwork. Depressing visits to Strake Senior. Meals at Shep's. Avoidance of the coffee which had to be tea with coal dust in it. Nothing much happened until mid-April. When a farmer called about his silo.

As a boy Strake saw a lot of farm violence. In the daily rituals of feeding, castration and random death. His dad kept a small farm. About thirty acres. Twenty cows and a few horses and a chicken coop. A heifer might not let her calf nurse. It would die shrieking through an entire night of dreadful noise. In the coming days his father gave him a shovel. Together they would dig a hole for the tender body. Barely yet alive and already dead. Dumped in, covered with red dirt. Black snakes slithered into the coop. They sat gnawing on eggs as the hens clucked in the corner. Reptile grins. His father shot at groundhogs digging up the land. Castration was the worst. It traumatized Strake for many years. Worse than any human suffering. But nothing quite prepared him for the silo.

They had to climb a side ladder.

Old Bernard Neely couldn't move fast with his limp.

Still scaled the rungs at eighty. These old farmers lived forever.

Probably all the fresh garden cabbage they ate.

Strake was just waiting for him to topple on his head as he climbed.

At the top there was a little metal ledge. They could both stand there to rest. Another ladder went down the inside.

In the corn grain were fat rats like pepper on scrambled eggs.

Then there were bigger bodies.

"See em?" Bernard pointed down.

"How many, you think?"

"I count two. That we can see."

Strake looked closer. "Is that blood?"

"Looks to be, yes. It ain't maple syrup."

"My gosh. How the heck did they get in here?"

"I doubt someone carried them up here on that ladder."

"Probably not," agreed Strake, startled from his easy paperwork (which he wished he was doing now, instead of dealing with this corpse garbage).

"Mind if I climb down inside there, Bernard?"

"Go ahead."

"Thanks."

"Can you dig out the rats too?"

Strake looked up, stifling laughter. "Sure. I'll toss them."

The farmer stared down at him as he sunk into the soft corn grain to his knees. A dust cloud caused him to sneeze. Before dealing with the bodies he tackled the "easy" job. Strake grabbed a rat by its tail. Heaved it up for Neely to catch. It fell right back down into the corn. He flung it again, harder. This time the farmer caught it. Spiked it below like a football. "Ha!" he shouted.

Strake found nine more rats and did the same removal. He had a little trouble with the seventh. It, to his surprise, was living.

Snapped its toothpick teeth at him, curling backward. As it sailed through the air Bernard reached up to swat it down, speeding the alive rat's descent. Rats. Wonderful. I love my job, Strake mind-muttered. Once they were tossed, the sheriff contemplated his morning grits as he wondered about nesting, smothered rodents. Gross.

Now, the bodies. He wiped corn grain away from their faces. The heads of two big men. The backs of their hair smeared. With a raspberry jelly of blood. Gruesome holes from gunshots. He dug more around one guy's shoulders: a black suit. Hm. Same with the next one. Black suits, white shirts and wide black ties with Windsor knots.

It was easy enough to reach into their jackets. Find their wallets. He stuffed them in his front pockets. Could identify them back at the office. The cumbersome bodies had to be removed. How? More stirred corn dust made him cough as he scaled the interior ladder. A chorus of flies hummed around his face. Bernard waited for him. They talked for a moment on the metal ledge as three bluebirds darted.

"Any ideas?" Strake asked.

"Never seen them. My friends don't have suits."

"Strange."

"When did they do it? I'm here all the time."

Bernard had a little trouble hearing. He might have slept through a car pulling up, gunshots. Bodies likely unloaded in the middle of the night. Alive before they climbed the ladder, probably with a gun on them. Offed in the silo. Made sense. Tracking down the killers might be easier than figuring out how to extricate the murder victims.

At the bottom of the silo on the ground were the dead rats. The still alive one gnawed on the stomach of one of his friends. Neely stomped it with his heel. After thanking the farmer at the Chevelle, Strake headed back to the office. To make some phone calls about the wallets he had found. Two men dressed in black suits. Killed in a corn silo. Each with identifications. From addresses in the Bronx. Strake's first idea was that it had something to do with Bartholomew Reed. But he wasn't alive anymore. Unless . . .

I'll bet you anything, Strake thought to himself, that the Reeds did this before the pawn shop fiasco. No one else in town had business with suits from out of town. Except Bart. Witnesses saw men going in and out of the back of that pawn shop many times, usually reported to Strake. Reed cousins had taken over the pawn shop since the three murders.

It was still open. Time for another visit. The toothless wonders of the Reed cousins made Bubbo and Fletcher look like film stars. Cross-eyed, more than one of them. Some with no teeth, only pink gums and flapping tongues. Their mouths had eschewed dentistry for quite a long time. If they had hair it was dotted with popping lice they scratched. Strake entered the pawn shop not looking forward to the discussion. They knew he had something to do with the Reed murders. Suspicious of him the minute he walked through the door. The place hadn't changed a lot in a couple of months. Blood stained the white tile. He knew what that was from.

"Sheriff," one man said with a nod. They were also very afraid of Strake who had his sniper rifle with him. He pointed the barrel tip at the floor, leaned on the butt of the gun like a cane.

"What are you doing here?" another lisped. His tongue rolled out of his toothless mouth like it was too thick to ever go back into it.

"Well, boys, hi, nice to see you. I missed your shining faces and . . . gums. Seems like we found two dead men in a silo on the Neely farm."

He liked to watch guilty idiots squirm as they tried to figure out what lie to tell next. Lifted up his M40 a little and stared at the sight for extra effect. They held the silence for a few moments. Strake whistled "Fly Me to the Moon." There were five cousins working at the shop. Ten paranoid eyes tried to challenge the sheriff. Desperate to look at one another to see what to do.

"Get out," one replied, pointing.

Strake tilted his gun against the glass case. A new one by the looks of it since the other had been smashed. Pulled out the wallets.

"I found these. Now, what morons would kill two men in a silo and not take their wallets?"

"Ah," one waved his hand, "blow it out your nose."

"Never seen those wallets," one insisted. Others nodded.

"Of course you haven't seen the WALLETS," Strake goaded them, "because they were in the JACKETS."

"What do you want, Strake?" the smartest of the lot said.

"Well, not much, I just want to know about your shop's dealings with the suits. And when the five of you might hit the dentist."

"And if we tell you?"

"The truth always helps."

"We didn't do it."

"Go to the dentist or kill them?"

"Didn't kill them."

"No?" Strake scoffed. "Why should I believe you?"

"Because," the "smart" one said, "you need to talk to your wife."

"Mary Mae?"

"Yeah."

"What ever for?"

"Sheriff," he said, "she works for the suits."

After EmEm took off, he just didn't have a good feeling. It was the same sensation he often had around her. Dread that something worse was coming. She worked with the two men in suits? Who later showed up with bullets in the back of their heads in a farmer's corn silo? Sheesh. For some reason he believed the Reed cousins. Around town they were known as the Inreeds. He felt sorry for the poor. Hated to judge them, what with EmEm's past.

Being brought up around so much poverty she could never shed. Maybe these suits were a type of escape for her. Was she involved with Bart Reed's business? Something tied to New York? No word from her in the months since he had returned in January. He needed to find her. Rats had chewed around the men's faces and eyes. From what he could tell the bodies hadn't been devoured by vultures due to the curved silo roof. The dead rats had suffocated in the corn, halting their feast. He stopped by to tell Meyer.

"That won't be easy, getting them out."

"Can't use pulleys?"

Strake waited for the coroner to consider the idea.

"Nothing in town that high."

"Are you telling me what I think you're telling me?"

Meyer sighed with a reluctant yes nod.

"I'll get us some help," Strake said, and called Basil at the motel. They drove back to the silo in the police car this time, Strake not using it much since he had come home. He had stored the Chevelle in his garage for the moment. Meyer rode in the passenger seat, Basil in the back after they got him at the motel.

"How's the trumpet?" Strake joked, not expecting the answer.

"Funny you should ask. Been taking lessons."

"Lessons?!"

"Off the back of a matchbook. Correspondence course."

"Um, how do you play the trumpet if the music teacher isn't there?"

"They sent me a technological invancement called the cassette tape."

Meyer stifled a giggle.

"You just pop it in a player and a man talks you through the trumpet."

"You learning it then?"

"One thing you cain't do is blow out your cheeks. That's for amateurs. Unless you're Dizzy."

"On a first name basis with him, I see."

"The trumpet world is very small. Dizzy sent me a postcard."

Both Strake and Meyer sucked in their lips to avoid impolite guffawing.

"You'll have to play us a song."

"Just doing scales for the moment. Hurts my lips if I play too much."

"When you're ready," Strake said.

"I have a six-year plan."

Meyer turned to the sheriff. "Tell us about these bodies."

Basil leaned forward, his chin on his knuckles on top of the front seat. Strake gave them the information. He didn't mention Mary Mae. At the silo Strake opened his trunk. It creaked and bounced a little. Meyer lifted two metallic tools brought from the coroner's office stash. He handed Strake his. Meyer gave Basil a stainless steel scoop to carry. The three ascended the ladder rungs, the sheriff first, Meyer second, Basil third. In the corn the sheriff and coroner stood over the dead bodies.

"Toss it down," yelled Meyer.

Basil gently dropped the stainless scoop. They spent the afternoon removing the large men. Of all the jobs he ever did this one was the worst visceral imprint on his hallucinating mind. One man's nose was gone. Didn't matter, considering the bloodbath about to happen. Technically not much blood due to coagulation but there was oozing. The gruesome slicing and hacking noises were what stayed with him. Basil stood on the ledge at the top with black garbage bags. Strake and Meyer went at it. The coroner was a pro so Strake watched his work on the first dead man before he started on the second one. "Clear out the corn for me. Need to see the top of the shoulders."

Strake dug with the scoop and tossed the corn grains away from the head. It was hard to maneuver to the neck. The sheriff would never forget that industrial medical hacksaw first touching the neck as it dug into the skin. Meyer sliced, sweating from his forehead. Above, like a curious lesser god Basil grimaced but kept his eyes on them. Back and forth the saw went like a file on fingernails and Strake thought: I bet he's done this so many times.

Old blood gurgled a little from the neck like poisoned champagne. Soon the head was off. Meyer sat in exhaustion. Strake lifted the severed chunk and heaved it up to Basil. Who was instructed to keep each dead man's body parts in separate bags to identify them later. Meyer told him it would be best for Strake to keep clearing corn instead of sawing.

"Too hard to get any leverage slipping around."

The sheriff nodded. "I understand."

Maybe this was one man who had seen as much death as he had. Probably more. Next: the right arm of the man, easier at the shoulder to cut.

"Leave on the clothes."

Strake handed up the arm, still in the shirt cotton under the suit wool, to the motel clerk. They worked in silence. Without complaint. The heat in the silo was much worse with the noon sun. It was an elevated hell. Strake scooped corn. Meyer cut body parts. Basil put them in black bags, taking them down when they got too heavy. Eight hours of amputating the dead.

After the two bodies were removed, piece by piece, Strake did one last drop into the silo grain, millions of corn kernels. A black strap was now visible from the top of the ladder as he descended. What was that? His feet sunk fast in the corn. Up to his thighs. Using the scoop he cleared out some space around him. He jammed in his arms to fish around the kernel grains right below the black strap. Felt like a leather bag. He lifted from below since he had no leverage with the strap from the top. Out it came. Expensive, smooth leather. Maybe lambskin. He sat the bag on the corn grain. Unzipped it, expecting a human head with his luck of late. Nope, bundles of fifties. No one was at the top of the silo watching him. On the money was a passport. With reluctance he opened it. Mary Mae Strake.

"Oh boy," Strake mumbled.

He back-pocketed her document. EmEm, he muttered, shaking his head. As Strake wiggled out of the corn, his foot touched something hard.

"Oh no."

Setting the bag down he grabbed the scoop again. Made more room. He reached down as far as he could. And touched hair.

"I don't believe it." Up the ladder he climbed. "There's more!" he shouted, setting the black bag on the ledge. Meyer stared up at him. So did Basil. They looked like children. The dread to come was unbearable. It seemed that this silo had been a graveyard for some time. There was no other way to stack bodies in this way. After they found the third and fourth dead men, they had dug a deep hole in the middle of the silage. Meyer never fatigued. He was around the dead so much and used to sawing cadavers. Strake could not show he was tired, even though all he did was to scoop grain to make space for the slicing.

It was one quiet afternoon where no one felt like speaking. They bagged the third and fourth bodies. Strake reached down as Meyer stared at him. "Two more."

They somehow worked faster despite their own bodies faltering. The desire to be done impelled them. With some luck they did not find more bodies after the sixth. Dusk was on them by the end of the day. It was kind of cold. The labeled black bags fit in Strake's trunk. They rode over to the motel to drop Basil. With his head down he walked in a slow way to the front desk where he still had to work. Then the sheriff and the coroner drove to Meyer's to unload the bodies. They had to open the bags and put the limbs and parts together for examination. They pieced back the six men on six metal tables.

When they were done Meyer said, "I'll look at them tomorrow."

"Okay," said Strake.

Back at his desk. He had wanted to tell Meyer about EmEm. Her passport was in the bag. This implied the money was hers. That was clear enough. Plus, she intended to travel out of the country. Some details made no sense. The killers left the men's wallets in their jackets. Making the six easy to identify. And why not just take the bag of money while killing the men in the silo? Unless . . .

One of the men had a very baggy black suit. Easy to hide the bag underneath since he was obese anyway. It was not a bulky bag. Could have fit around the fat stomach of the biggest man at the top. Maybe the bag fell a bit as he sunk? Leaving it near his knees buried in the corn. Sounded like Strake's wife worked for these men from the Bronx. They came to check on her, work with her, kill her, who knew? The Reed cousins, while maybe not lying, were not telling him everything. Mary Mae was, after all, the daughter of Bartholomew.

Strake remembered the conversation with himself about his own inheritances from his father. He had a lot of time away from EmEm and knew very little about what she did. Now, he sort of knew. It was probably simpler than he imagined. The Reed trio who had died in the pawn shop months ago had probably arranged for the cousins to kill the six men.

"These bottom men have been in here longer," Meyer told him.

It could not have been Bubbo, Fletcher and Bart, but the deceased trio might have warned the cousins about the Bronx contingency. That meant the suits had come for the three main family members *before* they died in the pawn shop. Heightening the Reed trio's paranoia. If this speculation was right, then the trio was probably about to die anyway. How about this? The suits were supposed to come to Georgia and off the three. They came too late. By then the Reeds were dead. Where did Mary Mae fit into this cruel mess? It seemed like it was her bag of money. Subtract out the dead Reed trio as the killers of the six suits. That really just left Mary Mae. Or somebody else. On a whim he called Basil at the motel.

"Say, Basil, Strake here, question for you."

"Shoot . . . but aim to the right so you miss my head."

"Ha, I will. That trumpet. A suit left it? When did he stay at the motel?"

"Back in January, right around the time you came home, as I recall. He came and went. Was here nearly every month for a few days."

"In a suit? Like those six dead men?"

"Yep."

"Did you recognize the guy from the motel in the silo?"

"Could've been one of them, I guess. All suits look alike to me."

"Did you see anybody else while he stayed there?"

"Hmmmmmm. I try to give guests their privacy."

"Come on now, Basil, this is pretty important."

"You know wut?"

"What?"

"It might've been more than one in that room, now that I think of it. I just kept seeing a lot of black suits coming in and out of the same room door and thinking, man, that guy is going to the snack machines a lot."

"Oh boy," Strake grumbled.

"Anything else."

"Yeah, I'm coming over. Be there in fifteen."

Basil was at the front desk.

"Can you get that trumpet case for me?"

"It's right here."

He lifted it onto the counter. Strake noticed a postcard on the wall that certainly looked like Dizzy had signed it.

"That guy just left this case here?"

"They didn't pay, remember? I found it in the room."

"Open it up. Take out the trumpet."

Strake turned the now empty case to him. Lifted the top part.

"I don't believe it," Basil said.

"I do."

At the bottom was another pile of money. Bundles of hundreds.

"Last question," Strake said, "did you happen to see Mary Mae around the motel before I came home, maybe prior to January? Before these men stayed here?"

"Sure, all the time."

"All the time!"

"Ash rye."

"Basil, what have you NOT been telling me?"

"Welllllll, I promised her I wouldn't say anything."

"Jesus. What now? Do I even want to know?"

"No, I'm pretty sure you don't want this knowledge."

"Tell me anyway."

Sighing, Basil looked at the sheriff: "Different men. She brought a bunch here. Gave me twenty bucks extra every time she left."

He could believe it. Maybe he could understand it. He took the money, left the case.

"Thanks for being honest, Basil."

In the patrol car dejection smacked him with a fast open palm. It made more sense. Still hurt. He leaned his face into his upturned hands. Too much. One technique he had when solving cases was to ask: what doesn't matter? The dead suits. Didn't matter. Sort of explained. The money, immaterial. Kind of obvious. Mary Mae's involvement. This was what mattered. It concerned him because she had fled. She could have murdered the suits. Yes, there was a flaw in this timeline. She would have to be back in Georgia to do it. He had assumed that she had flown elsewhere to get away.

What if she had dropped the rental at the airport to give the illusion of leaving? She had never left! What mattered here? Mary Mae. And the motel. Damnit Basil! He drove back to talk to the clerk. Basil, holding his trumpet, winced a little. "You know why I'm here again."

"Don't be mad, Strake."

"Which room?"

"Number four."

He knocked, heard a moaning of sorts, knocked again.

"Em?"

"Wait."

She opened the door. Didn't seem surprised. Wore only a bra and jeans. A white bandage taped to her stomach. Strake stood in the threshold.

"You can come in," she told him.

"Found this," he said, pulling the passport out of his back pocket.

"Thanks."

"Tell me about the six suits."

"Dad was skimming them. They came down for a little visit."

"What happened to you?"

"Got stabbed," she said, but it seemed like a lie.

"Which suit was it?"

"Not sure. Came in here while I was sleeping."

"Who killed them?"

"You're not going to like it."

"Your cousins?"

"No."

The sheriff sat on the bed by her, waiting.

"I told him not to get involved."

"Please say it isn't Harris."

She looked up at him with weakness and pain. "I couldn't stop him."

Strake nodded. "I found some money."

"A black bag?" she brightened.

"Yeah, and some in Basil's trumpet case."

"I need it. I have to go."

"I thought you had left."

"I should have. Almost flew out to Mexico."

"Why didn't you?"

"I can't really say."

"But Harris?"

"He found me here, injured."

"How?"

"You don't want to know. Take me to the airport."

"If that's what you need."

"It is."

He drove her to Atlanta.

"Did you really get stabbed?"

No answer. She had the stacks of fifties and hundreds, all in the black lambskin bag. EmEm got out of the passenger side. Shut the door to the patrol car. Moving slow with her gut wound. She had not said goodbye. They had talked little during the ride. He had an idea but not a clear one. That she had always despised him. But in that moment it occurred to Strake that she kind of liked him. She was crumbling human damage, not her fault. Had absorbed the nausea of family treachery. Walking, scarred daughter. He drove home. Wondered when he would stop worrying about her.

As he headed back to the office, not wanting to be in a vacant bed, he knew he had to talk to his son. Basil's ongoing duplicity and random trumpet playing gave him a chuckle. He pulled out an old record player Strake Senior had bought to play his jazz. There were some 33 albums. He thought of 33 Beer. Of Hanh and what she might be doing. *Count Basie at Newport* from 1957. Roy Eldridge on trumpet. They called him Little Jazz. He placed the needle on the record. It whirred with static before the beautiful brass screech of music filled the office. He stared at the bars of the tiny holding cell. Hardly ever used. He and his son should probably be in that cell. Everyone close to him was on the nebulous inside of justice.

Harris

Being a Strake was filled with assumptions. Even as a boy Harris noticed a certain grooming his grandfather and father gave him. Pretending he was Little Sheriff. Giving him guns. Hunting. Forced to watch animals die. He believed he was immune from Strake violence. That he could repel it. Or ignore it. He was too gentle to kill anyone. But in his mind he worried that he was like his father whose life was murder. It concerned him that maybe he *was* like Sheriff Strake. A gnawing that never left him. A pulse of something inchoate, to spring out of him at some point. The town assumed Harris was made of the same blithe viciousness. Automatic filial legacy. *Harris will be sheriff just like his dad and grandad.* Many town eyes had voices, as if the pupils were open mouths. The whispers of assumption. They were proud eyes. *Harris will take care of us.*

As a boy he bought into the cowboy identity. Loved it for a while as Strakes Junior and Senior doted on him. Something was not right though with the cool masculine fervor he intuited. It was an exterior. Bad people dropped with fists or bullets. In high school the Reed clan messed with him often but never too much, enough to feel bullied. Always protected by his father. This glow of power moved with him as a Strake. His father was often gone, helping out the government, vanishing for weeks at a time. Then to Vietnam. Things at home with his mother were never right.

She had much affection for him but had been ripped apart as a person by her relatives. Harris realized that if he focused too much on his parents it just led to sadness. So he read Grandpa Strake's mysteries, ordered ways to make you believe that everything is solved, when it never is. The mystery novel was an omnipotent falsity. Still, if you read enough of them you thought you could solve it all on your own.

He picked the most mundane, antiseptic job: a bank. Where he got to know Betty. He knew her from high school and they fell in love seeing each other every day at their jobs. She had been hounded by the Reeds for years and was weary of them. Everyone was. They were hyenas. If there was a right thing to do, they did the opposite. Only, his mother *was* a Reed. Which meant Harris was half-Reed. There was murder on both sides of the Strakes and Reeds. The former was in the name of what was supposed to be right. The latter: justice's wrong side.

Grandpa Strake and Bart's quarrel had endured for decades. Passed on to his dad and now to him. It was folly trying to escape it. Fletcher and Bubbo harassed Betty in an endless manner. In the halls and fields of the high school. They came into the bank and lingered. Leering at her. Tormenting Harris who wanted to believe that he would never act like his father and retaliate. The molesting increased daily to the point that Betty suffered mentally. Fearful of leaving her house. Harris only wanted for them to be left alone.

It happened at the tail end of his father's time in Vietnam. He pulled up to Betty's small cottage her parents had helped her buy. Only to see the Reed trucks surrounding it. A body appeared at his car window. Fletcher stopped him from opening his door. He was in a panic. What were they doing to her?

He remembered the words: "Stay put. It'll be over soon."

As quickly as the door had been blocked, the whole thing was done in minutes. Bubbo ran from her front door, pulling up his overalls. He and Fletcher peeled away. As Harris went inside he knew that he was changed, reversed. He now understood. She had been beaten in the face, her pale skin bruised. Her black hair yanked out in clumps, leaving bald spots. It was late December

1969. He had received a postcard from his dad that he would be home soon. When they met later at the diner, he could tell Strake knew something was wrong. So he talked to him alone after Betty went back to the bank. Harris told him what had happened. They sat in silence in the booth.

"I'll take care of them," Strake assured him.

And he did handle the Reeds. But there was still the problem of his mother. Harris found himself sometimes going to the motel. Picking up his bruised and pummeled mom. She would heal at his house. Only to go right back to the motel. This had gone on for over a year. Everyone in town knew what she did there. It was kept quiet for the most part. Until the suits started to appear. More and more. He had let his father handle the Reeds in February 1970. Still falsely believing he could avoid personal revenge.

He was not above it. His mother had been stealing money from the suits. They were lowlife pimps who came down from the Bronx. Filmed her for Times Square peep shows. If she didn't do what they said, she was raped and beaten with brass knuckles. Once Sheriff Strake was back home, though, his mother asked Harris to promise not to tell his dad that she was at the motel. Things were dire and he thought she would die soon, the way they hurt her. He resisted what was in him for the longest time.

At last he broke like a spray of vomit he couldn't keep inside him any longer. It felt like puke too. A wretched disgust in him that had to gag its way out of his body. She had been hoarding stacks of fifties and hundreds to help her get away from her soured life. She had a plan to go to Mexico and never return. She needed Harris' help. At the same time she didn't want him brought down with her. Many times he nursed her back, only to watch her embrace the mauling once again. It made him ache with an agony he could not forget. Soon, he was in it. He was ready even if he hated himself.

To become your father when you had been trying to avoid it all your life, this was wrong. It was not what he wanted. Yet what he wanted no longer mattered. Justice was nothing more than action against what you perceived to be incorrect. Everything was felonious now. He knew his mother wanted to leave. He also knew that she seemed to expect abuse. She went back into it whenever she had healed. Her raped and lashed body, it could not endure the violence much longer. A number of men in black suits came to the motel often. Piggish degenerates who all looked the same. Usually they drove down from the Bronx to pick up money bags throughout the South. Illegal slot machines, prostitution, drugs.

His mother had disrupted their cash flow. They were mad about the inconvenience. Cash piles had been vanishing as she stocked up for her lam. The motel became a familiar sight for Harris. Those men could never find out where she hid the money. They could only rough her up so much because they needed to find it. After his dad left for Vietnam again it almost seemed like spite that made his mom do what she did in her motel room. She appeased some of the men in suits by letting them sleep with her. They were onto her ruse though. It was only a matter of time before she either had to leave abruptly. Or stay and die.

"Where's the money, Mom?" Harris asked her while she was in bed with a face full of purple bruises.

"There's a silo . . ."

"You need to leave here. I can't keep watching them do this to you."

"I don't care."

"Don't you want it to stop?"

She stared at him. Maybe, he thought, she didn't know if she did. The suits were sick of waiting for their money. When he came to the motel, she had a bad gut wound. Wouldn't go to the hospital. Harris helped her in that stale motel room. Then knew enough was enough. He had to do something. His father had seen to the three Reeds with his swift blurry justice. There was a lingering problem though.

As his mother winced in bed Harris realized that he had to tell someone about Betty. He had not given the full truth to his dad at the diner, only details about the rape. Now, it was March 1970 and it was time to share the other news. Strake would be a grandfather, yes, but he didn't yet know that it wasn't his son's. Harris knew it wasn't his because they had agreed to wait until marriage in June. So the baby was a Reed aberration. Product of a gang rape. Betty, sweet as she was, insisted on having the child. He loved her so much that he could never say no. Still, this Reed corrosion had a way of rusting what it touched, even though they were dead. This is when Harris knew that people could keep on killing you long after they died. He told his mother in the motel room. Since Fletcher and Bubbo were her brothers, all she could do was apologize for them. She felt bad.

"My family is demonic," she told him. "Just when you think you can get away from them, they are right there."

"Mom, we need to get you out."

"It's hard to move when you're stuck."

"I'll help."

"How?"

"Grab what you have and go. There's no other way."

She thought for a moment, her stomach bleeding.

"Why do you take it?" he added.

"I'm not right. Never have been."

"Don't you want to live a life that's not filled with this?"

"It got away from me," she admitted. "I never expected it to get so ugly."

She closed her eyes.

"It got vile too fast. I just didn't see it coming."

"Mom . . ."

"The only way out of this is impossible. You can't stop their machine."

"What do you want me to do?"

"I wanted you to not be a part of this mess."

"Well, I am now. So what's next?"

She told him about the leather bag of money in the silo, the trumpet case of dough. Also about seeing one of the nervous suits leaving one afternoon. She followed that man. Had been keeping an eye on all the suits. They came in and out of her room whenever they wanted. Not being able to take it anymore she watched the nervous one. He had no car. Many of them came to the motel in airport cabs. He looked scared. Waiting outside for his taxi. He was focused on his ride. She ducked into his unlocked room. Saw the trumpet case. Knew what was in it because she had seen the suits stuffing in bills one night. She left it. Basil would see the case and likely hang on to it, not suspecting there was money hidden under the instrument. After some time the man's cab arrived.

She followed in her El Camino. Not the most inconspicuous car but she had no choice. The man looked back a bunch. She kept her distance. He had seemed worried at the motel. She had guns and money. Thought, right then, about getting out of town. Why did she stay? What made her remain in southern hell? She might have been addicted to the pain, she told Harris. It was familiar. She had never known a day without hurt.

"What happened next?" asked Harris.

She followed the green and white airport cab. At some point she realized that fully reaching the airport was not an option. She had a piece of luck when the taxi stopped for gas. Pulling up right beside the back seat she forced the man into the El Camino. He was not one of the violent men. He complied. Even seemed contrite, like he wanted to make amends and just get away from the other suits.

She told him about the silo. Said the bag of money was deep in the silage. She needed help finding it. It was lost. If he helped her, she would let him go. He offered little resistance anyway. Or so it seemed. At the silo he climbed up first. He was eager to find money that was rightfully the cash of the suits. But then things turned strange. He hopped down into the corn and sank, furiously digging with his hands.

"I've got the strap!"

Mary Mae had tossed in an empty bag as a diversion. Other suits had the actual lambskin bag and passport. She stood on the inside ladder.

"Let's see."

She tried to balance herself when she slipped. Instead of the bag of money he lifted his own piece and aimed. All of a sudden a bullet thunked into her gut like a baseball connecting with a bat. Falling into the sinking yellow grain she was able to grab her gun. As she fell on her side the back of his head was a clear target. A bullet ripped into his skull.

"I thought you got knifed," interrupted Harris.

"I lied." Used her energy to just climb out of the silage. She made it to the ladder and back to the motel. Where she dug out the bullet herself.

"You need to be in a hospital."

"I can't."

"Is it infected?"

"Yes."

"Mom."

"Son, you have to understand something. I don't care about dying. In some ways I welcome it."

"It doesn't have to be like this."

"I'm more harm than anything else. Being gone can stop the harm."

"That's not true."

"It is, I'm afraid."

"So you had planned, what, to just die in a disgusting motel room?"

"If I can last, I'll get some help in Mexico but not here. I can't leave. The suits are on me. They might have even followed me and that man to the silo."

"So they know about the dead man in there?"

"I can't say for sure."

"And let me get this straight, they have your money in a bag somewhere and in that trumpet case?"

"Yes, that's right."

Harris put the palm of his right hand over his eyes.

"The body's still in there?"

"Yes but I know Neely. He fills it gradually. It's the perfect spot. That body is near the bottom with the fake bag."

"How many suits are still here at the motel?"

"A bunch of them had to drive back to New York. Maybe five or so?"

"Which room?"

"Six."

"So you need that money?"

"If I plan to leave, I do."

"Okay. Let me handle it."

He looked at her.

"My passport is in that bag, don't forget. I can live with just the bag. Don't worry about the trumpet case or Basil will get suspicious."

The next week, nothing much changed at the motel. His mom's wound was infected so he had to act as fast as he could. He had his car warmed. Ready and idling. He blackjacked a suit, surprising him from his mom's room with a whack on the forehead. The man fell and he dragged him into his trunk. Harris drove to the silo and waited. He climbed up and in and saw the dead man at the bottom. According to his mom Neely would add more corn in increments. The silo was about a quarter full. The farmer didn't like to fill it to the top because he cleaned out rats as he went. He lowered himself on the ladder and fell into the corn. Up to his waist. Infinite corn kernels kept him from maneuvering with any agility. Harris needed to test how difficult it was to move around in what was a kind of quicksand. He took the fake bag with him. To get out of the silo he had to lunge up to the bottom rung of the inside ladder. Down on the ground again he braced himself at his Chevelle, a gift from his dad similar to his father's car, a bribe to become sheriff that he never fully bought. He did love the car though. The man was still groggy in the trunk.

"Your friend is up in the silo," he said.

The man blinked a few times and rubbed his forehead in pain.

"I'm in a suit. I can't climb a ladder. My shoes is too slippery."

"Go look."

"Why not? I'm a dead man anyway."

"How so?"

"They sent a posse from the Bronx after us."

The man scurried up the ladder in no real rush.

Harris had some sudden rapport with this goon who had accepted his fate. And had given him information he could pass on to his father. It was an odd moment in Harris' life. Knowing he was watching a man climb a ladder into an absurd pile of corn that was about to be his grave. He followed him to the top. The suit climbed over to the inside in a clumsy move with slick shoes.

As he jumped off the ledge like a kid about to do a cannonball in a pool, Harris aimed his pistol at the back of the head that rose into the air for a second. Life fell out of him as he dropped feet first into the grain by his murdered friend. Body sinking. Blood spread on the yellow and white infinity that almost looked like sand. Harris knew he needed to get out of there before farmer Neely's hearing started working. He didn't want his mom to go. But she had to get out of here. More thugs were coming from the Bronx, the man had said as much. It had been his first kill. He did it four more times. The suits were compliant. They wanted to find their friends and climbed the ladder.

Harris stacked the men in the silo. Five total kills. He had checked the grain store to see when Neely's deliveries would be. Timing the silage to cover them in a mass, vertical grave. His genetic lust for murder emerging. So caught up in the killing he forgot to frisk the men. However, he saw the bulge of the bag on one of them. Hidden under his jacket like an abnormal gut. In the end his father found it as they dug out the bodies. Got the money and passport to his mom.

A few months later he was at the bank with Betty. Three people with weapons, a girl, a teenage boy and a young bald guy. They came in to attack them with a Colt pistol, a hatchet and a long white knife. All he could think was that she would no longer need to have the baby from the Reed rape. He knew it was a submission. He had no resistance. Since there was no way to fight and win. He saw this when they came into the bank, armed and ready to kill. The three of them were just a symbol of loss in his own life. Or moreover, futility. His father would have fought and killed them.

Harris wanted an out, a way to leave a filial violence he couldn't escape. It gave him some peace as the hatchet came down on them both. First the blade on him more than once. Then the hammer on her, repeated. Many things were in his mind as he bled from his throat. He was free from worrying about justice anymore. The hatchet blade sunk in his neck, saturating his white shirt in blood. He felt the young boy yank it out of him. Twist around the handle. Bash it into the forehead of his wife with the hammer face.

It was all right to have no future. Betty seemed to understand too. This was a chance to leave life without further pain. It was in their eyes as they looked at each other. Harris stared at the hole in her forehead. A black hollow. One that was also in him. How could he feel relief when he should have retaliated? His five murders of the suits assuaged him.

He even felt good as he was dying. Then the guilt came for feeling so good about it. It was not an immediate death. Contrary to what the killer probably thought. There was a numb pain mixed with a wrenching in his body. It was sopor and it was torment. He felt a strange quiet, a muffled sense. Almost as if his hearing had been cut in half. He saw the bald man's Colt shoot his manager, Roger. The girl's white knife slashing Dolores. Murder was a visual opiate. It was calming to leave life. He had been slashed in the neck three times. Couldn't move. But could see it all.

A flash: a Colt, a white knife, a hatchet. Three killed, him soon the fourth. Harris knew he would be dead in minutes. The body paralyzed into ice. As if he were freezing everywhere. Except his eyes. No, his eyes were not ice yet. Almost. He saw them leave. The boy with the hatchet stole a typewriter. Why? The event was a flash. A popped bulb of light. Then the bank was empty with three dead bodies. And he almost there too, number four. To know you will die softened the unknown in a way. Most of his life Harris had been anxious about living. He had no desire to survive. Or fight anymore. Or be his father. Everyone had hoped he would be another protector. He was not. Well, maybe for a moment. Around his mind floated the air of blood gushing. The soundless sounds of ending. He felt his thoughts could not last. Despite the body ice, he lifted his hands toward him. Touched what washed down his chest. Pouring from his neck like a baptized demon. Freezing and warm.

In his head was an army winter march of thinking. Men blew white breath in the cold. Steps of impressions. Foot-pounding images of his short life. He looked down at the bib of warm red that had emptied from him. To leave hollow veins. His eyelids closed for a moment. There was so much pain that it was past feeling. Only a few minutes occurred after the killers left. He was thinking this all in only minutes. But his mind seemed so absolute and grand. How could seconds be so vast? Splashes of ink came at his pupils. Before the ice blinded his eyes to white redness he saw his dad. Walking in too late. He only saw him for a second or two.

Maybe Strake saw him alive, maybe not. Hard to say. He blinked. Strake stepped closer but was not fast enough. Then Harris could no longer keep his eyes open. Empty in a few moments. Maybe he had been empty, dead the whole time. As he bled he knew what he had missed. He had forgotten his stupid soul. No wonder he had been a nobody. A bare image without meaning. A quasi-man. To fail an ideal that was not your own crippled you. Not because you had failed. More, because you had not had your own ideal in the first place.

It was better to go when you had already left.
There had been nothing to him.

Strake Undone

The Nihilistics had come through town and were finished. It was later in 1970. October autumn around Georgia, delight. False dying of the leaves. Color meant death. He drove his Chevelle north. There were other things to handle. He was not sure in what order to do them. The car let him think.

His town was not calm. The Reeds were gone, most of them. However, bad still came in many forms. Mary Mae had vanished after he had dropped her at the airport. No word from her. Somehow drugs filled the area even with the Reeds not there. A hippie commune had a homeless camp.

Beautiful girls and boys in wild bright clothes roamed the streets. One man defecated right on the double yellow line of the road just on the outskirts. These were gentler criminals. Criminals nonetheless. He floated in his ride through many states. He had no particular plan. Or maybe he did. He did have things to do with no idea how they might happen.

There was a house. He had heard about it from the Reeds before their demise. A house in a city of millions. This place was an aorta of the suits. One big problem with the house was that it was many houses. The house kept moving from one to another. And, maybe after all, there *were* many houses. Then again, maybe only one. By himself Strake could only do so much. He had his M40 and many other weapons. The way he saw it was this: the Reeds were only a clogged artery off the suit heart. Gut the heart. Gut the suits. He thought of many plans as he drove. He could keep heading north to a place where he never saw another crime.

Beyond the Bronx. Crime was a calling though. You were tapped for it.

He couldn't quit, as good as he was at what he did. He took his time. A few cheap motels along the way. Rooms that stank of people ghosts and cigarettes and sex. Sheets coarse like paper bags. In the Bronx he found another such motel. And waited. For a few days he did nothing. Then he began to follow a suit he happened to see coming from a bar. It was afternoon. The drunk man blinked as if the sun spat light into his eyes. He wobbled along a horrible street. It had a bail bondsman, off-track betting. And wizened Italian men playing dominoes on the sidewalk.

Strake watched the drunk suit. No houses anywhere near. Strake himself had donned a black suit. Like them. White collared shirt. Black tie. Soon he could see he was in the vespiary. Wasp men dropping from their nests. One man turned into five. He was near something. Only they were very good at not going anywhere in particular. As if they crisscrossed each other to give a certain illusion of movement. He saw that drunk man in the suit come out of the bar. The rest appeared out of nowhere.

Because there were so many he knew he was under the nest. But where did they go? Where was this supposed house? Strake had gotten enough info about them to know the general area. He was here now. That was the easy part. The hard issue was maybe not even finding that house. Yet it was certain that he would. It had to be infested with men.

And Strake: only one person. Who else could he bring anyway? Sheriff Neaves? Possibly. He had his hands too full with his own town. Houston was dead from that Bald Drifter, one of The Nihilistics. Sheriff Crowley was too conspicuous since he was so heavy and was having health problems. No, Strake was on his own. He triangulated a central point where he saw most of them. The "house" had to be a basement in a shop somewhere. Not an actual house. Strake got back in his car and went to the motel a few miles off.

That night he wondered. Everyone's dead, he nearly said aloud. Would he continue all his life to explain vengeance? Like what he was about to do to the suits? Where did his justification come from anyway? A woman screamed in pain in the motel room next to him. Might be sex. Might be murder. He didn't care. The next few days were similar. Watching, noting, deciding. He blended into the city well. How easy it was to put on a black suit. Did he hope to be marked? Perhaps. It would be one way in.

Now the suits multiplied. Ten or more but each one looking much like the rest. They seemed to stay on the sidewalks. He never saw them go inside any buildings. Were these ten or so men lookouts? Hard to say. If he followed one, that man simply ran into another suit. They talked. They both moved on. Maybe these were the above-ground pawns. Sure, they drew attention but also deflected it. How better to not be suspicious than to act normal. Yes, Strake thought, there is a basement somewhere. He just couldn't figure out where it was.

After a week of watching he almost gave up when he saw the man again, the first suit he had noticed on day one. Drunk this time as well. No surprise there. Another problem the sheriff had: he wasn't sheriff here. He was not in a war either where he did what he wanted. He couldn't snoop around in bars and betting parlors to see if the basement housed criminals. How to surprise them? He decided to focus only on the drunk man. The rest were diversions. A gamble, sure. Then again, what progress had he even made?

He knew the general area but he was aware of that before he even came to New York. At stake here was history. These men, and the men behind them, were the source of so much death in

Strake's life. Not that he was any better for setting out to massacre them. Crush the wasp's nest. Sever the aorta. The heart was a vespiary. He might die trying. After following the drunk man to no avail one full day, he moved to the second thing on his list. He would come back to the suits later. Right now he had to drive to JFK. Then something strange happened. As he was about to get in his Chevelle to leave he saw the drunk man lying on his back near a stop sign.

What had happened? He approached, slow. Hundreds of people walked this way and that. Red sopped his white shirt at the stomach. Strake stood about thirty feet off but could still see the blood. These suits were quick. The sheriff had no idea how he had been wounded. Now he would miss driving to JFK on time. He had given the person a back-up plan in case he didn't arrive for a ride. He approached the man who looked alive. The dying suit grimaced, held his belly with both hands. Strake stood above him: "What did they do to you?"

"Who's that?" he winced, maybe confused by a blond stranger in a similar black suit. "I don't know your face."

"I'm looking for the house."

"The house, hmm."

"You know what I mean."

"I do," the man admitted.

"Where is it?"

"Take my wallet. Inside my coat."

"They stab you?" Strake asked, reaching inside the suit jacket.

"Yeah. And shot me in the same place."

"Stabbed you *and* shot you?"

"Did it at the house. They thought I was dead, but I ran."

A circle of blood spread on his stomach, red wine on a white tablecloth.

"You'll find what you need in my wallet."

Strake opened the billfold. He was about to ask the man another question when he looked down. To see him dead. He moved, leaving the body. Indifferent people didn't stop to help. Strake found a little alley to examine the wallet. There it was: an address on the back of a business card. By the time he emerged from the side alley he saw four suits. Picking up the body and tossing the dead man into the trunk of a long white limousine. As inconspicuous as he could be, Strake made it to his car.

Followed the limo. It turned onto streets and avenues with no logic.

A white car that long was salient and easy to spot.

Why be so ostentatious if you only wanted to keep a low profile?

He followed the car to the outskirts of the Bronx.

Unsure of all the little parkways and highways. But he stayed caught up. Soon he was at the edge of water, a river. Could see them even though he was half a mile in the distance. Four black suits stood from the parked white limo. They removed his dead man from the trunk. Two held the wrists, two the ankles. They heaved! Dropped the body in the water. Another odd thing happened. Two of the suits, the ones who held the wrists, flashed pistols and blasted the two who held the ankles in their foreheads. They dropped to the ground, were heaved by their arms and legs in the water as well. When the remaining two men stood, they were in for a surprise.

Strake had aimed his M40. Pop. Pop. His timing was perfect. Two spits to the head. They were at edge to look down where they had thrown the bodies in the river. So they both leaned forward and fell in the water too. Dead like that. Quick and ugly. Strake looked up at the blue sky. He closed his eyes for a second. Shook his head. Only the beginning. He spent the day at the Bronx Zoo. Perspired in his black suit. Able to think as he stared at animals. Nothing seemed to be secret about these men. White limo. Abandoned dead suit left in the street. So overt. But the house had been elusive until now. Why had he come here alone? The men seemed to be multiplying.

At the bison, close to the Fordham Road entrance, he swore he noticed four more black suits. Staring at him? Was he paranoid? He moved through the animals, suspicious. Headed to the other side of the zoo. Came to the sleek panther in a glass cage. Saw a pattern on its black coat. Never realizing it was also a leopard. The problem was that he had come to this place with no plan. Amorphous ideas, yes. Nothing with any architecture. It was a futile move because he didn't know what to do. He had trouble figuring out the next step. This was because he came in anger. Rage punctured clear thought. He couldn't discuss it with anyone. It was in his head, not a good place for rage. Maybe he would find the house. Then what?

Since the death of Harris he had been bored but filled with a strange vigilantism. The Nihilistics had nothing to do with the suits. Utterly separate and random. But the Colt, the hatchet and the bone knife had blurred his son's five murders prior to the bank robbery. It was hard to separate them though, suits and Nihilistics. Partly because Harris was in the middle.

Harris had died in the bank with three others. But before that he had killed several suits in the silo. The suits, while in the Bronx, had been somehow connected to the Reeds' gambling and prostitution around Georgia. If The Nihilistics hadn't come, Harris would be alive.

That could have been a bad thing. It was also bigger than his son. The suits and the Reeds had been ruining his town with drugs and no telling what else. Strake was tired of it. It was amateur business. Small-time mediocrity hooked into urban money. The source, at first, seemed to be just the Reeds. Then Mary

Mae's prostitution. Her work tied to the suits. Who came to his town to find money she hid. His son Harris learned of his mom's life. Saw it too close. Those suits dead in a silo, killed by Harris.

He stared at the eyes of the panther. No one had followed him to see this big cat. He waited. Peered out into the open area. None of the four suits he had seen earlier. He too had been conspicuous since being in the Bronx. Walking around the area in his suit as if he were one of them. Maybe they had seen he was a fraud. Followed him to the zoo. He would wait with these yellow eyes still staring at him. Black dots in the middle of each. Hard stare. A trapped, alert beast. The panther turned its head. Began to pace back and forth. Strake kept his gaze on the open area. A suit appeared. Then a second. They pointed in his direction. A third came. Then the fourth.

The sheriff knew what was about to happen. They had him cornered. Probably had guns. Maybe they had damaged his car? He looked at the panther who had stopped pacing. The cat yawned vampire teeth. A pink and black mottled tongue. Strake kept waiting. He knew that if he moved from this alcove he was done. They were not leaving. He was not moving.

The four men moved together.

Pretending to have a friendly chat as they walked. Strake watched. He was thankful for the mild October air. It was an empty day at the zoo. Not many people. One man headed where Strake stood. A piece of luck. It looked like the other three were keeping watch. Strake remained in a narrow outdoor hallway of sorts. In front of the glass cage. The path was made of dry mulch chips. It was wide enough for two people to pass each other and view the panther. But it was a tight fit. The area was a bit hidden from view.

The four men had seen Strake come in here. Now he needed to watch this man coming for him. While keeping an eye on the three to make sure they didn't rush him in a gang. He could hear the obese man panting. Charcoal hair, waves of it. This first bold suit stank of a pungent cologne. Strake was ready. He just couldn't budge. A second felt like a minute.

Time had long ago changed for him. He knew that it never meant what you thought it did. Especially when there was a chance for panic. The line was fine: don't become chased, always be the pursuer. But if you're cornered you can't do either. You're no longer chased because you're caught. And you can't pursue because you're stuck. He was immobile. There was no other option than to breathe and stand and wait. He couldn't think about the other three right now. So there he remained, focused on one man. Unable to move. Impossible to be the forward attacker. The mistake would be to make any move. Now the man was near, very near. Yards off. There were some fake trees by the glass cage. He appeared. Saw Strake. They didn't speak.

The man with the charcoal hair tilted his head to the left. Cocked up an eye as if to figure out if Strake was one of them. The sheriff's suit threw him for a second. Then the fellow smiled. Seeming to turn back to yell over at his friends. This is when Strake saw the massive target of the belly. He slid out the white bone knife. A parting gift from one of The Nihilistics, the girl. Jabbed it deep into the man's gut as he oofed. Gasping but unable to speak. It was slick and fast. The first time he had used it. A second stab in the heart. Still not over.

Two men came over next. They had to be close. They saw their friend dead on the ground. Looked at Strake. Went for guns in their suit jackets. Again, the bone knife. With two of them he could do nothing but hope for their proximity. They closed in on him. Strake leaned the back of his head against the glass. Panther pacing behind him. Would they risk shooting him and making noise? Could he kill the two of them quickly enough? Somebody would win here. Strake decided to focus on one man at a time. That's all he could do. Maybe he would die from the other. These men were trim, not fat like the first one. Odds were not good.

"We can't kill him here."

"Why not?"

"Are you insane?"

"Who are you?" the second suit asked. "You're not one of us."

Strake gave no answer.

"Look, he's up against a glass case."

"So?"

"So, you friggin moron, you want to break the glass? Plus, I like dis panther. Dis panther's good."

While the second and third suits turned to each other to argue, Strake made a quick lunge in the throat of the second one. Yanked out the bone knife as the suit dropped his gun. The third one stared in awe as the sheriff slid the knife across his throat. His gun dropped too as his white collar soaked fast from the long split on his neck. Strake leaned down and pocketed both weapons. The fourth man was on the way, tired of waiting. He saw the scene. Flashed a pistol and fired multiple times. Shattered the glass as Strake ducked. It rained shards. Strake ran at him with the bone knife and plunged it into the fourth man's belly. Yanked at the blade, but it stuck. He had to yank again as the man fell on his back. He had to get out of there. Thank god the zoo was empty. He walked fast without running to draw attention. Prayed he would get to his car.

About twenty feet away he looked back to see the panther digging his mouth into the bloody belly of one of the suits. He couldn't see which one through the fake trees. Just caught a flash of the uncaged black cat feasting on something. He could hear the gnashing of teeth on flesh. The parking lot felt so far from him. He gasped for breath. Moved forward. Soon he was in his Chevelle. No security officers had followed him. His car had not been damaged. Jesus. This is what happened when you had no plan.

Was he trying to die? Maybe he was. Amateurs had a way of turning you into an amateur as well. He breathed for a minute. Waited. An electric shivering vibrated his skin. The juice of murder. He turned the key forward in the ignition. Eased out onto Southern Boulevard. He was becoming like them, The Nihilistics, using the bone knife. Remembering the girl's final suicide with same weapon, he had a fondness for the torture he knew she felt. She was in his shadow now. Where was he? So easy to get lost in the Bronx. He pulled into a gas station for fuel.

Should he go back to Georgia? To the airport? He couldn't. He only wanted to find that damn house. Men were dying fast, not his intention, but he figured it would happen. Not a surprise. He pulled over to the air pump. Parked. Waited some more. When you knew what you needed to do, it was simple: you aimed and did it. But he was inert, not able to go forward or backward. Maybe a plan was impossible at this stage. He tuned his AM radio orange line to whatever voice he could find. A baritone voice crooned words like warm honey. "And this just handed to me: a panther is loose in the Bronx. Four men are dead. Be on high alert if walking. Zoo officials are trying to tranquilize it." So they had not contained the animal. Lucky he fled when he did. He stared at traffic rolling with indifference down the busy street with too many stoplights. It was an empty world filled with everything.

Sometimes light was too audacious. His eyes hurt. He was thirsty. There was a Coca-Cola machine. He walked over and bought a small bottle for fifty cents. He gulped it back, left the bottle next to the machine for the deposit. Sweet caramel coldness made his teeth ache. So much sound here. It never stopped. A locomotion of noise. Back in his car he leaned his forehead on the top of the steering wheel. Turned off the radio knob. Quiet. Perhaps this was an escape, coming north. It had a purpose, stopping the poison of the suits from infesting his town. Maybe some revenge for Harris. For EmEm. Who was he fooling? He was play-acting, even in a costume. He was bored and stupefied after the war. If he answered the question in a true way, the answer was that he didn't want to be home, for now.

As he looked up he was shocked to see the panther trotting down the middle of Southern Boulevard. A zoo van was not far behind it. Cars stopped and let this cat Moses part the sea road. Strake smiled. Probably thinks he's free. Wonders what happened to all the broken glass. It was a sight, that big black panther bouncing along on his fat paws. They had the satin beast in sight. The van pursued it. The panther stopped, sat on its hind legs, gazed around. It was getting further away, but he could tell that the van had stopped. A man jumped out. Squatted to aim. The panther flopped over to its side. The van drove up and loaded the animal. So much for freedom. Strake sat, couldn't move. His eyes widened. Something felt strange. Or familiar. He just hadn't felt it in some time. Killing so close excited your nerves. You shook like it had been predatory sex.

Take a second, Strake, he thought. You're okay. Got lucky back there. Waiting for the men had been tense, worse than the killing. Each man he killed was in the dark part of him now. That shadow was blacker. It was overall absence. Subtracting others from living. He had done it so many times. Never had it not been justified. That was the problem. He could keep on and never feel bad about it. Alone, he was emptied of guilt. He was empty of all things. You had to be vacant to kill.

The zoo van came back the other way taking the panther home. I like that cat, he reflected. He drove to his motel and slept in his suit for a day or two. He had no idea how time had passed. A plaintive fatigue came after killing. It absorbed his eyes and was mind morphine. The miracle was that no one had found him in his room. They followed him to the zoo but not here? Hm. No suits had shown up yet. They would soon. Or would he have to kill again as he located the house? Why wait? Refreshed, he found a diner.

The yellow omelet was dry. If eggs could be a paper bag, well, they had succeeded with this arid dish. He chomped some white toast with butter swirled in grape jam. A cup of hot black tea he sipped. The booth was red fake leather. The Italian waitress had brown eyes and an overbite but it was cute on her, a feral sexual look. She wore her black hair in a ponytail that bounced as she trotted around the diner.

He left a ten on the table, thanked her. Worst meal ever. He was in a lazy mood and still had not changed out of his suit. It reeked of his sweat. Part of the suffering. He would keep on this black suit until he found the house. Then he would shower when the job was done.

A few days passed. He tried to keep out of sight. Didn't see any suits on the street. No white limo. He still had the dead drunk man's wallet with the address. Had gone to that address. Found nothing. Not even a business. No house. The address was a dud. But why keep it on the back of a card? He covered his eyes with his palm. I'm an imbecile. The address on the back was not it. It was the business address on the front of the card. Idiot.

Answer there the whole time. Hadn't even considered looking at the address on the *front* of the card. This was clumsy. Which worried him. If he was slipping on small things, wouldn't he slip on a kill too? His focus was blurry. Amateurs never thought it through right. They just went at it like he was doing. Oh, and why don't we let a panther loose in the meantime? Good grief. What were the knowns? Had they followed him to the zoo? Or just been curious because he looked suspicious?

It was to be considered. Either way they seemed to have intentions to hurt him. Here was the other question: were the rest of them after Strake now? Tomorrow he would go to the address on the front of the business card. He would find the house. Go inside it and face the suits. But he needed to clear his head this evening. At the motel he slept in his clothes. He rested his bloodshot eyes. In the morning I will find them. The morning. He waited for endless night. What was this he felt? A small part vengeance, some boredom and lots of stupidity. Terrible human concoction. He sighed.

Then the puking came. The shivers. Cold and hot on his sensitive skin. He vomited all night. Only one culprit: the jaundiced omelet. More punishment. Once the poisoned food was gone from him he cried about his life. His breath was hot with bile and acid. Infinite night. The polyester of his black suit had a stench. He had some dreams. About what his grandson would have been. What if you lived only looking backward? Never setting another forward goal. Always ignoring the future. His future was a graveyard of bodies. That he killed. Then again so was his past.

Face at the toilet. He retched. A gag convulsed out of him. Sprays of wet chunks blew from his mouth. Why had he not just gone to the airport? Avoidance. He could only think of one thing: the house. His shadow would never be white. It would be a thrill to vanish. Instead of facing what was in front of him. Sometimes the deaths wearied his body. Not the killing. The dead after the kill. I remove life from them. Why is this what I have to do? He wondered.

To be good at what you did meant you maybe didn't love it so much. He was on his back on the bathroom floor. Looking at the light glare above him. Think of it in steps, Strake. Find the house. Make your plan. Try to survive. Go home.

A sharp pain jabbed his side. He shivered. Tried to sit up. Couldn't. The body did not know how to be warm and cold at the same time. One time in the war he ate some rancid prawns. Stumbled around hallucinating in a nauseous stupor. Vomited for days. He would be all right. Why so fixated on that house? When he had no idea what he would do when he got there? The Reeds had been pulling him into the small time. He loathed the small time. Nothing worse than piddling humans. Strake couldn't abide mediocrity. He watched so much of it in his small town. Lives misused.

No, you couldn't even say that since misuse implied they had used them in the first place. There was no use, and he saw the double meaning. His mind was on the panther. Although he couldn't see it bite into the dead men he imagined those vampire fangs. A meal of four men's stomachs. An escape into the street, for a few moments. Had it really happened?

Strake was a little worried that he was not thinking clear. He had come with no plan. Not like him. He always knew what to expect. But he had just rushed into this. No idea why. The emptiness at home forced him to drive to New York. He was tired of watching his town succumb to the small time. Humans moving backwards. Regressing to blobs of no use. Now he was here. Killing followed him. Perhaps he followed it too. But it followed him, no doubt. He wondered about the zoo. When did he get food poisoning? Time was too mixed. No longer linear. He was in an odd sphere, not a line of time. He stood up and walked to the bed.

On the nightstand was a needle and foil. Oh boy, he muttered.

He sat on the mattress and stared at the heroin. When? He had forgotten. This wasn't good. Unbuttoning the white shirt cuff he slid back the jacket and then folded the sleeve. The dots on his arm were like pepper. Christ. A strange fissure ripped down the middle of his eyes. This cracking ran through him. Split him inside. When he had even found the drugs? Had he been in this motel room in the Bronx the entire time? No, he had seen the drunk man die on the street. A quick look around the bed turned up the card the man had given him.

The white limo. But the zoo? It could have been recent. At the gas station by the air pump. Yes, he had seen that panther. It hardly seemed possible. The four suits who attacked him by the black cat, yes he remembered them. It felt abnormal. The men. The panther strutting down the street before a tranquilizer downed it. Now he wondered if the cat was a he or a she. Whew, okay it *had* happened. It was palpable.

Strake bought gas. That's right. I pulled up by the air pump. That's where he started using. In the car after they caught the panther. He stared now at the drugs. Shook his head in disappointment. It was a little better than it being an illusion. Not much though. For a minute there . . . Still there was a little lapse. Where he had forgotten some time.

He needed air. Walked out to his car. Opened the trunk. M40. Horse bone knife. Then he saw two more things that disturbed him even more. The hatchet. And the Colt Government. He had never wanted to admit his affinity for The Nihilistics. Especially after what they did to his son and daughter-in-law and the two others in the bank. Yet he flashed back to Becca's self-death with her knife. Knew he was like her. Exactly so. To take their weapons sealed it. He was one of them. He had been one of them before they had ever existed. Strake had the blood of nihilism in him in many small veins of his body. To some it could seem horrific, using their three weapons. To him they had died so he could get them. He was awake now, even with junk polluting his blood. He needed to handle that. Falling apart could kill him.

Was that a car watching him across the street? He felt better, if not weakened. No longer sick. Not so fatigued. Yes, he would change out of this rancid suit when he found the house. Once he realized the address was on the front of the card, he knew he was not quite ready to do anything about it. So . . . the location of the dead man's card was right. Here was the problem: if he just appeared, he would ruin it. In fact they seemed to already know he was an outlier. That was obvious from the zoo fuster cluck.

He also didn't see a lot of other blond men up here. He stuck out. And he hadn't seen any other blond man in a suit. Mostly black hair, Italian-American. All the suits fit this description. Carbon copied men. He had an idea, possibly one that might work. Leaving his car in the motel parking lot he walked until he found the Mount Vernon train station. It was a long walk. He had never oriented himself here. Didn't want to. As he waited to board the train he felt groggy. Thought the poisoning had passed. He had a white packet and a needle with him. How had he gotten back on this stuff? So groggy that he was on the train in the wrong direction heading to Manhattan. He took it to 125th and stepped off, stared at the ugly buildings and angry people shooting past him.

Not to worry. Just get back on the other side and head north. Strange eyes stared at him. He was lost. Right now he wanted to be lost. It could be fatal to show up at the house. This was wrong. He walked down the steps. Came up on the other side. What was that? Across the platform was a black suit. Looking right at him. The Metro-North train on Strake's side slowed between them. Instead of getting on it the sheriff waited.

Weren't they going to keep following him? The man was there. Staring. Not moving. Strake stared back at him. The sun was a warm lemon dripping noon heat in yellow streaks. His mouth was parched. He swallowed. Another train flashed between them on the middle track. The man was gone this time. Appeared next to Strake after the minute it took to go down the stairs and back up on his side. The man said nothing. Just stood about six feet from him. Strake turned. The man did not look at him.

For many days the sheriff had been asking himself what he was doing. To drive up here into chaos with no clear aim. The man was armed. The platform had emptied except for a couple of homeless men sprawled near a bench. The suit turned. Walked a few steps closer. But kept his body facing the tracks. Not looking at Strake. Then the man looked around in a furtive way. Lunged at him with a long silver blade. The side of his head was met with the syringe needle. Strake jabbed it hard into him. His mouth opened in a gasp, knife dropping from his hand. Kicked quickly onto the tracks. Wide brown eyes shocked that he was about to die. Choking for air.

Strake revealed the Colt Government. Rammed the barrel as far in the mouth as he could. To muffle the sound. Gun barrel stuck in the back of the throat, a hole in the back of the head exploding outward. Brains seeped on the concrete as the man fell to his side. The homeless men never noticed. He had a thought and dragged the body over to them. Dumped him by the bench with the sleeping bums. They never stirred. He approached the platform. Stared down at the knife about to be destroyed under locomotive wheels.

A train came. He headed north again. A few stops. To Pelham. He walked many blocks, sweating. In front of the middle-class house with yellow aluminum siding. It looked empty. But it was not. This was it. He walked around the back. No suits. Could he have caught a break with no one here at the moment? The back door was cheap and flimsy. Shouldered it open.

Inside the house he had a sickening feeling. He came to the front of the place. Four dogs stacked against a wall, dead. Bullet holes in their heads. Yet . . . no smell. Strange. There were no men. He walked up the steps. Nothing up here either. Several bedrooms used for basic sleeping. He came back down. Saw a basement entrance. Not even a door. Only an opening to the steps down. "What a surprise," he said. "Another hell."

He was about to descend them when a man in a slick ebony butcher's apron covering his arms startled him. Standing at the bottom. There was a moment of uncertainty. This is when his suit finally helped him. Before, it had only marked him as a target. "You're here. Good. Come on down."

He walked in a slow way as steps creaked under him. As the man stared up. The fellow had white hair and a pink face. He wore safety glasses. The black apron splattered with who knows what massacre. "In here," he motioned. He pointed to a similar black apron on a hook. "Grab one."

The sheriff put it on as he followed him through the dank rooms. Very cold air induced a shiver. Safety glasses in his right pocket. Strake lifted them out and looked at them. "Yeah, put dose on. You'll need em."

On stainless steel tables were the bodies of many dead men. Lying with their faces to the ceiling. Suits. He leaned closer. Were these the men he had killed at the zoo? Sure looked like them. They were. He knew these faces.

"I need you to get their clothes off."

Strake did what he was told.

"You're new?"

He nodded.

"We're losing a lot of men lately," the man informed him.

Strake was taking off the suit jacket of one man. Trying not to hurt his back as he lifted the awkward body.

"Why's that?"

"We don't know. But we have back-ups to follow anyone going in for the kill. If the killers are killed, the back-ups get the bodies out quick as possible, bring em to me. Only one problem, the killer gets off because we're collecting dead bodies instead of chasing him."

Strake had most of the jackets off. He moved to the shirts and ties. Then shoes. Pants. Underwear. Soon there were four naked bodies. And a pile of clothes on the cement floor.

"Okay, dat's good. Throw their crap in the incinerator in the next room. I'll tell you what to do next."

He did and returned after tossing the garments into the blaze that toasted his face. Maybe an hour had passed, maybe two. It had taken longer than he had expected to remove all the clothing. But it was a cumbersome process. He heard a noise. Upstairs.

"What's that?" The man didn't answer. Down the stairs came two suits carrying another dead one.

"Put him on dat empty table."

They lifted the new body. Without a word they left back up the stairs. "Same thing with dat guy." Strake nodded and looked down to see the man he had just killed at the train station. Clothes off. Five bodies. All due to him.

"Now the easy part," the man joked.

"Easy?"

He brandished the longest hacksaw Strake had ever seen. Gave it to him. No, no . . . thoughts of the silo returned. Then the man found a hacksaw for himself as well.

"Come with me. Need your help with something."

Strake placed his saw on the chest of one of the naked men. The red-faced man put his on another man. The two men walked into a third room, not where the bodies were, not where the incinerator was. This room was filled with saws. And large hampers with wheels.

"Help me roll one of dese."

They moved it across rough cement to the room with the dead men.

"You come from Upstate?"

"That's right."

"You can sleep in one of the beds on the second floor. After we're done."

"Thanks."

"You'll need it."

It began to dawn on Strake what he was about to do. With Meyer in the silo he had only scooped corn. Meyer had sawed the dead bodies. Now Strake was about to do the same. Poor suits. Seemed like it was their fate to be hacked into pieces after death. Strake didn't believe in coincidences; it was all just repetition.

"Start with the feet. They're the easiest."

He nodded. And began. He sawed for what seemed like a full day. It was hard to tell with the basement having no windows. As he went at it, the man did the same. The parts dropped into the hamper. Severed feet first.

"When we get to the torsos," the man wheezed, "we'll just toss em whole into the fire."

"Okay."

The two in bloody aprons and safety glasses never stopped working. Red splattered them, blood sliding to the gray floor to stain it and fill it with puddles. An arm fell, sawed at the shoulder. The hamper packed with bleeding human parts. They rolled it into the incinerator.

"You can toss em in," the man offered. "I don't enjoy dat part."

And you enjoy the *rest* of it? Strake thought to himself. He heaved in the limbs to the basement crematorium. They crackled and burned. They were down to the head and torsos. Nothing needed to be said in this horror. Strake started on a neck. Watched the throat sliced and hacked. The first head fell on the floor. He picked it up. Dropped it in the hamper. The man from the train station. Needle mark on the side of his forehead. The red-faced fellow worked like a butcher slicing meat at a deli. Another head fell.

"Can you toss dat in?"

"Sure," Strake said.

Three more heads fell in the next hour.

Together, they lifted the five remaining torsos into the hamper. Strake rolled it in and burned the heads and torsos.

"Good job," the fellow said to him. "Get some sleep. Decent shower on the second floor."

Upstairs in the shower blood cascaded off his face and body. Swirled down the drain at his feet. Should he risk it and stay in the bedroom? The full-body apron had done its job. Hard to work in but it covered his clothes well. After his shower his cheeks were still red from blood splatter. During the job Strake had not removed his suit jacket for fear of staining his white shirt underneath. There were no visible blood smears on his shirt or suit though.

He dressed again. Thought. Yes, he said to himself, I need to stay. This is unraveling now. And I'm in the middle of it. He had found an "easy" way in. The white-haired man would vouch for him. What was next? Wait. He lay on the bed in his full suit and shoes. Dreamed of the abattoir of men he had just created. The dreams came fast and torturous. He winced at times. But felt clean from his shower. He almost slept. Would there be more bodies tomorrow? Or would staying here keep him from killing anymore? Why were there four dead dogs in the entrance? This was the house. It was the address on the front of the card. A place of casual death. Men killed. Bodies brought. Animals and men. Crucifying. It was all crucifying. I'll close my eyes. Just for a minute. He flashed back to his drug and/or food poisoning. A wave of nausea surged but didn't last. He was where he should be.

Tomorrow it would begin. Today was research. He had walked in at the right time. Then a thought struck him and turned him cold. Wasn't an actual man from Upstate coming? The man who was supposed to do what he had done with the bodies? If he was right then that man might come into the house any moment now. Strake sat up in fear. He went downstairs in haste. The man with the white hair was not in the house anymore. He checked the basement. Strake stepped outside and looked. It would be another suit. Coming from Upstate. Train? Car? He guessed car. Sure enough an old green Dodge Dart pulled up in front. A suit emerged. Strake waved. The man approached. "I'm here for the clean-up."

"Not needed. We got it done." A weird moment of tension.

"Done? Already. Wait, who are you?"

"They called me in. You were late."

The man's lips vanished as his brow furrowed in confusion.

"Well, okay, only a little. I got hung up in traffic."

"It's fine. White-hair told me to tell you we're good."

"You mean . . . I can go?"

"It's covered," Strake said, his hand ready for the Colt Government.

"Fine with me! I got another job in Jersey anyway."

Strake pulled out a wad of bills and gave him two hundred in twenties. "For your trouble." The happy suit waved behind him as he headed down the sidewalk. Waved again before he dropped into his driver's seat. Then he was gone. Close one. Something wasn't right about that guy though. Strake had a bad feeling about him. All these suits were duplicitous and shady. Was this house just a charnel to get rid of corpses? Or a meeting place? He had to find out. That meant he was probably on hack duty again at some point. Where was the pig pink man? Could Strake just leave and show up whenever? No, he needed to station his body here. And wait. No matter how gruesome it was to be in the horrible place.

He had paid ahead for his motel. The Chevelle was safe in its parking lot. Yes, wait. Wait and suffer. All he needed to do was gather them here, spray gasoline on this hell. Maybe they would come. Maybe only dead bodies came. He was about to find out in the coming days. Inside the house he stared at the four dead dogs. Shook his head in disgust. Random dead animals piled in a corner. A sick crematorium in the basement. What kind of place was this? Man, Strake thought. Tomorrow would take a long time to come. That was all right. He had time to kill. And some men.

Thirty minutes passed. Looked like an empty night. Then he heard a noise. A car? He stood at a front window. The white limo parked. Suit after suit appeared. They smoked cigars in the gray yard grass. About ten of them. Strake needed a number. How many of them were there? He made a gamble and opened the door. The men looked. They seemed to model themselves on one another. Many of the faces looked fat and Italian. No way these idiots, who did nothing to hide, were the mob. They were something. Just what, he didn't know. Minor league.

"Wait, who are you?" one raised his voice, coming at Strake to the door.

"Here to work in the basement."

"You're not Harry."

"From Upstate? No, I'm not. He couldn't make it. Sent me."

"I don't like this."

The other nine men approached en masse.

"And where's Strother?"

"White-hair?"

"Yeah, that's him."

"He left after we finished on the five bodies."

"Okay. Good. There's six more in the trunk."

Six!

"We'll bring them down for you."

"Tables are empty."

"Watch your step. It's slick on the cement."

One suit walked over to the trunk and opened it. More suits came to help. And still Strake was bewildered by their casual behavior. Bringing in dead bodies. A car that stood out in a ridiculous way. Even the suits they wore: conspicuous. Strake smelled jacklegs. He walked over to the limo trunk. They were lifting out the bodies. He saw another dead dog. What the hell? They carried in the suit corpses. The fifth dog was thrown with the other four. He was back to work. The man with the white hair never returned. Maybe felt like he had a decent replacement. Meyer's silo tutorial had apprenticed him. He had not killed these new men. No, this was from something else. The sheriff felt a calm strangeness as he sawed off limbs. His life had been a ticker-tape bloodbath. Why should this be any different?

Some sort of meeting was upstairs with the ten suits. In his black apron which covered his arms and chest fully he realized one thing. It was time. He had focused on one body. In the man's jacket he found an ice pick. Skin and tendons and gristle as the neck was sawed. His head fell on the ground, eyes blank, tongue half jutting as he finished the rest. One down, many to go. At the top of the stairs he must have looked deranged. Still in his black body apron. Bulky, yes, but able to move around with surprising ease. Maybe designed that way for slaughtering large bodies.

The men discussed Times Square porn. He even heard the Reeds mentioned. Or was that just his imagination? Now he had to get close to their faces. And move quickly through them. Lifting the Government he aimed. Shot at seven heads before they knew what was what. That left three to attack him. He dropped the empty gun. Went on a rampage with the ice pick. Focusing on the three he had not shot. He stabbed at their hearts and eyes. Then one by one he plunged the ice pick. Into the tops of all ten heads. To be sure. He did the same in their ten chests.

He dragged each body to the top of the stairs. Pushed it down clunking and flipping. Ten bodies. He had finished only one suit from the earlier six. So that meant fifteen. Five left from before. Plus these ten. What else was there to do? First, out of annoyance he also tossed down the five dogs. Those went into the incinerator. Poor bastards. Next, the torso and head of the first man from the trunk. He worked on those other five. The time passed and his body ached and his teeth gritted. The butchering hypnotic. He filled up the hamper.

His hacksaw ripped apart flesh for hours. It was a good saw, sharp and beautiful in its quickness. But he was tired. He had no idea what he was doing. And yet he had done what he thought needed to happen. This was easier than facing heroin. He would have to go home soon. The fire roared with body parts. When the last torso was lifted and dropped into the blaze, he took off the black apron.

Hung it on the hook. Collected his Colt on the floor upstairs. His. Hmm. One of The Nihilistics had used it to rob the bank in his town. He stared at it in his palm. Agent Pierce had been right about the Bald Drifter. But had been skinned and killed by the girl in Basil's motel. He decided to take the ice pick. Needed a new weapon of his own. Not the hatchet. Not the bone knife. Not the Colt. Yes, the ice pick was all his.

The keys were in the white limo. The house empty. Except for the human inferno in the basement. Some of that fire he took upstairs . . . he waited. It only took lighting brittle curtains. First on the second floor. Then on the first floor. The house was a big shanty anyway. He walked into the yard. Through the front entrance. Door left open. He watched flames rise. Fire belched out of a window by the living room, a god burping scorched arson. Time to move.

As he drove to his motel he had images of slicing that saw through bone. The bones of men. So easy to rip apart with no resistance. He came to an obvious chop shop in an industrial hell. Chainlink fence. Four salivating Dobermans yanking their necks taut on chains. He stopped the ridiculous stretch of a vehicle. Four Latinos and two black men ran up to his window.

"Want it?"

They smiled. "How much?"

"On the house, my friends."

He walked several miles until he found his bearings. Made it back to the motel. He had no syringe anymore. That didn't matter. The urge would come again. Soon. Was he done here? Yes, maybe. The disorganized suits were clowns. Too obvious, easy targets. Those ten in the house. The main ones? Likely. It would send a message. How had they not recognized him at the house if they had been following Strake, like at the zoo and train station? Maybe all the men who had seen him were dead now. Of around twenty of them it was possible that two or three knew his face. Not anymore. After a stale shower and a coarse towel he fell on his bed.

Remained there on his back with his eyes open. Sleep would come. Not before many flashes of the past days blinked before him. He was a dark movie. Half to sleep he viewed his own film. His friend the panther. He really loved that cat. Sprays of red aerosol. The killing. The crunch of slicing dead men into chunks of meaningless flesh. The shooting at the train station after stabbing him with the syringe. The seven shootings in the house. The three stabbings with the ice pick. The final fire.

It weirdly lulled him in a violent cadence. He felt just. If he had not felt just, he might not have slept like he did. A day passed. Maybe two. He woke with a clear mind. Dropped his motel key at the desk. Sat in his Chevelle. And thought about the long, long drive home. How many days had passed? Not that many after all. He wanted to believe that the suits were gone.

If he understood his son's story about the silo, then these men were more like drones who did whatever anyone told them. Hence the ease with which Mary Mae made the first man climb the ladder. She had intimated that maybe the guy knew he was a dead man. That other suits were coming after him for the money he and his cohorts couldn't recover. Harris managed to get five more of them in the silo corn. Maybe because of the bag of money. Maybe just to check on their missing friends. However he did it, his son had persuaded them. The suits were a flock, sheep men.

This might explain why they let themselves remain in the open streets in the Bronx. Not worrying about being seen. It was why he could quasi-blend with him in his faux suit. But something didn't add up to a final sum that made sense. Yes, they were an illusion. Disposable people. Not covert. Willing to die. There was a reason the house was easy to find. Easy to enter. It made sense why an abattoir was in the basement. The assumption was that many of these men were an army of bodies prepared for death.

If that was the case it was macabre planning. By whoever was at the head. Knowing you had all these goons who could be killed any minute. What do you do? Start your own funeral home butchery. This also might mean there was an internal war in New York. He had walked into a battleground. In a black suit. And turned into a triage medic in a basement with a hacksaw. Except the goal wasn't to save the bodies. The objective was to chop and burn the dead ones. Now, you're getting somewhere, Strake. Only one conclusion emerged from his thoughts in the parking lot of the motel. He had sat thinking. Not able to move. Staring forward. Waiting for food poisoning and heroin to leave him. His work, he realized, was not done here. There was a shepherd, had to be. Maybe he could still go to JFK. Not critical though. Focus on the critical.

While a grim dread had followed him during these ghastly days, not much time had actually elapsed. He was not too worried. There was always the chance he might not make it to the airport. The person he was meeting knew what to do in that event. He couldn't think about it right now. The shepherd. The aorta. The heart itself.

He kept assuming the house was the central flow of corruption that oozed south to his town. Maybe not the case. He had five weapons. M40. Colt Government. Bone knife. Hatchet. Ice pick. His mind kept returning to one question. How had they not traced him to the motel? He could only intuit that they themselves had no real plan. No concrete research about him. So when they followed him to the zoo, it could have just been random. What about the train station? A single man who noticed him and thought something was off? These guys were everywhere, endless numbers. How much of a dent had Strake made in eliminating them?

Immobile in his Chevelle. Inert. Unable to drive forward. Only able to sit. In many situations like this an outside thing always occurred to change the inaction. He heard a knock on his window. He rolled it down. It was the clerk at the motel. A pale young guy with a goatee and pimples and greasy red hair. "I forget something?"

"Oh no, no, but I did. I meant to tell you before you left."

"What's that?"

"Well, it was weird, maaan. Last night I was emptying some garbage in the dumpster and I saw these two guys. By your car."

"In black suits?"

"Yeah . . . but here's the weird thing: one guy was UNDER your car."

Strake's eyes widened.

"Move!" He flung open his door.

"Go!" he yelled at the young man. "Find some cover!"

Strake hustled to his trunk. Opened it with the key. Grabbed his bag of weapons. The M40 had a strap. He wore it around his chest. Looking around he saw them in a brown car a half a block away. I knew they were watching me. Smiling. Two men. One shot him a middle finger and mouthed a two-word obscenity starting with f and y. He was about to push a button on a remote. The young man had already bolted into the motel. The sheriff rapidly put as much distance as he could between himself and the damned vehicle.

With the explosion of the Chevelle behind him, Strake was sprinting up the busy street, bag in his right hand. Many cars double-parked in the middle of the road gave him cover. The men were not expecting this. A tidal wave of fire blasted higher than the tall buildings. An orange and crepuscular eruption. Nuclear twilight thunder.

In one quick moment Strake kneeled. He hid behind a car in the middle of the street. Aimed his M40. Took out the driver. A flash of a head shot. He ran to the car. The bag was unzipped at the top. He felt around for a weapon. The suit in the passenger seat was standing by his door. About to run on the sidewalk he fumbled in his jacket for a weapon. As the hatchet blade came down full force on the top of his head. Strake chopped a few more times. More out of rage than a need to assure the kill. He reached into the man's jacket. Took his wallet from an inside silk pocket. Strake tossed his bag into the window of the passenger seat.

Threw the blood-stained hatchet on top of it. He ran around to the other side. Opened the door. Fished out that wallet too. Yanked out the man with the bullet in his head. The body thumped onto the asphalt. He removed the M40 strap and tossed the gun in the back seat.

Strake started the car, noticing the remote that had detonated the car bomb. He chucked it. Drove off in a slow way, nothing frantic, no screeching of tires. The odd thing was that the sheriff felt a placid calm absolute in its hushed logic. Because, before, he was not certain of being a target. Now he knew. They *were* after him. With a purpose. The zoo and the train station were not random. All the more reason to find the shepherd.

Behind him he caught a glimpse of the dead suit lying on the street. And the one on the sidewalk taken down by the hatchet blade. In his rearview mirror he could also see flames rise behind him in this filthy city. After a minute he stopped looking back. Only forward now. The brown car was indistinct, mid-sized. He would blend right in to the urban grime and mass of aimless humans.

He needed to get out of New York for the moment. He would be back. He drove north toward Connecticut. Found himself on the Merritt Parkway. He veered off an exit in Greenwich and down North Street then headed left on the Post Road, keeping north. At a convenience store in Riverside he bought gas and snacks. In the parking lot he went through the two wallets. He searched the glove compartment. Chewed on a stick of beef jerky.

Times Square was a possibility. The shepherd obviously knew about Strake. The bomb was evidence of that. He was thinking that the pimply boy had saved his life by coming to the car. The men saw him approach Strake's Chevelle and had to wait until he left. But Strake had been sitting in his car for a while. Why didn't they just blow it up before the guy walked up to his window? A simple answer: they were faux mafioso.

Then again, Strake assumed he had been sitting in the driver's seat thinking for a long time. When it may have just been a few seconds. So disordered was his sense of time that he didn't know. Whatever the case, he had been deeply lucky. Most prostitution operations were in Times Square but would the shepherd live there? Probably not. His money was on the Bronx. It was outside of Manhattan away from the scum around Forty-second. The crematorium of a house had been in the Bronx.

He needed to stretch his legs. He opened his door. Stood. Bag first. Into the trunk. When no one was looking he quickly grabbed the M40 from the back seat. Tossed it into the trunk as well, slamming it.

He drank a Coke and kept his focus on the two wallets. In the glove he had found a car registration that might help down the line. Specifically he looked for more business cards. But would the shepherd be stupid enough to pass them out to his hoodlums? Not likely. Nevertheless, they were perhaps connected, these cards, to other criminals. He could be methodical and pay visits to the offices. No house addresses on the cards though. Just offices.

He was rubbing his eyes in annoyance when he noticed something in the two wallets. The same card was in each. Only a

P.O. box listed under the name. In the Bronx. No phone number. Had to be it. A start at least. Painful fatigue made Strake grimace at the steering wheel. He needed rest. Real rest. Greenwich looked like a rich town. Four parts, all in Greenwich with their own train stops going north. Greenwich, Cos Cob, Riverside, Old Greenwich. He drove around and came close to the water. Long Island Sound maybe?

A random inn was on the right, some kind of converted mansion. The rest of the huge houses were homes. He pulled in and parked the brown blob. From his bag in the trunk he got a pair of jeans and a white t-shirt, which he had not yet worn even once. They were still clean and his only change of clothes but he had to get out of this rancid, moist suit. He walked inside with just the jeans and t-shirt rolled up in his right hand.

A pretty older woman with grayish streaks welcomed him at the door with a half-smile. "Could I get a room for a week? Do you have any?"

"It's off-season, sure."

It was expensive. He pulled out a wad of bills and paid in advance. Her eyes opened in surprise but she took the money.

"Is there a dry cleaner nearby?"

"Yes, you passed it in Old Greenwich as you came in."

"Ah, I did notice that little town, sorry."

"Been traveling?"

"Yes, kind of tired."

"It's quiet here. I'll give you a back room upstairs."

In his room he removed his suit and tie and shirt and boxers. He showered for nearly thirty minutes. Steamed followed him from the bathroom. He slept naked for what must have been at least two days. The ocean at Tod's Point washed beautiful perpetual sounds that kept him lulled in sopor. When he did come down again he wore the jeans and the white t. His suit and shirt and tie were balled in his hands.

The woman was not there. He remembered that the town was not far. Could he walk? It was about a mile or so on a sidewalk through the gorgeous purlieus of suburban palaces, a life he would never live. He found the dry cleaner and gave him the rumpled mess of clothing.

"Sorry for the smell," he said. "On the road."

"No problem, no problem, smell okay," the Korean man with clean tan skin assured him. "Tomorrow, tomorrow."

Strake walked toward a cafe. Saw a red and silver train rush past over a bridge. Cars came and went underneath it. Inside he had a coffee and a bagel. Everyone seemed rich. He made his way back to the inn. Slept some more, another full night of delicious rest. The next day he walked again to the dry cleaner for his suit. He still had several days to wait. It was fine to do nothing for the moment. He was clean. His suit and shirt were clean. No telling how many blood stains had blended into the black.

The most amazing thing was his white collared shirt: he was proud of having no blood splatter. Red stains were okay on the black suit. You couldn't really tell. In a few days he would move. For the week that he had paid he sometimes walked out across the street and stared at the water of the Sound. It was part of someone's house, private with a small beach of sand. But he could still stand in the grass by the road and look at the waves. He had come to the right place. Soon there would be more violence.

He didn't even want to think about driving back to Georgia now that he had no car of his own. Maybe he could fly? Take a bus? He would worry about that later. Maybe just keep the brown one. The time in Old Greenwich was empty and pleasing.

He never saw the older women from the inn again. She seemed to trust him by offering her absence. He was the only one there.

At the end of the week he left. Drove the one last time through Old Greenwich's town. Underneath the railroad bridge. Back to the Post Road. Heading south this time. After the Merritt Parkway the crisscross of smaller parkways caused him to be lost several times. Just head south, he kept telling himself. Finally, he found the Bronx again. He was back in his suit. He searched around, asked a few people for directions.

Then he found the building. And waited. It could be days before anything occurred. That was all right. What home was there for him anymore? His father was still alive, humorous in his longevity. His son, gone. His wife too. It was a blur when he was in the house shooting the seven men with the Colt then ice-picking the other three. He knew he took some blows to the head as they attacked him. He didn't remember much and he had been wearing that apron and those goggles, looking like some sort of horror madman in a film.

He just knew he had seven shots. And seven heads. The ones who didn't take it in the brain came after him. His spiking and impaling with that ice pick, maniacal. A lunatic. They did beat on him, maybe with their guns or fists. He couldn't be sure. He was so quick even in the apron that they had no time to react, for the most part. His memory was slow and his head was bruised in places. But the rest in Connecticut had relaxed him.

He kept the hatchet under the passenger seat.

The ice pick in the glove.

The bone knife under the driver's seat.

The Colt on the seat beside him.

The M40 was in the trunk to not attract attention if someone walked past him.

He was at 558 Grand Concourse. He noticed a couple of sculptures on the side of the building front. They were up on the outside wall itself. He decided to lock the car and go inside. Checked the two business cards. He searched around and located the boxes. Too far into the interior of the place. If he stayed here to keep an eye on the P.O. box he lost sight of the car.

He would have to go back and forth. A little time in the post office. Followed by sitting in the car. Or just pacing around the block with his eyes always on the front door entrance. Parking was an issue but he didn't care. Not his ride. Ticket it all you want. He worried about being towed with the ten or so confusing signs that made no sense.

Kind of a plan but also with some variables that could derail it. First, he wanted to assume that they checked this box on a regular basis. What if they didn't? What if it was just once a week? Did it matter? Did he have anywhere to be? Nope. He considered the terroristic absurdity of his casing the government building. But, once again, his suit saved him. Clean and pressed, he felt new and ready for this last phase.

The first day yielded little. No visits to the mailbox. He waited. Dozed in his car. Found a pizza place and had a slice with ham. He might raise suspicion since he had no change of clothes. Well, he did have the jeans and white t-shirt but nowhere to change. He'd take his chances and stay in the suit; it had served him well so far. Especially if another suit appeared, it would help him fit in and approach the man.

By the third day he was weary. He didn't want to lose his parking space so he stayed in his car. Took quick kips. Dozed for just minutes here and there, even at night. No tow trucks came despite the threatening parking signs. His damp suit was clammy again, fusty.

Patience, Strake.

On the morning of the third day he was just opening his eyes from a nap, sitting up in his driver's seat, when he saw a familiar sight. A suit. Ha. You morons need a new uniform. He locked the car and hustled into the post office. The man was furtive, looking side to side, and once or twice back behind him. He went to the mailbox. Opened it with a key.

Strake was about to come at him when he paused. No. Wait. The man collected mostly letters, a tall stack. He shut the P.O. box and turned to leave. Strake waited just out of his sight. Hundreds of people in a crowd hid him well, but he lost eyes on the man once or twice. The suit was headed for the exit out of the front entrance. Strake followed. A fast stroll but made to look like leisure. No matter, everyone rushed around like mad ants on fallen jelly.

Outside the man stood at the top of about ten concrete steps. He waited. Strake was just out of the door and he aimed for a spot also at the top of the stairs. But about twenty feet away from the man. The suit eyed his wrist to see the time. Looked irritated.

As far as the sheriff could see, his ride was late. That meant he would stay in his spot until it came. Strake turned and walked toward him. The man stared ahead, jittery. He held the stack of letters. Strake moved closer. Close enough to hear him muttering to himself. A little bit closer. Then the man turned. Seemed to notice another suit. He smiled in a weak way but without threat. "Oh, hey."

"Hi," Strake said, keeping it laconic.

"They sent you too?"

"Yeah. Some trouble at the house."

"I heard. Trying to be careful. I guess."

Strake nodded. "They're picking you up in a different spot."

"Where?"

"Just over there."

Strake pointed at "his" brown car stolen from the dead suits after the explosion. Would the man recognize it? "That Lashner's ride?"

"The ones who planted the car bomb?"

"That's right."

"Yeah."

"What happened to Lashner and George who rode with him?"

"I heard they didn't make it. Something went wrong."

"But I thought the explosion went off fine?"

"It did, but they gave me this car, told me to come here to tell you."

"Hm."

"When's your ride supposed to get here?"

"Supposed to be ten minutes ago."

"I'll wait with you."

"No, I don't like this. We stand out too much. And I don't know you. You look new."

"I can go sit in the car. I'll wait in case your ride doesn't come."

"Oh, he'll come. He may be late but he always shows."

"Suit yourself," Strake said, waving. He pretended to go down the steps.

With the ice pick he gutted the man in three fast jabs. Right in the soft middle of the stomach. It had to be quick because he needed the stack of letters. As the man fell, Strake yanked the pile from his clenched hands. He stuffed half in one side pocket of his jacket, half in the other side. There were no bushes to drag him behind. Couldn't be helped. The crowd around them ignored the man now sitting hunched over on the penultimate top step. Strake had the letters. He reached down and found the P.O. box key in the man's white shirt pocket. His eyes searched the street. There it was. Black limo this time. Leaving the poor suit to die he ran over to the long car. A door opened. He stooped down to avoid hitting his head. Landed in a capacious back seat beside a glistening crystal bar of alcohol bottles. The car drove.

"Letters," a jowled man said, sitting sprawled across from him in an opposite seat. Strake pulled them out of both side pockets and handed them over to a man with the biggest head he had ever seen. He wore a yellow velvet suit with a frilly tuxedo shirt and he had a mohawk. He was maybe three or four hundred pounds. In his mouth were two cigars smoked side by side as if they were one. The red splotches on his face looked almost leperous. The man didn't open the letters, just flipped through them with indifference. At last he looked at Strake. Tilted his massive egg flab of a face and seemed bemused. "Where's the normal guy?"

"I'm him today."

"No . . . you're not."

Strake lifted up the key to the post office box as proof.

"You look different."

"I am different. They do send me here and there. He had the day off."

"Oh. I didn't know that."

"Lots of attrition lately . . ."

Sigh. "Yesssssss. I don't know what to do about it."

"What can be done?"

"Do you want me to tell you a secret about me?"

Strake didn't answer, just waited for a little bit.

"I can't leave this car anymore."

"What do you mean?"

"I'm stuck in here. I can't get out!"

"Why not?"

"I've been in here for weeks. Just riding around. Looking at the city."

"Why don't you stop and get out?"

The man gaped at him with disbelief at the audacious question. "I'm telling you, I can't! My legs don't work. They just stopped working!"

"Oh."

"I get the reports. I feel like I've lost twenty or more men in the last couple of weeks. Someone is closing in on me."

"Can I help?"

"It's the end. I saw it coming."

"Saw what coming?"

"We've lost so much money. Cash just disappears. I have very little left except this ridiculous car."

"I heard about the house burning."

"That's the least of it."

The man poured himself an absurd drink of gin. His glass was large enough to take half the bottle. Instead of sipping the clear alcohol he gulped it down his throat.

"Ahhhhhhhh."

"Quite a drink," Strake thought but was smart enough not to say it.

"Yessssssss, the house."

"How many men do we have left?"

"Not many. Oh no, not many."

"Twenty?"

"Oh no. Just you and the other guy supposedly getting letters today."

"Wait, only two of us left now?"

"And myself. And my driver, Goodis."

"How is that possible?"

"It's possible because *you* made it possible."

"I did?" Strake challenged.

"I think I know who you are now."

Strake took in some air through his nose.

"Ah, almost forgot. One other person."

The sheriff sort of knew the answer.

"Strother," the mohawked man said. His butcher partner in the house.

"What about him?"

"Well, he came to me after you arrived."

So that's where he went.

"But we've been following you since you got to New York."

"Have you?"

"Oh yes, we have. Or *had* until you killed us all."

"What about the guy from Upstate who was late coming to the house? Isn't he one of you?"

"Nah," the man said, waving. "Called in as a favor. Not one of us."

"So you're telling me that it's just you, Strother, your driver and the man I replaced at the post office?"

"And not even the latter since you likely killed him too, isn't that right?"

"Three of you left."

"Three only."

"Your entire posse is gone?"

"Mostly yes."

"What will you do?"

"I have scabies, hence this derisory haircut. Lamentable, isn't it?"

"I was in Vietnam around some prisons. I've heard about how bad scabies can get."

"I'm a modern day leper! Look at this ugliness permeating me!"

"And you're really stuck in this limo?"

"Purgatory, isn't it? Riding around a putrid city. Unable to move. Stuck watching. Getting updates, one after the other about more and more death."

"Tragic," Strake joked.

"All my men are dead! Because of you my friend. We knew about you from the day of your arrival. What you see is a dead blob of a former man. I have been waiting for you. You seem relentless and lucky. Why target us?"

"Two words: Mary Mae."

"Ohhhh dear. Strake."

"Ohhhh yes."

"I knew the Georgia license plates would haunt us. I just knew it!"

"You probably heard about Bart Reed? And his sons."

"Yes, I heard. Your work?"

"Mine, yes. My father helped."

The man scratched his neck in misery.

"This is making more sense. Mary Mae, we had our hands full. I never had a good feeling about her."

"She killed one of your suits. My son followed with five more. After that I realized I needed to pay a visit and find the shepherd."

"The who?"

"The blood line to it all."

"And you think that's me?"

"I know it's you."

"Maybe it is. Maybe it really is."

"I need your driver to stop the limo and get out."

"Why? Oh. Goodis, pull over!"

The long ostentatious ride came to a halt in the middle of the street. Were they in Manhattan now?

"Where are we?" Strake asked.

"On the south side of Central Park," Goodis said.

"You can go," Strake instructed him.

"Go ahead Goodis. You're free. I don't need you anymore."

"You sure, boss?"

"I'm sure. We're at the end. Strake is the period."

Goodis scurried to Fifth Avenue and vanished. He was in a black suit.

"What happened to Strother after he came to talk to you?"

More scratching. "He'd suffered enough in that house. No longer with us but I didn't kill him. I let him go as well."

"So you really are the last then?"

"I am. I am the last."

The fat man's eyes bulged like twitching roaches. They were wide and sad. But they were targets. Strake leaned forward, just a foot or so from the gruesome visage. Pulling the Colt from inside his jacket. The barrel tip pressed to the eye on the left. The trigger pulled. The bullet sent. He moved the gun to the right of the man's nose. He pressed it on the other eye.

Trigger pulled. The final bullet. The last needed. This car would be the man's temporary tomb. He left it. He hailed a yellow cab that took him back up to 150th near the post office. Found his brown car with an orange and white ticket on the windshield. Blew his nose with it. He wanted to head to JFK but still had the M40 in the trunk and these other four weapons. JFK was a tentative anyway. With no suits left there was no one to follow him. He could take his time. Maybe ditch the car at a junkyard back in Georgia. He aimed south. Hey, they destroyed his ride. The least they could do was let him use theirs.

As he drove he found himself on the George Washington Bridge. Then the Jersey Turnpike. Looking behind him always. His life would never be without a rearview mirror. He had time to think on his memory absences. As he drifted through time. The road was fairly empty. It veered off to the left to Cars Only as the semis shifted to the right and vanished for a moment. A city of hell, he thought.

Much of his reflection was fragmented. Some from heroin. Some from violence. Not much waited for him at home. He was sleepy. A stolen car filled with weapons. He kept the ice pick close these days. On the seat beside him. The M40, the Colt, the bone knife and the hatchet.

Merging him into The Nihilistics. He was no different. Worse even. They had struck randomly just a couple of times. He lived in terrorizing nihilism. The suits, mostly handled. Mission finished in the Bronx. They would certainly think twice about coming to his town again. But crime was a long list. You checked off one thing done, only to have five more appear. A life of long chores. He was very tired now and needed to pull off for a moment.

A rest stop sign appeared after a few miles, but he had to drive a few more to get there. He found a parking space away from the restrooms and snack machines. Turned off the car. Closed his eyes. Leaned back on the headrest. I am not a good man. I can never become one. Were some of his killings gratuitous? He wasn't certain anymore. It was quiet as he half-slept.

Then a prismatic glass blast sprayed on him. And he saw the butt of a rifle. His window had shattered on the side of his face. The rifle butt nearly hit his temple. He reached for the ice pick. Stabbed at the hairy old hand in blindness. Glass flecks had filled his left eye. He shouldered open the door onto the person who grunted backward and fell on his rear. Aiming his rifle at Strake to shoot at him, missing. They fought. With only the ice pick close Strake had to move in a quick way.

He grabbed the rifle on the barrel and yanked it from the man, tossing it in his back seat. He looked around the rest area.

No cars close to them. A few semis idling in the distance. The hate in the man's eyes was like an unholy mask. Strake aimed his heel at the face. He pummeled the nose until it was only blood. The man was not fazed. He smiled with bloody teeth.

"I thought you had gone," Strake said. "Why are you coming after me?"

"I do what the fat man pays me to do."

"The fat man's gone."

"Maybe," he slobbered, as red filled his lips.

"I thought we shared a sweet moment at the house sawing bodies."

"Funny."

Strother stared at his hand that had been ice-picked.

"Others *will* come for you."

"Will they now? You mean more amateurs like you?"

"I'm not an amateur!" he spat.

"Sure you're not. One sec."

Strake walked over to his trunk and grabbed the Government. Standing over the dead man sitting, he fired into his forehead a few times. Too tired to worry about the body, he wiped the glass off his seat and sat down. He left the rest stop. Merged onto the highway. Stopping along the way he took his time. Maybe a few days passed. Maybe he did some heroin. Possibly a week elapsed. More empty motel rooms stale with past filthy souls. His included.

But it was done and that was good. He thought of the panther's momentary freedom. This gave Strake a smile. Still, it was not over. Only contained. For the moment. Leaving had been sort of simple. Coming home was not easy for him. It never had been.

THE GOVERNOR'S NIECE

PART III

"... I went out into the crooked street again."

Dashiell Hammett,
"Corkscrew"

New York, it had wasted him. His drive back to Georgia cleared some of his head. Only some. The rest of his mind was gray. His eyes blurred in and out of clear sight. What was left of him? A stinging body. Accumulating weapons in the trunk. Turning into the thing he was supposed to be fighting, nihilism. A town he didn't want to return to. Murdered son and daughter-in-law. Missing, likely dead, ex-wife whose ties to the suits started it all. Home was a terrible place, full of hornets. His job an absorption of atrocity.

Sheriff. He had looked up the word once on a bored afternoon: from "shire" and "reeve" under King Alfred. Before 1066 and the Norman Conquest. Shire-reeve. Evolving verbally to *sheriff.* His curiosity led him to also look up the roots of "shire": *scīr* which was Old English for "office" and *scīra* from Old High German . . . "care." A sort of care of the office.

Mundanely, office work. But the *care* stuck with him. He did care for his town that no longer had a center after the ravagement of The Nihilistics. Three of them came in the bank and killed four. Then the three themselves died in odd ways. How did you shake such an image? Somehow he ended up in the Bronx picking off the suits, becoming a bit nihilistic himself. Even keeping the weapons of the three killers.

He kept thinking about his evolution. Moreover an acceptance that he was pretty much the same as all killers. Doubtful he was evolving. Just realizing the truth about himself. Part of him wondered why he had gone to New York. Had it really been to avenge something? Or to escape another thing? Perhaps both. There was always that both yanking you in half. Never just a sole thing that made somebody act.

Whatever little mafia the body of suits thought they had was now like a dead bull filled with darts. Dragged on its thick side from the arena. He drove to the office, first thing, expecting a pile of the worst. It was the opposite: nothing had happened while he was gone. Envelopes of mail tilted in a tower stack like big saltine crackers. There didn't seem to be anything urgent. Office care. Zzzzzzz. He was focused on his desk and whether or not he should sit and conquer the pile when he heard a rustling. Maude? His pet hen. Deeply neglected in his absence.

Meyer had been looking after her, as he always did when Strake traveled, sometimes leaving her to wander the sheriff's office and just coming over from the coroner's to feed her corn pellets, assuming his human abattoir might not be the most fitting spot for a chicken.

But . . . no Maude. Hmmm. His vision had been blurred by the violence in the Bronx. His eyes were not always hurt but they were not clear either. In that moment they seemed to notice gray smudges. Then they were better, a bumped film camera that had to have its lens refocused. A young lady was leaning against the bars of the small jail cell. He knew the face; it was familiar. Yet he couldn't pinpoint it. A newspaper article? Had she been in New York? Very possible.

The Bronx had been an annihilation. A battle of the dead, one suit after the other dropping. That house up there, the butchering. Not usually prone to terrible flashbacks, Strake was having them now. Violence to him was almost a casual avocation. His nerves rarely suffered. This trip had been different though. His body fiercely ached, especially his neck. Parts of his shoulders creaked and his elbows popped.

Several times in a day he found himself lost in a daze for a few minutes, staring with his mouth open at a white screen of death blotches, every kill he had ever sniped. This reel played in vivid blood, reminders of each shot, every forehead explosively yanked to die quick. He could not stop thinking about the panther. A moment of freedom on a city street. What a sight! He doubted he would ever have amnesty, not even a moment of it. One of his kill films strobed in front of his eyes right now.

It slowly ceased and there she was. Her sharp face had appeared. Eyes wide and green and not leaving his. The blood movie dimmed her for a minute. Then he could see her. She was a blond diamond. He was slow to speak. She was fine to wait and to keep his stare. Who are you, he thought? Were you following me up there? "I do know you," he said aloud.

"Do you?"

"I think so."

"Keep thinking." Her look, it made him feel golden. For a moment he thought of a short-lived television show called *N.Y.P.D.* and this wavy blond actress Gretchen Corbett. She was on one episode some time in 1968 and he remembered the character's name: Darlene Welby. The episode was called: "Case of the Shady Lady."

"Strake?"

"Yeah, I'm him."

"This is my third time here."

"I was . . ."

"We know."

"Ah! You're Cafflee's niece."

Cafflee was the Georgia governor.

"What gave me away?"

"Aren't you a reporter? I think I saw your photo once or twice in an Atlanta paper."

"I have reported, yes, mostly as cover."

"No longer?"

"Well, I took some time off to work on a book."

"A novel?"

"Possibly."

"What's it about?"

She looked away for a moment, at the ground, around the office.

"Oh come on . . ." he scoffed.

"I have been researching you a bit for my uncle."

"I don't really want to revisit all that."

"Seems to me like you've become one of The Nihilistics yourself?"

He looked at her, having just thought the same thing not an hour ago.

"Wait, how would you know?"

"Like I said, government research."

"What do you mean?"

She shrugged.

"Did Cafflee tail me to New York?"

She turned up her hands in front of her, lifted her shoulders in a coy gesture. Adam Cafflee. State senator straight to governor. He was older than Strake, a young man who went gray fast then lost his hair over a recidivist druggie son hidden in prep schools around the world.

Why did all these rich people have such idiotic progeny? It seemed like the curse of lucre and power. Strake knew little about the son and was afraid to ask. The governor's brother was Douglas and this was his daughter. What was her name? Ella? No. It would come to him.

"My uncle needs you, yes. He's gotten himself involved in some unfixable stupid intricacy and isn't safe at the moment. He did ask me to come here. That's part one."

"And part two?"

"I get to come along and write the book about you."

"Come along? Where?"

"Wherever, I guess."

Flirt.

"Nothing is happening here for you. Come on, look at the dust on your mail. The Nihilistics destroyed your town. There's nothing here anymore. It's dead. And you will be too if you stay."

He sighed. Sat one leg on the corner of his desk and folded his arms.

"I'm sorry about your family," she said. "I am. Uncle Adam knows you don't like him much. He thought I might be more persuasive."

Strake rolled his eyes. "What's he mixed up in?"

"You'll have to go to Atlanta to talk to him."

"With you, I expect."

"Yes, with me. I'll be driving you."

"And writing my bio."

"Or novel. We'll see if you're interesting enough."

"You're not *really* a reporter, are you?"

"I trained like you, in a way, at a place in Virginia whose acronym I cannot tell you but one that you obviously know."

Strake smiled. You little spy, he thought, acting the soubrette. "And why me?"

"Because you have a pet chicken? I think you know why."

"Bad?"

"It is. Connects even higher than state government. Starts here, yes, and there is a lot for you and me to handle with Uncle Adam, but that's just stanching blood to a gushing artery. It's a corporeal mess. Someone vivisected the body politic. Family stuff hasn't helped either."

"I prefer a stoic narrative with fewer extended metaphors like that one."

"We'll focus on Georgia first before the hemorrhaging floods the state."

"When do we leave? The metaphors, I mean."

She hid her lips in her mouth to avoid smiling, then said: "I so rarely get to use them."

"That's probably a good thing."

"Car's running."

"Ava." He pointed his finger like a gun. That was it.

"Right. Only took you twenty minutes."

Outside he asked if he could go see Meyer real quick. She leaned against the black car. In her black suit reflecting almost purple in the sun. Fine blond hair, a splash of green eyes that stared at you just a little more than normal, maybe not to cause discomfort because she was merely curious but you felt the extra seconds of staring anyway.

There was Maude pecking on top of the chest of a man's pale dead body. Meyer appeared. "Strake!"

"Hey buddy."

"You're back."

"I was."

"Off again?"

"Keep by your phone for me. I'll call you later with more details. Cafflee's leaning on me."

"I bet he is. You may not be able to help. Atlanta's in trouble."

"What do you know?"

"I hear his son has caused a real mess, but don't quote me on that."

"I thought the kid lived abroad."

"He did. That was some time ago."

"I don't know much about him," Strake admitted.

"No one does. I think he was in jail in Switzerland at one point. Only rumors though."

"Switzerland?"

"After that I never heard much scuttlebutt about him."

"Just kind of dropped off the radar, I guess."

"Astounding what you can censor when you have money," Meyer quipped.

"So you think it ties all back to the son?"

"Can't say for sure. We have other things to worry about anyway, Strake." Meyer nodded toward the table. Strake leaned over and lifted Maude in his arms. She purred. The hen who was a cat. He looked down at an egg on the stomach of male cadaver. It took him a second to notice the face.

Meyer: "I was about to tell you."

"Shit, that's Neaves." His sheriff friend he'd known since high school.

"Yeah, sorry."

"What happened?"

"Well, that's the thing. I came in here yesterday morning and he was just lying on the table."

"Dead? Just lying there?"

"And I doubt he preemptively decided to get a jump on his autopsy, if you know what I mean."

"Oh boy. Someone brought him there then?"

"I think it was the suits," Meyer offered.

"I hope not. I took care of them. I have to go. I'll call you later."

"Give me some time. I still need to figure out what happened."

"I don't see any bullet holes."

"Me either. I'll look into it. Get going."

Before he knew it his body was a moving warp in the passenger seat with a slender stranger whose cute face never moved. She might have been voluptuous had she not seemed so hollow. All the beautiful flowers have poison, he thought. He could smell no perfume. There was the absence of something. The only time she animated was when she had a motive, in this case to ask him questions about the book. He would get sucked in by her allure only to realize he was spilling information he shouldn't about the Bronx, Vietnam, his town after The Nihilistics murdered four people at the bank. Then he would silence himself and turn the questions back to her.

"How is Doug? I always liked your dad."

"Dad's mixed up in this too. Not so innocent as we thought."

"Really? I thought he avoided politics."

Doug was an art magazine editor in Athens.

"He certainly tried."

"And you. Are you mixed up in whatever 'this' is?"

"I'm still on the outside. For the most part. I kept my distance."

"But aren't you on the inside now?" he asked her.

"Maybe. I don't know. It's hard to tell anymore."

In her tone he heard perhaps a gloom she wanted to hide. He also sensed attraction within both of them. The interior of the warm car was erotic. Governor Cafflee was maybe trying to distract him. He stared ahead like her, but it was hard. Sometimes he had to turn and look at her profile, a perfect little nose with almost invisible freckles. She was young, too young to be involved in it. He knew that she felt him staring at her face. Ava Cafflee. Exotic disaster? Gorgeous distraction?

Her uncle could have sent anyone. Why her? Man, and I had just gotten home too. And Neaves on top of it. He wanted to scream. Adam Cafflee was not a tall man. One might assume his wrecked appearance contributed to his rise in government, for his slouch and balding head with sprigs of moist ashen hair strands often put folks at ease. He was like everyone else. Sure he was. The guy was a sketchball.

He had climbed the staircase of Georgia leadership rather quickly to Strake's bewilderment. And the higher he rose, the less pretty he became. Some men evolved into gnomes as they aged.

Most men. What bothered Strake was that he had no choice because if Cafflee needed him, it was assumed the sheriff would help. But "help" was always a convolution, an inconvenience. These were not philanthropic people. They were, rather, silky mercenaries. Strake was what he was. He accepted his wasness.

Politicians were television screens though. They were not what they were. In a government plexus was a market of chicanery. Strake knew it well. He tried to stay outside of it, never fooling himself that he was still in it. Strake's help was an assumption from his Vietnam days when he had agreed to always be on standby for his government. However, that was a federal deal. So Cafflee must have pilfered a favor to have the sheriff come in at the state level. Now he was in the governor's office which looked like the man's wife had swallowed (and regurgitated) a coffee table book on baroque design with curvy white sculptures of cherubs and one Medusa that ripped off Bernini. The furniture seemed to upchuck Versailles.

Oddly enough, in that moment, as Strake thought of stomach ejecta comparisons to art and architecture, his guts rose from his belly and sprayed across the governor's desk like a putrid net capturing an animal.

Ava, to her credit, kept her stoic face immobile, not even a smirk. Her blank robot affect. Strake made a note of it. Good in violent moments to keep her cool but not so much for daily life where emotions were needed. Adam surveyed Strake's fetid liquid mess spreading over likely crucial documents. "Damn Strake. Let's get you off the smack first."

"It got away from me. I'm sorry."

"Can you do it?"

"Not sure. What did you have in mind?"

"We have a room for you here."

"In the mansion?"

"Yes. A guarded room."

"Let me guess. The plan is for me to stay in the room and not leave."

"Your extra sensory perception has given you the answer again."

"And after?" Strake asked.

"After . . ." said the governor with a malicious rictus, "we need to sit down and for you to not spew lunch on my desk."

"We'll keep an eye on you, feed you," added Ava. "There's a doctor here."

"Let the rehab begin," Strake said. "Didn't mean to make a mess."

"I know you, Strake. I also need you. I can't have you sick. Maybe you can handle it when you decide to go all renegado like you did up in New York. Maybe not. You look like some splattery manure that gushed out of a heifer's ass. How you're still walking is beyond me. Ava, can you get someone to clean up this delicacy Strake here left on my papers?"

"I see you still have no taste in sculpture," Strake said, contemplating the white statues.

"Ha ha!" Adam hooted, shooting up from his desk and finally standing to come over to the sheriff. "Yeah, these oversized marble carbuncles. My wife went to Italy then came back and bought them at some tourist place off a Georgia highway thinking no one would know the difference. Bad, right?"

Strake stifled a laugh and refrained from agreeing, but the agreement was all in the stifling.

"I missed you, Strake. But we need to get you better. Now, I don't want to force you, but think of it as a little vacation from the pain. Once you're better we'll find some new pain for you."

"Aw, how can I say no?" He batted his eyes.

"You can't."

"I figured. I guess I could use a break. Where's my room?"

Ava had returned with a maid who grimaced at the stench on the governor's desk, holding back a gag as she tried cleaning it, to little avail.

"Come on," Ava said, and she touched her hand on his back.

A strange frisson spread like warm water over his skin. Or more like heroin in his skin. He knew she knew it too. Maybe not a robot after all.

"I'll explain the job later," Adam told him as he left the room.

"Your son?"

"Later, Strake, later."

"Your brother too?"

The man jumped up with piercing eyes.

"Later then." Strake lifted a hand behind him in a weak wave and didn't look back at the governor again.

"Impressive work there," she said, walking in front.

He stared at her bottom. "Indeed," was his reply. Her head turned and caught his lecherous glance. Had she wanted him to look? In the hallway they meandered then stepped down flights of stairs with more halls leading to an elevator. Until he found himself in front of a door with two bloated security dolts who grunted at him in unison. They appeared to be made of red meat. Their ripe cologne and cigar smoke battled under Strake's nostrils.

"Hey guys. You two must be Mickey and Goofy."

A humorless silence was their collective response.

"You two make me laugh."

Not even eye blinks.

"Okay, I'll edit my material if you two work on smelling better."

Ava smirked and followed him into the room. "This won't be easy, but we need you to dry out fast as you can. We need it to stick; it can't be rushed."

"Are you sure I'm not just a prisoner?"

"Who knows?"

"Why take the time to help me?"

"Adam has always liked you. He's a little obsessed with you even. He also *can't use* you if you're, well . . . the desk."

"That was unfortunate. Unless of course I did it on purpose. I've always wanted to throw up on the government. I feel bad for the maid though."

"He's known about your heroin for some time. It's been an accepted response after your time during the war. We know you've dried out a few times on your own, only to return to the addiction."

"You sure know a lot about me."

"You may think you've had freedom to kill like you have, but you've been watched in a scrutinous way the whole time."

"I figured. Just was waiting for it to catch up to me. I guess this favor for your uncle is my comeuppance."

"You'll still be helping."

"No one can help the government," he said. "I smell something rotten."

"Something *is* rotten."

Strake sat on the edge of the bed in a room decorated in quasi-baroque like the upstairs office.

He covered his face with his hands. The space darkened for a moment.

"You all right?" she asked.

"I'm all right. The coroner had a close friend of mine on the table when I went in to talk to him."

"I'm sorry."

He removed his hands and looked at her. She could tell he wasn't good. He felt bloodshot.

"Try to rest for a few days, to start."

"I've done this before. I know what's ahead."

"Except this will be longer. Can I help?"

"Just drop by for a talk when you want."

"I can do that," she said, but he knew she wouldn't. Even so, there was something electric in her words that made him feel better.

"Good."

"The door, we have to lock it from the outside."

"I know."

"We'll make it as easy as we can."

He gazed up at her and blinked for a long moment. His eyes burned. They opened again so he could look at her.

"Okay." He nodded. He would give himself a month. Although with the current rigor, he knew it could be done in less time. Ten days. Maybe the governor knew this from the doctor and was counting on it. The first few days were always a stunning slam to the body, fists to the face, teeth crunching. He had done it before in a week but then he was back at it, never fully healed. He might give himself more time now. Two weeks could solidify him. A month . . . he doubted he had the luxury.

What bothered him was that he would be back to the killing. He was certain that's what Adam needed. Even if it wasn't direct murder, he sensed death had to be involved. A past killing needing to be researched and rectified? As his body floated in days of visceral pain and uneaten food rolled in on carts bright with silver covers, he wondered what the governor needed. Usually, a client hired you with a clear purpose. Nothing was clear at the moment. He was sure the governor had killed someone or that he wanted someone eliminated. It couldn't be anything else unless it was to cover up a past crime.

Toxic shit oozed from him; his eyes dripped glue. Or he thought they dripped. Gushing eyes. Of course the bad dreams came, recapitulations of his own murders in the Bronx, how he barely justified them, knew that they were wrong, his vigilantism no better than the Bald Drifter, whose gun was still in his car along with the hatchet and the horse bone knife of the two others. Along the way Strake had become a Nihilistic. With the realization that, in truth, he had been one long before that. Amazing what you could get away with when you were on the right side. Hell, he was even encouraged. Look where he was now, called up to do some nasty work.

Here was something: what if Governor Cafflee had *not* talked to the feds, the ones who typically called on him to do this kind of work? What if the governor didn't have approval to use him? He should have asked, but Strake had a suspicion that this was the case. In his mind was a steel filter gushing violence through him. He was a man who happened to be insouciant about killing. On a normal level this disassociation made him a quasi-psychopath. But what was a **normal** level? Had he ever been on one? If you were already nuts there was no more crazy to go to, right?

Even the pain he would feel for the next couple of weeks numbed him with indifference. His body hurt, sure, because it never stopped hurting. It ached to walk so he sat on the floor with his forehead leaning on his kneecaps. Filmic memories of his personal wars clicked in slow frames yawning as if his eyes were two backward projectors beaming images of killing light onto his brain. A forced detox just to clean him up for the next deaths. What was the point?

Couldn't quit a purgatorial job. A gun would be in his hands forever. He was never removed from it. He didn't eat much. To eat was to be sick. Better to wait. He then lay on the floor facing up and gazing at the ceiling. Blank, nothing. Images shot backward from his eyes. They were slow yawns forcing him to stare. Or think. He saw Hanh. Wait, Hanh, wasn't he supposed to meet her at the airport in New York? Did she ever make it? Did he forget to get her? Was it Hanh who was supposed to come? Or did he just wish that it was because he missed her? Many questions. All, of course, with no answers.

Random facts surfaced, from where he didn't know. Heroin, popularized 1898. Queen Victoria died 1901. Mostly Strake knew that he never wanted to die. It was, then, an assumption that everything else would be fairly easy. But was he . . . happy? Yes, he loved killing bad individuals. He had to admit that. He liked killing for the right reasons. He also could not even think of killing for the wrong ones. It never occurred to him. Inside him was something moral. Just didn't feel very moral when you were sawing up men in suits and throwing them into a furnace. He shuddered.

Yes, that was ugly up there in the Bronx. To be a Nihilistic it seemed that you had to kill for the wrong reasons. And he never did that. Then again, he also made many assumptions about whom to kill in New York. Were all of them right? He wasn't certain. Only he could be happy lying on a floor with a graphic murder movie playing behind his face, realizing The Nihilistics were very different from him. They, however, had been seeking fun in random deaths. Where was the line though? Sniping innocent men in the war? He justified himself all the time.

Never questioned whether what he did was wrong. He hated no one. Not even the suits. It was office work. Vomit shot straight up from his mouth like a geyser and splashed right back down on his face. He wiped his eyes, blinked out the stinging bile. Sat up. Creaked to standing. Walked to the bathroom. Washed his face with cold water. In the mirror: a wrinkled man.

"Sloppy," he mumbled.

He tilted his head to the left. The duplicate of his face moved. Yes, he was alive. Sort of. He leaned his nose to touch his nose, crossing his eyes. What was the Strake clone in the reflection thinking?

Days rolled in and out like the carts of more uneaten food brought by the security men. Soon he might be healed. But it was only part one, the set-up. Man comes home from killing binge. Man gets off drugs. Man goes back on another killing binge. The conflict was around the corner. The resolution never likely.

He needed a plan inside the plan they had for him. An anti-plan, as it were. The governor would tell him what to do. He would find a way to appear to do it while not actually doing it. First, he had to know what was asked. Already he knew there was something strange. He was never called up unless the wrongness was so layered that no one could ever slice through it. And what about his father? He hadn't even visited him after coming home.

The image of Neaves on the coroner's table with Maude's egg on him. Had the suits come after his friend? No way. No time. They were mopping up the bloodbath Strake had delivered. He had reduced their numbers. Nevertheless, they had connections in his town. No, paranoid. Stop it.

Neaves had to be separate. Maybe a message but not likely. Another mystery to contemplate, the timing of which did seem parallel to suits revenging themselves on him. Up in the air. Could be suit-related. Possibly not. He couldn't think about it right now. Another enigma was knotted in his forward future. Let's think about this. The governor needs you. He sends his beautiful niece. One, who, incidentally, wants to write a book about you, inflating your ego as a diversion. She takes you to the governor. Her uncle. Tells you along the way that there is a political mess you need to scour clean. She gives you just enough information but nothing more. Nothing really specific. They provide a detox room for you. They need you. For something ugly.

Soon they will tell you what that is. By healing you, they will feel you owe them this favor, which likely will involve killing one or more people to get them out of the way. Strake shook his head to the left and right quickly, trying to jostle these ideas. Or . . . they're just hiding you, keeping you from doing anything. Not entirely unlikely. Weeks passed, maybe a month.

He had never been so sick. His body frame shed pounds, maybe thirty, when he was down to his worst. All day he tried to do pushups, starting with ten, now up to a hundred. He ate omelets at first from the cart. Soon he added the turkey sandwiches and cheeseburgers. He requested blueberry milkshakes and they made them. Every day he drank two or three shakes and the cold fruity milkiness made him feel better. The pushups increased in indirect proportion to the vomiting's decrease. More food came into his body. He gained back weight.

An appetite returned and made him not ignore the food cart. Screaming when the rage smacked him. He added black coffee and croissants and chocolate muffins. He stopped lying on the floor when he slept and found comfort under the covers of the bed. It was a rich man's detox. He needed to make it stick. He hated heroin and the blissful love it falsely gave him. Strake wondered how he had allowed this stupid weakness in his life. It didn't help that everything was lost. That as soon as he had healed over one killing, he had killed again. And again. How many? No idea. Triple digits for sure.

Some nights he dreamed of a mass grave. Two large bald men stood at the top of the crater heaving bodies by swinging their arms and legs. Strake was at the bottom of the abyss, looking up as the men toyed with him, swinging the bodies but not letting them go. Once they did, the corpse would land fully on him, jolt him awake. The dream recurred. The grave filled.

One morning he found himself back on a normal schedule, not perspiring through the dark nights as much, eager to pour coffee and sink his teeth into a chocolate muffin. Was he better? This was a heroin delusion, sort of like a false peak on a mountain where you think you've made it to the top, only to have another incline to scale when you feel your worst.

The heroin false peak. Sure enough he retched and barely made it to the toilet. But he would go higher, in the right way this time. It was an expected setback. He needed another week.

One morning the governor's niece came to talk to him. The doctor had been mapping his progress. "You should be ready soon."

"I think so."

"We'll try my uncle's office again for a meeting in three days."

"I'm sure I'm not gonna like it."

"No, you most likely won't."

"Why don't you tell me some more?"

"I can't, Strake."

"Can I at least ask you to look into a couple of things?"

"Sure, what?"

"Neaves' death, for one. He just appeared on Meyer's table, dead, no gunshots. I didn't have time to look into it because I was leaving with you."

She looked uncomfortable. "Okay, anything else?"

"Yeah, my father. Also didn't have time to check on him."

"Will do. That all?"

"Not quite. I was with a woman in Vietnam. Her name is Hanh. During my spree in New York, I was hallucinating and thought I had to meet here at JFK. But I'm not sure. I'm worried she may have come and that I didn't pick her up."

"We'll look into it."

"Thank you."

"Take a few days and enjoy the plush service."

"I will."

"You look so much better," she said, formal.

"Do I?"

"Yes . . . you do." This time, more girlish.

He and Ava took in each other's warmth in an unspoken way, lingering close to each other for more than was probably allowed. Then, wordless, she left.

The question was: am I being cured and prepared for some mission bloodbath or simply being locked up so I don't go off on my own again? The governor was certainly controlling him. Cafflee. What was he up to? And was Ava already writing about him? One wondered. In the timeline of him there were empty places. How was his dad? What happened to Neaves? Was his father in trouble? Would Ava look into these things? Doubtful.

Wait, was that wise, mentioning his father and Hanh? Maybe not. There was a shelf of books in his rehab room and he grabbed a dictionary to look up the word "mystery" and its etymology. "Mystic" was one origin. From the Greek "musterion". Something hidden. That made sense. The hidden needing to be found. What did *he* need to find?

One, what was the status of the suits? Two, who killed Neaves? Three, was his father okay? Four, had Hanh come to the airport? Let's see, he thought, riffling through pages to the back with foreign words. "Tego" was Latin meaning to cover or protect. Tegere, texi, tectus. Ah, to protect. Tectus. This seemed a more likely definition in the governor's mansion. By the laws of simplicity it was probably the governor, his son, his brother. Or his brother's daughter, Ava. The governor's niece. Or the four together. Now, if he could only figure out what the crime was they were protecting. Or covering. Or hiding. Man, I'm solving a felony that may not even exist. He had it narrowed down to four people and trusted none of them. Didn't even know the son.

Wait. Memories of a vanishing man came to Strake.

A car under a Georgia highway bridge five years ago.

Yes, that's right.

Strake's father had investigated.

The young man who owned the car had gone to Cafflee's high school. This came up because Cafflee, who was not governor at the time but on the rise, visited the sheriff office personally to see if there was any progress. Apparently, the young man was Adam's friend. Apparently. Now, this was interesting and why did Strake only just remember it? Well, he had had a lot of time to think of connections between him and Cafflee. And this was one of them. Could be nothing. Could be something though. He needed to talk to his father. They didn't let him use a phone here.

Around 1:00 a.m. Strake opened his eyes looking up at the ceiling in the dark. He couldn't leave through the guarded door. The windows were nailed shut. It was too high to jump. Whoever had killed Neaves might be after his dad though. With a little system he had been removing sealant in each pane a bit with his pocket knife after his arrival. At first it gave him something to do as the poison dripped out of his skin. Then it became his sole escape idea, if it came to that. After Ava's visit earlier, he knew it had to be this night.

He could hear their voices outside the door, so that meant they knew the small noises he made too. He carefully removed the nine glass pane sections and hid them stacked under an armchair. No more tic-tac-toe with his fingertip on the moist glass in the mornings. After he removed them, which took over an hour, especially since he had to remain quiet, there was just the frame.

With the dry rot it was no problem to push them. The key was not to make a single noise. He sweated as he removed the splintered window pieces and slid them under the ottoman in front of the chair.

He was on the second floor. A problem. A very tall bald cypress tree was his good luck, but it was six feet away from the top. This meant he had to stand on the ledge and somehow jump. Either way he would land *somewhere* on it. And it would sting and hurt. He stood on the ledge. There was no good way to gain momentum. Move Strake! He squatted a little then lunged. But his toe caught on the ledge and he was upside down, his face aiming for the middle. Maybe better anyway for a softer landing. He closed his eyes and braced himself for a concussion, throwing his hands above his head as he nosedived. Blow after blow was like a whip strike on his cheekbones, but he was in the tree and grasping at wood covered with sap that stuck to his palms. He sat on a limb, inhaled a breath. Let it out. Looked up toward the house. Noiseless. He had turned off his room lights so no one noticed the missing window frame. As he shimmied down the branches he kept looking up at the mansion. How would he get back into his room?

It wouldn't be necessary. He couldn't stay there anymore, who was he kidding? Now that his body and mind were clean, he no longer needed them. They needed him though. Would come after him. But he had to see his father first. That young man's missing car under the bridge, his complete disappearance stank of the suits, a job they might do. And the suits had been around forever. They multiplied and bit like fleas.

On the ground he stood, his hands sticky from sap, his face scratched and in pain. He had twisted an ankle on his left foot and a knee on his right leg, but they were minor sprains. Still, he had a little limp. His next part of the plan was simple: find a ride. The affluent street area around the mansion was empty of vehicles. So he hoofed it. He thought of walking over fields during the war, which had never seemed difficult. He was only a few hours from his town. Maybe a bus? But not likely this late.

Strake moved through rich streets with colonial mansions and magnolia trees, lawyers, dentists, doctors, senators. He liked the dark and thought of the noir novels his father gave him as a boy as "the only truth" he would ever need to read. So that was it, the young man's car under the bridge. The governor had something to do with the disappearance and likely brought Strake here to see what he knew. Who was that young man? He couldn't remember his name. But, yes, the body never appeared. Just the car under the bridge. All this time later, could that be the reason? Preventative? Keep Strake close in case he knew something?

More worrisome was that his father definitely knew the case. Had they brought Strake to the mansion to take care of his dad? Walking in the dark was quiet, in this neighborhood at least. Soon he was somewhere different, on back streets that did not look safe. He found himself walking behind a tall black man. Who turned and pulled out a gun, then saw Strake and lowered it, continuing to walk on until he was gone in a side alley. The smell from garbage was thick with nauseous odor.

A horsefly buzzed around his ears, revealed under a street light when Strake snatched it in his hand and squished it in his palm. Gross. He wiped it on a lamp post, still trying to figure out how to get the cypress sap off him. More black men and women appeared and stared at him as he passed a neon Chinese take-out, closed but with many standing in front of it. Steam rose from a manhole cover, hell miasma. No one bothered him. Strake was not the kind of man you messed with at 3:00 in the morning and they seemed to know it. He could have asked for a ride, but he wanted to walk. For the moment. He had felt trapped in his room, wanting to stretch his legs.

However, he needed to get home before the governor's men came after him, which would be soon, right around when they dropped breakfast for him, around 7:00 a.m. "Hey," he chanced, asking a random man who was smoking a Lucky Strike.

"Yeah?"

"Can you give me a ride?"

"Yeah, yeah, sure, lemme just get my limo." Sarcastic quip, a stranger who feared nothing. The brown eyes of the tall man were not kind. He somehow blew cigarette smoke out the side of his mouth while making it shoot upward. This, with more smoke rocketing down his nose.

Strake handed him a hundred. "Few hours drive."

"Yeah, then I have to come back." He and several other men chuckled at what he said.

Another hundred was held up. "I'll give you this when we get there."

"It ain't a limo."

"What is it then?"

"What it is, is not a limo."

"I see."

"Around the cornuh."

They walked together. The riddler smoked and assumed Strake was legit with the cash. Strake knew the man wouldn't mug him. Or would he?

They arrived at a jacked up Nova whose bright yellow paint glistened even under the dim street lights. Strake nodded in appreciation.

"Where to?" the man asked.

Strake's teeth made a rare appearance in a smile.

"Close to Athens."

"Got a stop to make first," the man said, "on the way."

"Sure."

Strake looked behind him. He didn't trust the two guards at the mansion. Somehow he felt their presence even though they might not be following him.

"Running from something?"

"Something, yes. But I prefer walking."

"Hah. Yeah, you don't want to be running around here."

A police car blooped its siren and could be heard in the distance, maybe a few blocks off.

"So they after you?"

"Not yet . . . maybe."

They were in the ride now. It was smooth and fast even when it moved slow. In about ten minutes his new friend parked in front of a cinderblock hut with metallic jazz blasting out the windows and men and women falling drunk over each other amid the musical frenzy. "Come on in!"

Strake stood, bumped into him for a reason and followed the man as the sweet smell of booze and sex sprayed on him like cologne when they were inside. He was the only white man. A piano player in a suit and insane hat, my god, was that Thelonious Monk?? He slammed his fingers down on the keys like he was hitting them. Wait, no. Art Blakey behind him on drums. Strake's eyes had to be blurry. He knew about the Monk trio and had seen him once with his father many years back. So, would that be Gary Mapp on bass then? What was this place? It was Atlanta after all but the dive looked like one that fell into a pool of empty water and broken concrete.

Chicken and hot dogs and cheeseburgers flew around on trays that looked like flying saucers. The waitresses were tall and nearly naked in black one-piece swimsuits and bikinis, their arms rising above the heads of working men in overalls and bald men in cheap suits. A cheeseburger fell off a plate and was about to hit the floor when he snatched it and sunk his mouth into the bread, meat and cheddar cheese that oozed down the sides of his lips.

Painted directly on the walls was an orgiastic melee of bodies dancing. It almost looked as if the people in front of the mural had come alive from the art, carnal dalliances surrounding him. Arms and legs and brass. Maybe by the end of the night the dancers would turn back into art.

The man who was driving him, whose name he didn't want to know (and vice versa), was up near the bandstand simply watching Monk play and dance around the piano. At first Strake thought this might be the sole errand, to see the trio, but then he saw the man meet another guy. Figured as much. That new guy stared back at Strake and he knew he had to leave. They were on to him. What a shame. Thelonious Monk, damn. I will forever be on the run or running after someone. Never anything in between.

He made his way outside, still enjoying his juicy burger. A large woman with hair like a clown balloon stumbled out right after him and disgorged her liquor on the cinderblock wall. A gnarled mutt in his dog-eighties limped over and slurped on it. Strake moved back to the car. His earlier "accidental" bump had been preemptive, as he assumed this very thing might happen.

At the Nova he found the pickpocketed keys and unlocked the door. Soon the two men would be on his tail and the car was too bright yellow to be discreet. He had to roll and roll fast. It would not start in a subtle way, as it was a loud engine, but he was as cool as he could be, standing out as the only white man for miles. He should have realized they would notice him. Had gotten too caught up in the jazz. He eased away and didn't see the men come out of the building.

He had to find his way to his town without a map until the shops opened later. Strake always had stores of cash that he never knew what to do with, from the sniper jobs. Piles of money in the bank where his son and daughter-in-law had worked. He always wore a money belt filled with hundreds. Most of his pants had bills in the pockets. So he was never without walking-around money, which served him well.

The tank was full. He opened the glove and saw what he needed to see. He floored the pedal. As he meandered around and got lost, also hoping to lose anyone behind him, he finally found 78 going east and aimed for the signs to Athens. All of it seemed fine until around 4:00 a.m. when he could see a car with two silver eyes for headlights staring at him, the vehicle rising. With the Nova's gas pedal depressed, he still couldn't lose them. It had to be the owner of the car with some friends.

There was a small chance it was the governor's guards. Doubtful. And the suits were always in the back of his mind. It was possible. They had ways of knowing what you never expected, like his time at the mansion. Maybe they knew. Maybe they had him surveilled the whole time. Were the two guards possible suits? Paranoid thoughts blinded him to the current moment. It was amazing how your distracted mind could lose sight of what it needed to do.

In a moment Strake opened the glove, grabbed the pistol, slammed on his brakes and a scream of a long skid burned rubber in his nose as he stopped, opened the door and rolled out fast on the pavement with a thud. The unsuspecting car behind him crashed into the bumper sending the four men inside lunging forward, the front passenger's head popping through the glass, severing his throat that bled over the glass shards like bourbon over ice.

Strake aimed and fired at the owner of the Nova, now standing and screaming about his car but not for long as a bullet sunk right into the tip of his nose and killed him quick, while two bald fat men in pink tuxedos and frilly white shirts (from the Monk crowd) emerged from in the back seat and walked down the highway with shotguns firing at Strake.

He aimed bullets at their stomachs. They kept cocking and firing as their white shirts pooled with blood. Soon they fell forward dropping their guns and Strake ran over to finish them off with close bullets to the foreheads. Both cars were useless now.

He dragged his friend back to the yellow Nova and set him in the driver's seat. Walking back over to the carnage, he stared down at the collective eight hundred pounds of dead men on the road and simply said, "Nope." Not putting them back in the car. He took a moment to look at the fourth man, the one whose head was gushing in the windshield. He wiped the pistol and just tossed it on the road by the two fat men, about fifty feet away. Then he started walking. The sun would come soon. He still had the dusk of early dawn to give him a little more darkness. It was a quiet part of the road but soon there would be cars at some point. He needed to hustle.

How many highways like this one had he ended up on by himself in the middle of the night with dead bodies in his wake? He walked faster. But he didn't run. What was the hurry? For about an hour it was calm and he made progress, distancing himself from the scene back there. He just needed a pay phone to talk to his dad. To see if he had been harmed. It only cost a dime. No phones in sight though.

Strake noticed a field ahead. There were about thirty tents with cars and trucks and vans surrounding them. It looked like bad news. A stench of feces came with the camp that had a viral air. Just a sense. Something felt sour. Definitely not right.

The smell was rancid, the people kind of oddly feral. What was going on here? A shirtless young man in jeans and a baseball cap with the Braves on it stood by a dark-haired teenage girl in khaki shorts sending fireworks horizontal, not up. The light streaked through the tents as if he were trying to catch them on fire. Pink, purple and yellow lines crisscrossed from his hand as he lit them and held the wicks to fire. They noticed Strake; he didn't deter them.

The sheriff approached. Even in the blurred morning that was still night, he could tell they were junkies, possibly living in their cars. Somehow you always knew. The young man finished his fireworks show and nodded. The girl stared. She was Mexican. So was he. Strake saw the emaciation of his naked torso and poked arms, a trail of holes making a path up to his shoulder. He was a boy, maybe fifteen. From his back pocket he seemed to reach for another firework but held up a needle to Strake. Kind of a firework after all.

A shiver spread through his body. He was as clean as he could ever be after his forced rehab. He needed to stay like that. He indicated no, closing his eyes and moving his head three times to the left and three to the right, counting to remember that he could refuse.

The boy shrugged. "You need a ride?"

"I do," Strake said.

"Got any money?"

Strake found a hundred and held it up with his index finger and thumb.

"Okay," the boy said, turning to the girl who walked over to a tent and unzipped it and disappeared inside.

The car was a white 1966 Mercury Comet Cyclone, two-door. They bumped over the field back onto the highway. Strake gave him the name of his town. They passed through Athens.

The two talked about the Braves and their move from Milwaukee in 1966. The boy had gone to some games with his father before the man had to return to Mexico. He and the girl worked in Georgia and North Carolina turkey factories gutting the birds.

Soon he was in his town and happy to be there. He gave him the hundred and the boy saluted with it, then he was gone, driving slowly. Strake stared at his father's house. Breathed. And went to the door. He'd been remiss in not visiting him when he was back from New York, but had there even been time? Ava appeared at the office and swooped him off, perhaps to keep him from seeing Strake Senior. Too many things were coincident (or just repetitions): coming home, intercepted at the office, the murder of Neaves, leaving before he could deal with any of it.

Ava. Full of omissions. She would be here soon enough. He hesitated at the door. Did he want to see what was inside? His father would know about the empty car and missing body. Wasn't Strake putting too much on his dad though? Couldn't he just find out this information with a little asking around on his own? If that was the case, then maybe his dad wasn't in danger. Could be the old Strake fear on alert. It was early, but Strake Senior had his coffee on the percolator around 5:00 a.m. The sheriff nearly knocked but didn't. It took a moment because his legless father would have to seat himself in his contraption to come to the door. Strake paused. He thought of how sore his legs were from walking.

How sweet the heroin might have been with the boy and girl. He was in a morning reverie, almost happy. As a boy he had thought his father was titanic, solving crimes and still reading mysteries at night that he shared with his son. Strake never wanted to be anything else but like his dad. What would happen if he didn't knock? If he left his father out of this. No, not possible. There was a threat. The panicked governor could easily make an old man go away. Ava began to feel more sinister, not just a ghostwriter. Her android eyes were empty. He knew that look. In a way, he had the same one.

You had to be empty to kill. Nothing could touch you. Killing was like any other errand. Of course that was not true, but it's what it was. He had only been standing there a few minutes, although it had seemed longer. Maybe he was simply afraid of finding his father dead. Sighing, he lifted his hand to knock and gave the door a tap tap tap.

His father never minded if he just came in, but he thought it best to announce his presence. When the door opened, he was already sighing relief because someone was here. There had been the idea that maybe they could have taken his father. But the door opened.

"Hey Dad," Strake was about to say when a woman's head appeared.

At first he saw the part in her hair. Something he remembered. As his mouth fell open, the door widened. Her brown eyes met his. Hanh. She fell into him. Her head on his chest. He found his arms pulling her deeper into him. There was guilt about not remembering, but that New York time was a fog. He had written her that things might intervene, might keep him from getting her at the airport. Even in spite of that he felt bad. He should have found a way to come for her. Because she had come to him from so far.

There had been a plan, that's right. He had given her his address and his father's. He had sent her money. He had also wired money at a Western Union in Manhattan, just in case. She had been on her own through all of it, but somehow she had made it here. The disbelief stunned him. He had not been expecting to see her at all. Much of that was his fault as he stumbled out of New York to Connecticut to recover, then made his way home.

"How long have you been here?"

"Few days."

"Is he . . . ?"

"Yes, fine. Sleeps."

"We need to wake him. There's something I have to ask."

They were inside now. He walked to the bedroom and pushed open the door. His father's turbo-wheelchair by the bed. The old man's eyes opened and he shook his head in friendly disgust, "About time."

"I was sidelined. Cafflee."

"Cafflee! That corrupt shitball?"

Strake updated him on Ava being at the office, his rehab at the mansion and his escape once he found out what they were doing, adding in Monk.

"You saw Monk!"

"Just for a few minutes."

"Man! Monk!"

His father sat up in bed and flamed a cigar, gesturing to his son.

"Can't do a cigar before sunrise."

"Wimp. It's a lot healthier than eggs. Cigars kill viruses. Tell me more about this missing body though."

"Well, you were on the case, right?"

"I'm trying to remember."

He stared at the ceiling to think.

"Some friend of Cafflee? They found his car under a bridge but they never located the body."

"That's right. That's right! It's coming back to me. High school friend of the governor."

Strake explained his idea that they were keeping him away from Strake Senior for this reason.

"I doubt they're that smart, son."

"You really think they need me for something?"

"Not sure. Maybe. Why did you suddenly remember this case?"

"No idea. They yanked me through a pretty hard detox and I had all kinds of thoughts flying through my head. Something residual."

"Could be nothing, you know?" his father politely warned him.

"I know."

"And she claims to be writing a book about you?"

"Yes, mostly about The Nihilistics and how she thinks I've become one myself after New York. Maybe I always was one."

"May be. I'm sure I was one before you."

"I need to talk to Hanh."

"Yeah, she showed up a few days ago at the door, said she knew you. She's been sleeping in the guest room."

"Thanks."

Strake was thankful his father didn't judge him in that moment.

"Wait, son, do you think that body could be close to where the car was? I always thought that, then they closed the case from up top and told us to let it alone. I didn't ask questions at the time because I had too much else going on. It was fishy for sure."

"Suits?"

"I'm sure. The suits make sense for a disappearance like this."

"That was Talton Bridge, right?"

"I think so . . . yes, it was."

"And the name of the car owner?"

"That was Norman Something. Or Something Norman."

"Not Jessie Norman?"

"Jessie! That's it."

"Jessie Norman," Strake muttered.

"You find that body, and the trail leading to it, you might find yourself locked back in that room at the governor's mansion."

"I'm sure they are on my tail as we speak."

"You know, there is that Creek burial ground near that bridge."

"Not Cherokee?"

"No, Creek for sure."

"Okay, I'll check it out. Had you heard about Neaves by the way?"

"I had heard, yes. Sorry."

Strake still couldn't believe his friend was gone.

"Hear anything more around town about it?"

"I think he went on a similar rampage like you did, only kept his local."

"What do you mean?"

"Can't be sure. Just rumors. But he's been hunting down the families of suits, kids, moms."

"That doesn't sound like Neaves."

"He might have snapped."

"I don't know."

"You asked. That's what I've heard."

"Sorry, I'm sure it's possible. I snapped."

"We all snap at some point."

In the living room Hanh lay on the sofa reading *A Suspension of Mercy* by Patricia Highsmith.

"Practicing English," she said, holding up the book. Strake noticed the pocket dictionary on the coffee table too.

"I remember Dad reading that novel and giving it to me. I think he has the American version around here somewhere." He went to a tall shelf of noir, thrillers and mysteries and scanned the spines. "Ah, here it is. *The Story-Teller*." He also noticed a space to the left of it where maybe her copy had been?

"Same book?" she asked.

"Yes, same. The one you have is British. This one was published by Doubleday, same year, let me see . . . 1965. Very good novel. Wait, how did you pick this particular book?"

"Outside, I find."

"Outside?"

"Yes."

"Not on the shelf here?"

"No, outside, on steps."

"One sec." He walked back to Strake Senior's bedroom. "Hey Dad, you remember this Highsmith book?"

"Of course, one of her best. Her eleventh. Why?"

"Well, Hanh has the UK version; she said it was lying on the porch steps when she arrived."

"Impossible. I haven't been reading them, and they would have been shelved beside each other."

"Hers had been removed."

"And just left on the steps? That can't be right."

"Could be the governor's niece might have a sense of humor after all."

"What do you mean?" his father asked, sitting forward.

"She may have been here. I did tell her to look in on you."

"I sometimes stay in bed for days. And I do leave the door unlocked."

"Superb security."

"Ahh," he grunted, waving his hand at his son.

The cigar smoke hurt Strake's eyes and he felt woozy.

"Either she's a big Highsmith fan or she was killing time waiting for me and forgot to return the book. Or she came inside, got this specific novel and made a point to leave it outside for someone to see."

"I can't fault her taste," Strake Senior noted, impressed. "That is one of my top noir novels."

"If I recall," his son said, "it's about a freelance writer in Britain, right?"

"Not only that, but the guy is separated from his wife, working on a crime show and acting like he thinks a murderer would."

"That's right . . . Ava is a writer."

"Writing about you, correct?"

"Yes."

"All writers have a screw loose, lesson one."

"All of them?"

"Every last one. Actors too."

"Why do you say that?"

"Writers are anti-social pariahs who sit by themselves in their underwear all day typing up insane thoughts."

"You do make a point."

A vision of Ava in her panties in front of a Hermes 3000. He shook himself out of his lustful vision.

"Son, what you might have here is simple."

"What's that?"

"A fan gone bad."

It hadn't occurred to Strake that Ava was unstable.

"So she's flirting?"

"I wouldn't say that."

"What then?"

"I'm thinking stalker."

"Stalker?"

"Yeah, can't distinguish between books and reality, shows up at your office like some rich psychotic blond in a Hammett novel, comes to my house and leaves a weird book about murder on the steps. You know the type."

"Oh boy."

"You want to know my theory, after what you told me?"

"What's that then?"

"I don't think the governor is involved with this. I think it's all her, making up some excuse about governmental machinations to kidnap you."

"Now *you* sound crazy."

"Do I, son?"

"Adam did say he needed me."

"So he says."

"What about the missing body and the car under the bridge?"

"What about it? You said yourself that you had a sudden idea, one that you haven't even researched. Maybe the governor is tied to it. Maybe it's just a coincidence. One thing's for certain: the governor's niece is at the center of everything."

"But that's just a hunch?"

"Possible. But I didn't leave that book on the steps. You said Hanh found it when she got here."

"That's what she just told me."

"Then Ava put it there so you would know she had done it."

"I wonder why."

"I know what I would do."

"What?"

"Reread that novel."

Strake came to the sofa with Hanh and he read his American copy while she worked on translating with the UK one. The Planners, not dissimilar to The Nihilistics, were an idea in the book. There was also a character created for television called The Whip. So she had come into his house, picked out a specific book and left it outside for him to notice. He had never trusted Ava. Something too vacant about her. He popped back in his dad's bedroom and said he needed to go talk to some people, could he look after Hanh?

"I gave her a gun; she's fine."

"Oh."

"I have one too."

"Well, the house is suitably armed then."

In the living room as he was leaving he leaned over and kissed Hanh's lips and his eyes closed right before he saw hers up close.

"I have missed you," he told her.

She had a way of putting life into him with her breath.

"Can we talk later?"

"Don't have to talk," she assured him.

"We don't?"

"No. I will be here. When you ready."

"I am sorry."

"If you ever ready."

She watched him leave.

He had a few stops to make, first his house to pick up the brown car. As he left his father's he walked and thought about the young boy in the field who had offered him heroin. It was a coward's life to think you could feel good all the time. The more you thought that, the worse you were when you were off the stuff. At his house he stepped around a buckled wooden piece with rusty nails jutting down like rotten rat teeth. He bent over to look at it closer. Need to replace that, he thought, gazing around at the other twenty boards that required the same. Paint on his house chipped like dandruff.

"I have to come home more," he said aloud, to no one.

He took a second to yank up the nailed board so he wouldn't step on it later. Sat it on the railing. Then he did the same with a few more. He was about to open the door. But he had a weirdness you feel when you know something is different. How you know this is another thing, but you know because of a sense. It is the slightest feeling, barely perceived. Kind of like trying to pet a skittish cow who runs away at the last minute if you move too close too fast.

He had almost stepped too close when he decided to look into his front window. The two security guards from the governor's mansion were sitting on his sofa. He never had gotten their names. Where was their car? How close behind had they been? Had they seen what happened back on the highway? Strake needed to get his stolen car, but it would make noise. He had to wait so he inched around to the side where he could still see them in another window. What happened next caught even him by surprise. It took about fifteen minutes. He kept his eye on the door.

The men talked casually inside as if it were their own home. But he was not about to go inside. So they *were* after him. Maybe just to contain him in a room under the pretense of detox, but even so they were still following him to keep him from doing something. Ava had first intercepted him at the office.

These two gorillas had simply assumed he would come home. Luckily they had not gone to his father's and seen Hanh, both of whom would have probably shot them had they tried to trespass like this. He moved his legs to keep the blood flowing. He glanced in the side window from time to time.

Then it happened. The door opened. Strake heard it. He looked. It was someone wearing the mask of Elvis. He squinted to see clearer. What in the world? The body at the door moved through the room as the men stood in protest, looking alarmed and reaching for their guns on the table. Too late, boys. Instead of a gun the unknown body swung one of the boards he had just ripped up, a rusty nail aimed at the head of the one on the right, connecting and sending him down. The nail of the board was stuck in the side of his head as his tongue fell out and blood spread its black liquid.

The other man had his gun and was about to fire when the body ran right for him and gutted him with a long white knife. Was that the bone knife? No. Impossible. It was in the trunk of his car. With the other weapons.

It *was* the bone knife.

The second man's stomach spilled out in front of him as he looked down in grief and tilted forward by his friend. The Elvis mask turned and left, leaving the door open and taking the horse bone knife. This was a fabricated crime scene if there ever was, designed to put Strake at the center of the blame. He thought quickly. The body with the Elvis mask had somehow broken into his car. Likely the same person who left the Highsmith novel at his dad's. But would Ava be so . . . obvious? Or was she actually helping him by getting rid of these goons? Hard to say. Several of his theories needed to be red-penciled.

He had to check on his ride. Well, not his, the one he had jacked from the suits in New York. It was wise not to move in this moment. Let Elvis have some distance. He could clean up the bodies. Or leave them. Find Ava or stay focused on the car under the bridge and the missing body. Hey, that was a thought: did the car under the bridge still exist? Hm.

That might be a better starting point than blindly going to the bridge for nothing or to the burial ground, also for nothing. More theory emending. The car . . . Junkyard? Police impound? As he stood outside his window watching yet another tableau of viscera flash across his eyes, his adrenal impulses fired. He had to be calmer. He could not rush a decision here.

And what the hell had just happened? Someone in a mask had just put a nail in one man's brain and a knife in another man's stomach, the same knife one of The Nihilistics had used to kill at the bank and to kill his GBI friend at the motel. The same knife he had stolen on his own path to nihilism. He let out a breath through his mouth, a long one. From his pocket he found a stick of Juicy Fruit and folded it into his mouth, the sugar melting around his tongue as his teeth shivered.

Hanh was okay. His father was fine. They could protect themselves. This killer had been on foot. No cars had ever appeared around the house. In a way, Strake couldn't move. Part of him didn't want to. A bigger part was frozen in place. He chewed his gum until the sugar faded then spat it into his hand. He balled it and held it warm in his palm. In a few minutes he would either go inside and take care of the bodies. Or he would leave here to find that dead man's missing car, perhaps the nucleus within such a baffling case. Maybe he would do both, clean up the bodies, locate the car from the bridge. Right now, he didn't want to do a single thing.

His shock was deep in him so he was able to ignore it, as he had been trained to do. Jarring nonetheless to see two men assaulted in such a manner. What was the right thing to do afterward? Who was he kidding? There was never a right thing when murders like these were involved. He moved around to the back of the house, certain the weird Elvis effigy was gone. Can't be too sure, he thought. In the end he made his way into the house. What he noticed was that both men were still alive. They looked up at him. Neither could speak.

Instead of calling an ambulance he dialed the governor, hanging up before anyone answered. Strake bent down to the man whose guts bled.

"Go," the man was finally able to rasp. "Someone will be here in a minute." In that brief statement it told Strake they knew he hadn't done this to them.

Made sense. If the governor had sent these men, then he would likely be expected to clean them up and look after them.

"Any idea who that was?"

"None." The hurting man closed his eyes.

Feeling bad about leaving them, he moved to the door with one final look back and went to his stolen car. He opened the trunk. All the other weapons were there. Except the horse bone knife. Frustrated, he drove to a local police station to speak to a sheriff's assistant. Many of the local sheriff friends of his had died. This was the only lead he had at present. Strake explained about the car under the bridge.

The assistant was a young man who wore a black three-piece suit and horn-rimmed tortoise glasses. His name was Delman. Whether that was a first or last name, Strake did not know. He seemed to recall Meyer mentioning him. The man seemed recognizable. He had that southern country-club familiarity, as if the sheriff had run into him within local circles.

Delman took off his glasses. Put the temple tip in his mouth. The nose pads had left small bruises between his eyes. He was younger than thirty but he looked tired. However, his boss Neaves had just been killed. Strake would ask about that in a bit.

"The car, that's right," he said, after a minute. "I remember something about that one."

Strake waited.

"Neaves talked about the case."

Oh man, he thought. Maybe that's what happened to his friend.

"He did?"

"Yes, recently."

"Do you remember why he brought it up, Delman?" Strake was betting it was his first name, not last.

"I don't. Give me a sec. We have so many cases. This one was older?"

"Correct."

"Wait . . . you don't think?"

"Maybe. Could be related to Neaves' death."

"I never put that together."

"It's an obscure case, if you remember." Strake sat down finally on a metal folding chair that was cold on the seat. "The car was left under the bridge but the body was never found."

"Neaves and I definitely talked about this in the last month."

"What did he say?"

"Nothing much. He just asked if I could find the file on it. I did. I gave it to him. It's probably still on his desk."

"Do you mind?"

"Um, not at all. Go ahead."

They walked into the dead sheriff's office. Strake didn't have trouble finding the file; it was right on the top of the inbox.

"Did he bring it up again?"

"No, he didn't."

"Then he shows up in my morgue."

"Oh, you saw him."

"I did."

Delman covered his mouth with his purlicue, seeming to chew on the soft place between his thumb and forefinger in contemplation.

"We need to find that car," insisted Strake.

The fellow seemed upset and was dazed for a moment. "Sorry," he said at last. "I never thought something like this could happen to Neaves. I thought he was immortal."

"What is the likelihood of finding the car?"

Delman thought for a moment. "It was so far back. I can't imagine it's still there, but there is one spot. It's like a dead-letter place where vehicles are taken after they're in the impound lot for too long. I'm not even sure it's legal. Neaves kept it going just to move away orphan cars."

"Where is it?"

"I'll drive you."

Delman's car was a cabriolet 280SE Mercedes; the top was down. It was a gorgeous ride and Strake whistled, wondering how this young man could afford it.

"Gift from Dad," Delman said, after hearing the sheriff whistle. "Kind of embarrassing."

They drove around back roads and ended up on what was no more than a dirt path. A black hellhound crouching on the shoulder lunged at the front passenger tire, gnashing at the rubber to no avail. A disturbing omen nonetheless with visible teeth bared.

"Every time," Delman said, "that dog tried to take out one of my tires."

Strake wondered if they were coming into the inferno. Close. They pulled up to a junkyard where derelict vehicles were pancaked by the car crusher. A man was currently in the machine maneuvering a flattened Chevelle as easy as an arcade claw crane. The magnet was released and the car dropped with a stunning noise, like a thousand dishes crashing on the floor. Strake and Delman stepped out of the luxurious convertible. The man in overalls and a Red Man cap stepped down and walked over to them. His face was a sight to behold. In his right cheek it looked like a bulbous tumor but was a wad of tobacco. He spat and the stream hit the dirt with a small splash. Flies swarmed the brown spit pool.

"Butch try to eat yer tire again?"

"He's determined," Delman admitted.

Cataracts milked his eyes bluish white. Fat warts like forgotten ticks on a dog's back dotted his face. The two top front teeth were gums as were the two bottom ones.

The man spat again looking at Strake: "I know you. Yer Strake's boy?"

Strake nodded and shook his hand that felt like leather sandpaper.

"We're looking for a car from some time back," Delman said.

"Which'n?"

Strake spoke up and talked about the missing body and the car under the bridge, not bringing up the governor's connection.

"I don't disremember it, but I also can't quite place it. Let's have a walk around. I might know a place it could be parked. I disremember ever scrapping it."

They moved through the junkyard, piles of cars and trucks, some probably with dead bodies in them. One thorough investigation might yield answers to plenty of cold cases, Strake thought. He also saw another car he knew as well. It took them about an hour. Delman recognized what he thought might be the one. They approached it.

"Lemme see something," the man said.

Strake did not have a good feeling. This gut sense turned out to be right. They could all see the key still in the trunk. The man turned it. Strake and Delman moved closer to look at the decayed corpse.

"Well," the man said, "guess we found yer body."

The first thing Strake thought: somebody wanted this to be found. Keys were in the trunk.

"Tell me about this car," the sheriff said.

"Well, it just showed up. I don't ask questions. The owners do what they want. It had a note on it not to scrap. From Neaves."

"How long has it been here?"

"About two months maybe?"

"We need to go," insisted Delman.

"Why?"

"We just do."

The sheriff looked into the distance.

A cloud of dust appeared back on the dirt road.

Strake looked at the young man.

How did you know?

"I'll be back in a bit," Strake told the old man, eyeing that familiar vehicle he had seen a few minutes ago. The junkyard fellow seemed to understand. He flashed a toothless grin dripping with slobber from the gums.

"I'll be here until they kill me."

In the convertible Delman floored it. Just as they came to the dirt path, they passed Ava's car on the way. She u-turned fast and followed them. Her car was no match for the power of the Mercedes and Delman lost her.

"What was that all about?"

"No idea."

"But how did you know to get out of there?"

"I heard a car, just being cautious. That place gives me the creeps."

"That was Ava Cafflee, the governor's niece."

"Strake! We need to focus on that body in the trunk."

Suspicious subject change accompanied by shouting.

"I know. We have our missing body. Seems a little easy, if you ask me."

"Or lucky," Delman countered.

The open top caused the sun glare to burn the sheriff's face and neck. He shielded his eyes. What next?

"No telling what Ava's doing back there," said Strake.

"You think she'll tell him to get rid of it?"

"Not sure."

"How did she know we were here?" Delman asked him.

"I had two security guards after me. They were attacked at my house. I'm sure they want to pin it on me."

"What happened?"

"Some freak in an Elvis mask took a nailed board to one head and the other was gutted with a horse bone knife that The Nihilistics had used."

"Sheesh. And you think it could be Ava?"

"No idea. She seems to be wherever I am."

"How do we get back to that car to investigate the body?"

"I'm not sure we can anymore if she has anything to do with it."

"What do we do?"

"We have the file on the case. I say we read it a little more closely."

They were back at the sheriff's office, which felt empty without Neaves. They shook hands in the parking lot. Delman went inside looking shaken. Strake had the file and was about to throw it in the passenger seat of his car when he noticed his trunk lifted slightly. He walked to the back. Lifted it. Inside were all the weapons, including the horse bone knife that had been returned, covered up and down with dry blood.

A note on an index card said: "From The New Nihilistics."

Beside the print writing was a small sticker that looked just like the Elvis mask. Strake tilted his head upward and let out a breath. He wanted to damn the brutal gods, if there were any.

Had to be more than one to come up with this anarchic chaos. He wondered about his next steps. Go back to the junkyard? Meet with Ava and confront this once and for all? It was clear whose body it was and that the corpse was hidden in plain sight, easy to find. That was not the mystery then. A dud end. What was the why?

The New Nihilistics on top of everything. Ava, Adam, two security guards attacked, body in a car, book left on a stoop. You could juggle the elements; they just fell to the ground. Everyone seemed tied to Governor Cafflee. Neaves dead, throw that in. And let's not forget being trapped at the governor's mansion for a supposed rehab. His head had been fuzzy, eyesight too. He assumed they dosed his food and drinks every day. He drove with an aimless daze, not wanting to go home or to the office. What other leads did he have? He decided to head over to Meyer's and see how Neaves had died.

When he entered the metallic room, Maude clucked over to him. He picked her up and gave her a hug. She gurgled and moved her head back and forth.

"Hey Strake."

"Any ideas yet?"

"I found one thing."

"What was it?"

"A tiny injection point."

"Where?"

"Under the back of his long hair, hidden. Took me forever to find it."

"And?"

"Yeah, he was poisoned and brought here to tell you something."

"I figured. What poison?"

"Gasoline."

"Seriously?"

"Yeah, sorry."

Strake had another feeling. The motel in his town. Every time something bad had happened recently, Basil was involved. He drove over and parked at the deserted place. The owner practiced his trumpet scales at the front desk.

"Hey Basil, sounds good."

"Strake."

"Anything weird here lately? Now, just go ahead and tell me and save me some time."

"Come to think of it, yes, there was a woman in a nurse's uniform."

"Pretty recent?"

"Yeah, she stayed here about a week, always had a doctor's bag with her. I thought she was passing through, traveling nurse or something."

"What did she look like?"

"Blond, green eyes."

"Oh boy."

"What?"

"Don't worry about it."

"I think she was just a nurse. I'm not trying to say anything."

"Sure you're not."

"Hey, I'm playing at the bar now. Wednesday nights. Got a trio."

"I'll try to drop in."

"One other thing."

"Do I want to know?"

"Not sure, Strake. It's just that after the bank shootings I have seen a lot of loud teenagers rolling through here."

"Drugs?"

"Ash rye."

"Hmm."

"You can see them all over town too."

"All right. I'll check on that."

Strake drove back to the office, trying to think about what Basil had said. Almost in that very moment he passed the bank to see several hippie teenagers posing in front of the place where his son was killed. They had expensive shooters, German from what he could tell, and was that a film camera as well? One young girl in a purple stocking cap that covered her ears had a Polaroid and white squares slid from it that she fanned and handed to the others, one after the next. Strake parked the car on the street and watched. It was a lurid circus.

A young man held the film camera and focused on the exterior of the bank in one moment then back on the crew: he filmed the photographers. Their antics seemed devoid of morality, but who was he to judge them. He felt guilty for relaxing his police work, avoiding the bank for a while now.

This wouldn't be happening if he had been in town more. And he couldn't approach the amateur paparazzi; they would certainly film him and he needed to keep quiet, at least for a little while longer. So someone who looked like Ava had dressed as a nurse to attract suspicion as the holder of the needle that killed his friend. He felt like his mind zigzagged. Had to be another diversion, the nurse outfit.

And gasoline!? Who injects gasoline in someone? It was too random. There was so much disorder in the crimes, yanking his thoughts away from a logical center. For this reason he had to think with illogic. He had to be as senseless as they were. At least until he trimmed off the manic fat. There was logic somewhere. Too many players blurred it. They acted with different forms of evil, which meant learning their tactics. The more involved, the more eclipsed the coherence was.

It was like playing multiple sports at once where they only gave you the rule book at the last minute. You thumbed through it trying to catch up. Impossible. You never would. Meanwhile, everyone ran around you. They had encircled him and he was in the middle. He had to sink his teeth into the meat of what could be three or more cases bombarding him. The one sense he did have was that it was all the same thing, dovetailing. It was one case, not three or four. He assumed it was because everything had happened so close together. It coincided with a certain harmony. Whenever he dwelled on the elements, it synchronized. Not with as much perfection as he would like. Enough though. Didn't mean he knew every answer.

It was a Möbius strip where your eye moved around the band of three dimensions. Not a simple flat circle. A twisted loop of self-contained infinity that messed with your sight. Nevertheless it was singular. You just had to get inside it. Or see it in the correct way. He was in a kind of judgment labyrinth and it was easy to be lost. Another visual came to him: a maze inside a Möbius strip. This is what it felt like. No wonder he did heroin. The mind raced around infinite tangles when he didn't shoot up.

The Nihilistics were an exception. They announced their plan and wanted to be caught. Usually the idiots known as criminals tried to stay quiet. They didn't want to be seen. So where was all the explicit attention coming from? The New Nihilistics. Who were they? In front of the bank they looked like homeless kids caught up in anti-hero fame. Were they some of The New Nihilistics? Basil had talked about seeing them at the motel more. Strake hadn't thought too much about them. Assumed they were idealizing the first trio of killers without knowing why.

But could the Elvis mask be one of the kids photographing and filming at the bank? Strake chuckled to himself about Basil and his motel where the answers sometimes occurred. Maybe he should just live there? The Nihilistics had been young. Three of them. What disturbed him was that they could never be forgotten. They were in his memory and now others wanted to copy what they had done. Details spat in his mind like bullet shots in a target.

The Nihilistics.

The Bald Drifter.

A horse bone knife.

A hatchet.

A Colt Government.

The Bronx.

The furnace.

An ice pick.

The governor's niece.

The forced rehab.

Thelonious Monk.

Men killed on the highway.

Heroin addicts who gave him a ride.

The motel.

His former wife.

The suits.

Hanh.

His father.

Neaves dead.

Teenagers turning The Nihilistics into icons.

The body in the car at the scrap yard.

The two security guards attacked.

The New Nihilistics.

The horse bone knife stolen from his trunk, used and returned with a note.

Strake was inured to the chaotic; in fact, it was quite normal to him. With his brain fog though he found it hard to move. To act. To do something. He thought too much. He was in his head all the time. The world was backwards. People did not care about how they acted. To that point, right as he opened his car door to stand on the sidewalk, two obese women walked past him with three slobbering aggressive dogs.

The women chattered and sipped on large sodas, ignoring their pets, one of whom lunged at Strake. In his mind he drew his gun and shot the idiot canine in the forehead. Clueless humans had little regard for manners. Instead, he kicked the dog right under its mouth, not something he wanted to do but the cur was about to sink its teeth into his arm. And he was not letting that happen. The indignation of the mannerless women was legendary. Strake knew one human doctrine: stupid people never apologized. Rather, they flipped their idiotic behavior back to the person on whom they had already inflicted their egregious actions.

"Did you just kick my dog?" The moronic pet whimpered close to her.

"I sure did. It was about to bite me. You weren't paying attention and I know it was so important that the two of you drink more soda. That soda is sooo important."

"I drink this for my diabetes!"

"Don't you mean that you have diabetes because you drink it?"

The women's mouths were black holes of awe.

"You are out of line, mister!"

"I'm out of line? Interesting. That's not how I see it. I see unobservant people with three dogs they can't control. One dog tries to bite me, but you don't even notice. This represents a safety issue, and since I'm the sheriff in town I have to actually write you a ticket. Don't worry. It's not a felony but you will have to be in court to explain why you have an unsafe dog. I can assure you that I will be in that courtroom to make sure you pay a large fine and possibly do a day or two in jail."

Suddenly the gormless duo turned ashen and polite at the same time. Strake leaned back into his car. Found a pad. He began to dramatically scribble two tickets for misdemeanors.

"Now, if your dog ever tries to attack me on the street again, know this: I have a hatchet in the trunk and I will use that next time. Hieu?"

"Haiku?" one said.

"Hieu? It just means 'understand?' and is a little word I picked up as a sniper in Vietnam."

"We understand," the other spoke for both of them.

"That's great, ladies. I'm having a rough week and I really don't need to be bitten by a dog on top of it. See that bank with all the photographers? Notice the guy filming them? That's where my son and his wife were killed by The Nihilistics. Ever since then, everyone is dying on me. Hell, I had to go up to New York to kill a load of suits and I took out quite a few of them. Now I'm back and I have the governor on my ass, including his niece who claims to be writing a book about me, but also seems to be involved in something nefarious surrounding a dead body we just found in a car. As you can imagine, all of this death is stressful. And I like to be able to walk down my street without being attacked. I don't like impolite people either. You just got in my way. You made my day worse. I like dogs, I really do, but I don't appreciate ones that want to take a chunk out of my arm. Sorry, I'm rambling. Am I talking too much? I notice that the two of you like to talk, so much so that you don't even pay attention to what's happening around you. If I hadn't've kicked your jackass dog, it would have bit me. I hope you understand my little tirade."

As he ranted he casually ripped off each of the tickets and handed them to the ladies.

"Oh, I'm sorry about the hatchet. I wouldn't use that. I have a bloody horse bone knife that would debrain your dog much better. It's also in my trunk and was just used on a guard from the governor's mansion. By the way, there is a group calling themselves The New Nihilistics who stole that knife from my trunk to stab one of the guys (they used a board with a nail on the other). Also wore an Elvis mask. Crazy thing! They put the knife back in my car with a note after it was all done. Phew, so you can see the day I'm having. Man oh man! Death sure piles up sometimes. I would just hate to add a dead dog to that because two bafflingly oblivious nitwits have turned the world's propriety upside down by not taking accountability for their behavior."

At this point the women had turned into silent statues, their Cerberus trio also now docile to match their owners. They held their tickets with a dejected look. However, Strake never got an apology. He never would. The stupid did stupid things. Apologies were absent from their lexicon.

"I want to thank you both. I had a lot on my mind and it's sooo nice to talk to someone! While we've been chatting, you may not have noticed that I have more pressing things to handle, like those young kids in front of the bank. Harmless seeming, right? Not the case. You've helped me stand here while I observe them so it doesn't simply look like I'm overtly staring."

He yanked the tickets from their trembling hands.

"Don't worry about these. I needed to use you as a diversion. Even still, your dog sucks. Learn better pet etiquette and keep walking. Scoot. Come on. Go. Take it easy on the sodas too. They're sugar poison."

The bewildered women scurried away with their hellhounds.

"I feel better," Strake said, inhaling.

He felt slightly bad but not that much; the women deserved a social slap. But he had needed to look in front of the bank without seeming to directly watch them. This was important. Now he had an idea of some faces of the teenagers. What was most disturbing: the heroin addict who had given him a ride was one of them. He didn't see his girlfriend.

The sheriff got back in his car and drove. Meandered. Thought. Too much thinking but then again sometimes the bullet shots on the target hit right where they were supposed to. Strake felt that he could not stop moving. He had to stay in motion the rest of his life. When had he last read a book like the Highsmith? As in, sat down in a quiet place and simply read for pleasure? Rarely. To be in motion was to move forward. You could not stand still. Reading required stillness.

Murder meant movement. It was about fluid observation. Each thing led to the next thing. All the things were bad. He saw the target in his head. He heard the shots spit into the circle. Right now they were just a bunch of holes. Soon the shots would form something new. A constellated target with gunshot holes he could understand. It would take time. He knew only one thing for sure: the bullets would not stop.

Strake was on a back road. He stopped the car. Why was he still driving this stolen vehicle from New York? He wasn't thinking right. It should have been abandoned when he came home. Vehement memory strangled him, the hands of it on his throat. It blinded him and those same hands pressed his eyes into darkness. He had not given enough attention to Hanh.

The trauma of his past was a morgue of bodies, not lying but standing shelved like tall books around a capacious metallic room. Staring at him in his dreams. It was also a mass grave to toss in another memory of death. Piles and piles of death with no respite. A normal person might see a couple of dead bodies their entire lifetime. For him it seemed weekly, sometimes daily. What was next? What was left?

There was hardly anyone left to die. The governor's niece was in the center like the incestuous Minotaur. A god-cursed product of the wife of Minos and a bull. She had come to him. For what true reason? Many aspects of this bizarre multi-case simply did not make sense. Plenty of clues but no solution. The answer would likely be a hybrid mongrel. It couldn't add up to anything pretty, that was for sure.

The supposed clues were impossible riddles. Would Ava have come to his town's motel dressed like a nurse to kill Neaves? And been so explicit? Strake didn't buy it. Basil *did* notice what happened; he wasn't always right. Strake maybe wanted it to be her. What if it was simply a traveling nurse? Then again, what if it was Ava? The suits were still possible for Neaves' bizarre gasoline injection. He couldn't rule that out especially after word spread about what he had done to them in the Bronx. He also felt bad about his excoriation of the two women and three dogs earlier.

Then again, his uncharacteristic preaching had formed a bifurcated plan, one fork aimed at the paparazzi in front of the bank exploiting the four murders there and the other tine stabbed into some entitled ladies whose unconscious behavior needed a sucker punch. He comforted himself by saying that if it had been men, he would have sucker punched them just as hard.

Soon it was dark. In his car alone thinking for, what, five hours? He had some theories but this seemed to be the simplest and thus most accurate: The New Nihilistics had to be the bank teenagers. Who else? They liked the eclat of, say, an Elvis mask and a duplicate crime just for kicks, as evidenced by their behavior earlier to publicize their efforts with images.

Neaves had been taken down by the suits. The nurse at the motel, she still could have been hired by them. Misdirection on my part because I'm attracted to Ava and wouldn't mind seeing her in a nurse's uniform. This means the traveling nurse might have played a part after all. Question though: did the killing of Neaves connect with the governor's niece?

The body in the car at the scrap yard. He had the folder. Best guess: the governor is a suit. When they were younger, his dead under-the-bridge friend did something stupid and the governor (or his security men) offed him. But since the security men were monkeys, they might have botched it.

What a knot. Sheesh. The French had this word, denouement, which for a long time Strake thought meant to tie up loose ends or something like that, implying that you would take the strings and tie them together correctly? Which never made sense to him. Because he had it backwards. It was the other way around. Denouer in French meant to **un**tie the knot. To unknot. And he had a complex knot the size of a fist. There were knots tied around knots.

One way through was like Alexander the Great when he sliced the Gordian knot with his sword, but that was a cheap solution. The only satisfaction came from when the tight rope unraveled, tantamount to an orgasm of sorts. Maybe Strake could use the horse bone knife to slash the Möbius strip. Stab the labyrinth right in the middle. Aerial view of the Minotaur. Parachute in and take out the enigmatic bull. Knots, mazes, Möbius strips. None of these comparisons helped him anymore. His mnemonics were even distractions. Better than heroin, he supposed.

Strake knew he was close. No one had taken him out. Yet. They had come to his house, only to have the random intervention of an Elvis-masked nihilist thwart the security guards. Perhaps the governor wanted to frighten him into silence. No, not possible. He only remembered the car under the bridge while he was locked in that room at the mansion. No way. Very random thought that happened to be connected to this political clan. He just got lucky by associating anything he could to the governor.

And would evil people be this transparent?

The governor had been genuine about helping the addict sheriff.

What worried Strake was that his paranoia drove most of these assumptions. That's all they were. Assuming. An optimistic spin would untie the knot quickly. The governor needed him for a favor. Strake needed to heal before he could do it. Ava really was writing a book about him. The body in the car was a stray idea of his while losing his mind off the heroin.

But wait. Why would Ava show up at the scrap yard? How did she know they were there? This meant that the dead body *was* related. And come on, Neaves dies while investigating it? He had almost forgotten that part. Of course the dead body in the car mattered. He was blurring again. Shifting from what he knew was wrong due to doubt. The answers were right there. They usually were. Just buried. Probably under the Minotaur. In a maze. Surrounded by a Möbius strip. Strake chuckled to himself. He was a scatterbrain. If his hunch was on the money and the dead body was a former suit, then soon the other suits would follow. Diminished in numbers from his one-man attrition up north, they would still gather down here somehow. Was the governor a target then? Was that the reason for keeping Strake close?

During their first meeting at his office Ava alluded to knowing about his renegade vigilante trip; this meant her uncle knew as well. Okay, now he had a finger in the knot and could feel it loosen. He needed to see Hanh, but he wanted to see Ava. Either way, he didn't want to be in a house right now. In truth houses gave him the creeps. He also needed to get rid of this turd brown car. Strake closed his eyes for a moment and crossed his arms in front of the steering wheel. He slept a little. Fingers of memory choked him in his short nightmare. At this point, though, the nightmares were not that bad.

Funny, he had never considered suicide. It just never occurred to him. Self-killing. No need to hurry the process. Life was death. The nap was brief. Sleeping, a good way to practice dying. He blinked. Then drove back into town. He parked at the bar. Inside, he saw Basil leading his trio. He sat on a glitter red stool and gulped on a warm Pabst from the tap. Tomorrow, he thought, this will be clearer tomorrow.

Trumpet and drums and piano, blap, smack, ding. It was not as bad as he had expected. The bar smelled of life and piss and perfume. He missed Hanh. She was in his town and yet he still missed her. He thought of their quiet time together in Vietnam. Maybe that is what he missed. Another time. Sometimes you couldn't be with a person even when they were right in front of you. Part of him was afraid to go home and be with her. He wasn't sure he knew how to feel good anymore. Bad had become a habit.

Outside, he was vigilant in the parking lot. He noticed a car, a face that looked familiar. Shook it off. Paranoid again. He drove away. His eyes tilted up to the rearview mirror. Was that car following him? He would have to wait until morning, but he knew where he needed to go next. In the meantime he drove back to his same spot. Parked. Crawled in the back seat to sleep. The hands blinded him this time and it was almost as if memory was a murderer.

He was at the junkyard after sleeping through the day. It was around 4:00 in the afternoon. The old man welcomed him again.

"I'll trade you," Strake said, pointing at the car he wanted.

"Throw in three hundred?"

"Deal."

Strake handed over the brown car key and got his new one. He transferred the weapons.

"Say, did a blond woman come through here after us?"

"She did."

Strake had noticed that the dead body car was still there.

"What did she want?"

"No idea, just drove up, looked around and left."

"Didn't mess with that body?"

"Nope."

"So it's still in there?"

"Far as I know. I try to avoid cars with dead people."

"Heard that."

"You'd be surprised how many have them."

"Yes, I probably would be."

"I ain't messing with it."

"Okay, thanks. We'll have someone clean it up later."

Strake started up the convertible Impala. It wasn't that he wanted to look like The Nihilistics by using the exact same car they had. Instead he would lure The New Nihilistics with the image of him in it. And get some answers. Plus, it was a sweet ride, even with the morbid association. He had not driven far when he saw her. Maybe she had been parked near the scrap yard. Watching. She followed him for some time and he wasn't sure he should stop. But he did. After he got back to his sleeping spot. He watched her in the side mirror, not turning yet.

Her black car pulled up close behind him. She opened the door. Stood. Dressed the same as when he first met her. Black pants suit that didn't stop her curves, even from the little distance off in a small mirror.

He now moved his eyes up to the rearview. She moved closer, her high heels firm around the gravel on the shoulder. Her white shirt had a collar spread to show her neck and the slit between her cleavage. For just the slightest second he thought she might pull out her gun. Shoot him in the back of the head. It was an erotic vision of how he wanted to die. Even though he knew it was not plausible. She could not have been in the Elvis mask, who was clearly a shorter male. Was she simply a writer taking notes on her elusive subject? Staying close but never too? She stopped, for what reason he was not sure. Framed in the rearview. What did she want? It was kind of a cold day in late November. When it grew darker early. Was it almost December? He really didn't know.

Dates were a blur. July, Nihilistics. October, Bronx. November, rehab. Something like that. They were under some old oak trees. Finally, she came to the door. A yellow jacket kamikazed around them. She swatted it down and gave it a stomp. No necklace. No earrings. No rings. A bare body. Killer, he thought, even the small things. He wondered what big things she had murdered. "Hi."

"Ava." He had turned to the left to gaze up at her.

"Nice car," she said. "Looks familiar."

"It has a purpose."

"Which is?"

"A lure."

"A lure?" she said, skeptical. "For what?"

"The New Nihilistics."

"What do you mean?"

He told her about the note, the bone knife returned after being used.

"My uncle needs you back."

"I won't be going there again."

"You don't have to, but do it for me."

"For what?"

Ava stood over him like a female shadow. She resembled him. Perhaps they could be brother and sister at a glance. Blondie and Clyde.

"He'll tell you. He can meet you wherever you want."

Ignoring her he said: "How's my book coming?"

"Oh, it's coming. Writing itself."

"I'll bet it is."

Her hand touched his left shoulder.

"Can I sit down with you?"

He motioned to the front seat. She came around to the other side and opened the door. Slid her bottom over and stretched her long legs in front of her. They sat quiet for a little while. Staring forward. "The New Nihilistics," she mumbled. "Hmm."

"Adds some complications."

"Indeed," she added.

"How are Mickey and Goofy doing?"

"Alive but mangled."

He thought about the truth in that instant. How it was like those spider web lines your face runs into in the early morning sometimes coming out of the house or out on a hiking trail. They smack your eyes and wrap around you and you're always afraid you might be bitten. One time he was. In a basement. A wolf spider took a chunk out of his side, but many babies dotted his face with bites that took forever to heal. Trouble was: you never saw those webs and they hit you when you least expected it. The truth was something like that. Right there on your face but wiped away too quickly to avoid the bites. So you missed your chance.

He turned. "You know about the body at the scrap yard?"

She nodded. "For some time."

"What's the delay?"

"Can't talk about that."

This time he nodded. More quiet.

"What is it you really want from me, Ava?"

She gave a coy shrug without looking at him. Somehow the hours passed in that Impala convertible. Soon it was dark.

Stilted conversation had turned into flowing guesses. They watched the sun go from orange peel to iris purple. Blending blue and yellow and red in the distance. A trace of moon cuticle appeared. It was now dark enough for them to touch each other. She moved closer. He turned. There was impending warmness. Her shoes, she slid off. But still there was light. He watched her face like a boy on a playground seeing a girl for the first time.

Cold air was still humid and sensual in Georgia. Steam moved between them. It was nearly too warm to bear. Her. In their almost hot sweat. Cool late fall in some way colder than winter. Her body neared his. They were touching now through clothes.

"You think I'm involved?"

"I know you are," he said.

She leaned her head on the top of his right shoulder. Still no smell. No perfume. She smelled of nothing. Some kind of absence. How was that? Strake considered all the parts of what had been happening. Body, Neaves, security guards, New Nihilistics, Highsmith novel.

Around the periphery, not in the center, was the governor's niece. She *was* the Möbius strip. Made sense. Had wrapped herself around the maze. You wanted to find the bull in the middle, so you focused in the wrong spot. She was the infinite loop. A spiral. There it was: the perfect spiral.

"You're overthinking it."

"I am?" he said, startled from his useless retrospection.

"I can tell you something," she offered.

"What?"

"Something you're missing."

"Would it help?"

"I don't know. The mystery is only the half of it."

"What's the other half?"

"My uncle. In a way he's both halves."

"Kind of like apparent and true wind."

"What do you mean?" she asked, leaning back over against her door in a pout of feigned frustration.

"True wind is the real blowing."

"Mmhmm."

"Apparent wind, the one you feel when you move."

"The true wind," she echoed.

This time he slid across the seat line and moved to her. What had looked like her moving away was only to reach down to her pants and undo them. The black cloth slid down her legs. She finally took off her jacket. Her naked legs stretched to the floorboard.

"I want you to hurt me," she told him.

His mouth moved closer to hers. She was in her white panties and white shirt.

"How?"

"You're the killer. You tell me."

His left hand found her skin.

"I won't hurt you." It was a whisper.

Their bodies were wet with moisture. She pulled off his t. Touched his chest. Soon his jeans were off. She lay on her back and spread her legs as he slid his hands over her.

"Promise to hurt me."

"No."

It was a night with the unlimited in it. She gasped and his breath was on her. He could not believe how pretty her body looked. They drank each other in a rush. She bit his neck. Would he hurt her like she wanted? Yes, he would. He said he wouldn't. But he would. Biting each other until they died. She let him yank off her collared shirt and he tossed it into the back seat.

The three who killed his life had driven this car. Their weapons were in the trunk.

Wait, what was that? He saw headlights. They were moving fast.

"Ava."

"I see."

"Hang on."

Strake had started the car and they were off.

"I know that car," he told her.

It was close behind them.

"From where?"

"The bar last night, parking lot. I knew it!"

"New York plates," she said, looking back and not bothering to dress.

The naked niece in his passenger seat. She turned to see the pursuer. Her slender body dripping on the threshold of coition. He didn't have time to dress either. They drove nude and hot. She sat back down, smiled at their bare skin. Didn't seem to be in a rush to clothe herself either. Strake found the road as Ava asked, "Who do you think it is?"

"I have an idea," he said. He pressed the gas pedal and they sailed like they were on water. With the top down there was so much to feel like it was a boat. The car behind them edged closer. Strake could only see one man, the driver. So only one person. Who was he? I know that face. The man's arm appeared with a gun that shot at them, hitting the rearview right in the middle like an asterisk.

A little too close to my head, thought Strake.

Ava leaned over the front seat to grab her jacket in the back. Her gun appeared. Before he could stop her, she fired five shots into the man's windshield. His hand dropped the gun on the road where it bounced. The New York car slowed. They stopped.

Turned back around. Pulled up to the now immobile Chrysler. Naked, she stood from the Impala and trotted over to the attacker, gun in hand. Strake wasn't as bold and slipped on his jeans, stepping barefoot to see who it was.

"Goodis," he said.

"Goodis?" she responded. "I know that name."

"You do?"

"How did you know him, Strake?"

"He was the driver. For the fat man stuck in his limo up in New York."

"The fat man?" she asked. "The one with the crazy suit?"

"Yep. Seems like you know more than you're saying."

"I never said I didn't know anything. I just never said it."

Strake stared at the dead suit who had been killed with bullet perfection, a few shots clustered in his neck. "Nice shooting."

"Aw thanks, daddy-o." She kicked out a hip.

"Can you put on some clothes?" he chuckled.

"I don't think I wanna." She pranced around the car like a boxing match beauty holding up a round number. Only it was the gun held over her head. She fired a shot into the air. She was female fireworks.

"You're something else."

"My uncle had hired this goon."

"I don't understand."

"Adam, he used Goodis all the time for jobs up north."

"He did? Why?"

"You tell me," she said, leaving the statement hanging like a pulled tooth still attached by a pink gum string.

At that point Strake made the obvious connection that Adam was a suit, not that he was surprised. He had considered it. This made more sense now since the sheriff had reduced their numbers in the Bronx.

"Does he know about the house? The governor?"

"In the Bronx. Yes."

"I get it. No wonder he wanted to keep an eye on me."

"That's right," she said. "There's nobody left up there to help him. And now Goodis is done. I think that's all of them."

"Okay, this is starting to add up. Adam never needed me?"

"Not quite like you think. In fact, I think he was looking for a chance to kill you in that room, or maybe let you kill yourself in an accident during detox."

"So you lied about him needing me?"

"He will need you. That's not a lie. Things are about to splinter. You won't be able to help him much though. No one will with what's coming."

"Good thing I left when I did. Hey, I can't concentrate if you just stand there naked with a gun."

"Are you going to hurt me or not?"

"You really want me to?"

"Yes. I do. Don't think about it. You have my permission."

"What do we do about Goodis?"

"Leave him. I'll call Adam. The body'll be gone in two hours."

She returned to the car, her body bare and warm and young. He touched her thigh with his palm as his fingers glanced off her fresh skin.

"We have to get out of here."

"I know."

She spread her legs for him.

"You want your car?"

"We'll get it later." She closed her legs. Then spread them again. Her mons a flash of curls.

"Tell me what you know about Neaves."

"Your sheriff friend who died?

"Yes. A blond nurse who strangely resembled you was at the motel."

"Coincidence. Wasn't me. I promise. I'm not into killing for no reason."

"I wonder who then."

"I think you know. You just haven't put it together."

The Impala moved through the night, Strake still shirtless, Ava stripped and staring at him waiting for anything. She leaned back against the passenger door and opened her legs for him often, a body so tempting, a blooming soul. He wanted to pull over and return to what they had been doing, but he knew he had to stay on the move.

"We can't stop," he told her.

"Yes we can," she challenged, "but we won't."

"No, we won't. Not for too long anyway."

"Find a pay phone at least. I need to call Adam about the dead body."

They pulled into a dead town and saw a phone on the corner. Strake fished out some dimes and a nickel for her. He gave her a quarter too. She walked to the phone in her sublime nudity and made the call.

"You're never getting dressed again, are you?"

"I'm just fine for now."

He found the highway. They moved through the night space without much reason. It was a dual feeling that they needed nothing. Many looks went between them. She liked to stare at Strake. She was giving him a visual that would last him forever. When would they stop, they didn't know. It was fine to roll forward without a future. Maybe they had none. A thought occurred to him. That they were doomed. So why not drive and not think about the quietus? Everyone was nihilistic. This car was a moving bed. It was a boat chopping over waves.

She was exactly who he was. She knew it too. Into the darkness the car slid. Top open. Bodies ready to touch. Not yet though. When? All they needed now was a third person and a bank and they would be no different from The Nihilistics. Goodis dead. Ava innocent? Or not. Who killed Neaves then? Oh man. No, it couldn't be. He looked closer at her face. He had the answer, one of them at least.

"Figure it out?" she said, as if waiting for what was inevitable.

"I did."

"Stop the car up here."

There was a side road, gravel, maybe crew parking for highway work. He was off the highway and hidden. Then, he hurt her. As he did what she asked, she was now his in a different way. Lying back she was under him, staring up, knowing. He was in all of her. She absorbed him like an animal's foot in a trap. He yanked as much as he could to free his limb but it was no use. The teeth clamped down on him, sunk into his flesh and she was his. She had him. They would fuck until light, bare bodies endless. Hurting her was nothing. She knew how to pretend. This was thirst at its finest. Full throttle lust. Garroted, both of them. They bruised each other. They fought and succumbed in blissful torture. Could it stop? In a final couple of breaths they sat up naked in the morning sun, crushed to beautiful pain.

"Don't stop hurting me," she said, finally clothing herself.

"I won't."

"I need this to never stop." She touched his face. "You are the man I have always wanted."

He didn't know what to say to her. She liked that he said nothing.

"I know what you have to do now," she said.

He had finished dressing as well. "Okay. Let's go."

They drove back toward the town where Neaves had been sheriff. He thought of those webs hitting his face, the truth, right there but wiped off too fast. The silk lines and grids of a web were a maze. The web was a labyrinth. It was a better comparison for everything. A thick web had the exterior of an infinite loop. The spider was the bull's eye. An arachnid Minotaur. The bull was a spider. The spider, a tiny bull.

They got to Neaves' office. It had an eerie sense around the place. That death ghost lurking. The sleek German convertible was smashed into a pole. Still running. Its front guts dripped green and black fluids on the gravel. The face grille punched and tooth-less. Strake reached down to turn it off. They had out their guns as they came into the office. Not needed. A bullet nearly spoke from the mouth in his forehead. Delman had seen it coming.

"Poor kid," Ava mumbled.

"I never put it together."

"That's why I followed you to the scrap yard. I was trying to warn you."

"The Mercedes should have given it away. That car stood out so much. I knew it! Too slow."

"Can you call Adam?"

"We'll get someone to call your uncle," he assured her. "I don't want to do it either."

"He never liked his son much. Delman was a troubled person."

"I'm sorry about your cousin."

"Don't be. He killed Neaves."

"I guess Neaves was getting close to that body in the trunk."

"Right. Delman was in the middle. Something stupid and drunk I'm sure. I believe he killed the guy in a drunken rage."

"Why do I feel like solving this means nothing?" Strake said to her.

"Because it doesn't," she assured him.

"I think we need to pay a little visit to the governor."

"In time. Not right now. I'm kidnapping you."

"To where."

"I don't know. But you're my prisoner for one week. We have to do something first though."

"One sec." Strake made a call to tell Meyer to phone Adam. He imagined Goodis had already been removed.

"Delman's life was an ongoing accident," she said.

"I'm sure."

"There's still the matter of my father."

"Doug? What's he have to do with this?"

"His affection for Delman got out of hand."

"Oh."

"Adam never saw it. He ignored the problem."

"Man."

"I told you it was messy," she said.

"Did he ever ask for help, Delman?"

"I don't want to talk about him anymore."

"Sure, okay."

Strake didn't have much more to add, although in hindsight he could tell that Ava's cousin had a wounded look about him despite the veneer of his suit, glasses and car. His eyes spoke of harm done. Neaves had gotten too close to those injuries. Had gas injected in his neck.

"I saw it and never did anything," she barely sobbed.

"Don't worry about it anymore."

"That body in the trunk . . . it was nothing. Delman was blind drunk and ran into him. He didn't want anyone to know about it because it would circle back to what Doug did to him."

"Did your father ever . . ."

"With me, no. He knew better. I was too loud. Delman was passive."

"I hate the South sometimes," Strake said. "I see this go on so much in families and everyone pretends it doesn't exist. My own wife was subjected to it. The same men, her brothers, raped my daughter-in-law. She was pregnant by one of them, I finally figured out. This sent my boy Harris down a bad road against the suits."

"I didn't know. I'm sorry."

"When The Nihilistics came into the bank and killed him and his wife, I can't explain it. I . . ."

"Felt comfort?" she tried.

He nodded. "Hated to feel that way. Seemed wrong."

"It wasn't wrong, Strake."

"There's never any real relief. From anything."

"I know. It won't stop for us."

"It never does," he agreed.

He hugged her.

"Don't hurt me," she whispered.

"I will," he said.

"Okay," she moaned.

He drove and they spoke little, somehow comforted that even though they had both seen so much, it didn't feel as bad when they were together. He wondered if he loved her. He thought he did. He hoped so. It could just be recognition, the mirror of her in female form. A mirror was empty and insufficient though. A fake image in silver. She thrilled the worst out of him. It escaped with a growl. She had leashed the black dog's neck with a hard yank. She was staring at him. He turned to meet her gaze.

What feeling the eyes contained like small thumping hearts. It was that leash, her stare, snatching the gloom and panic out of the sheriff.

"What's your take on the suits?" he asked.

"What about them?"

"Should we still worry?"

"Somewhat. You want my true opinion?"

"I'd prefer that to a false one," he said with a straight face.

"The New Nihilistics are the neo-suits."

"That's a mouthful."

"Many of the teenagers sprung out of the suits with their drugs and prostitution. In some ways the N N (less of a mouthful) were the offspring of suit corruption."

"Riveting theory. I believe you're right."

"They may not be wearing suits but they're the same."

"I still worry about the stray suit suits, the originals."

"You should," she warned him. "They relentlessly multiply when you least expect it. Or there's always one you forgot about sneaking around."

Her last sentence got him thinking about loose ends.

"Good point."

"That's why you and I can never rest. Our backs are moving targets for the rest of our lives."

"Thanks for the halftime uplift. I can go out and win the game now."

"You're welcome."

"Am I?"

"Yes, you are."

He shook his head in amusement.

"If you say so."

"I do say so," she said, sliding closer to him.

Their next stop was brief. Athens. To the magazine building. Similar tableau to Neaves' office. Her father Doug slumped at his desk. Bullet in the back of head this time. Strake could see Delman's penultimate act and the reasons for it. Then his own final moment a little later. The web covered Strake's face for a second. He wiped it off. The sheriff called the governor and left a message with his secretary.

Back in the Impala they were free for a few minutes. He drove down to the Georgia coast. They found a huge pink hotel on the water. Some island. A breeze touched them with a cool cold feeling.

"True wind," she said. "Apparently."

"Not always apparent."

In their room they hid from it all. From the guns and death and the people close to them always finding a way to vanish. For days they ordered omelets and cheeseburgers and beers and wine. They ate and fucked and fucked some more until they hurt. It was a kind of savage sex. Their skin felt carnal as if they had to be ruthless.

Righteous gangsters, no better than the ones they fought with knives in the sin circle surrounding them. She was tied to him. And he to her. They were hostages within their jobs. Her hands wrapped around his back as if she might enclose him in her darkness. He could not press her to him hard enough. The pull of each other was a haunting magnet. The lure of her was salacious. It was to cut a throat with every touch. Yet they sanitized them, the cuts. Blood was water in their case. The more of it the better. Juices washed them clean. Rabid feeling didn't make them animals. They sweated in submission. Licking skin pristine with their hot tongues. She stuck her forefinger into his bellybutton as if she could turn him on and off with it.

She probably could. Ava had the power to kill him too. As their bodies lashed, killing was never too far from their thoughts. She had a hard time walking and so did he, both for different reasons. She begged him to hurt her more. While he said he would he never really did, but she liked to tell him and he liked to pretend. On the beach they walked and held hands and said little, just staring at the other's face with longing. They were a kind of art, the two of them, handsome and gorgeous and blond and strong. Nude in bed they were color. Framed in sex and a desire to never end each other. Two violent things smashing and somehow becoming gentle.

In many ways they pretended to hurt. In a few they did actually cause pain. The ache was delicious though. Her body was genius. It couldn't be real. She couldn't be here, as she was. She never existed.

If she left the room she was gone for too long. His guilt for not being with Hanh surfaced here and there. Never enough. Ava was what he was. She was him. Could two people stay in a hotel forever? Not possible. She was also transitory. A glimpse of what he would never have. So too was he, for her. They were brief photographs of each other, not films. To be a film with her was nothing possible. Impossible glimpses, they were. Impressionistic snapshots. This is what memory was anyway, never a movie, always scattered pictures that were elusive.

She hopped on the bed, naked and pristine. It wouldn't last. Where next? Probably back to the governor for some answers. His past had killed his future though. What could ever be next when what was ahead would never happen? He wondered if Ava wanted him after this week. She probably thought the same. It struck him that she had no future either. And what about her book? He decided not to ask.

"Strake," she said, touching his chest.

He smiled at her.

"Do you want me forever?"

"**Is** there a forever?"

"No, but if there was, would you want me for it?"

"I think I would."

"We have to go soon," she said, with frustration.

"Do we?"

"Yes, you know we do."

"What's stopping us from staying here?"

"Events."

"You're right," he admitted.

"Events will always take over. They just do."

"I guess so."

"What's left to clear up?"

"More than you realize."

They showered, dressed, packed. They ripped off their clean clothes and fucked themselves dirty again. But this time they knew they had to leave. Out in the Impala the sun hit them. They were movie stars without a film. A film was only moving photographs anyway. He was lucky to have a few pictures of them. He pulled away from the hotel. The ocean hissed in the distance.

"Atlanta?"

"Yes," she agreed.

"Do you want to eat?"

"In a bit."

"Okay."

They drove on in no hurry with the top down, compelled to stop for sex on the side of the road as she straddled him in the middle of the front seat. In Atlanta they were not ready to see the governor. They found *The Seducers* showing in an empty sex theater, a bizarre Italian film that had Ava on her knees in front of his chair. At one point they were naked in the sticky aisle. They later fell asleep in the car for an hour. Then it was time for the real again.

What presented itself next to Strake and the governor's niece was nothing he could have expected. Certainly not to the degree it played out. They drove around Atlanta in angry fun-love, talking about what to do. She made several calls from a pay phone. Couldn't reach the mansion for some reason, busy signals every time. He did the same, finding out his town had emptied. The activity at the bank with the copycats had stopped in an abrupt way, Meyer told him. His was a town of only ghosts now. No more photographers. Or filming.

He wondered why. He would soon learn. The thought was to go to the mansion and talk to Governor Cafflee. What would they even discuss? His two bodyguards were in the hospital. This probably left Adam without any security. Arrogant as he was he perhaps didn't understand the level of tragedy about to happen. Strake had wondered about The New Nihilistics. N N, as Ava had coined them. Not just a few people either. If the paparazzi in front of his bank were any indication, he imagined their numbers were deep. And young. Insane and bored and with a false purpose to mimic the original three Nihilistics. During his excoriation of the two women with their dogs on the street, he had overheard riotous talk. There were ten to fifteen people pretending to enact the horror of the bank robbery. He imagined there were more of them lurking somewhere. Strake explained what he saw to Ava.

"What's your theory?" she said.

"I think it's heading toward the governor."

"How so?"

"It's like a gang. You saw what they did to Mickey and Goofy. They leave clues about themselves like with the Highsmith novel on my dad's doorstep."

"So . . . what might be next?"

"I guess we'll find out, right?"

"You think it's unsafe to see Adam?"

Strake considered his options.

"It might be, yes."

"Why would they target him, this new group?"

"I don't know. They've already hit his security guards, so they must know who those two guys are, working for your uncle."

"I see. That could be bad."

"In other words they were the warning shots."

He didn't like her grin. She knew something. She could tell he was aware. She kind of liked it, her secrecy. What was she up to?

"Let me make another call. See if I can get through."

She was hiding intel.

Strake knew it.

Okay, let's see what happens. Withholding was her game. He could wait. Everything was unfolding anyway. It was only a matter of waiting. They had been sitting in the Impala freezing with no way of pulling up the top of the convertible. She stood and called at the phone they had been using for multiple calls. Her look grew serious, she nodded. Coming back she let out a breath of worry, but for some reason Strake thought it was phony. He was back to mistrusting her.

"I got someone at the mansion just now. They said there was some abnormal rioting outside."

"How abnormal?"

"Very."

"How many?"

"Thirty or so."

"Dang. That's not good."

"All of them are armed."

"Okay that's useful recce."

"What should we do?"

Strake didn't speak for a few minutes as he sat in the driver's seat. Still smelling her scent in his nose that gassed him with lust. I can't think straight, he thought. This woman is crazy as I am.

"Sounds like a full on riot about to happen."

"Certainly looks like it," she said.

"And why do I have a feeling that you knew about it already?"

"The Planners?"

"Ah, so you did know."

"I always knew."

"There's just the two of us," he noted.

"Us might be able to take them."

"Are they violent?"

"They will be."

"I can snipe quite a few of them."

"You may have to."

Strake put it in D.

With reluctant urgency they moved toward what they knew would be more injury. Sex had inoculated them. It turned their bodies into power. He had never moved with a body like hers. It was almost ugly how pretty the fucking was. She knew him.

"What did Adam do?" he asked.

"Everything," she responded.

They were silent in the miles to the governor's mansion.

"We can turn around," he suggested.

"Can we?"

"No," he said, "I guess we can't."

"Adam's in his office."

"So thirty kids in the yard. I wonder what they want?"

"They want nothing. And everything at the same time."

"I sort of know what you mean."

"We need to make a show of protecting Adam, even if it will be futile."

"I wish you would tell me more."

She rolled her eyes and let out a huff.

"You already know, Strake. The suits. Adam is *the* suit. He was the first suit. We saw what your boy Harris did at the silo. We followed you to the Bronx. I was there. I tailed you the whole time. Even when you went to the inn in Greenwich."

"You did?"

"Yes."

"For what?"

"My uncle simply wanted me to follow you. He never said to kill you. I think he wanted to know what you could do. And he found out."

"You were there?" he said.

"I was there."

"I wonder why he didn't tell you to stop me."

"Because. He wanted to get rid of the suits as much as you did."

"I see."

"The Nihilistics came out of nowhere during all this, you have to realize. He didn't see them coming. Nor did you. He certainly didn't expect there to be a new sect of thirty forming a mob on his yard. So while he needed you, he also wanted to get rid of you."

"Makes illogical sense."

"Adam is stupid. He's been poisoning the state for years with drugs and illegal prostitution. Throw in gambling. The guy thinks he's mafioso. Ha, you can't be the mafia in the South. You just can't. He's a hoodlum who found some power and did all the wrong things."

"You want him dead?" Strake asked.

"Who do you think got this little mob to convene?"

"Wait . . ."

"That's right."

"You? You've been organizing them?"

She said nothing.

"Which means," he said, "that it **was** you. The Highsmith book, the guards with the bone knife and the nail board."

"Not me exactly. But me nonetheless."

"You're something else. I knew it!"

"No you didn't. You thought you knew. But you knew nothing. Which is what this is all about. Nothing."

"It is a bunch of nothing," he admitted.

"All of it," she agreed.

"What will they do, this mob?"

"You'll see soon enough."

After her confession Strake had no idea what to think. At the center of The New Nihilistics was the governor's niece. The cold wind of late November blew their hair and froze their ears. He was not looking forward to the last mile of driving. He dreaded it. Ava had planned the entire plot. Half of him thought she had done it to amplify the content of her book about him. A biography, by the way, he had never seen her writing. He guessed it was fiction, as in: it never existed. That she had been in the Bronx . . .

How had he missed her? She was stealth. Kind of like that panther. No image of her following him ever surfaced in his mind. A mind of a thousand thoughts. He slowed as he neared the mansion. They could hear the bruit before they saw them. Pornographic chants about what the governor could do to himself. Ava had fed their minds with his vice. She was enough to cause the street fight about to happen. They were a few blocks off, Strake and Ava. The two of them watched. He drove another block, staying far away enough to not be noticed. They would know their lightning rod, Ava. She had to avoid notice. They knew him too.

"We don't have a lot of options."

"No," she said. "I know that."

"You think Adam will do something foolish?"

"He could have called in the Guard, but I doubt it."

"Why?"

"Not sure but I think he's afraid of being exposed. He wants to contain this group. They are uncontainable however."

"Armed well?"

"Yes. I trained them."

"When?"

"Last few months. Remember that field you passed when you were fleeing the mansion? Where that kid gave you a ride?"

"I remember him. He was in front of the bank too with the cameras."

"That field was a main base. Looked just like addict hippies. Some of them are addicts. They have nothing to lose. And nothing is what they will have."

"Nothing, either way."

"Now you're getting it."

"It all seems to come down to a blank," Strake mused.

"You and I are doing the same thing, babe."

"How so?"

"You killed off The Nihilistics and the suits. In your own way. I just saw an opportunity, a groundswell of angry children with killing mapped onto their minds in a glorious form. Empty souls who have no capabilities beyond copying others, even if to copy means to murder."

"What's your hope here?" he asked.

"Look," she said, pointing.

"Is that him?" A door had opened and Governor Cafflee appeared with his palms facing the irate audience. Thinking he could talk them down he was clearly asking for them to leave.

"What's he doing?"

"Something stupid."

"I mean, is this a killing mob?"

"Yes, very much so."

"What in the world did you teach them?"

"Everything. Remember, I've been following you for some time now."

"But do they have guns?"

"Yes. Let's get out. We need to move closer."

Strake opened the trunk and found his M40. He pocketed the ice pick and the horse bone knife. Ava had her own gun, maybe more than one, but he gave her the Colt Government anyway. She grabbed the hatchet.

"So you're planning to go nihilistic on your students?"

"They're empty, remember?"

The scene of him and her was absurd. A near perfect mimicking of what The Nihilistics had done when they robbed the bank in town and killed four. Pulling the same weapons out of the same Impala trunk. The weapons of The Nihilistics killing The New Nihilistics, probably how it should be. Ava, their leader. How could he be mad? It was symmetrical justice. She was taking out the ultimate suit. Who happened to be her uncle. Partial revenge for Delman too.

Strake had done the same, only it was reversed, one man versus many. Now it was many versus one man, the governor. Flailing his hands at his door as if that could calm them. It couldn't. These kids were ready to die and to be proud for doing so. Nothing added to nothing was not anything. He and the governor's niece, armed like past criminals who had inspired the melee in front of them, moved forward. This was the plan all along. Foment a ridiculous mutiny. Subtract the governor with the uprising. Kill the uprisers for killing the governor. It would look like group suicide. Their feet stepped.

The sheriff and the niece. Only hours ago in a luscious musk inside naked fire.

What would happen to them after this ended? His time with Hanh could not be repeated. He felt very bad for her. She was better for him, or was she? Ava *was* him. Did he need another him? Hanh balanced his violence. Ava encouraged it. They heard the voices. It was raucous discord. Strake saw the boy who had given him a ride that time. The chorus of screams, manic and shrieking. These were broken kids who cared for nothing. Strake and Ava stopped, not yet noticed. Adam kept ranting. Waving his hands. He was in a three-piece suit. He was trying to calm the crowd. They moved toward the governor. Knives appeared like musical notes sung at the same time. The blades gleamed. They were long knives. They had what looked like an old army line of bayonets, minus the rifles.

Adam luckily shut the door and disappeared inside. It was clear he had no security. Why in the world had he come outside? Not a good move. Strake thought Adam was safe for the moment. Suddenly another wave of teens came. This group with hatchets. The New Nihilistics multiplied. The ones with knives parted. The hatchets worked on the doors and windows of the mansion. Soon they had split the door, chopped it to pieces. The hatchet mob torpedoed into the house. The group of knives followed. Another group, again from nowhere, stopped in the lawn, ten of them. Sure enough Strake could see they each had a Colt Government. These young men, no women, kept watch in the yard. Screams were heard inside now with the downstairs windows hatcheted open. Upstairs more windows were smashed, the tomahawks flashing like bird heads.

"What do we do?!" Strake hissed.

"We do nothing," she assured him.

"Nothing?"

"That's right. Absolutely nothing. Not yet."

The house turned into a horror circus. It was clear they were doing systematic damage to the interior. Only minutes elapsed. Strake bit his lip. She was correct. What could be done? She had already set them in motion. Taken out his guards so that the governor was alone. Still, it was difficult to watch. He never hated Adam, but he now knew the extent of his involvement. The first suit. Damn.

This was Ava's battle, not his. She had been tailing him, learning from Strake. She also liked him. Thank god. Glass crashed and the house was now on fire. The New Nihilistics filed out the front door and pushed back out of the yard to avoid the heat of the flames, which fanned a lot quicker than Strake could ever believe. The last five boys with knives forced Adam into the yard. The governor was on his knees. First the knives stabbed him. It was a gruesome swarming of hands and blades. Adam took many stabs in the back, the front, his arms. They're leaving the head, Strake thought. Oh no.

After this the knives formed a half circle to watch the hatchets. Each aimed at the top of his head. Some chopping into the forehead, some the back, some the sides. North, east, south, west bolts ripping the man's brains with the short axes. Finally the Colts. Ten men. One by one they each put a bullet somewhere in the governor. The body thumped around on the grass.

"Now," Ava instructed him. "You take the guns."

Strake pulled out his M40. Mowed down the Colts first. Ten dropping, their minds absent from his cruel gift of the gun. He had a mean skill. Ava moved closer and fired on the hatchets. With no Colts to protect them, it was easy. Once Strake had killed the guns, the hatchets saw Ava and knew she had betrayed them. They fled like scared cows. Bullets spat in the cold air. Young bodies dropped in the yard. As the house flames rose and boiled near his face. He saw the boy who had given him a ride. With a knife. The boy saw the sheriff. Strake couldn't kill him. He let him run.

Others escaped too, some of the ones with knives. Hatchets and knives were on the yard.

"Let's go," she said, wincing.

"Go?"

"It's enough. We have to go!"

"Where?" he gasped.

"To nowhere. We're going nowhere."

They ran back to the Impala and tossed their weapons in the trunk.

Strake peeled off.

"That was . . ." he tried.

She was wordless for a second, looking away before she spoke.

"You started this," she reminded him.

"I know. I can't judge anyone."

"Good, glad you know that."

"What now?"

"Nowhere. Remember?"

He saw her hand on her stomach.

A bullet had gotten her, soaking her white shirt.

He couldn't speak.

She asked him to drive.

"Do you want anything?"

"No . . . nothing."

In the Georgia night they moved in the topless car inherited from killers. After an hour or so she asked him to pull over to the side of the road. It was an empty highway. Always take the side roads, he thought. He put it in P and waited. Her eyes closed in slow motion.

"Strake?"

"Yes."

"Do you want me to die?"

"No."

"You want me to live?"

"Yes," he said.

"You're the only one."

He couldn't argue with her. She was probably right.

"What do you want me to do, Ava?"

"I want to look at you."

"That's all?"

"That's it," she said.

"Nothing else?"

"Nothing."

Strake was torn. He couldn't take her to a hospital. Then again, it looked like she was outwardly longing to be gone. She was drenched in a curse of her own making. Yet she had merely copied him. He felt bad about it. A fan, like his dad said. No, not that easy.

Adam was corrupt. Her family was a contamination. She had created her own N N to deflect from what she wanted to do herself: excise the governor. Merciless in the process. Training teenagers to do her dirty work. Pretending to protect the mansion. Quite a plot. Ava. Bleeding to death. In a limbo time. Might live, might die. Might not be Strake's place to even help. She stirred. Her lids opened again.

"I can't look at you," she muttered.

"Why not?

"My eyes won't stay open!"

"Is it done, what you needed to do?"

"Yes. It's just you now."

"Do you want me to help you?"

"I don't know. The end seems so easy. Why not go to the end?"

"Are you ready for it?"

She squinted hard and blinked her eyes a few times.

"I think I need you," she said, as if it pained her.

"What's wrong with that?"

"Everything."

Strake stared forward, glancing up at the cracked rearview from Goodis' bullet. Fractured diamond.

"I don't feel good," she told him, sighing.

"Isn't it over? What you planned?"

"I guess."

"Let me help you."

"I haven't decided. You could step out of this car and be done with me."

"I don't want to be done with you!" he yelled, out of his mind.

"You don't?"

"No."

"The world is nothing," she said.

"It can be. Doesn't have to be though."

"You're a smartass."

"I'll wait, whatever you want to do."

"I don't want to do anything right now."

"That's fine. Just bleed to death like a moron."

"Moron," she giggled. "Funny word. I knew you cared."

He put it in D.

"Let's get you some fresh air."

Again they went on a pathless road. Top forever down. Highway there and not there. Just a road that could be nothing if you let it. Strake drove back to the hotel on the beach, proffering a stack of hundreds to the clerk for an unlimited stay, a healthy lagniappe for him if the staff promised not to bother them. The awed clerk pocketed the jumbo tip, multiple bills the sheriff stuffed into his palm. "You'll need to replace some linens and towels." Strake counted out more hundreds and laid them on the counter.

"Not a problem, sir. Understood."

He handed him the key with a number on it. Back outside in the parking lot. At the Impala he opened the door and lifted her. She could walk a little. Barely. Drops of blood dotted the pavement hitting the white lines like sickening rain. He had to make sure none fell on the hotel floors. He removed his shirt and balled it against her stomach. She held it in place.

In the lobby the clerk was gone. They rode up a slow elevator to the top floor. He inserted the key in the knob and turned it. He guided her over to the bed where she sat in a daze. Then she lowered herself back and let out a painful breath. Strake made a call in the room. Waited. She had not wanted to remove the sopping shirt. It took a few hours for their visitor to arrive. She didn't say much.

"I was supposed to take you out."

"Assuming you don't mean a date."

"Adam wanted me to kill you. In New York. Not just tail you. I lied."

"And why didn't you do it?"

"I couldn't. When I first saw you, I knew I never could."

"What changed your mind?"

"I was looking in a mirror. I couldn't kill myself."

"So you followed me from Georgia to the Bronx?"

"Yes, but I only saw you at a distance at that time. It was when I met you in your office that I lost myself. Even from far off, I had no way to breathe near you. I want this man, I thought. I want this man like no man has ever been wanted. He is the first man for me. Up close to you, I suffocated. It was like being smothered. I had always wanted to be strangled by love. And there you were with your hands on my neck."

"Well, hurry up and get better so I can asphyxiate you."

"Ha. You better."

"I should have let you die."

"There's still time," she said.

"There will never be enough time for you."

"Afraid of losing me?"

Her words stayed in the room. She knew the answer was yes.

Meyer drove down and dug the bullet out of her gut. That was the first step. He cleaned the wound and gave her a morphine injection. Left more for Strake to give her later. Strake had stared at the needle stuck in her skin and didn't miss heroin. The needle withdrew. She slept. The coroner was about to leave after Strake gave him many hundreds in the parking lot.

"Thank you, Meyer."

In the room Strake lay on the bed beside her. Eyes to the ceiling. Finally he dozed some. Dreams of negation assailed him. He was cut right in half, the two sides split. A suspended needle and thread tried to sew him. Each poke hurt. He remained split. At what point did a dream turn into a nightmare? How did you tell the difference?

And could a nightmare ever change back into a dream? It would be waiting now. The worst of it was at a certain completion. Meyer said Ava would take some time for her body to heal. Gut shots were delicate.

"No abrupt movement," the coroner had let him know.

In and out of a dream nightmare his head swayed. Certainly it had to be a nightmare to be split open with a needle unable to help you. Why did he feel good then? A dream was supposed to be good. A nightmare bad. He felt good. Therefore, it wasn't a nightmare. He knew why. A blond dream lay beside him. Also the opposite of a dream. Soon she would open her eyes and feel a little better.

Days would turn into weeks. They spent a month at the hotel not being bothered. Strake kept the perpetual tips going. They walked on the beach, like before. She limped along at first. Soon her stride returned. Her confidence too. He kissed her stomach assuring her that it was healing her faster. She doubted it but said he should continue, just in case. It was a little hideout. No one had followed them. Only Meyer knew they were here.

What could possibly occur next after this asylum? Off-season, the hotel had no guests that Strake noticed. Often he lay on the bed staring up and finding himself lulled between reverie and tragedy. Flashes of everything, the blood of bodies. Then the feeling of her near him. He never was sewn together. Didn't matter. It was fine to be split. He was fragments. Pieces. Fragments could never be whole again.

Food came. Soon she healed enough and sex returned in a slow way. Their isolation was quietly manic. Her body had to take it easy.

"Don't hurt me . . . yet."

"I won't."

"Yes you will."

"How come I have to be the one to hurt you all the time?"

"Because that's just how it has to be."

"You're very demanding, I must say."

"Must you, though? Must you?"

"I must."

"Must less, okay?"

"Lust mess, you said?"

"You're pretty clever for a dumb sheriff."

"What do you think is next for us, Ava?"

"I'd like to not think about that question at the current moment."

"Same here."

"Don't you have to go back to Hanh anyway?"

"Not necessarily. I don't know if that's possible."

"Why not?"

"We found each other at a time when there was nothing else."

"And that time has passed?"

"I believe so, yes. She understands."

"So there's only me then, right?"

"There is only you."

"For how long?" she asked.

"No idea. Hoping for long."

"Were you scared of losing me?"

"I was."

"Strake, I can hardly talk around you. It really bothers me."

"Can I tell you something?"

"No."

"I'm telling you anyway."

"Oh allll right, what is it?"

"I'm kind of the same. It's hard to speak when I'm near you."

"Take it easy now," she warned him. "We're nihilists, remember?"

"Are we?"

"Yes, the originals."

"I wonder."

"We've lost all of it. Everyone is gone. This is true for both of us."

He nodded.

"Can't argue there."

"Let's go be inarticulate somewhere. You drive my mind and body crazy." They found the bed again and again. Skin brightened as they touched each other. Naked bodies in a hotel on the beach.

News trickled to them through the phone with Meyer's updates. The New Nihilistics had stopped with the death of the governor. The coroner heard no more reports about them in their month hiatus. Too easy. Some had escaped. Where had they gone? When the trauma never stops it is difficult to rest easy. Pauses were nice but fake. It was not like he and Ava could just go back to his house and live a sweet little life. Not an option for them. His guilt about Hanh was on his mind. How would he handle her? Uncertain. Ava felt stuck as well. No more protection from her uncle. Her family, no more.

"There is no possible plan for us," she said, frustrated.

"What about double suicide?"

"Funny."

A month passed. They had no idea what to do. So it turned into another month. The hotel room grew colder even with heat. The rare visitor stayed a night and left. He never felt alone with her. It snowed on the beach and was not expected. White glitter a kind of eye manna. By early February it was clear that her stomach had not only healed but bulged. They didn't want to go anywhere. Did they have to? It was paradise, sand and snow. Cold waves that mesmerized their sleep.

"Looks like that bullet got me pregnant."

"Magic bullet."

"You want to have a baby, Strake?"

"Is it allowed? With us being so nihilistic and all."

"It's probably allowed," she said, "in certain states."

"I hope so."

"One question."

"Shoot."

"How the hell are we going to get the top of that car up?"

"I think we need to leave it behind," he said. "I'll find us another."

"You're right. Last time I checked, it was full of snow."

Ava: "I'm scared to have a kid."

"Me too."

"I mean, where can we go?"

"Anywhere and nowhere."

"Doesn't help narrow it down."

"No."

They watched the snow shake down on the beach in the distance. He put his arm around her. He hadn't told her about something that had happened a week ago. Walking by the water one afternoon he had that old feeling, an interrupter of the bliss he knew was vapor. Never let the lull fool you. One of his rules. He had just been at the Impala feeling paranoid. He checked the weapons in the trunk often. A beach is a type of desert. It is sand. And an empty beach gave an arid impression despite being beside the roaring ocean.

With the winter season and lack of tourists, it was easy to notice a new person. There he was, the young New Nihilistic, his heroin baseball friend, his ride home that time. The first time he saw him, he was shooting fireworks. He had something similar in his hand but it was more powerful this time. Strake wondered when Ava had turned the boy into her own weapon against her uncle. What was he doing here? How had he found them?

There was no point to it. For a minute he wondered if Ava had been in touch. No, not possible. That would be a deep betrayal. He stood ten feet from the sheriff. It was enough. Not close range. Yet. The gun was pointed at Strake, one of the Colt Government pistols used at the governor's mansion.

"Got you," the boy said.

"You sure?"

He fired out of control. Strake had already ducked. The boy had trouble with the trigger for a second shot. Strake sprinted fast at him and sunk the ice pick in his throat with repeated jabs. The kid's stunned eyes dilated in fear. It was a grisly pummeling. His throat shot out liquid like coins from a slot machine. Strake had smacked the gun out of his hand down into the wet sand as salt water washed over it. Soon the waves would do the same to the body. The boy collapsed to his knees. The sheriff brought the ice pick straight down on the top of the head. It sunk into the brain in an unholy death. No one should die this way. The boy fell with his face in the water. A shame. He had let him live once. Why didn't you leave it alone?

He watched the waves do their gradual work. Cold winter water bathed him in a reverse baptism. His coffin would be vast ice and salt. He waited for the body to disappear. It took about thirty minutes. He watched the ocean with reverence. Such an elegant killer. So big and unrelenting. What was it like to contain so much? Such water was a heroic monster. He felt terrible about the boy. This was the problem: motivations were skewed. Nobody knew why they were doing anything. They did things, but the actions were anarchic. Nothing clean. No clean kills. Only ugly ones. Disorder.

Satisfied the body wouldn't leave its abyss, he headed back to his room. He would miss this small heaven. It had helped them a lot to stay here. The ocean rumbled behind him. He liked the harsh purring sound. Strake never told her what happened. He called a tow truck later. They watched as the Impala was hooked under the front like a big fish and reeled away. It would be crushed to nothing, as it should be. Up in the room he found the Yellow Pages and located a car dealership.

Strake: "We'll go tomorrow. I don't feel like it today."

"Does it matter? I'm kind of afraid to return."

"I have to go home," he said, "for a while."

"I know."

"And I want you there with me, if you can sit still."

"I can. Eight minutes is my record."

"We'll work on your numbers."

"Is it safe? You know, to go home?"

"Maybe. Maybe not. It's about the only thing we can do right now."

"You're probably right. I fear safety anyway."

"We can come back here as much as we want."

"Can we?" she said, hopeful.

"I like it in the winter."

"This was our little place, wasn't it?"

That night they slept well in a cuddle.

In the morning a cab picked them up.

They found the dealer.

With his large bag of weapons Strake saw the truck and went straight for it. 1970 Dodge Dude D-100. Red with white stripes, long bed.

"I figured you'd like that one," she said, trotting up behind him. "You man person."

The salesman in a tan polyester suit and wide paisley tie strolled over. Strake looked at the sticker. "Used?"

"Just slightly."

Strake handed him three grand in one hundreds. Snow fell more and more. He quickly tossed the weapon bag in the truck bed to not attract attention. The surprised man took the money and handed him the keys. "Title's in my office. Give me a minute." Strake and Ava stood under the cold white dots that they liked to feel on their faces. He wiped off the windshield with a cold hand.

The salesman returned with a clipboard. "Just sign here." He handed Strake the title. They thanked him. The truck purred alive.

Off they drove. To home. Or what was left of it. It was hard to return to an imperfect place. Especially one bathed in massacre.

They arrived at his house, but neither one of them could make themselves go inside. They sat in the warm truck, staring at his home as if it were a perplexity. She tilted her head to the side. "It needs some work."

"I never have a good feeling when I come here."

"Is it that bad?"

"The house is all right, but every time I leave it, bad happens."

"I see what you mean," she said. "I don't even have a house."

"No?"

"Moved around so much. Adam always put me up in hotels."

"We need to get you to a doctor first."

"It can wait. I'm sure your child will be a small man-horse neighing out of the womb without any problems."

"Man-horse?"

"You heard me."

"What you're trying to say is a centaur."

"Whatever."

"Let's give it a try. We'll have to name him Chiron."

"His name will be Strake."

He turned off the ignition. They opened their doors. Strake grabbed his weapon bag.

"Here we go," he said.

"We are going here, yes."

"Look at us stating the obvious and being normal people."

She stretched upward to kiss him. He opened the door, some carnage remaining from the injury of the two guards.

"This is it." He dropped the bag on the floor and turned to hug her in a long embrace, feeling her bump against his own belly.

"We'll make it into something," she said.

He was skeptical. A life that is a dark hole has a sickness. Strake believed this and never felt he could be free of who he was. His identity would eventually lure him back into a homicidal space. Where were the consequences? How had he gotten away with so much? A murderer didn't have perpetual luck, even if he was sheriff. He hated these perceptions because they were followed with the bad. It was almost as if his thoughts occurred right when the opposite of them happened. He was about to say something when he was certain he heard a noise. Could be Maude, his pet hen. He walked toward the bedroom and there was his wife, Mary Mae, sleeping like she had never left.

"And who's this?" asked Ava almost with a snicker.

"That is my wife. I had no idea she would come back."

"I feel so special."

"Nothing to worry about."

"And yet, here she is, another woman in your bed."

"We have been gone for quite some time," he noted.

"I did a little research. I know her part in the suits."

"She might think it's safer to be home. I'm sure she heard about the clean-up."

"Now," Ava said, having fun, "where am I supposed to sleep?"

Strake shook his head, slightly amused himself. Another absurd episode in the television show of his existence. He had been so focused on dealing with Hanh that he hadn't even considered EmEm would return. He wondered what she wanted. She hated the house. She hated him. When he dropped her at the airport that time, they had parted on good terms. No hostility. A detente of sorts. She had been through a lot.

"I'm afraid to wake her."

"I would be too."

They watched the sleeping woman with curiosity. She was under the covers so only her head was visible. Strake inched closer. Ava followed him.

"Um . . . Strake."

"I know."

She had no eyes, only two gouges. He peeled back the cover to see that there was not a body.

"What the hell?" he muttered.

"Jesus," she added.

There was orange spray paint: THE NEW NIHILISTICS. Ava had not expected this to ricochet on Strake, but it had.

"This is my fault," she said.

"No it's not."

"It might be. I feel terrible about it."

"We need to go check on Dad and Hanh."

"Probably a good idea."

It wasn't far to Strake Senior's. Strake pushed open the door to a spooky creaking. He held the Colt. She had her gun. A body lay on the floor.

"That's one of them," Ava said.

"I saw him at the mansion with a knife."

Strake Senior had armed Hanh. Would she be alive? He moved through the house feeling tense. In his father's bedroom the man was on the floor, dead. But no Hanh. This was what he feared. No end. They would pursue him forever. Strake guessed his father had killed the boy after the kid shot him. Afterward, the teenager came out of the room and died. The boy had grabbed one of the Colts from the mansion yard. It was near him on the wood floor.

It could mean that Hanh hadn't been here at the time of the killing. Months had passed. He didn't blame her. She had waited long enough. He went to the kitchen looking for any indication she had remained. Or left. There it was. A short note sitting on top of *A Suspension of Mercy*:

January 10, 1971
Strake, it was not our time.
Hanh

Whew, he thought. She had not been in the house when Strake Senior died. He headed back into the bedroom and looked at his dad one last time. Then he called Meyer. He needed to give that guy a raise. Ava had her fingers on her mouth in baffled chagrin. It was another unfortunate skill that murder sobered his mind. Something bothered him. He initially thought that the New Nihilistic had killed Mary Mae and staged her head, then went to Strake Senior's and killed him. He ran this by Ava.

"I see what you mean," she said. "Decapitating her means a body needing removal. As far as I could see, that was a clean severing (if there is such a thing)."

"And there's another thing," he added. "Was she in the house . . . or did they find her traveling somewhere and *bring* her here? As far as I know she had left this town for good when I dropped her at the airport."

"Maybe she came back and got in the way."

"I don't know. Seems quite elaborate."

"A few of those New Nihilistics did escape from the mansion."

"True, true."

"Strake, how can I help?"

"Damnit! Nothing makes sense."

"Calm down," she tried.

"Why would she be back at the house? Plus, you saw it, there was no blood anywhere."

"We didn't check everything."

"You're right," he said, with reluctance.

They went back to his house.

"My bet's on the fridge," she offered.

He opened it. "Ugh."

Squeamish mystery unriddled. His wife's chopped limbs and torso had been stuffed by the rotting food Strake forgot to empty. Organs had been stacked on the top shelf.

"Home is where the heart is," she quipped. "I think I see the heart right there." She pointed. "I always wondered what that cliched platitude meant."

"And now you know."

"Strake, I'm sorry to joke. I can't believe this. I'm not trying to make light of it."

"It was bound to happen. After what I've done." He was too fascinated by the scene to close the refrigerator door. So was she.

"Death has been following me all my life," he sighed.

"Do you think this will end?"

"Not likely. One of the reasons I didn't want to bring you back."

"I understand." She put her arm around his waist. "I love you."

"Ava, I love you more than anything. I didn't want a welcome like this."

"Some welcome."

"I'm just glad Hanh wasn't harmed. I should have treated her better. It wasn't in me. I couldn't go back to Vietnam and she was the country I left."

"Um, do you think we can close the door now?"

He chuckled and shut it slowly.

"Dad was in pain. He had lost his legs. I can't say I'm not relieved."

She moved both arms around him and pulled Strake toward her.

"What should we do?" she said.

"As usual, I have no idea."

"You believe the suits killed your wife?"

"I don't think the kid took out Dad. Too complicated. He was alone."

"So, the suits?"

"It makes sense. But which ones?"

"That is the question."

"I stirred a nest up there."

"Loose end?" she tried.

"I'm sure there was someone I missed."

"Agreed. I mean, that house up in the Bronx. I followed you once. I looked inside. I knew about the furnace downstairs. They chopped up bodies. You told me you did too. Can we stay here and be safe?"

"I don't know," he said.

"Everything's been taken from you."

"Same for you. Hey, wait." He seemed to be thinking about an idea.

"What?"

"You came to that house when you were tailing me?"

"I saw the bloodbath. You also told me about what you did."

"You're right. Who else would cut up a body in this manner?"

"Exactly," she said.

"A possibility comes to mind."

"Tell me."

"We're dead," he whispered. "I didn't see it coming."

"Who!?

"The man who did this," he said, pointing at the fridge.

They heard the front door open. It hadn't been locked. Footsteps of boots. The two scurried into an open door of the side dining room where they could watch. A man appeared, chewing gum. He had not expected to see anyone because he walked in a casual way into the kitchen, opened the refrigerator and surveyed his work. Liver, looks good. Heart, mmhmm. Very nice. The odd thing was that Strake had finally realized it could be him at nearly the same moment. He was never fast enough in his deductions. This man could have been creeping around for a while. The job on Mary Mae would have taken days to do it right. This loose-end man was the period at the end of an impossible sentence. Strake had been waiting for a final punctuation; he knew it was missing, but he also didn't know what it was. Strake appeared in the doorway and startled the fellow.

"You," said the butcher, grinning.

The governor's niece showed herself too. Strake fired the Government at the man's smile. He aimed for the teeth. His body fell.

"I don't recognize him," she said. The gun's smell was thick in the air.

"You wouldn't," he told her. "I only met him briefly."

"Who was this?" She pointed at the man who had smiled his last time.

"He was the original guy who was supposed to do my butchering job, cutting up the bodies."

"What happened?"

"He was late, so I paid him and said they didn't need him. He took off. I didn't think much of him."

"He has to be the last," she said.

"I don't know. They keep coming."

"With Adam dead, I don't think that will happen. My uncle may have even called him before he was killed. He was desperate. Could be a leftover. No offense meant to your wife in the fridge there."

"Ha, you really are a sick woman."

"Thank you. I studied it in college."

"Apparently majored in it."

Meyer would come soon with his assistants and clean up the slain. Three bodies, one head. His father was a blow; it hurt to think about what happened to him. The New Nihilistic who shot Strake Senior. Mary Mae. Not a surprise. Sounds like the Bronx fellow he just murdered had hunted her and brought her to Strake's to make a point. If he was the last, though, why even bother? Leftover orders from the governor sounded right.

He couldn't take more. This had to end it. There was nothing left. No more bodies to die. The funeral for Strake Senior, sheriff before him, had a fine turnout. Mary Mae had none, cremation, dust, forgotten. Around March his world turned quieter. He stayed on as sheriff, for now. Ava's miscarriage left only the two of them. She was sad, of course, but her bullet wound had not helped. They didn't mind in the end. They were supposed to be nothing at this point, crushed. Quite the opposite. The pulverizing had been theirs. Yes, New Nihilistics were a threat, depending on who remained. Compared to the suits, though, they were trivial particles. But the suit infections were no more. They might build themselves up again. They always did.

For now they were down a dark hole. He had buried them. In some ways he was relieved about his father and Mary Mae. Not glad they were dead but strangely mollified that a price had been paid. Getting away with everything never felt fair. It left you looking back over your shoulder. He could aim forward. Looking back was for amateurs who failed to see. Nothing happened for a while. It was he and Ava. The cases were small. She helped. Small town boredom had returned. He didn't mind the feeling. Sometimes when nothing happens it's fine.

One day she came into his office. Handed him a pile of white typed pages. *Sheriff Strake* was the title. He asked her if she ever figured out if it should be fiction or biography.

"No idea," she said. "A mix of the two."

"Fictography?" he tried.

"Exactly. Or should I say, not exactly."

"Am I supposed to read this? I mean, I already know what happened."

"I'd like you to read it."

"How long do I have?"

"Starting . . . now."

"You want my opinion?"

She kicked out a hip. "Not really," she said. "I need someone to line edit the book before I send it off to my editor-editor, you know, my *real* editor."

"Mm hm. That makes me the fake one then, I suppose."

"Exactly-not-exactly."

"I don't know. I have to rescue a cat from a maple. After that I need to give some speeding tickets. My afternoon is quite full."

She closed one eye in pretend thought scratching her chin with her thumb and forefinger.

"Uh oh," he said, "looks like she's thinking about something."

"I'll pay you," she offered.

"How much?"

"It's about four-hundred pages. I don't know. Eleven dollars?"

"Make it seven and we have a deal."

They shook hands and he pulled her into his lap.

"Do you think we're a bleak noir novel?" she said.

"Noir?"

"Yes."

"By noir do you mean callous cynicism as you might see in a dark film with lots of people killing one another with guns?"

"Don't forget the ominous malevolence," she added.

"How could I? But you left out the shadows and lack of remorse."

She nodded in agreement.

"It's in my book. You know, noir, to me, is akin to the old definition of tragedy, where everyone dies, versus comedy, where no one dies."

"Everyone died on us," Strake confirmed.

A sadness passed through them like chilled air. She stood.

"I kind of didn't tell you the truth."

"You're prone to do that, I'm noticing. About what, this time?"

"My agent in New York; he has already sold it."

"I'm assuming you met him while following me around up there."

"I, in fact, did show him the first half in Manhattan. I had to finish the second part here after everything settled down. Naturally, I also had to wait until our story came to completion."

"I'm sorry, what lie did you tell?"

"That I needed you to line edit it."

"How so?"

"It's about to be published in a month."

"Seriously?" he said.

"Oh, and Sidney Lumet has optioned it. He read the galley proof."

"I bet he did. I just bet he did."

"Jealous?" she cooed. She batted her eyes fast like a hummingbird.

"That he read it? No. I loved *The Deadly Affair* by the way. His best."

"So you approve, Strake?"

"If it means I don't have to read this book, then yes."

"You still have to."

"One question."

"Shoot," she said. "No scratch that. I should never say that to you. Go ahead is what I meant."

"How come he got a galley proof? That's a step up from these random pages you plopped down in front of me."

"These, my friend, are the original typed pages. Likely they will be ensconced in a museum corner one day."

"Can you maybe take them there now?"

"Funny. I want your impressions. To see if I caught you right. I think I did. I mean, I *know* I did because it's about to be published, probably a bestseller and hit film."

"A noir movie, I suppose."

"What do you think?"

He let out a long fake sigh. "Let me have ten minutes. I'll give it a skim."

"I'm honored that you will speed-read it."

Now, he stood. Faced her.

"I am sure it is amazing work, Ava." He leaned his forehead down hers. "Just get Steve McQueen to play me in the picture and we're good."

"I'll do my best, Strake, but I think they will want someone who's less attractive, you know, for reality's sake."

"I see how it is."

"Great," she said, "I'm glad we're on the same page."

"Speaking of pages I have a book to read."

"Thanks for doing it."

"Oh, I didn't mean your fictography. I keep trying to read *Ripley Under Ground,* but I just haven't had the time. That's what I meant."

"When you're done with the Highsmith, you can read my masterp—"

"–potboiler. You bet."

"Who do you believe would win, between us, in a gunfight?"

"Tough question," he mused, stroking his chin in feigned cogitation. "Better not answer that one."

"You're smarter than you look."

"We would both die at the same time, I'm guessing."

"It makes me sad that we're the last two standing," she said in a mild despond. "Lots of it flashes at me when I sleep."

"Me too," he said, touching her face.

"I like when you touch me. You don't do it enough."

"That's because you're getting Dustin Hoffman to play me instead of Steve McQueen."

"Continuing to dwell on that, I see."

"Can I get a cameo at least?"

"Doubtful. I'll talk to Lumet."

"Sure you will."

"No," she said, "I will waste no time doing it."

"Comforting. Glad you're on my side. I'd hate for you to be my enemy."

"Good news is that my agent said Lumet is talking about filming here in your town. Nothing for sure, but he likes the idea."

"Here?"

"Maybe, not certain. Quite likely they will at least use the same bank that The Nihilistics savaged."

"I will be reliving these deaths one way or another for a long time."

"I'm sorry."

"I relive it anyway. A book. A film. They don't make a difference. Things are in me forever."

"I know, babe. I'm the same. Remember, we're the same."

"We are." He kissed her with sweetness.

"I'm here to comfort you," Ava told him. "I love you more than god. I know you feel the same."

"I do," he assured her.

"We need to keep talking about it all. Not bury it. You bury it, you die."

In a few months her book sold in a popular flourish. Lumet came to town to scope locations. He talked to Strake about what happened at the bank and everything after it. Left to work on the script. The director returned one afternoon in the summer. "We got McQueen. He wants you in the film."

"He does? Playing who?"

"His double."

"So they'll never see me?"

"In a way, no."

"That's fine," Strake said, with a grin, "just fine."

Later, he bragged to her about becoming a star.

"I think you mean black hole, don't you?"

"Hey! The back of my head is about to be very famous."

"I'm sure it is. Your scalp will be known worldwide."

"I pretty much carry the movie."

"Sure you do. Film stand-ins are legendary. I can name so many."

She touched her fist on his chin in slow motion.

"I liked you better when you weren't an author," he said.

"I can't help it if I'm the famous one."

"Just wait until my invisible stand-in role is known. There's no stopping the back of my neck."

"It's important to repeat that to yourself a bunch. Eventually you'll believe it fully even if it is completely impossible."

"Your support is remarkable."

"Thank you," she said.

They gave interviews here and there. He and Ava fended off questioning reporters during the shooting. Shooting, Strake thought. Ironic. The film was shown in their town. Black and white. Many films had played in Strake's mind. What he watched on the screen was a tad comic to him. There he was twice. Once in McQueen who had kept him close and learned who he was. Once as the double, his back to the audience. There was Ava later in the picture. Most of the scenes from his life including Vietnam. It didn't hurt to watch it, this cursory dream of someone else's creation. In a way he felt as if it were nothing. Multiple photographs moving fast, speeding through light. Light was just air, wasn't it? After the movie the sheriff and the governor's niece were the only ones left in their seats. They waited for the cinema to empty. An empty white screen was colorless once the film stopped. It looked so clean, he thought. Moral almost.

"How come we didn't die?" he asked Ava, turning to her.

"What do you mean?"

"Us."

"In the film?"

"No," he said, "us."

"We're accidents, Strake. Accidents don't have to be death."

He considered what she said for a moment. The house lights were turned on by an usher. He and Ava stood and walked up the inclined floor to the lobby. They headed outside onto the sidewalk. She was quiet. He flamed a match and held the end of a cigar to it. Bluish smoke floated off like a ghost made of steam. She watched it. Then him. You keep looking at me, he thought. I don't mind.

"Did you like the film?" she asked, knowing he did.

"Isn't everyone supposed to get killed in noir?"

"Some live."

"Some," he reflected.

www.ingramcontent.com/pod-product-compliance
Lightning Source LLC
Chambersburg PA
CBHW030527120726
47904CB00005B/1659